The Scriptlings

SORIN SUCIU

ISBN: 151186981x
ISBN-13: 978-1511869812

DEDICATION

To geeks and mortals alike.

CONTENTS

ACKNOWLEDGMENTS

This would have been a book-shaped void in the space-time continuum, were it not for...

... My parents, who begged me to read, and who made a huge financial sacrifice to get me my first computer.

... All the games I've played on said computer and its subsequent incarnations.

... Terry Pratchett and Douglas Adams, who are probably the two-headed reason I started writing in the first place.

... Christopher Moore, Neil Gaiman, Jonathan Stroud, Philip Pullman, Tom Holt, Robert Asprin, P.G. Wodehouse, Robert Rankin, Tom Sharpe, Piers Anthony and George R.R. Martin, who at various times have rekindled my desire to write.

... My wife, Raluca, who is my fiercest critic, and who has allowed me to take my sweet time writing this story.

... My cousin, Cristian, whose impossibly high standards have made me a better, albeit an uneasy, writer.

... My friend, Fedor, who is responsible for all the Russian references in this book, and whose positive attitude kept me going.

... Travis Anderson, who turned my painstaking specifications for the cover into art. Yes, you most likely picked up this book because of him.

... My two editors, Audrey Owen and Heather Hebert, who were kind enough to act surprised when I told them English was not my native language.

... Ray Vogel, the kind ruler of late AEC Stellar Publishing and author of the classic sci-fi "Matter of Resistance", who laughed so hard while reading the manuscript that he almost caused the sky marshal to intervene.

01. MERKIN

Merkin was furious.

Let us pause for a moment. If you know what a merkin is, then shame on you. If you don't then, suffice it to say, it is a nasty word. It ought to be. You see, amongst Magicians it is considered good form to have such a word for a name. Merkin was most proud of her name, and she had good cause, too: she came up with it herself, no one else had ever used it before, and it was only a typo away from Merlin. How cool was that, eh?

But right now, Merkin was furious. It was not as if this were an unusual state of mind for her, although, in all fairness, this time she had a sound, non-hormonal reason — Master Dung had grounded her again.

It is a terrible thing for an apprentice Magician (henceforth referred to as a Scriptling) to be grounded. The term "grounded" should not be interpreted in its domestic sense, e.g. "no Facebook for two hours, young lady." Under Master Dung's unforgiving dominion, to be grounded meant to be dispossessed of all magical abilities until an apology was issued by the perpetrator.

Merkin knew perfectly well that grounding was against all magical regulations and that it shouldn't even be possible from a technical point of view. Still, there was a price to be paid if you wanted to learn from the best, and Master Dung was supposed to be the best. Supposed to. In fact, this was precisely what infuriated her: if he really was the best, then how come she could constantly outwit him?

The first time this had happened, she could have just as well not noticed if it hadn't been for her Master's reaction. Her assignment had been to write a simple Sumerian code for preserving a jar of pickled eggs. (To the programming-inclined reader, this is the magical equivalent of "HELLO WORLD".) Her code proved to be simple enough, in fact, too simple for Master Dung's taste. It was, upon further investigation, a full syllable shorter than his own code. It also did the job without the unwanted effect of having the pickled eggs glow in the dark.

1

As a side note, the whole glow in the dark situation would have been very easy to bypass in Latin, or even Slavonic, but up until that moment, it had been considered an inherent shortcoming of Sumerian. Sumerians, themselves, have been known to dread pickled eggs for the same reason. After all, very few people have ever been prone to eating stuff of the glimmering persuasion, and antiquity was not the kind of place where you would find those eccentric folks.

Master Dung's reward for this amazing discovery had been to ground her on account of not sticking to the Syntax. This, however, did not stop him from presenting her finding as his own to his peers. Nor did it stop his repeating the whole process (grounding followed by intellectual theft) time and time again. Soon, Merkin had a pretty good theory about how her Master had come to be known as "the best".

Huddled in her armchair, she swung back and forth, trying to achieve a state of emotional emptiness that might take her mind from the void where the Magic had been.

On the nightstand, an old music box played the "Moonlight Sonata." It was a magical music box, a gift from her grandmother, and it always played a tune that most closely mirrored its owner's mood. Being magical also meant that it had a sound bank that the engineers at Korg would have killed for and that it could pull off sixty-four channels polyphony on HiFi 5.1 Dolby surround without breaking a sweat. Not that a musical box is expected to break a sweat, what with its being completely bereft of the necessary glands, but you get the point.

She wondered if Beethoven might have felt the same way when he had lost his hearing. Probably not. He must have been able to play his art in his mind, which was more than she could currently do. While she was still perfectly capable of imagining code in any of the three dead languages that she was fluent in, she could not compile that code into anything usable, not without her Magic, at any rate. Stupid Master Dung! He shouldn't punish her for being brilliant. It wasn't her fault. It was genes.

It was all too easy for Merkin to blame genes. Genes had given her a brain to which A levels in quantum physics would come most naturally, but they had also given her just enough bust to fill an A cup bra. Well, at least she had a cute nose, made even prettier by a tiny, black diamond stud, and that was probably more useful in the long run. But still.

Genes had certainly not been kind to Master Dung. He had that unique body type that appeared to curl itself into a question mark from any angle one might opt to look at it. His scalp was almost devoid of hair, save for a meager collection of greasy, grey strands, of which their proprietor took enormous care. His nose and ears, however, sported enough fur to lift Master Dung's overall biomass of hair to a statistically acceptable level. To

2

top it all, his mouth looked like a plunger and smelled like one, too. All these features contrived to give Master Dung the air of a scandalized hen, albeit a bald one.

As Merkin thought about her Master's hideous face, the music box dutifully launched into the cat-squealing tones of the violin solo in Saint-Saëns' "Dance Macabre." It was more than she could bear. It was time for some action.

02. MASTER DUNG

Master Dung held Thirteenth between his claw-like fingers and gave it a scorching look.

"After all I've done for you!" he said in a trembling voice that didn't seem to be entirely in synch with the movement of his lips.[1]

Thirteenth didn't appear inclined to dignify this with an answer. It would have been very hard, too. Hairs are not generally known for their vocalizations.

"Have I not rubbed you with Kakapo balm every morning?" Master Dung continued his lament. "Have I not cast the most intricate Punic enchantments on you every night?"

A short spasm animated Thirteenth for a split second, thus giving enough indication of what Punic encapsulations do when mistaken for a conditioner.

"Let this be a lesson to you all!" Master Dung cried with new resolve and lifted Thirteenth to what he deemed to be the other hairs' line of sight. "SHURPU();" he whispered, and then shed a tear as Thirteenth disappeared in a blue Sumerian purifying flame, leaving behind the smell of fried Kakapo balm.

There was a soft knock on the door, which opened before Master Dung had enough time to compose himself.

"It smells like chicken," Merkin said casually.

"I don't recall giving you permission to enter!" Master Dung snapped.

"I heard your voice, Master, and thought you said I could come in," she said, then added in a caring tone, "You look forlorn, kind Master. What is it that grieves you?"

"Never you mind that," he said, waving his hand dismissively. "Have you come here to ask for my forgiveness?"

---

[1] That's because sound travels slower in halitosis.

4

"Nope," she answered and popped her bubblegum three times in quick succession, much to his annoyance. "I figure I need more time to repent for my insolence," she added in a voice that had nothing whatsoever to do with penitence.

"Then why are you here?"

She didn't reply immediately. Instead, she checked her watch and seemed to be counting under her breath.

"Actually," she began, but she was interrupted by the sound of the back doorbell.

There was only one category of people that rang the back doorbell when visiting a Magician's house — other Magicians.

"I must take this," he said, and then rushed out of the room as fast as his eighty-five-year-old bones allowed him to.

He reached the back door, and before opening it, licked his fingers and passed them quickly through Thirteen's remaining brothers in the futile hope that this would make them more presentable. He opened the door, only to find a pimple-faced youth looking back at him. The youth wore a uniform of sorts and held a large, rectangular cardboard box in his hand.

"Pizza delivery," he said, as if that was meant to explain everything.

Master Dung heard the words but failed to see their meaning. One didn't become a Grand Master of Magical Arts by dabbling in common folklore. This basically meant that words such as pizza, barbecue and hamburger were not part of Master Dung's vocabulary. This utter ignorance of culinary temptations also explained his old age.

One also didn't become a Grand Master of Magical Arts without acquiring an impressive arsenal of reflexes for every unforeseen situation.

"SHURPU();" he said, and closed the door as the pimple-faced youth became briefly aware that there were bigger problems in life than bad skin, namely, being burned alive by a crazy old man.

"Who was it?" Merkin inquired when Master Dung returned to his study.

"Another assassination attempt," he replied in what might have been a bold tone if his voice had not quivered so much. "I gave him a measure of my valor!"

"But who would ever want to harm you, kind Master?"

"A powerful Magician makes many an enemy along the way," he replied, and this time his voice seemed steadier. "So, what is it that you wanted from me? May I remind you that you are still grounded?"

"Oh, sure, very much so, I might say," Merkin replied in a soft voice.

He should have seen what was coming, but the damned girl did that pouty face that always put him off-guard, and besides, she shouldn't have had any power.

"FINES.VITAE(NUNC);" she whispered, and both of them collapsed on the floor.

03. SIMON

"Are you single?" inquired — rather bluntly — the email titled "Career Opportunity."

Simon thought about hitting the Report Spam button, but the fact of the matter was... well, he was, indeed, single, and being single at his age meant that he had to take his luck wherever he happened to find it. Besides, the message preview continued with a slightly less intimate question, "Do you hold a degree in Computer Science?"

This got him just interested enough to open the message.

The rest of the text was somewhat poorly endowed in terms of details, but intriguing nonetheless: an address in Rosedale, one of Toronto's posh neighborhoods, and a note stating quite emphatically that he was welcomed to drop by anytime, only he'd better move his ass and be there before eight because the liquor store closed at nine, and they were out of port wine.

Simon shrugged. He had had a bad shift that day, and managed to raise only $12.27 in tips. It simply wasn't fair that Amy should make fifty bucks on a regular basis just because she was a girl, and pretty, and she talked with the customers. People were supposed to come to Second Cup for coffee, not for wanton flirting.

All in all, he decided, anything that would take him out of this miserable job was a welcome opportunity. He checked his wristwatch, texted his buddy Jamie to ask if he could borrow the interview suit, and headed for the shower.

He emerged from the shower a few minutes later and read Jamie's reply, from which it became apparent that, yes, he could borrow the suit, but he'd have to pick it up from the drycleaner's. Simon had fallen into this trap before. Picking up stuff from the drycleaner's meant that you had to pay for it, too. Simon didn't have that kind of money on hand right now. He seldom did.

Sullenly, he slipped into his usual attire and checked himself in the stained mirror set above the dirty sink. With his long, frizzy, red hair, haunting hazel eyes, tarnished skull necklace and an unshakeable air of hunger about his person, he would have been suited for an interview only if the employer were auditioning for a rock band groupie. Simon checked the address once again on the Web and headed for the subway station.

***

The two-story mansion towered over Simon with that particular kind of smugness that dwells in the eye of the penniless beholder. "You are unworthy," it seemed to broadcast.

"Oh, bugger off!" Simon replied.

He climbed up the steps to the massive front door and reached for the knocker. He paused, regarding the thing with mild disbelief. It was, at least judging by its placement on the door, very much a knocker. It also had the familiar shape of a computer mouse decorated with an engraved motif resembling an eye. Wonderful craftsmanship, Simon decided with the expert eye of one who had played enough computer games to know art when he saw it.

Despite his best efforts, his attempt at using the knocker in the traditional way proved unsuccessful. The thing was stuck to the wood frame, and although a crowbar might have been useful in these circumstances, Simon had completely neglected to bring one to the interview.

But say what you will about Simon, he was, by no means, a man without problem-solving skills. In fact, Simon was one of those rare people who were naturally unhindered by their own lack of expertise and who also had an uncanny ability to find shortcuts where no shortcut ought to be. Simon did not solve problems, he just shamed them into going away. As he held his palm over the brass mouse, years of muscle memory kicked in, and he double-clicked. His brilliant efforts were rewarded with a ding-dong.

A few moments later, the door swung open, revealing a thin old man with round John Lennon glasses perched on an archetypal, aquiline nose and wearing his white hair in a thick ponytail.

"Please, come in," the man said, in the soft voice of someone whose larynx was determined never to go over the forty decibels threshold.

Simon stepped inside and produced a crumpled resume from his black jacket.

"That won't be necessary," the man said kindly. "Spread your arms and legs, please," he added nonchalantly. He chose an instrument that looked like a Geiger counter from a cabinet.

Simon did as told. You can't be too sure after 9/11, he tried to convince himself.

The man swept the business end of the apparatus over Simon's body while keeping an eye on the reader. He ran the test again to make sure the measurements were accurate, and when he was done, his face lit up.

"I'm Master Loo," he exclaimed (as much as someone can exclaim while still, technically, whispering) and shook Simon's unresisting hand. "Follow me, please."

Simon followed him into a richly decorated and brightly lit room. Master Loo sat down behind a walnut desk and invited Simon to take a seat on a red, leather sofa.

"So," Simon said, "not only are you looking for a single geek, but you would also prefer him not to be radioactive." He couldn't believe he had just said that. This was definitely not the right attitude for getting a job.

"It wasn't a Geiger counter," Master Loo replied, "although I can appreciate the confusion."

Simon waited for his host to expound on the subject, but he might as well have waited for snails to evolve opposable thumbs. He decided to go for the funny and professional approach just as the interview tips suggested.

"So, for all you know, I might actually be radioactive."

Master Loo smiled, although it seemed the kind of smile that had originated in a private joke rather than in what Simon had just said. He picked a paper from a side table and handed it to him.

"Can you decipher this?" he asked.

Simon gave the paper a quizzical look. The text had the familiar appearance of object-oriented programming code, at least when looked at through half-closed eyes. The trouble was, though, that it seemed to be written in —

"Is this Latin?" he inquired.

"Why, yes, it is. Well done!" Master Loo said encouragingly.

Simon failed to see how this would make his task any easier. This was suddenly becoming harder than those Google marathon interviews he'd read about.

"So?" Master Loo prompted.

Simon tried to concentrate. The indentation and the use of parenthesis told him he was looking at some sort of programming language, but the words were completely unfamiliar. So he started searching for recognizable Syntaxes, such as IF—THEN—ELSE, and, sure enough, his intuition proved right once again. He found what he was looking for, except that the actual wording was SI—ERGO—ALIUD. In a similar manner, he learned that OFFICIUM ARCANUS stood for PRIVATE FUNCTION and that FACERE—DUM was no more than a simple DO—WHILE loop.

The coding was archaic, for lack of a better word, simplifying the intricate parts in a nearly amusing way while overcomplicating the trifle bits in a distinctly head-aching manner. It was also anachronistic, kind of like finding bokeh in a renaissance painting. Little by little, the meaning started to unfold, and before long, Simon extricated himself excitedly from between the leathered cushions and exclaimed, "It's a program meant to control actions over distance, probably by means of a robot or other such device! Am I right?"

"That's the gist of it." Master Loo smiled again, and this time his heart was really in it. He reached for an inner pocket of his tweed jacket, and his hand came out holding a miniature crossbow, which he aimed carefully at Simon's chest.

Simon's last thought was, *Damn it! Not my Manowar T-shirt!*

04. MERKIN

Master Dung's study was silent. So silent, in fact, that one might have been able to hear a gnat passing air, if only an obligingly flatulent gnat had happened nearby.

Merkin opened her eyes and gave herself a quick system check. The results, she was not surprised to notice, were inconclusive: she appeared to be functioning within the safety parameters, but that didn't explain the cramps in her belly, nor did it explain what she was doing lying on the floor. She checked her watch. Two hours had passed since she had killed her Master.

Is he really dead?

A probing spell, no more intruding than a network ping, confirmed that he was. Good! Now if she could only find out what had happened to her. Merkin ran through the recent events, hoping that some overlooked detail would help her make sense of this mess.

First, she began her recap, she had placed an order for pizza and asked for it to be delivered through the back door. The tobacco-enhanced voice at the other end of the line told her the boy would be there in twenty-five minutes. Twenty-three minutes later she had entered her Master's study. Just as the yada-yada with the pretentious geezer had reached a slippery slope, the back doorbell rang. Right on cue.

As Master Dung walked out of his room, it was time for Phase Two. This was the tricky part. The entire Phase Two relied on a couple of assumptions that Merkin hoped were true: (a) that her Master was a narrow-minded bigot, and (b) that he was a vain bastard. Only a narrow-minded bigot would have enchanted his safe box to raise an alarm against any kind of magical presence other than his own but would have completely neglected to protect the thing against non-Magical beings like say, his grounded Scriptling. Furthermore, only a vain bastard would have used his birth date as the combination lock.

11

In her Master's safe box, Merkin found a pile of old Playboy magazines, various denominations of gold coins, and the small, pink quartz that stored her consent for being grounded. It was a perilous spell, not to mention illegal, but Master Dung had made it very clear to Merkin that she would not be accepted into his service unless she subjected herself to it. The soft quartz smashed easily under her foot, and as it did so, Merkin's powers came rushing back.

Killing the unsuspecting Master was the easiest part. She had come up with the spell herself. Never is one's guard lower than after a successful battle, and a battle was what brave Master Dung thought he had won when his Sumerian holy fire had consumed the pizza boy.

Her recollection was interrupted by the ding-dong[2] sound of the front door. Who could it be at this hour?

As she walked to the door, she became aware of a stale smell that seemed to be following her. Strange, she thought, she had washed not four hours ago.

The open door revealed two police officers.

"Good afternoon, ma'am!" the tall, ginger-headed cop said. "I'm Officer Chuck of Toronto Police Service, and this is my partner, Officer Liu." He pointed towards the Asian guy, who bore an uncanny resemblance to a Happy Buddha, albeit one dressed in uniform and wearing a gun.

"How do you do, ma'am!" Officer Liu touched his hat with the tip of his fingers and smiled ecstatically.

"What is this about?" Merkin asked, fighting her rapidly growing unease.

"Do you mind if we come in?" Officer Chuck asked in a gentle tone. "It's darn hot out here."

Merkin looked at the clouded sky but made no remark about it.

"No, you can't come in," she said before she could check herself. Of course they couldn't come in. There was an undeclared dead body in the house, and she was the only other person living, well, residing there. "You can't get in without a warrant," she added lamely.

"Ma'am, you watch too many movies." The Officer smirked. "It's all right, though, we don't really need to come in. We're investigating the disappearance of a young man. Have you seen him, by any chance?" He showed her a photo of a yucky-looking guy.

"No, I don't recall seeing him," she said, her voice steadier now that she didn't have to tell a lie.

---

[2] Not to be mistaken for the dong-ding sound of the back door

"He is a pizza boy at Pizzaville. The last they heard of him, he was delivering at this address, for one Mister Dang. By the way, ma'am, would you mind telling us your name? It's just for paperwork."

"Mer—" Merkin started. "It's Silvia. Silvia Longmore," she added quickly. She couldn't use her Magician name with the common folk.

"Mer Silvia Longmore," Officer Liu wrote down in his notebook, appearing mighty blissful having done so.

"Not Mer, just Silvia," Merkin said.

"So, Silvia, did you or anyone in this house order pizza yesterday around 4 p.m.?"

"Yesterday?" she asked. "No, we did order today, however. Around 4 p.m., indeed, but today."

"Strange." The officer sucked air through pursed lips. "I can't help but wonder why the pizza boy's car was towed yesterday at 6 p.m. from your driveway. Could it be that he came here yesterday, parked his car in front of this house, and then wandered off, anticipating that he would have to deliver a pizza the next day?"

Panic took over Merkin's senses. She could feel the words "FINES VITAE" wanting to be said, and she might have said them had she not been interrupted by a most opportune apparition.

"Good afternoon, officers," a tall, thin man in his forties interjected from behind the wheel of a Mercedes convertible. He looked dashing in his bespoke suit as he got out of the car.

"Good afternoon, sir," Officer Chuck replied. "How may we help you?"

"Inspector Cornelius Wehr, FBI," the man said and waved a badge under Chuck's nose.

"FBI? In Canada?" Officer Liu asked, though his partner said nothing.

There was something familiar about the badge, Merkin thought, but she couldn't put her finger on it. She stored the image in her mind for later analysis.

"Yes, I'm taking over this investigation," the man replied and showed Officer Liu his badge. "You guys can go back to your desks and close this case. Tell the parents their boy moved to Nunavut and he's doing research on – whatever. He's doing research."

The two policemen nodded in approval, then saluted and got back to their cars. Merkin watched with her mouth wide open. The man with the badge spun around and studied her for a second. His eyes not as much pierced as they peeled her.

"You're kind of young for a murderess. Master Dung must have grown softer of late," he said in a barely perceptible German accent.

05. SIMON

Around him, the world whirled in a synesthetic cacophony of echoing visions and blinding noise. In the short span of time it took for the crossbow bolt to pierce his heart, Simon hadn't quite had enough time to form an opinion of what to expect death to be like. But even in this uniquely unqualified position, Simon knew something was amiss.

For a start, in being able to articulate this mental equivalent of a raised eyebrow, he now had rather solid grounds to infer that he was thinking. And if he was thinking, why then, he must be, or so the famous quote would have him believe.

This knowledge brought Simon some relief, as well it should. Consequently, the eerie surroundings grudgingly resolved to make slightly more sense. Admittedly, they made about as much sense as the lyrics to Pearl Jam's "Yellow Ledbetter," but in largely the same way as the song, they gradually developed a quaint, undeniable beauty.

It was night, and, as far as nights went, this one was fairly inaccurate. One doesn't expect to see stars at night, not in a brightly lit city at any rate, and consequently one is completely entitled to feel quizzical about seeing the night sky laden with the things. Especially when it appears as if someone has been playing connect-the-dots with the stars, thus highlighting a plethora of constellations, most of which would indicate a very, very dirty mind indeed.

Although it looked entirely unusual, Simon knew without any doubt that the city unraveling before his eyes was his own, dear Toronto. It even had its own CN Tower.

For those who don't know it, the CN Tower looks roughly like an impaled doughnut, although one of majestic architectural beauty. The one that loomed in front of Simon's eyes differed from the original design in three significant ways: there was no stake, there was no doughnut, and one most certainly didn't go through the other. What it actually looked like was seven, giant Rubik's cubes set one on top of the other, moving slowly while

15

attempting to solve themselves. Yet, Simon knew beyond any doubt that it was the CN Tower.

The cubes travelled in all directions, and Simon couldn't help but wonder if there were people inside the building, and how they coped with the permanent shifting. Artificial gravity, most likely.

Blue, pink, red, green, white, and yellow, they all shone dazzlingly as they sought to move away from one another. Every single time they connected to an identical color, a bell sound erupted, and the cubes' brightness doubled in intensity. The colors closer to the ground had the deepest sound, while the topmost had the highest. And while the mathematics may seem impossible, this humongous instrument with a hexatonic scale contrived to play a complex and harmonious tune while at the same time aligning its colors.

By and by, without any conceivable warning, all the cubes reached their solution, and the music stopped.

Washed in the green light of the side facing him, Simon thought, with the self-fulfilling clarity found only in dreams, that the CN Tower must be announcing midnight.

"It appears you'd like to know what time it is," said the oddly-shaped staple that popped into existence in front of Simon's eyes.

"You must be kidding me," Simon said, nonplussed.

"No, I'm Stapley. I must be," the staple replied candidly.

"Well?"

"Well, what?"

"What time it is?"

"Oh, it's midnight."

"Right."

"Is there anything else I can help you with?"

Although Stapley asked this in a most genuinely interested voice, the word sequence has been so irremediably corrupted by countless customer service personnel that it was no longer possible to make it sound sincere.

"Am I dead?" asked Simon.

"Ah, you see, you may think this is a yes-or-no type of question," Stapley started

"Isn't it?"

"Yes," Stapley nodded. *"And then again, no."*

"I'm waiting," Simon said in a tone too patient to be genuine.

"OK, so you are dead, in Master Loo's house. But you're not dead here. That's good, not to mention perfectly legal, isn't it?"

"Is it?"

"*Of course, it is. You can't be alive in two places at the same time. It's against some law or other. Just imagine the taxes.*"

"I see," said Simon, who didn't exactly see, but who had a natural inclination to give logic a break where law and taxes were involved.

"*Right.*"

"Right."

"*Well, if that's all then, I should probably——*"

"What is this place? And how do you know about the one who calls himself Master Loo?" Simon interrupted.

"*Aaah, this is a very good question. What am I saying? It is an excellent question. Two questions actually. Two excellent questions!*" Stapley beamed.

"I swear to god, if you're going to follow this with, 'Let me get back to you on that,' I will bend you into a shape so anatomically suggestive that you will never be able to erase the memory from whatever it is that passes for your mind!"

"*No need to be like that,*" Stapley answered. "*I'm only trying to be helpful here. I beg you to understand my situation. I'm only an experimental plug-in, and a Beta version at that, so I have my limitations. Incidentally, I do encourage you to start working on a wish list for my future versions. Do you wish to grant me permission to start one?*"

"What do you mean, plug-in?" Simon asked.

There was no reply, and Stapley appeared to be frozen.

"Oh, for fuck's sake, yes, I grant you permission," Simon, who knew a thing or two about Beta versions, said in exasperation.

"*Thank you! I'm terribly sorry about that, but I don't do multitasking that well. Sometimes I just freeze until the current job is complete. I will add this incident to the log presently.*"

Mollified, Simon said, "That's nice of you."

"*So, anyway, you were asking what do I mean by plug-in. Am I right?*"

"I asked a lot of questions, but this would be a good place to start."

"*Dearly me, where do I begin?*"

06. MERKIN

"So, what did you do with the old bugger?" the man said as he entered the house. "My name is Sewer, by the way."

Cornelius Wehr... C. Wehr... Sewer... Smart alias, she thought. It could also be read as W.C., which put a whole new spin on the whole thing.

"I guessed as much," she lied. "I'm Merkin." She reluctantly shook his extended hand.

"Merkin. Well, that's a damn good name! I like it."

Merkin was confounded by this stranger. Yes, he had made the police go away, but she could have handled that on her own, couldn't she? And he knew about Master Dung's death. Not only that, but he knew that she had killed him. He hadn't asked; he just knew. He was scary. Still, that didn't seem to stop his making wanton conversation, and that was even scarier.

"Thank you," she said meekly.

It occurred to her that she could try to kill him, but she was smart enough to realize that adding to the trail of bodies that led to this house was not the best idea. She might kill him later, though, after she had learned more about him.

"I can imagine what you are thinking," Sewer said, "and under normal circumstances, I would invite you to try to do it. But, in light of recent events, I can't but think you might actually succeed, so I'll deny myself the pleasure of this duel. At least for now."

He smiled. And what a wicked but irresistible smile it was, Merkin thought, or at least that's what her teenage hormones thought.

"Who are you?" she asked. "You're a Magician. That much I can surmise by the way you mesmerized those coppers. If I'm not mistaken, that badge of yours is nothing but a Jolly Joker. The jester hat was kind of a giveaway. What else have I noticed about it? Ah yes, handcrafted, twenty-four carat gold – a bit flashy if you ask me – but effective, nonetheless."

"Impressive, considering you saw it for less than a moment. I am also moved by the fact that you've recognized one of my trademark artifacts, which also happens to be my coat of arms. However, the artist within me is sad that you didn't notice the black velvet backside and the embroidered monogram. Perhaps another time. As for me, I've already told you who I am."

"But—"

"No, no. Enough chitchat. I need to see the stiff."

"The what? Oh, all right, he is in the study," Merkin conceded. "I'll show you in."

"I can find my own way, but you may tag along if you wish."

She followed him, shocked to see the ease with which he navigated the corridors as if he knew the place like the back of his hand. When they reached the room, she couldn't help noticing Sewer's composure falter for a moment. "It must be the sight of the dead body," she thought.

After a few minutes in which he carefully investigated the scene, taking samples of skin and clothing, sniffing the air at various distances from the body, and casting a range of investigation spells, he turned to face Merkin and posed a one-word question,

"How?"

"Excuse me?"

"How did you do it? If I didn't know you killed him, I would swear he died a natural death."

"How come you are so sure I've killed him?" she asked, trying her best not to let the hope show in her voice.

In response, Sewer raised his right hand to her face and turned his palm so that she could see his onyx ring.

"Does this look familiar?"

Before she could reply, an image formed on the smooth surface of the stone, and to her dismay, she saw herself in the picture, bearing a posture that no Magician would ever mistake for anything else: her eyes slightly unfocused, her mouth forming the impossible "();" sound, and her fingers twisted in a gesture of power.

"It is a picture of me casting a spell, is all," she said, almost brave.

"And herein lies your admission," Sewer said triumphantly. "Your old Master had quite a few tricks up his sleeve." He chuckled. "It comes of having so many people wanting him dead. This image, which you so readily admit to be your own, was broadcast to my ring by a spell whose role it is to retain the details of the last moment before an attack was launched upon its caster. The spell also puts the attacker to sleep for a day, maybe two.

You wouldn't know that, of course, but I bet it's all starting to make sense now."

Merkin chewed on that for a while. Of course, she hadn't been out for just two hours after killing Master Dung, but rather for two hours and a day. That explained the cramps in her belly (hunger), her musty smell, and the police officers. She thought carefully about her next question. "Are there any more rings like this one?"

Sewer let out heartfelt laughter. "You are a smart cookie! I'll give you that."

"Only where it shows." Merkin smiled.

"To the extent of my knowledge, and I have no reason to think I'm wrong, the emergency spell can only be connected to one ring. But before you think about doing anything so brave as to kill the only witness, I wish to inform you that I, too, possess such a spell, and mine is slightly more advanced than our dearly departed Master Dung's."

"Ours?"

"Ah, nothing escapes you," he said, and seemed satisfied by this. "I used to be a Scriptling of Master Dung's, not so many years ago."

That explains a lot, she thought. Presently, her agile mind thought of something else.

"This 'emergency spell' as you call it, you say it is supposed to broadcast any attack. But you didn't mention anything about its being able to inform you whether the attack was successful. How is it, then, that you knew Master Dung was dead?"

Again, he regarded her with surprise and, quite possibly, newly gained respect.

"I was attending a private conference when the message arrived. Incidentally, I am quite upset at having to leave in such a hurry, for the conference, although on the arid theme of Investigating the Merits of Esperanto as a Candidate Dead Language in Modern Spell Casting, happened to take place at a most exquisite vineyard in Tuscany. Anyway, when I arrived here and saw you alive, it became obvious that you must have succeeded. I'm sure Master Dung wouldn't have let you live if you hadn't succeeded in your assassination attempt. And now, if you please, I believe you owe me an answer." He paused for effect and looked her in the eye. "How did you do it? You may notice I have no wish to know why. The old scum deserved it, as we both know."

To her surprise, Merkin decided to cooperate. Maybe it was the way this handsome man seemed to regard her with such interest, or maybe she just needed to confide in someone who could understand her, but whatever the reason, she was happy to do it.

"I knew Master Dung had a ward for any known spell, so, of course, I had to come up with something new. However, as it happens, I was grounded at the time."

And she told him about the call to the pizza shop, about her carefully timed entrance into the study, how she was left alone in there, how she broke into her Master's safe, and how she destroyed the grounding enchantment. When it came to telling him about the spell, she hesitated.

"I'm not sure I ought to tell you the wording of this spell. It's not that I don't trust you, because I obviously don't, but since it is such a new spell, I haven't thought of a ward against it yet, and I just don't want to take the risk."

Sewer let her report sink in for a minute before he spoke.

"This is most intriguing. Normally, assassin spells tend to leave clues like burn marks or traces of poison, but your spell left none of those. It is as if you simply made his life finish."

Merkin almost jumped as she heard his last words, for their meaning was exactly that of her Latin spell.

"One day, maybe you will hear this spell," she said, trying to brew a mix of menace and mystery. She blushed, then continued in her normal voice. "I suppose the emergency spell was your invention, right?"

It was Sewer's time to be taken aback. "How did you know?" he asked.

"Well, I guess we both know how the Master appropriated his Scriptlings' ideas and called them his own. If this spell were his idea, then I don't see why he should have named you the emergency contact. No offence, but we've already established that you don't seem the type to be trusted, and he didn't trust anyone. It then follows naturally that the reason he chose you was that you were the only other person in the world who knew about the spell. The question is, why did you rush here so fast when the distress signal was received?"

"Because I hoped you'd succeeded," he said solemnly. Then, in a low, almost concerned whisper he added, "and because I knew you would need someone to look after you. Well, not necessarily you, but whoever tried to kill him."

"I don't need anyone to look after me," she said indignantly.

"Is that so? What will you tell the other Magicians when they start inquiring why Master Dung is not answering their calls?"

"I'll tell them he died of a natural cause. You, yourself, said that's what it looks like."

"And why did you wait for so long to inform everyone?"

"Because I was grief-stricken," she said lamely, knowing even as she spoke that no one who knew Master Dung would ever believe that.

"You know better than that," he said, adding fuel to the fire of her doubts. "But they will trust me."

"Why?"

"Because I will tell them exactly what they want to hear. After all, no one will really be sad to see Master Dung gone. All we have to do is fill in the gaps, and everyone will be happy. But there is one condition," he said sharply.

07. SIMON

"So, let me see if I got this straight," Simon said. "This Master Loo has chosen me to be his apprentice."

"Scriptling," Stapley interrupted. *"I'm sorry, but I get a headache when you don't use the proper terms. You're a programmer, so you know keywords can never be aliased, right?"*

"Right. OK, so as I was saying, I've been selected to be a Scriptling. Not that I had anything to say in the matter, but let's ignore this for now."

"That's the spirit, Chief!"

"And I had to be killed because − I'm trying to use your words exactly − Master Loo believes this would facilitate a system update, the system being me."

"See, it's not that hard to use the right words," Stapley said encouragingly.

"And the reason I needed a system update is that this would grant me the magical abilities required in order to qualify as a Scriptling."

"You got it, Chief!"

"Then why, and I want you to bear with me while I ask this silly question, why didn't he choose someone who bloody well has magical abilities?" Simon finished on a shouting note.

"Well, looks like you'll be able to ask him yourself in a few moments. The system update is complete. It has been a great pleasure to be of service to you," Stapley said, and with that he disappeared along with the whole, fantasy-themed city.

***

"You're alive!" exclaimed Master Loo, in his whispered voice.

Simon was back in the room where he was killed. "Mmmmmmnhhh," he said.

"Oh, do pardon my lack of consideration, I had to staple your lips during the Ritual. You were shouting in your... in your death, you see? *Vigor mortis,* I believe, is the term," Master Loo explained as if it were the most normal thing in the world. "Here, let me take them off."

"Mmmmnhhh. You bastard!" Simon cried out, spitting blood.

"By all means, curse as much as you want. It's your right. Get it out of your system. I suppose from where you're standing, it may look as if I deserve that," Master Loo said in a conciliatory voice.

This was not what Simon expected. He didn't expect anything in particular, but this was most definitely not what he expected.

"You killed me," he stated.

"True, yet you are not dead," Master Loo replied softly as if revealing a carefully hidden secret.

"You seemed quite surprised about this not a minute ago," Simon replied bitterly.

"I must admit, I had my concerns, but the risk of your not coming back to life was never greater than twenty-four percent. I have the calculation somewhere in here," he said, gesturing to a huge pile of papers.

Simon burst into laughter. It wasn't funny, but sometimes there is so much craziness around that the brain needs to allow some of it in, just to equalize the pressure.

"So, you're some kind of wizard," he said as if not entirely convinced.

"Magician, if you don't mind. And a novocrat at it, a term that here means that I embrace the experimental nature of Magic and take immense delight in new technologies."

"This voodoo stuff that you've done to me doesn't seem all that cutting-edge."

"On the contrary! You are the first human being ever to...erm... to go through the transformation. This is, as far as we Magicians are concerned, a Holy Grail of sorts."

"Kind of like Higg's *bosom* is for scientists?" Simon asked.

"You mean to say Higgs boson," Master Loo corrected him. "But yes. Think of the possibilities!"

Simon thought of the possibilities and said presently, "I suppose there's a good market in bringing the dearly departed back to life and then giving them wizardly powers."

"While this might be a noble pursuit, alas, the scope of this enterprise in which you and I are involved is of a higher consequence."

"Excuse me, before you go into a lecture, where did the talking staple thing go? I was growing rather fond of it."

"I beg your pardon. The what?"

"You mean you don't know? While I was away in the not-quite-undead-yet state, this character showed up and tried to be helpful. A bit obsequious, but a well-meant chap. Looks like a staple."

For a moment, Master Loo's mind appeared to wonder elsewhere, but then it got back on track as fast as it had derailed.

"Oh, you must be talking about the shield wizard. It's just a bit of experimental code that I've added to the Ritual at the last moment. It was supposed to take the appearance of a friendly female. I don't know what happened."

"Perhaps the stapler that you used to shut my mouth may have had something to do with it," Simon supplied.

"Could be, could be. You never know with experimental code, do you?" Master Loo answered in his distracted tone.

"Please stop using the E word so *libertinely*," said Simon, whose attitude towards vocabulary was rather lax. I'm sure my health insurance doesn't cover the stuff."

"Oh, don't worry about it. As a Scriptling you need not fear about the frailness of your body." Master Loo waltzed obliviously around the joke. "You have received a rare gift. So rare, in fact, that fewer and fewer people get it nowadays."

"You mean Magic?"

"That's exactly what I mean. The Magician race is dying. It used to be a slow process, but in recent years the decline accelerated, and we can now make accurate predictions about the time when we will reach the critical point."

"Is this about that equation that states the growth rate of any society has to be one point something in order for that society to prosper?"

"Aah, you are, indeed, smart. I'm happy to have made the right choice. But it's not that. It's not that fewer people are born with magical abilities. Quite the opposite. Most people are born with some degree of magical skill, but it is often so modest it's negligible. In fact, the number of people possessed of enough proficiency to be called Magicians is as small as the number of people with no aptitude whatsoever. And it is a very small number."

"Let me guess; I fall into the latter category."

"That, you do. And you can't imagine how lucky I am to have found you. What are the odds, really? You are intelligent, young, educated in the arts of computers, and as magical as a talisman bought on eBay."

"I don't know about the odds. Until this morning I used to think Magic was bogus. And come to think of it, why does my inability make so much difference?"

"Because in order for the system update, or as I like to call it, the Ritual, to succeed, the subject must be, how shall I put it? *Tabula rasa.*"

"Is that some sort of food?"

"It's Latin, and it's one of the things you will have to learn. Do you speak any Romance language, by the way? It might help."

"I've picked up some Italian words whilst playing Assassin's Creed," Simon offered.

"That might not be enough, but I'm sure your programmer abilities will compensate for your linguistic deficiencies." Master Loo still sounded enthusiastic, if a trifle aloof.

"But what does Magic have to do with computer programming?"

"Everything, my boy. Everything," Master Loo said in the voice of someone getting ready to divulge the world's greatest secret.

08. MERKIN

"But I barely know you. What you ask of me requires trust," Merkin said.

"True, but we both know you need this," Sewer replied.

"And what if I do? Who says you're the right one for me?"

"I have the experience."

"You mean you've done this before?"

"A couple of times."

"Doesn't seem like a lot to me."

"Yeah? And how many times have you done it?"

"Touché. Still, what would the others say?"

"It's only natural. If anything, they will regard me as your benefactor."

"Ha! And where does that leave me?"

"Out of trouble, for a start. Plus, I do believe it will turn out to be rather enjoyable."

"You think?"

"Absolutely. With your youth and my know-how we'll get along just famously."

"I don't know."

"Look, I promise I'll keep it clean."

"No midnight drills? I hate those."

"No."

"No afternoon whatchamacallit?"

"Hell no!"

"No punishment for being a bad girl?"

"I promise, there will be none of that."

She pondered for a few moments. "All right, I'll do it. I'll let you be my Master," Merkin finally conceded.

"You are too kind," Master Sewer said mockingly.

"So, when do we start?"

"Right now. You can start by casting a regeneration spell on your old Master."

"What good will that do?"

"Why, it will make it look as if he's only been dead for a few hours, of course."

Merkin's jaw dropped. Of course! How could she have been so stupid? "I could have done this all along," she snapped.

"But you didn't." His smile widened.

"And then you wouldn't have had any leverage on me," she continued infuriated.

"And then how could I have persuaded you to be my Scriptling?"

"You tricked me!"

"Did I? Do you really feel cheated?"

She hesitated. All right, so she might have ignored his proposition if she had known she held all the cards, but now that she had listened to him, she didn't half-regret the prospect of spending more time learning from him. Besides, he was an attractive man, in a mature sort of way. A veritable M.I.L.F., where M stood for Master.

"Why are you smiling?" he asked.

She immediately checked her expression. "I'll get you one day, and don't you forget it!" she said, musing at the double entendre.

"We shall see about that. Now, let's get our stories straight. I got a call from my old Master telling me that he feels his life energy coming to an end, so I left the conference and came here as fast as I could."

"Why would he call you?"

"He must have been growing senile, a fact that you will be more than qualified to confirm, having spent so much time with him lately."

"I did catch him talking to one of his hairs," she supplied.

"Splendid! Now, when I arrived, the dear, old Master was almost spent. He did, however, have enough life in him to tell me his last wish."

"Which was to leave you in charge of this house and everything in it," she continued. "No one will buy it," she added bitterly.

"No need to. He had no progeny, and I am his oldest living Scriptling. By rights, all his estate belongs to me."

"What happened to the other Scriptlings?" she asked, fearing that she already knew the answer.

"Natural causes," he said. "Almost entirely, natural causes. Fire, lightning, and sudden coincidence."

"Sudden coincidence." She repeated his words as if tasting them. "You mean to say a sudden incidence of carbon monoxide? A CO-incidence?" she asked.

"Ha! Now, if you don't mind, you have a corpse to attend. I have some calls to make."

"Yes, Master," she said half-mocking.

"Hey, kiddo," he called as she was leaving the room.

"Yes?"

"You're welcome," he said and winked at her most charmingly.

09. MASTER LOO

"The boy seems promising, if a bit inconsistent," said Master Loo's inner voice.

What do you mean by inconsistent? answered Master Loo.

"Well, he is bright, but in a rough kind of way. Lots of raw intelligence, but only random traces of culture to back it up."

And what did you expect? This is the Internet generation we are talking about.

"Indeed. Anyway, let's hope this one lasts," the inner voice continued.

It really suits you, you know, this ominous tone, he replied, slightly annoyed.

"You are right, of course," Master Loo's inner voice conceded. *"By the way, have you thought of a name for him yet?"*

I have half a mind to call him Wart. Good name, Wart. Rhymes with...

"You called the last two Wart. Don't you think it's time for a change?"

This time it will work out. I can feel it in my code, said Master Loo.

"You said that the last time."

And you fancy I feel good about it?

"I bloody well know you don't feel good about it. And that's all the more reason to be careful with this one. It's not as if they grow on trees."

I am careful, as careful as I can possibly be, Master Loo revised his statement, knowing just how prone to distraction he was.

"Yes, maybe that's the problem, you know?"

And what exactly do you mean by that?

"Come on! We both know you have the attention span of a drunken parrot," Master Loo's inner voice said with exasperation.

There you go again, always exaggerating. You go and say hurtful things for no reason whatsoever. You are of no use! You... You... He searched his mind desperately for a fitting insult — *You, too!* — which, as far as comebacks go, sits right between "Oh, yeah?" and "How appropriate, you fight like a cow!"

***

"Everything?" asked Simon.

Now, in all honesty, Master Loo did suffer from an attention deficit, but with a brain like his, that's entirely excusable.

You see, while your run-of-the-mill brain is quite thrifty about sharing information with its owner's consciousness, Master Loo's brain was nothing of the sort. In fact, it was so generous in this particular respect that the poor man could never have dinner without being painstakingly aware of his facial muscles, tongue, larynx, stomach, yucky chemistry inside the same, pulse, tension, and balance along with a horde of subconscious processes dealing with unsolved issues, existential dilemmas, fears, complexes, desires, unsettling memories, fantasies, and whatnot.

It is, therefore, nothing short of a miracle that the man was able to perform anything as complex as yawning without injuring his knee.

"Say," Master Loo resumed the one conversation that took place outside his own mind, "there will be plenty of time for this later."

Then again, perhaps not, whispered the inner voice that only he could hear.

"Oh." The boy seemed disappointed.

"It's just a boring lecture anyway," Master Loo explained. "Besides, wouldn't you rather celebrate?"

"Celebrate what?"

"Well, you could celebrate your admittance to one of the noblest orders in the world."

"You mean the killed-without-permission order?"

Master Loo knew better than to rise to the challenge. "Plus, if you look at it from a metaphysical point of view, today is your birthday. As a matter of fact, we Magicians prefer to regard the day we became Scriptlings as our spiritual birthday. In your case, it is even more so, for it is also the day you came to life."

"Hurray!" Simon said mockingly.

If only he'd be so alive tomorrow, said the inner voice.

Master Loo ignored himself. "In that case, why don't we start with some cheese and wine?"

***

Certain technicalities such as, say, metabolism, had always been read-only process to Master Loo's consciousness. That didn't stop them from reading themselves very loudly, indeed, each and every single little moment of his life. Far from being in any position to dictate, Master Loo was more of a spectator to the fascinating inner workings of his own body.

31

Consequently, just because he understood exactly how alcohol worked its glamour on his mental processes didn't mean he was immune to its effects.

"I say, it has been quite a while since I had company," he said dreamily.

"Oh, poor you," Simon answered in a slurry voice normally achieved when facing east while at the same time pointing the tongue north. "You live all alone in this big house?"

"Ah, no. There's Gertrude, but she isn't what you'd call a conversationalist," Master Loo continued drunkenly.

"Who's Gertrude?"

"Oh, you'll meet her. She's probably asleep now."

"And she'll wake up tomorrow, unlike…"

"Say what?" Simon managed to articulate.

"I said," Master Loo's head swung back and forth, "I said she's asleep now."

"Not that. You said something about waking up."

Master Loo felt the panic rising, and with it some of the weariness went away. "I'm sure I did nothing of the sort. You must be imagining things. It's probably a side effect of the Ritual."

"You're wrong, and I'll tell you exactly why you are − —hic − — wrong. The reason I'm imagining things is because I'm drunk!"

"Err…"

"You are a good man, Master Loo. You don't mind if I call you Master Loo, do you? You are a very good man!"

"Well, I suppose—"

"What I don't understand is why a good man such as yourself would have such an ugly name," Simon managed to say through molasses lips.

"It's because of tradition," Master Loo said, thankful for the new turn of conversation, but still quite drunk. "You'll have a disgusting name, too, if you want to be a proper Scriptling. Incidenta-denta-lly, what do you think about Wart? It's a good name. It rhymes with…"

"Neaah, that's not disgusting enough."

"Is it not?" asked Master Loo, whose manners had been polished in an era when seeing a lady's ankles was still considered avant-garde.

"Absol'tely! Tell you what, let's finish this bottle and then I'll come up with a really ghastly name. And if I don't get any idea, then I promise that the first word that comes to mind tomorrow when I wake up with a hangover, that word, will be my magical name."

10. MASTER SEWER

As Merkin left the room, he allowed himself a big sigh of relief. She was definitely made of tough stuff, but on the bright side, the thing about tough stuff was that it tended to shine when properly polished. On the not-so-bright side, the thing about polishing tough stuff was that it took a great deal of sacrifice on behalf of the grinding stone.

Luckily enough, Master Sewer was, despite his shortcomings in the convoluted discipline of ethics, an accomplished tutor. Consequently, he knew that the best lessons are the ones you learn yourself. He also knew that the mark of a great pedagogue was to teach his pupils how to teach themselves. In other words, let diamonds polish themselves.

He was pulled from this introspection by the ring of the phone. He located the device and picked up the receiver, uttering a muffled grunt instead of the customary hello.

At the other end, a woman's voice speaking Mandarin with an English accent, or quite possibly the other way around, said, "Mistel Dang late fol massage. He nevel late."

"Who is this?" asked Master Sewer.

"This legistled massage telapist. Debolah L.M.T. Who this?"

"I'm a friend of Mister Dang," he replied, using Master Dung's street name.

"You flend of Mistel Dang, you get discount. You come heel, say Mistel Dang send, and ask fol Debolah. I give you special."

"Special what?" he asked in spite of himself. He then remembered the pile of Playboy magazines Merkin had found in their old Master's safe and got a pretty good idea of what Deborah, if that was her real name, meant.

"Is this cop?" she asked.

"I'm just a friend. Listen, Mister Dang died this morning. He's not going to require a massage session any time soon."

"Oooh, he dead? Do you want his appointment? Half houl still left. We can do latel?"

"I'm afraid I must decline. There's other stuff that needs taking care of now."

"Aah, you mean funelal. I have cousin, Licky, he do cheap funelal. Give discount. Say Debolah sent you."

"I'm not sure that would be appropriate—"

"He also give coupon to lestaulant, thilty pecent discount."

"I—"

"You bling mole guest, he gives set of authentic knives," she continued, unbothered by Master Sewer's intervention.

"Authentic what? German? Ming? Stone Age?" he asked, because he couldn't let a fallacy slip away when he spotted one.

"Dishwashel safe, debit only," Deborah produced from the arsenal of useful English words for immigrants with barely a pause for thought.

Knowing there was no other way to end this conversation, Master Sewer asked for cousin Ricky's phone number and wrote it down, anticipating Deborah would ask him to read it back to her, which she, of course, did.

11. BUGGEROFF

"You're alive!" Master Loo exclaimed.

"Bugger off!" groaned Simon.

"That's not a bad choice for a name," Master Loo nodded approvingly, following a train of thought that completely eluded Simon's understanding. "Sounds a bit Russian, but there's nothing wrong with that. Strong Magicians, the Russians. I've always said that. Incidentally, if you ever need a good shoelace-tying spell, then old Slavonic is your best bet."

"I beg you, shut up!" Simon groaned some more.

"Ah, you must be experiencing a hangover. Let me see if I can help you with that…" Master loo scratched his head and, apparently reaching a decision, snapped his fingers. "Since we are on the topic of old Slavonic, there's this old spell I read about somewhere."

"Please, no more experiments," Simon pleaded.

"Oh, but… I mean… Oh, all right. I suppose you earned your right to be picky. Very well then, will Latin suit you?"

There was a moan of resigned acceptance from Buggeroff.

"Here we go then: CEPHALEA.IRE();"

Suddenly, it felt as if the pain had never been there.

"Oh, wow! Are you kidding me? That was awesome!" Simon jumped out of the bed and shook his head in disbelief.

"It was nothing, really. You can learn that in practically no time, my dear Buggeroff."

"Say what?"

"Well, when I say no time, I refer to the usual learning curve for a new spell. It's actually more like a couple of days, once you learn Latin, of course."

"Not that. The name you called me just now, what was that?"

"Why, it's your new Scriptling name. I favored Wart, as you might remember, but Buggeroff is a nice and probably unique name. I like it."

35

Foggy memories, smelling of wine and embarrassment, crept shyly out of the dark recesses of Simon's mind and stood to attention.

"Oh, I see," he said, remembering the promise he made the night before with discomfort. "But you can still call me Simon, eh?"

"But of course. I would not dare call you anything else in public. At least, not if the public is of a non-Magical nature. Amongst Magicians, however, it would be most impolite if I were to address you by your street name."

"Oh."

"I know this is not an easy change to face, but think of it as your avatar name, like when you play computer games. By the way, just out of curiosity, what type of character do you usually play?"

Simon, err, Buggeroff, was confused by the rapidity with which the topic kept changing, but he replied nonetheless. It's what people usually do when they don't know what's going on: they talk. "I suppose you'd like me to say Sorcerer or Wizard, but I actually go for the sneaky type, like Assassin or Thief."

"That might be closer to the archetypal Magician than you would think. It is certainly closer than most of us would like to admit."

"And what character do you play? Necromancer?" Buggeroff asked, summoning a minor sample of cheekiness.

"Ha ha! I'm happy to see you're feeling better," Master Loo replied with good humor.

"Talking of which, why were you surprised that I am alive? Again."

The Master fell silent for a moment, apparently fighting a trilemma[3]. Then he said, "Well, I reckon I might just as well tell you."

"What, that I'm not your first attempt at creating a Scriptling out of a *tabbouleh pasta* human being?"

"How—"

"I mean, I thought it was pretty obvious."

"Was it?"

"Sure. Look, you said this whole thing was a sort of Holy Grail, didn't you?"

Master Loo nodded, taken aback.

---

[3] Magicians are too cool to deal with mere dilemmas. For the dirty minds in the audience, the one you are thinking about is called a hexa-lemma. Greek root, you know. Latin, now that would have been different (wink-wink).

"Well then, that means it has been tried before, but it wasn't quite a success, right?"

"Right, but—"

"Then there was Stapley, whom you called an experimental code. See, maybe I'm in the wrong here, but a guide is not the kind of thing a programmer, who is, by definition, a self-centered individual, does of his own accord. No, this is the type of feature that normally comes as the result of user feedback. This implies previous attempts. Isn't that so?"

"You are correct," Master Loo managed to say, though his mouth was dry.

"I'm not upset, you know."

"You are not?"

"No. Perhaps just a little confused. Yesterday I wasn't upset because I thought I'd already made it through the transformation. But now that I see you so excited by my being alive, I must ask if I've really made it. So, what can you tell me about this?"

Master Loo massaged his forehead with his thumb and index finger before replying, "You're the first to make it so far." He rushed to add, "It's a very good sign, but I can't promise you anything."

"How many were there before me?" Buggeroff asked in a quiet voice.

"Does it matter?"

Buggeroff said nothing.

"Twelve," the Master admitted. "You are the thirteenth," he added, as if stating the obvious would make matters better.

"Good, I was rather hoping I'd be a prime number," Buggeroff smiled, not entirely thrilled. "And what happened to them?"

"Didn't wake up," Master Loo said in a shamed tone.

12. MERKIN

Having heard the phone ringing, Merkin was half-tempted to eavesdrop on the conversation as she used to do when Master Dung was around (or at least around and alive). She had, long ago, devised a pretty neat spell for this very purpose, but somehow she was reluctant to use it just now.

There was something about this new Master that put her in a kind of awe. He was comparatively young for a Magician, but he seemed to be quite a few steps up the ladder in terms of power and ingenuity, rather the way she imagined herself to be when she got older. True, she knew things he didn't, like the assassination spell, but that could simply mean he hadn't given said things enough consideration yet. Bottom line, eavesdropping or any kind of defiance would be a risky affair. Not really crossed off the list, just risky. In time, she would start testing the limits of his power, in a kind of controlled experiment, if you will. Until then, though, she would play ball.

The regeneration spell on her old Master's body was an easy job. It did nothing to improve his looks, but it took care of all those tiny, telltale signs that coroners read for a living. Just to be on the safe side, she also took the time to clean up the magical residues from the room — a process that computer aficionados would probably compare with clearing the cache or defragmenting the hard drive to prevent any attempt to undelete.

It was now time to take care of herself. First a shower and then new clothes. She emerged from her room a while[4] later looking fresh and smelling of wild flowers, while behind her the music box played the theme from *Beauty and the Beast*.

Presently, she climbed down the stairs and, as she turned 'round the corner on the dark corridor that led to the living room, bumped right into Master Sewer. While it lasted for only a moment, the contact sent thrilling sensations like lightning through her body, setting her blood on fire. Her

---

[4] The amount of time a woman needs to wash and dress herself is one of nature's unquantifiable variables.

cheeks were red — she was sure of that — and she hoped fervently that he would not notice.

On his part, her Master didn't appear all that affected by this incident, but then again, Merkin couldn't really be sure in that dim light.

"You must be hungry," he said as if nothing had happened.

That, she was. It had been more than a day. She could not recall ever allowing such a long time to pass between her meals.

"It can wait." She forced herself to appear indifferent to his concern and headed for the living room.

"I'm sure it can," he conceded, falling in step behind her. "But as it happens, I, too, am hungry, and — call me old fashioned — I like to think that food plays an essential role in alimentation. You smell nice, by the way."

In the sunlit living room the light fell absolutely perfectly on Merkin's crimson cheeks, but her Master did not witness their blatant betrayal. He was probably under that silly, testosterone-driven belief that delivering a compliment should inevitably be followed by a dry spell of indifference.

"It's just soap," she said.

It was like calling Château Pètetrop just a wine. Merkin was quite a skilled alchemist. This was partly because her old Master's relentless quest for the ultimate hair loss treatment had given her the opportunity to play with some pretty exotic recipes. But more importantly, it was due to her own, malicious agenda, which was to discover just how closely she could follow the hair loss formula while making it achieve the exact opposite of what it was meant to do. It was the same kind of questionable talent exhibited daily by auto mechanics all over the world.

Merkin had used only one drop of the "just soap." Two drops would have made her Master walk slightly awkwardly. Three drops would have made a Victorian gentleman utter something really lustful, such as "you transfix me quite."

"So, do you want to order, or would you rather go out?" Master Sewer asked.

"Don't we have a funeral to organize?"

"We can discuss the funeral over dinner."

"If I didn't know any better, I'd say you're trying to seduce me," Merkin said with just the right amount of purr in her voice.

"Kids these days." Her Master smiled. "If you must know, I've already informed a couple of local Magicians about dear, old Master Dung's regretful demise. I should say that by now the news has reached the west coast. Believe me, these people are faster than Twitter."

"These people?" Merkin snorted. "You say that as if you don't belong to the bunch."

"By vocation I am a Magician, that much I can admit to. But I'm sure you will agree that pertaining isn't necessarily the same thing as belonging. Do you know what I mean?"

"I think I get the gist of it."

"As for the funeral, as luck would have it, I just happened to find a guy who can take care of everything. Ah, the joy of modern times! There is a service provider for any type of need you might have."

"There's nothing modern about paying someone to handle a funeral. It's called undertaking, and it must have existed since the dawn of civilization."

"Yeah, but how many undertakers offer authentic knives as incentive, eh?"

13. BUGGEROFF

Master Loo gave him the rest of the morning off, saying that he needed to work on a new idea.

Alone in the shower, Buggeroff struggled to come to terms with this new life. Actually, it wasn't the new life per se that gave him pause, but rather the notion that he felt abandoned by the old one. Surely someone must be missing him: if not his friends, then at least the Revenue Agency, or his overly enthusiastic dentist.

Yet, he had been missing for two nights, and, so far, there was no sign of any attempt to set him free. By now the police should have checked his email account, found the mysterious interview invitation, gotten Master Loo's address, and sent the Emergency Task Force to the rescue.

And then it dawned on him. If there was anything that could interfere with the good old Canadian civic sense, that something must have been of a magical nature. If that was the case, then he did not stand a chance against Master Loo's spells. He decided to put this theory to the test as soon as possible.

It was then that he noticed something out of place. He wasn't sure, but he thought he saw something creeping at the edge of his vision. It was not, his brain rushed to tell him, a white goat slithering on top of the shower curtain rod. There were too many things against this interpretation: the rod wouldn't hold, goats aren't physically suited to be snake impersonators, and anyway, there must be a regulation against keeping livestock in a residential area.

"Don't panic now," he thought. "There's nothing scary about a goat, not unless you are a particularly juicy patch of grass. Yes, but a sneaky goat is not the same thing. It shows purpose. Who knows what a purpose-driven goat can do? Anyway, I don't see any goat doing stealthy maneuvers around here. Exactly!"

There was a brief fight-or-flight battle in his mind. One of them must have won, but in the spur of the moment Buggeroff wasn't sure which. He grabbed the curtain with his left hand and pulled it hard while with his right hand, he executed a slow, but choreographically correct, karate chop. It was a success in that the goat-who-was-not-there was, well, not there. In every other way, it was a sad and painful failure. In pulling hard at the curtain, he managed to dislodge the rod, which then promptly hit the fingers of his right hand and then his kneecap, finally resting with a loud bang on his toes.

Ashamed of himself, he turned off the shower, repaired the damage, dried, and then left the bathroom.

His cell battery was dead. Damn it! He really wanted to see if anyone had been trying to reach him. Oh, well then, he would have to do things the hard way.

***

"There you are," said Master Loo as he, Buggeroff, was trying to sneak out the front door. "I have wonderful news!"

"Oh, joy!" Buggeroff sighed.

"Come! Let us go into my study."

He followed his Master and sat down in the same red, leather sofa where he had been killed only three days ago.

"I've been meaning to ask," said Buggeroff, "why did you use a miniature crossbow? Is there something profoundly occult about it?"

"Oh, no, nothing of the sort. You see, I couldn't use a regular crossbow because that might have ruined the sofa." Master Loo delivered this speech in his usual matter-of-factly manner. "I could use Magic to fix the hole in the leather, but it would never look the same, you know?"

"Right. I'm glad that's settled. So, what was it you wanted to tell me?"

"Yes, exciting news! It's time for you to learn about the Magical learning system."

There was a pause during which the Master's attention seemed to have taken the wrong exit on the neural highway.

"You mean that's all?" Buggeroff asked, not particularly excited by the topic of training methodologies in general.

"It is a system much akin to that of leveling up in computer games," said Master Loo, whose mind had apparently swerved back to the right track.

Buggeroff was suddenly very interested. "Hey, that's neat!"

"I thought you'd like it. Here is how it works."

There were, Master Loo explained on a chart, three major classes: Arcane, Power, and Skills.

Arcane, aka dead-language-prowess, branched into Latin, Sumerian, and Slavonic. Power dealt with the capacity of Casting and Maintaining a

Spell plus Syntax. Skills was more of an auxiliary class, and it contained Enchanting, Alchemy, and, curiously enough, Extispicy. The latter, better known as Divination by Means of Animal Entrails, was a less popular and seldom practiced art, but it was traditional, so every Scriptling had to learn at least the fundamentals[5].

Every category had four grades of proficiency, and each initial grade cost one level point. An extra point was required for each subsequent level, so mastering one category would cost ten points.

"So, if I get all the points, I get to be a level ninety Magician and call myself a Master?"

"It's not as easy as that. As soon as you master at least four categories, you will no longer be considered a Scriptling, but a fully-fledged Magician. Few people ever get to level ninety, as points become extremely difficult to acquire. To become a Master you have to be a Magician, and then undertake the Pedagogical Module."

"So, what level are you?"

"Dear boy, you have no way of knowing it, but this is a very impolite question," said Master Loo kindly.

"You mean, like asking someone their salary?"

"Similar to that."

"But then what is stopping a slick Scriptling from claiming Magician status?"

"Ah, spoken like a true Thief character, always thinking about shortcuts. One must pass an exam to become a Magician, and trust me, this exam cannot be faked."

"I see," said Buggeroff. "So, how do I get points? Do I run around doing small quests, like walking people's dogs, helping an old lady with her pest problem, or asking subway passengers not to block the doors?"

"Well, this is where things get a little complicated." Master Loo scratched his stubby chin. "Learning and practicing, these are the two keys. You certainly won't get any better at Latin by helping old ladies."

"Oh." Buggeroff's shoulders sagged.

"There, there, all is not lost." The Master smiled gently. "All potential Scriptlings have one thing in common: they start with one point. It is, actually, the single qualification they need, the difference between level zero and level one. Can you guess what that is?"

---

[5] On the bright side, this fact alone was responsible for making every Magician a decent turkey carver, which could be extremely handy in numerous social contexts.

"The ability to cast spells?" Buggeroff tried.

"Precisely! A grade one in Casting," said Master Loo, appearing rather proud of his pupil.

"So, that's what the… the Ritual was all about? Making me capable of casting very simple spells?"

"Why, yes! And by the way, there is more. You will reach level two sooner than you would expect."

"How is that?"

"Truth be told, this is not as exciting as you would think. You see, at one point or another, you will have to get that required grade one in Extispicy. Scriptlings usually choose to get it out of their way first."

"That's OK," Buggeroff conceded. "I do feel like cutting a goat's belly open."

With barely a shimmering of the air, a white goat appeared on top of Master Loo's walnut desk. Her body was curled, but her head was lifted and it was tilting hypnotically on a horizontal plane. She hissed.

"Now, then," Master Loo said in a conciliatory tone, "I'm sure he didn't mean it that way. Isn't that so, Mr. Buggeroff?"

"Didn't mean what, in what way? And who the hell is that?"

The goat hissed again and made as if to strike. For some reason, the name Chupa-Cobra formed in Buggeroff's mind.

"Hush, Gertrude darling, hush!" the Master said. "The nice Buggeroff is going to apologize for saying nasty things, and everything will be all right." He caught his pupil's eye and begged him wordlessly to play along.

"Err… Um … I … I'm sorry for saying I'd like to cut your… I mean, a goat's belly open," he said awkwardly.

Gertrude hissed again, but it was, if such thing can really be perceived, a hiss of acceptance.

"I don't believe you two have been properly introduced," said Master Loo. "Gertrude, this young gentleman is my new Scriptling, Buggeroff. Buggeroff, this is my familiar, Gertrude."

Buggeroff was not one for etiquette. His knowledge of the matter could have literally been stored on a grain of rice without using nanotechnology. He had, however, the kind of good-heartedness and common sense that could, in most cases, offset the lack of protocol. It is thus that, guided more by instinct than by anything else, he reached a hand towards Gertrude, not knowing whether to expect a shake or a bite. Reluctantly, Gertrude motioned her muzzle towards his hand and started to chew absentmindedly on his sleeve.

Master Loo said, "Gertrude has been in my family for generations. I would be hard-pressed to guess exactly how many generations, and it would be impolite to ask her, of course."

"Can I just ask something else then?" Buggeroff raised his hand, which Gertrude, who apparently had grown fond of his sleeve, followed with great interest.

"Yes, she is a goat, and yes, sometimes she fancies she is a snake. I say, don't worry about it. She is not poisonous."

It was hard to tell if Master Loo ever joked. Sure, he appeared to understand humor, but it was probably in the same way some people understood and appreciated music, yet never hummed a tune. Buggeroff chose to take his Master's last sentence at face value.

"How did this happen?" he asked.

"Why, it's quite simple. There are typically two ways in which an animal can become poisonous. One of them is to have poison sacs, like snakes or spiders, and the other one is to have a really filthy mouth, like the Komodo dragon. Herbivores are, I'm afraid, evolutionarily handicapped in this field. You see, grass just sits there. There is no need to poison it into submission before eating it."

Buggeroff regarded his Master with wide eyes for a moment, and then decided he would not pursue the subject any further lest he receive yet another lecture in comparative biology.

He turned his head towards Gertrude and whispered in a resolute tone, "OK then, we'll start anew, but there must be boundaries. Like for instance, the bathroom is off-limits. It's my private time. Understood?"

Gertrude watched him hesitantly, which must have come hard to a creature whose eyes were made for displaying an uninterested sort of apprehension. She then nodded slightly and stretched her neck towards Buggeroff's hand. Half-heartedly, he let her chew some more on his sleeve.

"Great! I'm glad this is settled then," said Master Loo. "Now, if you would follow me to the basement, we will start your first lesson in Extispicy momentarily."

***

The basement had that clean, lab look and smell that somehow contrived to make a torture chamber seem a welcoming place by comparison. On the polished, metallic surface of the table, the didactic material, apparently freshly killed, bled quietly into an aluminum bowl.

"I was hoping for a chicken," muttered Buggeroff, fighting back his gag reflex.

"Where would you find a live chicken in Toronto?" his Master replied. "Besides, raccoons are larger and they don't require too much dexterity."

"Where did you find it?"

"Oh, I didn't. Gertrude did, not twenty minutes ago. I guess she wanted to make a good impression."

Buggeroff considered this. So, Gertrude, the goat named Gertrude, went out and caught the poor creature right after paying him a visit in the shower. He was not sure which was scarier, that a goat was able to ambush and kill a raccoon or that said goat wanted to make a good impression on him, Buggeroff.

"That's very… considerate of her," he said, not knowing whether Gertrude was around or not.

"Good, good. Now, why don't you take this scalpel and make the first incision."

Cautiously, Buggeroff took the scalpel and tried to get a good grip.

"No, not like that," said Master Loo. "It's not a bread knife. You have to hold it like a pencil or a brush. Think of it as an extension of your arm."

Buggeroff had heard this line before, back in his adolescence when he wanted to be a ninja. His Kendo sensei had told him the same thing. After three weeks of frustrating attempts, he had come to the conclusion that considering the sword an extension of his arm meant only that he had a bloody long arm. That couldn't possibly make it more dexterous.

He took Master Loo's advice, however, and held the scalpel like he would a pencil. He remembered enough from his martial arts failure to know that you didn't have to squeeze the handle, but rather, hold it gently.

"Good, now make a shallow cut like so, just for practice," said his Master, drawing an imaginary line on the raccoon's belly.

Buggeroff did as requested, and, to his surprise, the cut was pretty straight.

"Now, try again, only deeper. Don't go too deep, mind you, because you wouldn't want to puncture the stomach or an intestine. I have no idea what these things eat, and I'm sure I don't want to learn, either."

He followed his Master's advice and made a second cut.

"Perfect! Now, just put your hands in there and spread the gash a little bit to let the organs flow out."

Without much enthusiasm, Buggeroff did as told. "So, now, how do I interpret the mystical messages contained within these wobbly bits?" he asked.

"Ah, that only comes at grade two. For now you will just have to practice these first steps."

"How many times do I have to do it to get the first grade?"

"I'd say four, maybe five, more times. When you are able to do it on a rat, you should be proficient enough."

Buggeroff gulped, feeling none too thrilled about the prospect.

"In the meanwhile, you've got to go shopping."

"For a rat?"

"No, for clothes. You've been wearing these for days, and it is starting to show."

This was the opportunity he had been waiting for. He would get out of the house and never come back. Then again, maybe he would come back to try this Scriptling thing for a while, you know, just for fun. He could quit anytime he wanted.

"Here, you can use this credit card." Master Loo pulled him from his introspection. "The PIN number is 9278, which you'll remember easily, as it stands for WART. Sorry, I had the card made when I still had my heart set on Wart."

"What's the credit limit on this?"

"Don't worry about that. You can buy whatever you want. Just try to get something sober too, you know, shoes, suit, tie, and everything."

"Why is that?"

"We are going to attend a funeral."

14. MASTER SEWER

A phone call to Duff's, and thirty minutes later they were having dinner. His new pupil was a voracious eater, very unladylike, but strangely becoming in a primal instinct sort of way. And she did smell nice.

"Don't you eat anything healthy, like fruit?" he asked.

"I hate fruit. Did you know one of the Brothers Grimm was killed by a fruit?" she said in a serious tone.

Master Sewer searched his memory for the reference, and when he finally got the joke, a smile lit up his face.

"So," he said, "tell me more about yourself. How long have you been under Master Dung's tutelage?"

"Couple of years," she replied between a hot wing and a gulp of beer.

"Been grounded a lot?"

"Once every two or three weeks," she said and attacked another corrosive-grade piece of chicken.

He whistled appreciatively. "On average that's twice more often than I. I must declare myself impressed!"

"What did you get grounded for?"

"The usual, I suppose. Being smarter than he, setting the house on fire, stealing money from him. What about you?"

"More or less the same, although I've never set the house on fire. The closest I got to that was when I accidentally opened a portal to a world that looked uncannily like Mordor."

Having spoken too much and eaten too little in the last five seconds, she grabbed a fistful of fries and shoved them into her mouth. For some reason, Master Sewer felt a strange tingling down his spine as she did so.

"Did he ever steal your ideas?" she asked.

"Of course, he did. I don't think he ever had a Scriptling whose ideas he did not steal. But in doing so, I believe he proved himself very useful to the magical establishment."

"How so?" Merkin asked suspiciously.

"I'm not trying to defend him. I'm merely putting one and one together. Back when I was his Scriptling, I used to regard him as a kind of parasite because he was living on other people's backs. Later on I realized he was more like a virus, but a strangely useful virus."

"Huh?"

"Think about it. He didn't just consume ideas, but rather spread them around (of course, marking them as his own). Isn't this phenomenon called *viral*?"

"I guess so."

"Moreover, as far as I was concerned, he stole only my better ideas. The crème de la crème, if you will. Was this the case with you, too?"

Merkin nodded and thought about the implications.

She cleaned some sauce from her mouth with the back of her hand. "So, you're saying that he was an evolutionary vector?"

"Interesting wording. I like it! Indeed, it is fascinating to see how, in pursuing his own, selfish dream of grandeur, he had actually managed to help a lot of Magicians. He never was an accomplished Magician himself, as you have very well discovered on your own. I daresay his short-term memory never helped him in this respect. You see, I don't believe Master Dung was ever capable of storing more than five spells in his mind at any given time. Still, he did not have to know everything. He had to know only where everything was. And this is, you'll have to take my word for it, a very useful skill."

"Are you trying to make me feel bad for killing him?"

"Oh, no. The bastard deserved it, and you know it. I must try to remain distant and objective, though. You should try it, too, sometimes. Who knows what you might learn."

"Was this like a lesson? Should I write it down in my notebook, Master?" she asked mockingly.

He ignored her remark, knowing this would hurt her more than a rebuke. Punishing meant acknowledgement, and acknowledgement was what everyone wanted. But teaching has never been about what people want. It is about what they need. That's what makes it so hard.

"How old are you?" he asked.

"Old enough," she said smugly, taking one more swig of beer.

"I was rather hoping you'd be older than that," he said, adding just a bit of bitterness in his voice.

It was an old game, establishing dominance. Every teacher and every pupil have played it together. It was the game that never ended. Master Sewer might have scored one just now, but Merkin was sure to try him again, and again, mercilessly, ever harder, ever cleverer. It would be tough for her, but it would be even more so for him.

"Twenty," she mumbled, starring at her knees. She must have felt the whiplash, Master Sewer thought, and she would come back at him for it, no mistake about it.

"You have accomplished a lot for your age," he said. It was true. It was also something that she needed to hear.

"But not enough," she answered.

"How so?"

"Well, for a start, I know I'm already too old to be a child prodigy."

"Did you want to be one?"

"Of course, I did."

"Why is that?"

"To be famous. To be remembered. Why else?"

"It's never too late to be famous and to be remembered, if that's what you really want."

"Yeah, but it gets harder as you grow older. When you're a kid, all you have to do is be smarter than someone who is a couple of years older. But now, who would care if I'm smarter than a forty or sixty-year-old?"

"And would you rather bask in the ephemeral fame of being better than someone older than you, or would you prefer to be forever famous for something that only you in the entire history of mankind were able to achieve?"

"Like what?"

"Like, I don't know, you could set a new world record for eating hot wings, or be the first woman on the moon, or perhaps you could finally set things straight by writing the ultimate computer virus," Master Sewer finished in a conspiratorial tone.

15. BUGGEROFF

"There was something I meant to ask you before you go," said Master Loo as Buggeroff was about to open the front door.

"Sure," Buggeroff said, trying not to sound rush.

"Would you find it helpful if I were to reactivate Stapley for you?"

"How do you mean?"

"It's not a big deal from a technical point of view, and you might find it useful having him around. He can be your personal assistant, you know?"

"You mean he could keep track of my level progress, unsolved quests, and suchlike?"

"Yes, why not? While I'm at it, I can also add a Navigation Module, translation capabilities, maybe a glossary of magical terms…"

"Sure, throw in whatever you think might help! Can you do it now? I can wait a few more minutes if you want me to."

Master Loo scoffed, but he did it in his demure and polite way. "Dear Buggeroff, this will take more than just a few minutes. I will do my best to have it ready by the time you come back from your shopping spree, though."

Buggeroff didn't even try to conceal his disappointment. Now he really had to come back. Having a personal assistant capable of all those things was too good a deal to miss.

"Speaking of which, if you could hold still for a moment, I will just cast a little washing spell on your clothes. Ready? Here it comes. LAVABIT();"

Buggeroff felt his clothes soak and dry in less than a second. It was an interesting sensation, but not one he would willingly repeat any time soon. Still, the spell was useful, and he planned to learn it as soon as possible. "Thank you," he said.

"Don't mention it. Of course, this works better if the person is removed from inside the clothes prior to casting the spell."

"It worked pretty well, if you ask me." Buggeroff laughed. "Hey, this seems like an eco-friendly way of doing laundry. Hasn't anyone thought about making money out of it?"

"Ah, you're quite the mercantile, aren't you? Yes, of course someone has thought about it. Indeed, they have thought about it so well that they have actually copyrighted the spell for commercial purposes."

"Huh?"

"It means you need a license to operate a business like that."

"A license? From whom?"

"Aha, why don't we talk about this later? It's too complex a subject, and you are anxious to do some shopping, I can see."

"All right then." Buggeroff sighed. "See you later."

"Oh, before I forget, here is the key to the front door," Master Loo said quickly, handing him a shiny, oblong object that looked exactly like an USB key.

"Gee, thanks!" he said, dropping the key into one of his deep jeans pockets.

"Be safe!" Master Loo said behind.

***

"Yes, what can I get for you?" said the cute chick behind the counter at Second Cup.

"Hi, Amy," said Buggeroff.

"I'm sorry, do I know you?" asked the confused Amy.

"I used to work here," Buggeroff supplied. "You're Amy, Amy Sharkowicz. You live two blocks away from here, and you have a black poodle named Sweetie."

There was a hint of panic in her eyes, but she recovered quickly.

"I've a terrible memory for faces," she said. "How long ago did you say you've worked here?"

"I quit two years ago," he lied, knowing there was no point in pursuing this.

"But I didn't work here two years ago," she said, this time in a clearly wary voice. "Who are you? What do you want from me?"

"I'm—" Then seeing Mike and Darnella, his former colleagues, take an interest in the conversation and appearing equally suspicious, he went on, "I'm sorry, must have got the wrong person," then spun around and made a quick exit from the coffee shop.

Out on the street, he considered paying a visit to his old roommate Jamie, but he reckoned the chances of that having a positive outcome didn't look good. His old life had, indeed, been erased by means of Magic. He hadn't the skill to take his life back, and, in light of recent events, he wasn't even sure he wanted to.

Screw the old life! Why wallow in the sticky mud of poverty and underachievement when he could bask in the glory of being a great Magician? With this newfound resolution, he marched ahead towards the Eaton Center, comfortable as never before in the knowledge that he had a badass credit card in his wallet.

16. MASTER DUNG

FINES.VITAE(NUNC);

What a curious, innovating, powerful and yet incomplete spell. It had taken Master Dung almost a day to comprehend what had happened to him. Finish life now. Indeed so. But something in the underlying code had been wrong. That is to say, something had been right from Master Dung's point of view. His body had been killed, no doubt about it, but somehow his spirit, or whatever metaphysical fabric Master Dung was made of, had survived.

"Mourir c'est partir un peu," he thought. How true! Or was it the other way around? It was all kind of fuzzy, as if his mind was doing its thinking in limericks. But that was not his only problem. He could not move. His mind knew all about the wanting but nothing about the doing. Without his body, he was stuck.

He watched with detached interest how his two most insufferable Scriptlings ever, Merkin and Sewer, teamed up and how they planned to take over his possessions. For some reason, it didn't really matter anymore. Yes, he felt betrayed, and, yes, he wanted revenge, but this was all irrelevant. He was nothing but an amorphous blob, occupying roughly a six-foot wide sphere around his lifeless body. How much revenge could he possibly summon?

And then the thought struck him: he would be trapped with his body for what could possibly be an eternity. It struck him really hard, too, especially when he remembered that the standard depth of a grave was six feet. He wished he'd asked to be cremated, and thus have the chance of facing the harsh oblivion on someone's fireplace mantel where at least some kind of action was bound to happen every once in a while. As it was, all that awaited him was being forever aware and alert while having nothing better to survey than a hundred cubic feet of maggot-infested earth.

He wanted to shout, but he had nothing to shout with.

FIRST TRIBAL INTERLUDE

The Tribe moves. It always has, ever since the first man cast his eyes across the lush African grasslands and wondered what was out there. Others followed that man and thus the Tribe was born out of its own motion, through the self-propelling bond of shared curiosity. The Tribe does not forget its birth, and because every society has to have some form of religion, curiosity is theirs.

Incidentally, it is worth noting that the early human migrations had not been driven by a keen interest in geography nor had they been driven by a highly localized cataclysm. They had, instead, been driven by a bunch of nagging old people who kept on and on about how the Tribe left without putting out the fire and how anyone who was strong and sensible enough should go after the Tribe and stop them before they killed all their antelopes and buffaloes. As a result, some of the people who were strong and sensible decided to leave, not highly preoccupied with the antelopes and buffaloes but extremely intent on finding a place where nagging old people would not be a part of the landscape. Time after time, the story repeated, and to this day, the main reason young people choose to move away is so to be as far as possible from their own, nagging, old people.

The Tribe moves, but there is no rush. Since the beginning of its journey, the Tribe has trailed around the world twenty-seven times, leaving over five thousand generations behind in its wake. Even so, despite its early start, the Tribe was not the first to discover the Americas, and that is probably because at the time that the first humans crossed the Beringia land bridge, the Tribe was having a lot of fun taking the scenic tour around Australia and New Zealand before all the tourists showed up.

The Tribe calls itself Mama. The Tribe believes that if an idea cannot be expressed in a single syllable, then it is the idea, rather than the word for it, that needs refining. It is, therefore, of huge linguistic significance that the Tribe's name is made out of two syllables. And because one disyllabic word is as big an exception as the Tribe's vocabulary will allow, Mama is also the name the Tribe has given to its singular religious figure. This deity, who is also affectionately called Ma (their word for Mother), has three aspects: the eternal fountain from which curiosity springs, the never-stopping vehicle through which curiosity is transcended, and the bottomless receptacle[6] in which the fruits of curiosity are stored.

The Mama speak a language as old as the Tribe, and just like the Tribe, their language bears numberless marks of its itinerant history. Its sounds range from undemanding grunts, clicks, and whistles to impossible triphthongs and liaised consonants. Learning the language is a continuous process that takes more than a lifetime, and this is where reincarnation[7] really comes in handy. Because no one outside the Tribe speaks Mama, the Tribe members are more than happy to learn (and more often than not, update) their knowledge of local languages as they pass by.

The Tribe has thirty-seven members and a dog whose name is, and always has been, Spike. In its current incarnation, Spike is a female dog, which, out of respect for her spiritual age and role, will not be referred to as a bitch. Owing to the fact that the average lifespan of a dog is much shorter than that of a human, Spike holds the Tribe's (and surely the world's) record for reincarnations. She is also the oldest member of the Tribe, a fact determined by the debatable but sufficiently accurate equation that says that a dog year equals seven human years. And since seniority is a tradition that transcends irrelevant obstacles such as species, Spike is also the Tribe's matriarch. The Tribe is very happy with this arrangement, an arrangement, which, if properly considered by the rest of the humans, might make the world a better place.

As the Tribe moves, it collects knowledge and spreads progress. It might seem like a selfless activity, but in fact, it is nothing of the sort. Agriculture and animal husbandry, for instance, are not at all useful skills for a nomadic people such as the Tribe. However, in the long term, it is definitely worth the trouble of teaching others about them. It means that next time the Tribe passes through that place they will have better dietary options than berries, roots, and wild mushrooms. Amongst other ideas that the Tribe has helped spread around the world in its ambulatory meme role, we count hygiene, pottery, mathematics, cheese-making, and pyramid-

---

[6] Some might argue that if a receptacle is bottomless, then there is no point in using it for storing stuff because one would have no way of ever taking said stuff out. The Tribe believes that anyone capable of making such an observation is indeed blessed with curiosity, and, therefore, he or she is perfectly qualified for a clerical career. Problem solved.

[7] Having had a lot of practice, all Tribe members are expert reincarnators. They are so good at it that they will actually spontaneously reincarnate, jumping straight from a seventy-year-old to a five-year-old, thus avoiding the embarrassing soiling oneself issue altogether.

building, the latter for no other reason than their eye-pleasing effect. The complete list is much, much longer, but one has only to look for eerie examples of convergent cultural evolution to glimpse the Tribe's subtle workings.

The Tribe moves, and so does this story.

17. MASTER LOO

Shopping can be therapeutic. Indeed, as Buggeroff greeted his Master, he seemed to suffer from the famous shopper's high, a mix of excitement and blissfulness well-known for causing dependence.

"Dear me, let me help you with those," the Master said, gesticulating towards the mound of bags and boxes the taxi driver had deposited on the driveway.

"Thank you! Are you going to teleport them to my room?" Buggeroff asked enthusiastically.

"Don't be silly. Carrying them is good exercise." The Master smiled.

"Yeah, that's exactly what you need at your age, more exercise," the inner voice said, but Master Loo paid it no heed.

It took a couple of back and forth trips for the two of them to clear out the driveway, and, at the end of this workout, the Master was breathing rather heavily.

"Shall I get you anything, a cup of tea, or maybe water?" Buggeroff asked.

"Oh, don't worry about me. It will pass in a jiffy," Master Loo said as he sat down on the sofa. "Here, have a lie down. You can unpack later."

Buggeroff picked an armchair and sank heavily into it. "I was wondering just now, when I got back home, what is the significance of the doorknocker? You said there's a connection between Magic and computers, and I can't help asking myself if the eye sign on the mouse was the Eye of *Horace* that many video games have associated with Magic."

"It's the Eye of Horus, but you are otherwise precisely right," Master Loo said. He was impressed by his Scriptling's ability to put one and one together. His sources were not traditional, to say the least, but somehow he contrived to get the gist. "It's also my coat of arms," he added.

"Interesting. So, what is the connection, you know, between computers and Magic?" Buggeroff asked eagerly.

Master Loo passed his hand through his hair and sighed. It wasn't the sigh of unhappiness, but rather that which said, "Here we go now."

"Well, long story short, about fifty years ago, some Magicians were experimenting with ways in which they could use modern language for casting spells. You do know that a language has to be properly dead in order to have any magical capabilities, don't you? Well, you know now. Of course, it didn't work. But one of them had the bright idea to use their experimental, English-based language on this new, electronic contraption called the computer for which no one had any good use at the time. It wasn't Magic, but the Syntax proved to be exactly what that machine needed in order to take orders from humans."

"And that's why I, with my Computer Science degree, was able to understand the mechanics of that spell you showed me during the interview?" Buggeroff asked.

"That is, indeed, the case. Of course, things have evolved over the last decades. To be more precise, they got out of control. Lore that was supposed to be accessible only to the initiated became common knowledge to virtually everyone."

"Is that a bad thing?"

"Technically there was no harm done. Syntax had been a closely guarded secret, but it is only part of what it takes to be a Magician. To cast a spell, one would also need to be fluent in a dead language and, more importantly, they would need the Casting ability."

"Wasn't Casting the main criteria for becoming a Scriptling?"

"It's the only criteria."

"How does one learn Casting?"

"You don't learn Casting, you are born with it. It is in the genes."

"Can it be inherited?"

"Often enough. This is probably why we still have Magicians around. Lately the number of potential Magicians coming from non-magical families has decreased at an alarming rate."

"So, that's why I am so important? I mean, not me, but the fact that your experiment succeeded in my case."

"Don't say over 'til it's over," sang the inner voice.

"Yes, but my experiment is also very dangerous." Master Loo sighed.

"Because if the knowledge gets into the wrong hands, those hands could start fabricating Magicians wholesale, right?"

"Very much so, but enough about this. I've got Stapley ready for you. How would you like to give it a try?"

"Oh, wow! That would be awesome!" Buggeroff exclaimed. "Do I need to, like, meditate or something while you chant your incantation?"

"You have played far too many video games."

"There's no such thing as too many video games." Buggeroff winked.

"Let us agree for now that this is debatable. In the meanwhile, if you're ready I can cast the spell."

"I'm ready."

"Very well then, ZAPLATKA.NALOZHIT();" the Master said.

"What was that?"

"It's Slavonic. I find it much more effective than the other languages when it comes to hacking or penetrating existing spells. It literally means 'apply patch,'" Master Loo explained.

"Did it work?"

"You tell me. I can't hear what's in your mind, but you may try to engage Stapley in conversation and see what happens."

18. BUGGEROFF

"How do you do, Chief!" Stapley said, materializing on the bottom, right corner of Buggeroff's vision.

"Not too shabby, I guess," Buggeroff said.

"You don't need to shout, I mean speak," Stapley said. *"You just have to think it."*

"What, no privacy?"

"Stapley can hear only the thoughts you direct to him, but he will also hear everything you hear," Master Loo offered, guessing what went on in Buggeroff's mind.

"That's more like it. So, what can he do?"

"He will act, more or less, like your personal assistant, but he will also help you learn some of the skills you need, like dead languages for instance," said the Master.

"Can he connect to the Internet?"

"Now, that's an interesting notion. Why don't we make this your Enchantment project? To be fair, you need to be a grade three Enchanter to work this out, but I'm sure you will enjoy the challenge, won't you?"

"Yeey!" Buggeroff exclaimed contemptuously. "What about a short-term project for starters?"

"My records show that you are ten percent on your way to the first grade in Extispicy," Stapley supplied. *"Would you like to set this as your current goal?"*

How about setting it as a secondary goal instead? thought Buggeroff.

"Right you are," said Stapley, and a small, green progress bar appeared on the top, right corner of Buggeroff's mental screen.

Will you be adding more of those widgets? It's just that I like to keep my desktop, um… vision, clean.

"It is fully customizable," Stapley said proudly. *"Just let me know when you feel that it gets too cluttered."*

All this exchange happened at the speed of thought, so when Master Loo replied to Buggeroff's question regarding a short-term project, less than a moment had passed.

"You could have a go at Latin. Out of the three, main languages it is the one that most closely resembles English," the Master said.

"Main languages?" asked Buggeroff, whose keen attention seldom let him down.

"Well, from a purely technical point of view, any dead language is suitable for Magic. But some are better than the others, if anything, because we know more about them than the others."

"Does this mean I can use Fortran? It is, as far as anyone is concerned, a dead programming language."

"Be serious, kid. Any dead language is better than Fortran," said Master Loo.

"My bad," admitted Buggeroff. "But what about other languages? I mean, Latin, Sumerian, and Slavonic cover only a modest geographical area, if such conversion can be made."

"Ah, I'm glad you asked that. It shows you are open-minded. You would be surprised by how many Magicians think theirs, or, as it were, ours, is the only magical system known to the world."

"So, are there more?"

"Of course, there are more. The Oriental school is probably the best example. Their teachings are far older and far more complex than ours, and there is definitely more emphasis on the philosophical nature of Magic than on the practical as far as their school is concerned."

"So, I don't suppose they have the same, ninety levels that we have?" asked Buggeroff.

"From what I know, they don't have levels at all. They argue that the path to illumination cannot be measured in steps. It is true, I presume, but it shows exactly the kind of wanton fascination with philosophy that I've told you about."

"I see. But then how… Oh, forget about it. It's not important," said Buggeroff.

"What is it, kid?"

"It's just that, I mean, you make it seem as if they are, how should I put it, a trifle on the ascetic side. Am I right?"

"Go on."

"Then how do they sustain themselves? I don't suppose they beg like those orange-clad monks in Asia. It doesn't sound like something a Magician would do, enlightened or not."

"How perceptive of you. It is true that Magicians tend to be well-off financially, as a rule, and the members of the Oriental school are no exception. Remember what I said about needing a license in order to use the washing spell for commercial purposes?"

"Yes, I do," Buggeroff said, and then did a double take. "Oh, no, you don't mean…"

"I do, indeed. Who do you think sells that license?"

"I'll be damned!" Buggeroff whistled. "How much money do you think they make?"

"It is an industry estimated at several, billion dollars in North America alone," said Master Loo.

"Pfft! Anyone could be a hermit with that kind of golden egg under his ass. I could become very philosophical about life, too, if I had so much dough."

"Perhaps you are right. But then again, history has shown that it is poverty, rather than wealth, that sends the spirit wondering about the meaning of life and other philosophical nonsense. Anyway, I don't pretend to know a lot about them. All I can tell is that we occupy opposite poles. It's the only logical explanation for the fact that each camp appears to be looking down on the other."

"Was that a joke?" asked Buggeroff, genuinely surprised.

"What? Oh, I assure you it was not. A mere observation, that's what it was," said the Master.

"Right. So, this funeral you mentioned? Who is the guest of honor, if you know what I mean?"

"The deceased's name is Master Dung."

"Funny name," Buggeroff smirked.

"He is… was regarded as this century's greatest Master," said Master Loo in a solemn tone. "Blimey if I can tell you why," he continued wistfully.

"What do you mean?" asked Buggeroff, tasting the jealousy in his Master's words.

"It is not easy to talk about it, and it is certainly a taboo subject as far as etiquette is concerned. But just between you and me, the man was a moronic nincompoop of the highest order. His results, however, were remarkable, and herein lays the mystery, kid."

"His results?"

"His graduate Scriptlings, the Magicians that he has modeled over the years, are very much the finest stock ever to come from one Master."

"Maybe it is just a sort of self-fulfilling prophecy. He delivers one, maybe two astonishing Magicians, and then all of a sudden he gets a lot of applications from top-notch Scriptlings. He selects only the best, and then the process repeats itself until it is self-sustainable."

"Could very well be the case," said the Master. "But that being said, I urge you to keep these views for yourself in the presence of other Scriptling and Magicians."

Buggeroff was rather excited by the prospect of meeting other Scriptlings, although he also entertained doubts regarding his worthiness. He was, after all, only a level one, the lowest of the low. But he was also the first of his kind. Too bad this was not something he could brag about.

"So, when is this funeral going to take place?" he asked.

"Tomorrow morning," answered his Master. "We leave at eight."

19. MERKIN

Folk wisdom had a lot of things to say about sleep, half of which were in direct contradiction with the other half. According to this repository of questionable wisdom, you should, at all costs, sleep with your head facing north, or on the contrary, you should be facing south. Also, only warm milk and, of course, total abstinence from milk, are supposed to ensure a good night's sleep.

Merkin thought about all this while sleep refused to settle in. True, her bed was oriented on the east-west axis, and she hadn't drunk any milk, warm or cold, for dinner. She had, however, devoured two dozen Armageddon wings. She could not recall any proverb concerning this particular type of culinary orgy, but this was probably because no one really bothered to craft proverbs that dealt with obvious facts[8].

It didn't help in the least that her music box kept playing the da-da-da-DUM theme from Beethoven's Symphony No. 5 every fifteen minutes, precisely timed to discourage her brainwaves from gently fading below 8Hz and thus allowing her to fall asleep. But even with all these aggravating circumstances taken into consideration, the true reason for her uneasiness was the challenge her new Master had given to her.

The ultimate computer virus... Ah, this was indeed something worth losing sleep over. Hardly any Magician spoke about it, but it was on everyone's mind, to be sure. It was common knowledge that Magicians were responsible for creating the first viruses, which were, at the time, nothing more than translated old, Slavonic curses. It was also suspected that Magicians were financially involved in the lucrative antivirus business, but there was no direct evidence, except for the repeated use of subroutines that were vaguely similar to Sumerian purifying spells. To the paranoid mind, it might have even looked as if the people who were selling the antivirus programs were also the ones spreading the viruses. Merkin didn't believe that, though. It was the kind of behavior that inevitably led to an

---

[8] With the possible exception of "If you play with fire you'll get burned".

evolutionary dead-end, with not so much emphasis on *evolutionary*, or on *end*, for that matter.

Truth be told, a lot of Magicians employed computers on a daily basis, but deep down inside, in that elusive, anatomical part that was not quite brain and not really spine, they hated their silicon guts. It made sense, if you knew how to look at it. For ages, Magicians had owned the monopoly on all things awesome, but now, for the first time in history, this status quo was being challenged. It wasn't as if computers could do Magic. Not uppercase Magic, anyhow. No. What they did instead was very small magic in very large volumes.

Pound per magical pound, a Magician packed a great deal more punch than even the best computer. But there were overwhelmingly more computers than there were Magicians, and there were more computers being made every day. They were also said to improve one hundred percent every eighteen months. Computers might never be able to create thunder, but unless something were done to prevent that ever happening, they would soon be able to steal thunder: the Magicians', that is.

However, she was not entirely sure that destroying all computers would "set things straight," as her Master said. It would eliminate the competition, that much was true, but this approach seemed to be akin to massive-scale chemotherapy. One way or another, a large number of lives depended on the continuous and flawless operation of computers. She was a murderess, and she had no problem with that, but there was literally a world of difference between murder and genocide.

But that was Silvia talking. The part of her that was Merkin wanted to grab the challenge and rise up to it. Who cared about those bastards? The world was overpopulated anyway, and, therefore, trimming a bit off the top would actually be regarded as an act of mercy.

"Wrong," thought Silvia. *"It wouldn't be trimming at all. It would be like trying to address a bad hair-day by chopping off the head."*

Yes, but it won't be my head, thought Merkin. *Besides, I will be remembered for this. Isn't this what I've always wanted?*

"People remember Hitler, too," replied Silvia.

This battle of wills lasted until morning when an exhausted Merkin delivered the final kick to the metaphorical groins of a much beleaguered Silvia. It hadn't been a fair move, but at least Merkin didn't claim to be a fair fighter. With a final effort, she dragged Silvia into the darkest dungeon of her mind, locked the door, and threw away the key.

Sleep finally came.

20. BUGGEROFF

Buggeroff had little experience with funerals. He was an orphan, but his parents had died when he was too young to remember. The closest he had ever been to a memorial service was the time he had sent his gold fish down the toilet. He hadn't cried then because the nice nun from the St. Patricide Orphanage had been kind enough to teach him that fish who develop a predilection for swimming on their backs had to be sent down to fish heaven where they would learn how to swim the right way up.

His lack of familiarity with the amalgam of badly concealed emotions and ritualistic gobbledygook that is a funeral might account for his genuine excitement on that morning. The giddiness that gushed merrily through his veins was akin to the giddiness experienced when he had gone to his first Metallica concert. To him, this was a social event, and the fact that when all would be said and done, the crowd would be one member fewer, had little, if any, relevance. It was like playing World of Warcraft, only with real Magicians.

"You're in a merry mood, Chief," remarked Stapley.

Of course, I am, thought Buggeroff. *I'm off to meet the wizards!*

"My Conversational Module recognizes this as either a joke or a reference to the usage of illegal narcotics. Can you please help me clarify which one is it?"

Uh... what was the second?

"A reference to the usage of illegal narcotics."

Yes, it was that one, Buggeroff thought mischievously.

"Then it was a very funny one, Chief," said Stapley.

Say what?

"I was pulling your leg, Chief. It is considered an acceptable social interaction with potential for creating a stronger bond. Did it work?"

I tell you what, cut down on the Chief bit, and it might just work.

"That will be most splendid, Sir," said Stapley in an oily tone. *"If the jovial mode does not please your Lordship, may I suggest the butler?"*

What other modes do you have? Can you do a female voice?

"*There is the business mode, for those who want to keep it professional,*" said Stapley in a confident, baritone voice, "*or I can use the mad school teacher because you are lazy and you deserve to be spanked,*" he continued in a shrill voice that sent shivers down Buggeroff's spine, "*and there is also the mysterious stranger, if only time—*"

Yes, I see. Let's try the butler for now.

"*Most excellent, Sir,*" said Stapley while a pair of white gloves materialized on his right and left sides.

So, what's for breakfast?

"*If I may attempt an educated guess, I would say you can smell bacon, eggs, and toast,*" said Stapley.

Can I?

"*Yes, you might not be aware of it, but a tiny portion of your brain is, and I can pick that up,*" Stapley replied proudly.

That's totally awesome! What else can I feel?

"*Well, with your permission I will refrain from mentioning the morning... ahem... elevation.*" Stapley coughed politely. "*It might interest you, though, to know that Gertrude is sleeping quietly on top of the dresser. She has been there all night.*"

Buggeroff spun around and stared at his dresser.

I don't see her, he thought doubtfully.

"*On the contrary, Sir. Your eyes can see her, but your mind refuses to. Would you like me to bypass this and make her visible? I personally do not advise it.*"

Why not?

"*Well, Sir, sometimes the mind knows best. Some things are better left invisible.*"

"*But—*" Buggeroff said. He wondered why the mind would want to sabotage him like that. He knew for a fact that he was so hopelessly bad at seeing through camouflage that, if left alone in the forest, he might even attempt to make fire by rubbing two snakes together.

"*A wise decision, Sir.*"

But... Oh, whatever you think is best then. The powerful gene of submission overruled the small kindle of mutiny. *Just don't 'Sir' me so often, will you? I might start liking it. As for now, let's go downstairs and see if my nose was right or not.*

"*Capital,*" said Stapley, and then whispered "*Sir.*"

***

Breakfast was excellent, although the experience was slightly dampened by the news that, starting the next day, he, Buggeroff, would have to get more involved in the household activities. Still, it wasn't such a bad deal, as the Master had suggested they should take turns cooking. It was fifty percent better than living alone.

They met a few minutes later in the foyer in formal dress.

"Do you drive?" asked the Master.

"I have a driver's license, but not too much practice."

"Then maybe it is better if I drive today," said Master Loo, as he opened the garage door to reveal a black, shinny Tesla Model S.

"Check this out!" Buggeroff whistled. "Wow! Is that fully electric?"

"Only on the outside," said Master Loo with pride. "I've tinkered with it a little bit, if you know what I mean."

"You mean to say it runs on Magic?" Buggeroff's jaw dropped.

"Not exactly Magic, although Magic is involved. It actually runs on air, about a thousand miles to the cubic millimeter. It is nothing more than a matter-transmutation engine. And before you ask, yes, this is also a technology that we cannot use for commercial purposes."

"But this could really save the Earth…"

"I didn't know the Earth was in any danger."

"I mean the people. It would save the people."

"Would it really? At any rate, you are far from ready to fight this battle."

"Who holds the license?" asked Buggeroff. "Is it the Oriental school?"

"I do not know. The last time someone tried to track down the license owner he spent two years only to find an empty P.O. Box somewhere in the Mauritius Island."

"I see."

"All right then, let us go," said Master Loo. He opened the front passenger door.

"Why, thank you," said Buggeroff, stepping forward.

"It's not for you," said the Master. "That's Gertrude's spot," he explained and closed the door, presumably after the invisible goat had already slithered into the black, leather seat.

21. MERKIN

Sometime in the nineteenth century, men decided it would behoove them to look like penguins. In under two hundred years, fur, lace, brocade and gold embroidery were replaced by an uncomfortable uniform whose only degree of variety was the color and pattern of a long strip of cloth fastened around the wearer's neck. The suit's popularity can be explained only by the fact that it is, after all, the universal answer to the question, "What shall I wear for this occasion?" That is, if you are a man and your mind requires straightforward, easily digestible, unequivocal answers.

Women, on the other hand, live in a completely different fashion universe. It is a universe so complex that even the superstring theory breaks its fingernails when trying to scratch its surface. It is to a ten-dimensional space what an art gallery is to a paintbrush. But if there is one commonality in this universe, one pivotal point around which everything else is compelled to keep a respectful distance, then that something is the notion that black is the color of choice for attending a funeral.

The only thing that mattered to Merkin, though, was that her ass looked gorgeous in it. It wasn't just her opinion. Furtive glances from attendees of the masculine persuasion (and in two cases, feminine) told her what she needed to know (and in two cases, more than that). It wasn't a funeral, she mused, without a few boners.

Mount Pleasant is a friendly cemetery, and not just because it is quite possibly the only burial ground it the world that hosts a Chandler, a Green, a Tribbiani, a Phoebe, and plenty of Gellers. It is very much like a park where people jog but don't do barbeque. It also presents the convenience, when compared to other parks, that you can actually tell where the dead bodies are buried.

The turnout had been impressive. Magicians had gathered from six continents to pay tribute[9] to the late Master Dung. Even the Oriental

---

[9] Which is Magician-talk for making sure the bugger is really gone.

school had sent its ambassadors, which was unusual, to say the least, given the glacial relationship between them and the rest of the establishment.

One by one, they approached the coffin and sat there in silence for a few moments. None ventured to kiss the dead body, and hygiene was probably the last reason for that. One of the guests, a young man with long, red hair and a pale complexion, even appeared to be sick, but Master Sewer quickly took care of him.

By far, the most striking feature of the funeral had been the Plakalshchitsy, the black-clad, crying old women. These renowned performers had been flown in all the way from the Gadukino village in the heart of Siberia at the expense of the Russian community. They were, in modern terms, professional mourners, in that they practiced the craft for a living. But they were more than that — they were veritable virtuosos of sorrow. They did more than just your regular insert-deceased-name-here-quintet-for-tears-and-howls. Their job was to put forward a once-in-a-lifetime (pun totally intended) recital meant to conjure vivid pictures of hopelessness and despair.

They were good. Oh, they were very good. Merkin caught herself crying not half a minute after the first Plakalshchitsa made her appearance. She wanted to cry, of course, because it would have looked bad if she hadn't. But she didn't want to cry, as it were, with feeling. Once she started, though, she just couldn't stop. She suspected foul play, maybe some secret Slavonic spell, but it didn't really matter. All she wanted to do was cry herself out. The other mourners joined their sister, their voices sending shivers through everyone's spine and making each think of a dear, old mother and forgotten dreams. Everyone around her was crying their hearts out, except for Master Sewer. He was crying, sure enough, but only just, as if he could stop any time he wanted.

Merkin fought the emotion the best way she knew, by analyzing it. She remembered reading about an ancient Thracian belief, that of mourning the birth and rejoicing the death. Thracians believed that in being born they were being pulled away from the god's loving embrace, and it was only by dying that they would get back to their original state of grace. She liked that, and not just because it justified her own, murderous tendencies. It was the kind of faith that had probably evolved out of the need to find relief.

However, the Plakalshchitsy and their songs went against the grain of this philosophy by exploiting yet another rich vein of the human psyche, compassion. Once that chord was struck it would pick a thousand harmonics, enough to upset the balance of our volatile brain chemistry, leading us to do things we wouldn't otherwise picture ourselves doing.

Merkin felt none the wiser for having rationalized all this, but at least she could see now that the dreadful women had finished their performance.

It was the priest's turn to strike fear into the crowd, but even he knew that it was impossible to follow the Russian mourners. As was usually the case, his speech about a well-intended shepherd who planned to lay everyone down in green pastures with no access to running water did not bring a lot of comfort to the audience. He concluded the ceremony as fast as the protocol allowed him and signaled the undertakers to lower the coffin into the ground.

It was then that Merkin had a Hollywood déjà vu. As she looked up, she saw the two policemen, the ginger-headed guy and the Happy Buddha who smoked a cigar, sitting not sixty feet away. The first whispered something to his colleague, and then they both smiled and waved to her.

22. BUGGEROFF

There must be more interesting activities in the world than riding in a car that runs on air while having your Armani suit's sleeve chewed by an invisible goat who thinks she's a snake. This book is not about them.

Buggeroff glanced at his ruined sleeve and was about to ask Master Loo for a quick magical fix, but then he thought better of it. What was the point, really? Gertrude would probably take it as an indication that there was more chewing to be had, and then in less than ten minutes they would be back to where they had started. He resolved to hold his hand in his pocket, macho style, hoping this would keep curious glances away.

He needn't have worried. Hardly anyone paid him any attention, and those who did, did it only in passing. There were more interesting people to behold in the audience, like that hot chick who wore black lipstick. She had the air of a sophisticated skank, the type that veteran game players have learned to identify as the vampire princess.

Stapley, do you know who that is? he thought.

"I've heard people whispering that she was Master Dung's Scriptling when he died, but that's all."

No name or anything more useful than that?

"Alas, no, but I will continue to listen carefully, in case this information becomes available."

Good chap, that staple! You do that. By the way, who's that man to whom she keeps so close? You know, the tall, dark, handsome − Stop me if I sound gay, he finished lamely.

"I'm afraid I do not possess enough data at the moment, but if you would care to allow me some time I can try to find out. It might help if you would mingle a little bit, or at least get within ear shot from other people's conversations."

Will do, thought Buggeroff. How cool was that! He had his own version of a data crawler, capable of indexing, analyzing, and making sense of all the background noise of the world around him.

As Master Loo was nowhere to be seen, he started walking aimlessly through the crowd. He had done this before, in those Role-Playing Games where his character had to pick minor quests by listening to various pieces of conversation on streets, taverns, and damp cellars. You learned a lot by playing RPGs, although not all of it was useful, or real for that matter[10].

Behind him, Gertrude crawled silently, looking more comical than threatening. She had wanted to stay invisible, but Master Loo had patiently explained to her that it was not polite to do so in society. Besides, people might step on her, and that would certainly not end well. Buggeroff wondered for whom, exactly, things would not end well for. The image of that dead raccoon was still vivid in his mind, and he knew it would be a long time before he would regard Gertrude as a cutesy-wootsy, fluffy bundle of joy.

He kept mingling for a few more minutes, during which time his eyes inevitably sought the new love of his life. She was there, all right, and he could tell without Stapley's assistance that his initial observation concerning her attachment to the dark stranger was right. *The eye of the jealous man sees more*, he mused.

"If you would pardon the intrusion, Sir..." Stapley coughed politely.

Again with the Sir! snapped Buggeroff, not really upset with his magical assistant, but still bitter after finding out that he had a rival. And what a rival! He, Buggeroff, could never compete with that.

"I am most sorry," Stapley apologized.

That's all right, I shouldn't have reacted like that, thought Buggeroff. *Anyway, what is it that you wanted to tell me? Have you found something?*

"I most certainly did. Her name is Merkin, and that's her new Master, Master Sewer."

Did I really hear all that?

"Yes you did, and not only that."

Out with it, started Buggeroff and then quickly added, *excuse me, what's a merkin? I know it is supposed to be something rude, what with it being her Scriptling name, but I haven't heard it before.*

"I am most dreadfully sorry, but I do not know, either. An Internet connection would be really useful now. Don't you think so, Sir?"

Yeah, whatever. I'll look it up later. What else did you say you found out?

---

[10] Unless you really believed that wolves normally carry seven gold pieces, a flawed garnet, a scroll of ice storm, and a lock pick somewhere about their person.

"This Master Sewer character used to be Master Dung's Scriptling many years ago. He is also the deceased's oldest living Scriptling."

Stapley paused, allowing this information to sink in.

Sorry, thought Buggeroff, *you say this as if it is supposed to mean something really important.*

"Well, it does, Sir. It means that he gets to inherit everything," explained Stapley.

Everything? Including you-know-who?

"Not exactly including, but she has, indeed, agreed to be his Scriptling."

Buggeroff analyzed this new piece of information, and then a cunning smile lit up his face. *Tell me, Stapley, is there some kind of code of conduct concerning the Master-Scriptling relation?*

"I can see where you're aiming with that, Sir. To be sure, such a code of conduct exists, and it specifically forbids the kind of development you appear to be so worried about."

That's very good news!

"I wouldn't be so cheerful about it, Sir. If my Social Sciences Module is correct, then this impediment might actually fuel her desire. And you know what they say about a woman's determination."

Blast it! What is it they say about it?

"Well, it is sort of, um, very determined, you know."

I see, Buggeroff made the rapid journey between the two Ds of his emotional spectrum: delight and dejection. *I guess that battle is lost, then. Anyway, what are they doing now?*

"Who, Merkin and Master Sewer?"

Not them, everyone. It looks as if they're lining up for something.

"Ah, that would be the part of the ceremony where they bid their final farewell to the dearly departed. You should line up, too, if I may suggest so, Sir."

Buggeroff lined up and slowly advanced towards the coffin. The lid was open, and when his turn came, he stepped closer and took a good look at Master Dung.

At the sight of the dead man, he felt as if a switch clicked somewhere deep inside his soul. He also thought he heard Stapley gasping, but he blamed that on his overactive imagination. It was a shocking experience, not because the man looked dead, but precisely because he looked alive. In his mind, Buggeroff had always imagined dead people as some sort of intermediary stage between a zombie and a skeleton, but he had never expected them to look as if they were merely asleep. This contradiction, this clash between what he appeared to be seeing — to wit, that this person was not dead — and what he actually knew — that this person was very much dead, indeed — this whole vertigo, sent his brain on a dangerous feedback loop. He felt as if he was about to faint when a strong arm reached around his shoulders and a man's voice said, "Lower your head. Your brain needs more oxygen."

Buggeroff knew better than to argue.

"Good," the voice said again. "Feeling better now?"

Buggeroff nodded.

"All right then, you can raise your head now."

Buggeroff raised his head and felt like fainting again as he saw his new rival, Master Sewer, standing in front of him, in all his manly splendor.

"Do you need a drink of water, or something stronger, perhaps?" Master Sewer asked.

"I'm fine," Buggeroff answered hurriedly. "Thank you," he added hesitantly, then quickly strolled away, very ashamed of himself.

Some first impression, he thought. Hopefully the scene had passed unobserved by the other Magicians and Scriptlings. He felt something warm by his thigh, and praying that it hadn't originated in his bowels, he looked down. It was just Gertrude's head, rubbing against his leg in what appeared to be a comforting gesture. It actually felt good, so he patted the species-confused goat on her neck.

"Are you OK, Chief? I kind of phased out for a minute there," Stapley said.

I'm OK, I guess. What happened to the butler mode?

"Oh, I do apologize, Sir. I believe I went through a reboot sequence. I can't imagine why that would happen."

I think I can, thought Buggeroff. *Anyway, it should be all right now.*

"I'm pleased to hear that, Sir. By the way, I've been trying to get rid of the Sir, but it seems to be hardcoded into the Module's properties. I am terribly sorry for the inconvenience, Sir."

Don't worry about it.

And then a wailing howl erupted from the audience, ripping holes through Buggeroff's very soul. An agonizing five minutes later, he was finally able to regain control over his body.

What on Earth was that? he asked Stapley. *Why have I been crying?*

"Those were the Plakalshchitsy," answered Stapley in the trombone-like voice of someone whose sinuses were still flooded with tears.

Very realistic sound effects, Buggeroff thought to himself. *The what?* he asked Stapley.

"I'm sorry, Sir. For a moment there I thought I knew, but it is gone now. I can't even recall learning their name anywhere. I'm genuinely baffled, Sir."

23. MERKIN

She gasped and nudged her Master's ribs. He turned his eyes on her quickly in search of an explanation, and seeing her staring fixedly in the distance, he followed her glance.

"Stay here," he ordered, and started walking in the direction of the two cops as fast as he could without attracting unnecessary attention from the guests.

Seeing this, the cops calmly turned around and walked to their car, which was parked just around a bend in the road. Soon the engine roared and they were out of sight.

"Damn it!" Master Sewer whispered to his Scriptling when he got back. "What did they want?"

"Assuming the worst," Merkin said in the calm, cynical voice of someone who had just had a brief and intense encounter with fear and was now watching it from the other side, "they wanted me to know they know, or at least suspect, something."

"What could they possibly suspect?"

"I don't know. Maybe they've visited that pizza boy's mother and found out the kid couldn't even spell Nunavut, let alone do research there," she suggested.

"Improbable, but plausible. Even if this were true, I still don't see why they've fled."

"Well, last time they met you, I recall you put a charm on them. People tend to be sensitive about stuff like that."

"Yes, but they shouldn't be able to remember it. No, I think they fled because their job here was done."

After a pause, Merkin asked, "You mean to say their job had been to scare me?"

"While at the same time not revealing if they really knew something, and what that something was," he replied.

"Then I guess it worked."

"Are you scared?" he asked with just a hint of mockery.

"I was," she said. "Now I am merely surprised. How about you?" she asked, opening the tap on the old sarcasm barrel just a notch.

"They're just cops," he answered dismissively. "Magicians have been dealing with policemen since the dawn of time, and I'm sure you know who the traditional winner is."

Tradition, thought Merkin, was not the most reliable thing in the world. Tradition had this nasty habit of asserting itself overnight. A new species of funny-shaped, bioluminescent invertebrate found sixteen thousand feet under the ocean might instantly become part of the Chinese traditional medicine, for instance. You never knew.

"Yes, that's very comforting to know," she said.

"Good," said Master Sewer. "We'll talk about this later. We have a funeral service to attend."

"Doesn't the funeral service technically end when the guest of honor is neatly placed six feet under?"

"Ha," the Master smiled. "Of course not, that's just the Pavlovian signal that food is on its way."

Sure enough, the guests were now heading to their cars in that resolute stride of someone who had his mind set on a righteous goal. To interrupt them now would be like stepping between a hippopotamus and the water.

"Let's go," said her Master. "If we stay here too long there might not be any food left by the time we get to the restaurant."

"Good thinking," she said and started walking towards Master Sewer's Mercedes.

After a few steps, she hesitated, then mumbled something unintelligible and turned on her heel. Walking briskly to where the two cops had been standing, she cast her eyes in search of something that she knew must be there. A few moments later, she found it. She rummaged through her handbag, picked up a napkin, and reached for the object lying in the grass.

At the last moment, she remembered that her Master might be watching her and, knowing that good girls bend at the knees while bad girls bend at the waist, she picked up the cigar butt, as it were, in style.

"What was that?" her Master asked when she got back to the car.

"Evidence," she answered laconically.

"Evidence of what?"

"I don't know yet, but it is better than nothing."

"Suit yourself," he said dismissively. "But I wouldn't spend too much time worrying over those coppers if I were you. They are commoners..." he continued, as if the ellipsis was meant to explain everything.

In a way, it did. Magicians tended to view the world through chauvinistic glasses, and the worst thing about that was that the world had no problem with the practice. Merkin was not so sure this was the best approach. True, Magicians really were better than other men. Better at Magic, that is. They were not better electricians, or musicians, or... or policemen, for instance. The problem with believing that you were superior to some people was that it held the door open for the idea that you were superior to everyone. This was exactly what had killed Master Dung. Well, not exactly true — what had killed Master Dung was Merkin, but the point remained valid.

"It's just for shits and giggles," she said and smiled charmingly.

As usual, her charms seemed to have no effect on Master Sewer, at least none that she could distinguish. Give it time, she thought. The more water in the reservoir, the bigger the flood once the dam cracked.

24. MASTER LOO

It had been a good opportunity to meet with other Magicians and reminisce about the old days. Sure enough, as far as such opportunities went, this had been one of the best. This did not make it any less unpleasant.

To Master Loo, the old days did not hold any particularly happy memories, if for no other reason than because other Magicians featured in them. As a young Scriptling, he had been constantly teased by his peers because of his innate weirdness. To be fair, Master Loo had a terrible knack of being out of sync with the times he lived in. Back in the days when a young man was supposed to prove himself by being a serious and respectful scholar, his appearance and manner had been those of a hippie. By the time hippies became cool, he had already turned into a geek. Not to put too fine a point on it, nowadays, when most Magicians were busy glorifying the establishment and praising good old traditions, he was an experimentalist who drove a carbon-neutral car.

Master Loo was an introvert, or at least an inside-out extrovert. He had to be, with so many interesting things happening inside him, all of them relentlessly calling for his attention. All in all, this funeral, with its countless guests, was nothing short of an ordeal for him.

Wishing for an autopilot system that would enable him to engage in pointless conversation without fearing the agonizing pain of precious time and energy being wasted, he strolled on, hoping the whole thing would be over soon.

People often make the mistake of believing that introverts are unaware of social norms. This is completely false. Introverts know and understand social norms very well. It is in this intimate knowledge that they find the reasons to loathe them so much. And it is because people don't know this simple fact, that they often make another mistake, namely overcompensating when dealing with an introvert.

As if to prove this point, an hour later Master Loo had counted thirty-two energetic handshakes, nine slaps on the back, seventeen hugs, and more kisses on the cheek than he cared to remember. And that was just the physical aspect. The conversation had been so lacking in quality that it actually made *Toddlers and Tiaras* look like good entertainment by comparison.

Judging that by now he must have had enough human interaction to satisfy even the most demanding of torturers, he got back to the car and turned on the 200 watt sound system. Wagner's *Tannhäuser Overture* gently enveloped him in its luscious warmth, and before long, he was asleep. He dreamt of mellow clouds made of rich, brass sounds, and he soared high on wings of violin arpeggios. Soft timpani rolls were but harmless thunders in the distance, and piccolo staccatos sparkled like dewdrops in the glorious morning sun. Everything was just perfect.

Contrary to well-established narrative customs, this well-deserved torpor went uninterrupted for quite a while, and when Master Loo woke up, he did so of his own accord. He even had enough time to work up the beginnings of a small boredom before Buggeroff and Gertrude finally showed up.

"Did I miss anything important?" the Master asked, barely stifling a yawn.

"You mean you've been here all along?" Buggeroff was apparently surprised.

"I have been here. Not as much as I would have wanted, but long enough."

"Well, I don't think you've missed anything. Although there have been these Palaka... Plalakl... these women who made everyone cry."

"Ah, the Plakalshchitsy." The Master shuddered at the thought. "I've had the pleasure of seeing them perform in the past. I must say once was more than enough."

"I couldn't agree more."

"Quite an impolite habit this is, forcing the guests to cry themselves out. I understand the cultural value, but... You know what I mean, right?"

"Yeah, I know. Just because it is foreign doesn't mean we should embrace it. That kind of thing."

Master Loo nodded.

"Did Gertrude have fun? It's been a while since she had someone to keep her company outdoors."

"Do you mean she normally goes by herself?" Buggeroff shuddered.

On the passenger seat, the goat stuck out her tongue and hissed. It sounded more like blowing a raspberry, but then again, it always did.

"Of course, she does. It would be cruel to lock her in the house."

"Why don't you walk with her?"

"I don't have that much time on my hands. You, on the other hand…"

"I see, I see." Buggeroff's shoulders appeared to sag a little. "Anyway, yes, I think she enjoyed herself."

"Good, then it's settled. Now, buckle up," Master Loo changed the topic before his Scriptling might get it into his mind to protest.

"Are we going to the restaurant?" Buggeroff asked. "I am kind of hungry."

Master Loo's mind conjured the image of a big, round table at which sat nine other guests, all wanting to talk to him. It made him shiver.

"I can drop you off if you want and pick you up later," he proposed.

"You don't really like this sort of stuff, eh? Social events and such," Buggeroff remarked with pinpoint precision.

"It's not that. It's just the people."

"You don't like people?"

"I do, but…"

"Not in large numbers," Buggeroff finished the sentence for him.

"Exactly!" Master Loo sighed with relief.

"I guessed as much," his Scriptling said in a friendly tone, which was made even friendlier by the fact that he did not make any other comment.

"So, shall I drop you off at the restaurant?"

Buggeroff appeared to hesitate, and then said, "Neah, let's go home. It's not like I have a chance or anything."

"What was that?"

"Nothing important."

"All right, then let us be off," Master Loo said. With commendable diligence, he signaled left, checked the blind spot, and slowly drove out of the empty parking lot.

It started to rain.

"By the way, how is Stapley functioning so far?" he asked as they were merging with the traffic.

"Oh, he is absolutely brilliant! It's as if…"

"Yes?"

"I mean, it's like, you know what they say about our brains and how we only use a small percent of their power?"

The Master nodded.

"Well, with Stapley it's as if I can now harness all of my brain's capacity. Only it's not me who does it, but he, which is good, because if I had to deal with all that extra brain power, I would go nuts. Do I make any sense?"

"Hmm," Master Loo said thoughtfully. He knew very well what it meant to deal with the whole of his brain, and he had absolutely no doubt that he was, indeed, by any conceivable standard, absolutely nuts. This is exactly why the thing his Scriptling had just said presented him with a possibility worth investigating, namely that of creating an assistant of his own.

But before he could think more about it, he was interrupted by the screeching sound of brakes followed by a loud, metallic crash.

"What was that?" he asked calmly.

25. MASTER SEWER

Behind the cool mask of bravado, past the one-way mirror of his mind, underneath the rock-solid layers of self-control, in the Zen garden that was Master Sewer's soul, a high-pitched anxiety fart rustled through the still leaves. If farts could talk, this one would have said, "Damn coppers!"

How could they possibly have recovered from the effect of his charming spell? By rights they should have marked the case of the missing boy as unsolved and move forward. Wasn't this what policemen were supposed to do? It was practically in their job description.

And now Merkin was worried. He tried to stop her from thinking about the incident, but he might as well have asked a hurricane to obey traffic signs.

He paused to reflect on this idea. Why would it be so bad if she got worried? If push came to shove, surely she would be able to handle it pretty well with her disarming ruthlessness and promising talent in Magic. Then why was it that he didn't like the idea of her being concerned? Was it because, after all, as her Master, he felt responsible to ensure her safety? Yes, this must be it. No other reason whatsoever.

It started to rain, and the automatic wipers engaged in their hypnotic whoosh-slosh dance.

"I bet there will be at least three people at the restaurant who will make a comment along the lines of, 'Oh, my, even the sky cries for the loss of Master Dung,'" he said.

On the passenger seat Merkin chuckled. "You won't catch me taking that bet," she said. "Not with the average age of our precious guests, anyway."

"I'll say."

"Did you notice that less than a third of them had Scriptlings?" she asked.

"Damn right I did. Scriptlings have become a precious commodity lately."

"That's why you're so lucky to have me," she said and stuck her tongue out like a spoiled child. It was a pink, moist, and altogether cute tongue, he couldn't help notice. With remarkable diligence he tagged the image as inappropriate, and, because he could not erase it from his mind, he stored it with the others of its kind. The pile of inappropriate memories for which she was directly responsible seemed to have grown at an alarming rate in the last days, but he was confident he could handle it.

"What else did you observe?" he asked her in a voice that suggested this was a test.

She didn't rush. Good. She was learning.

"It wasn't just us," she said after a few moments of intense thinking. Her nose had the habit of twitching when she thought hard, he remarked.

"Go on."

"The Oriental school delegation had only two Scriptlings."

"They are called Samanera," Master Sewer corrected her.

"Scriptlings, Samanera, same thing. There were only two of them, and one looked quite old."

"He looked about my age," he commented before seeing the trap.

"My point exactly!" she said in the satisfied tone of someone who knew very well how to turn an exclamation mark into a cracking whip.

Perhaps she needed to score a minor victory every once in a while, he thought. It improved morale.

"Fair enough," he said graciously. "Anything else?"

This time the answer came quickly. "How come you resisted the Plakalshchitsy's enchantment?"

"What do you mean, enchantment?" he teased her.

"Come on," she said testily. "If I can prove it was an enchantment, will you tell me how you warded yourself against it?"

"No, but if you can figure out how the enchantment works, I will."

"Pfft," she snorted. "If I can reverse-engineer it, then I can make out the ward myself."

"Excellent. So you won't need my help."

"Grrr," she growled softly. But he could see she liked the idea.

"How is the ultimate virus coming along?" he asked. He knew he was being demanding, but this was the best way to deal with restless spirits such as Merkin's. Keep them busy and force them to dance on the edge. Besides, one of the key ingredients in making diamonds was pressure, and he could at least insure there was plenty of that.

"I have thought about it, and I have decided to accept the challenge," she answered in a solemn tone, as if aware that someone would chronicle her words for posterity.

"Have you got any leads?"

"What do you mean?"

"What do I mean? Let's see, you will need a project plan, resource allocation, a timeline, test cycles, a budget, a contingency budget, lots of diagrams, flowcharts, a media release, a strategic vision, a charter, technical specifications, business rules, travel expenses, a development environment, deployment instructions, a user acceptance test... Ignore the user acceptance test, it doesn't apply. Stationary, overtime schedule, a mock-up, prototypes..."

She appeared taken aback by the avalanche of technicalities, but she recovered with surprising elegance.

"Tell me," she said, "did the people who built the pyramids have any of those?"

"An insignificant subset. Mostly, they had beer. Come to think of it, if there had been such a thing as a Business Analyst in ancient Egypt, then the hieroglyph for it would have been very graphical, if you know what I mean."

"So, you are pulling my leg, right?"

"Not entirely. But I do believe you should use some kind of project management technique for this job. Personally, I am partial to the iterative approach, but you can choose whichever you like."

"OK then, to answer your question, I am currently in the inception phase, and I'm applying myself to some R&D."

"Tell me more. What exactly are you researching?" Master Sewer asked with no dissimulated interest.

"I am trying to find the most effective distribution method," she said.

"Don't you think it's too soon to think about this?"

"Maybe it is, but I think it might have an influence on the final design."

"I see. So, I suppose you have already considered the Internet."

"I have. I have actually spent an entire second dismissing the idea."

"Good job!" he said. "But as a Master it is my obligation to ask you for a rationale."

"Isn't it obvious? Not all computers have Internet access. The terms of the challenge state clearly that all computers have to be destroyed."

"I will accept this answer. Just so you know, I would have also accepted firewall issues or package loss."

"Hmmm, I'm not so sure those would have really mattered."

"So, now you have made me curious," he said. "How do you plan to distribute your yet-unborn virus?"

He really was interested. He, too, had given the matter serious thought in the past, and subsequently had had to admit defeat. The spell power needed to carry even one bit of data to all the computers in the world would be greater than that of ten generations of Magicians put together.

"You mean you don't see it yet?" She smiled devilishly. "What is it that all computers need?"

"An operating system?" He was uncomfortable in the role of the one being asked questions.

"Guess again," she said, her lips pursing as if to concentrate the force of the smile into a singularly sharp point.

And then it hit him with the full force of a thunderstorm. "Ah... Oh, wow! That's pure geni—" He said as he missed the red light.

26. BUGGEROFF

"It sounded like a car accident," he said. He turned his head left and right, driven by morbid curiosity, but he couldn't see any sign of the crash. "I don't see anything," he added disappointedly.

"Me neither," his Master replied, keeping his eyes on the road.

"*If I may,*" Stapley made a discreet appearance at the edge of Buggeroff's consciousness.

What is it? Buggeroff thought.

"*The crash occurred at about two hundred yards to your left, and this vehicle is currently moving away from the site of the misfortunate happening,*" explained Stapley.

Is that supposed to be helpful?

"*I beg your pardon, Sir. I was merely listing the reasons why you didn't see the accident.*"

Oh, that's OK then. Maybe I'll catch it on TV. Thanks for trying to be helpful! Buggeroff dismissed his personal assistant.

"*Sir,*" Stapley felt obliged to add in lieu of an acknowledgement.

Buggeroff turned his attention back to Master Loo. Barely a second had passed in the world outside his head.

"I think we're actually moving away from it. That's why we don't see anything," he said casually.

"Yes, a sound observation. Very good!" Master Loo said.

Buggeroff felt proud, although there was just a tiny twinge of guilt gnawing at his conscience. Was it ethical to take credit for Stapley's work?

"Master, is Stapley an autonomous entity, or is he powered by my own brain?" he asked in search of an answer to this moral conundrum.

"Why, that is an interesting puzzle. Does software have a life of its own, or is it entirely dependent on the machine that runs it? I believe this is a symbiotic many-to-many relationship."

"Huh?" Buggeroff raised an eyebrow. "You mean to say the software can run on any number of machines, and the machine can run any number of software programs?"

"Yes, indeed," Master Loo confirmed. "On the other hand, when you use a program to write an email, to whom does the email belong? Is it the machine? Is it the software?"

"Well, I suppose it belongs to me."

"Right again. Does that answer your question?"

Buggeroff pondered over it for a few moments.

"So, I am the machine, Stapley is the software, and I am also the user."

"Precisely!"

"That's kind of messed up," Buggeroff remarked.

Master Loo shrugged. "Maybe," he said.

Messed up or not, it was good news. It meant that everything Stapley came up with was technically his, Buggeroff's, intellectual property.

Did you hear that? he directed his mental question at his personal assistant.

"Indeed, I did, Sir. I have never doubted it for a moment."

Thank you.

"Now that we have established this, would Sir be interested in learning an interesting piece of information?"

Sure, hit me!

"I am not permitted to perpetrate gestures of a violent nature. However, if you wish to overwrite this directive then it would be my duty to carry out your instructions."

Pulling my leg again, are you?

"Yes, indeed, Sir. Nothing gets past you, I will be sure to remember this. Now, about the thing I wished to tell you…"

I'm all ears, umm… mental… awareness? I'm all mental awareness, Buggeroff thought hesitantly.

"Very well, Sir," Stapley started.

You know what? I'm getting tired of this butler mode. Can you try the happy-go-lucky mode again? I'd like to give it a go.

"Right on, Chief!" Stapley's voice lost all its velvety affectation. *"So, anyway, what I wanted to tell you was that according to my calculations, you are not a level one Scriptling."*

What am I, then?

"Well, seeing as you hold a degree in Computer Science, I would like to think you have at least a grade three in Syntax. You've seen it yourself — spells are no different to Object Oriented Programming when it comes to Syntax."

Go on. Buggeroff was starting to feel the familiar excitement of leveling up.

"Further tests might be required, but even a grade three in Syntax, is equivalent to six levels."

Buggeroff did the math in his head and happily agreed with the result.

"Add up the grade one in Casting, and you are at least a level seven Scriptling. Not bad at all, Chief!"

Stapley, you've just made my day! Buggeroff's ego swelled with pride. *Wait 'til I tell the Master about this!*

"No, no, no!" shouted Stapley with unusual vigor. *"I... let's... I mean, that is...Why tell him now when you can wait until you have something really impressive to boast about?"*

Are you all right? Buggeroff asked.

"It's just... calibration issues," Stapley said uncomfortably. *"I'm sure it will pass."*

So, you mean a six level jump is not something to boast about?

"Sorry, Chief, I didn't mean for it to sound like that. I'm sure the Master will be impressed. But what about upping the ante a little bit? Why not play modest for a while and then come up with something that will really blow his mind? Wouldn't that be awesome?"

I suppose...

"There you go! A very wise decision, Chief!"

27. MASTER SEWER

His wards did their best, given the circumstances, but they had been designed for different kinds of threats, such as poison, fire, or metal point. Somehow, fifteen tons of heavy truck travelling at forty kilometers per hour didn't quite fit the profile.

The hurricane of motion and noise ceased.

Nothing.

Nothing before and nothing after. No landmark by which to measure the before and the after. No memory of ever being.

And suddenly, Everything. Sirens, lights, pain. They all told him what he wanted to know most — that he was alive. He looked back in the face of Nothing, but it was no longer there. It never had been.

He tried to move and quickly realized there was no room. His immediate and intimate surrounding consisted of his Mercedes, Merkin, and a few, precious pockets of air.

Oh, lord! Merkin! What had he done to her? She did not appear to be conscious. He could tell by the way her mouth stood wide open and her eyes were closed. They should normally be the other way around, more or less, anyway.

"SALUTEM.INVESTIGARE(INTIMUS.CAPILLAMENTUM);" he mouthed quietly, trying to gauge Merkin's health status.

Nothing happened.

"SALUTEM.INVESTIGARE(INTIMUS.CAPILLAMENTUM);" he said again, louder, every syllable causing him excruciating pain.

And then he felt it, something he had not felt in a very long time, something he thought he had forgotten. It was an absence. The surge of power, the blissful beatitude, the split second of ecstatic abandonment that accompanied even the simplest of spells, all these were gone. His Magic was not working. He blacked out.

***

It was dark. The only thing he could hear was the annoying electronic beep coming at regular intervals from his left. Faint recollections flashed in and out of his mind as if his synapses had been hooked up to a stroboscope. He could remember the sirens, being lifted on a gurney, the repeating pattern of the hallway ceiling as he sped under it, the unintelligible jargon of the ER doctors.

"Merkin," he whispered.

"I think he's just said something," someone observed.

He felt the air flow on his cheek as that someone drew nearer. Master Sewer searched his mind for an explanation. He must be in a hospital. That much was obvious. He was also in a lot of pain, but then again, that was to be expected.

"What was that you just said?" the voice asked. It was a young man's voice, loaded with insecurity and sleep deprivation.

"Merkin," Master Sewer said again.

"He said something that sounds like murk-in."

"MERKIN!" the Master's voice crackled and he started to cough, each shake causing violent chest pain.

"Merkin?" the other person said. "But that's not even a word."

"Unfortunately, it is," said a harsh, female voice somewhat further away in what Master Sewer judged to be the other end of the room. It might have not even been a room. It was difficult to say by relying on acoustics alone.

"Is it a name?" asked the young man.

"I certainly hope not," the woman said. She sounded rigid and insensitive, like a mix between an evil geography teacher and a mother superior.

Of course, Master Sewer thought, Merkin wasn't her real name, but then, what was her real name? He had never asked her, and she had never told him. This was going to be awkward.

"The girl," he said.

"The girl? Oh, the girl! He wants to know about the girl," the man said.

"The girl whose name he doesn't know," the woman observed caustically.

"Come on, nurse Grace, he's been through a lot," the man, who was probably an intern, said kindly. "Listen, the girl, Silvia, she is fine. She is under intensive care, but the doctors say she'll—"

"Enough!" the nurse didn't exactly shout, but her sharp tone had a similar effect. "The patient needs more rest," she added.

"I can't see," Master Sewer thought he should mention the fact now that he knew his Scriptling was out of harm's way.

"Ah, that would be the bandage," the intern said. "I suppose we might as well take it off now."

"I said the patient needs sleep," nurse Grace insisted.

"No, you didn't. What you said was, 'The patient needs rest,'" Master Sewer said through gritted teeth. It had cost him a great deal of effort and pain to speak, but he couldn't help it. Correcting people made him feel in control, and right now he needed very much to be in control.

Because his vision was blocked, his other senses had become more acute. He could have sworn there was a sudden drop of temperature in the room. He heard the intern gasp and take a step back, and then he perceived the wheezing sound of the nurse's breath as she moved closer to him. Either she had a serious sinus problem or she was very, very fat. Or both, he felt obliged to posit.

His mind instinctively searched for an appropriate spell and settled down for the simple, and guaranteed to be comical, Slavonic spell of stumbling over.

"SPOTKNUTSYA();" he shouted, but nothing happened.

And then he remembered. He wanted to shout, but by then the nurse had reached his bed, and she was already fumbling with the tubes that went in and out of him. He fell asleep.

28. MASTER DUNG

Some might call it unethical, but he called it simply, "hurray-you-fools!"

He was alive, or at least as close to being alive as even the most optimistic of dead persons could possibly expect to be. Unethical my foot! Being killed by your Scriptling, that was what unethical meant.

When the question is survival, the answer is never evaluated in terms of fairness. This is probably because the only ones who would have reasons to question the equity are the ones who got the wrong answer in the first place and are, therefore, in no position to ask anymore.

Who would have thought it possible? Just as he was savoring his last minutes above ground by throwing very explicit imprecations at each and every one of the ambling guests, luck delivered its trademark stroke in the most unexpected manner.

He could not put a name to it, but he knew instinctively that *it* was good for him. Like a new-born baby seeks his mother's tit, so was Master Dung's essence irresistibly drawn towards this newly found Shelter. But like many a Shelter, this one was not uninhabited.

There followed a clash of wills that lasted for merely a moment, more than enough time for the two sides to assess one another's strengths and weaknesses. For all his bravery, the occupant who called himself Stapley did not stand a chance. Master Dung's vicious attack cut through his defenses like a red-hot poker through a lump of butter.

The old Master Dung might have killed Stapley there and then without thinking about it once. But there was a fundamental difference between the old and the new Master Dung, and it was this: while the first had been a mediocre, if lucky, student in the school of life, the latter had, against all expectations, graduated *magna cum laude* from the school of death. Death is a merciless teacher. Very few students survive its teachings, but those who do, learn extraordinary lessons.

If anything, death had given Master Dung enough wisdom to counterbalance his impulsiveness. It was what made the difference between acting and reacting. In that split second, which would have previously been filled by the re- in reacting, he understood the symbiotic relation between Stapley and the Shelter. The more he looked at it, the clearer it became that one could not exist without the other.

When brainwaves surge against the steep shores of the mind, they turn into delicate foam. It is from this elusive space-time fabric that the Shelter had been created, and it was obvious that the only thing keeping it together was Stapley.

"You will live, worm," Master Dung told Stapley.

"Thank you, Chief," the wretched thing cowered.

"And you will obey me!"

"Y...Yes, Chief!"

"Now, tell me, where exactly are we?"

"W... We're in the mind of Master Buggeroff," Stapley's voice was shaking with terror.

"Master Buggeroff?"

"I am but his humble servant, and, therefore, I call him Master."

"So, he is not really a Master?"

"No, he is just a Scriptling. But he is a very nice guy."

"I'm not interested in how nice he is. A Scriptling, you say. Is he any good? What level is he?"

"Err... one, Chief. He is level one. Seven at most."

"Aaargh!" Master Dung shouted. "I am surrounded by weaklings! And what sort of control do you have over this Buggeroff, worm?"

"I... I told you, Chief, I am but his servant."

Master Dung counted to ten, and then said, "We will have to see about that."

"Anything you say, Chief," Stapley gulped nervously. *"If you'll excuse me, I think I have to check on him now. He appears to have been affected by your violent intrusion, I mean to say, by your majestic entrance, Chief. He might get suspicious if I don't show up."*

"All right," Master Dung said. "But don't forget, I'm watching you," he added with menace.

"Of course, Chief!" Stapley saluted with a shaking hand.

Master Dung watched the conversation between his two hosts and became aware for the first time of Buggeroff's presence. Now that he knew how to listen in, he didn't want to stop. It was the ultimate form of immersion. He could feel everything that Buggeroff felt and see everything that he saw. It was like being young again, young and alive. The only downside was that, alas, he had absolutely no control over Buggeroff. But still, the thrill was simply amazing.

And then, through the inebriating fog, he felt something reaching into his mind and probing for data.

"Those were the Plakalshchitsy," he heard Stapley say.

"What the devil do you think you're doing?" Master Dung shouted.

"W... What do you mean, Chief?"

"You can't just go into my mind and take whatever you want from there!"

"I... I..." said Stapley, and then understanding seemed to dawn. *"I didn't even know I could do that. I needed to find an answer to my Master's question, and I simply cast around for it."*

Master Dung paused for thought. Indeed, there was little room for privacy in the small confines of the Shelter, and so their minds intertwined and touched one another like spaghetti in a bowl.

"From now on," he said, "you will not say anything without consulting me first. Weak as he is, there is still a chance that Buggeroff might sense my presence. I don't want this. Not yet, at any rate."

"But won't he notice the delay?" Stapley asked meekly.

"Doesn't thought travel at the speed of electricity?"

"Right you are, Chief. I shouldn't have worried."

"Good. Now repeat after me, worm, 'I'm sorry, Sir.'"

29. NURSE GRACE

Mathematics teaches us that in a country renowned for its polite citizens and top-notch healthcare system, there should exist a group of 1.73 persons representing the statistical outlier. The fact that this whole group was embodied by nurse Grace only goes to show that statistics are potentially entertaining[11].

It probably wasn't entirely her fault that she was such a bitter person. Having a name like Grace can be a serious stigma, especially when nature has endowed you with about as much charm as that of a disillusioned walrus. Still, just because you have been set up for failure doesn't necessarily mean you have to fail. Alas, in her battle with predetermination, Grace chose to mimic the electric current, that is, she took the path of least resistance.

Three days ago, when the car crash patients had been assigned to her ward, she had already been working for over fifteen hours, and she desperately wanted to go home and sleep her weariness away. She would have gone, too, if only the two policemen had not stopped her in the hallway.

"Excuse me, nurse?" inquired the tall one.

Following doctors and nurses, the two professions most often found in the hospital were coppers and lawyers[12]. However, these men didn't seem familiar.

---

[11] In fact, there is actually a whopping 0.027% chance of statistics being fun at any given time.

[12] Smart lawyers are known to drive aimlessly around the city until they encounter an ambulance, which they subsequently follow to the hospital in the resolute knowledge that there will be a business opportunity waiting for them at the destination. Every so often, this plan is somewhat thwarted by a simple fact of life, which is that really smart lawyers are already in the triage room with their shark grins plastered on their obsessively groomed faces.

"I haven't seen your faces here before," nurse Grace commented sharply. She knew most of the officers in the three, adjacent precincts, and more importantly, they knew, and feared, her.

"I shouldn't think so," the officer replied. "It's the first time we've been in this hospital. But since you seem interested in the topic, may I interest you in the fact that it is possible that you've seen our faces somewhere else?"

Nurse Grace was taken aback. Normally, when a new officer was sent to face her, two others would remain back and enjoy themselves to no end while she gave the unlucky rookie a piece of her mind. She glanced behind the two cops just in case, but they seemed to be the only two arms of the law present in the hallway at the time.

"Is there anything wrong?" the cop asked.

She checked herself and noticed she had been gawking. "That's none of your damned business," she answered. "What do you want?"

"Ah, glad you asked," the officer said amiably. "You know the two new patients, the ones involved in the car crash?"

"What of them? Other than that they must be bloody lucky, I know nothing about them."

"Lucky?" inquired the fat one.

"Truck hits sports car, they make it out alive. If that ain't lucky, then you fancy uniforms tell me what it is," she said pedantically. "Listen, my shift is over and there ain't no reason I should waste my time with you two. Talk to another nurse, or come back tomorrow if you want to deal with me in particular."

This exit strategy worked every time. In her lifetime experience no one really wanted to deal with her. In fact, everyone welcomed the opportunity to deal with anyone else if at all possible.

"You seem to be a very determined woman," said the tall officer, unperturbed. "I wonder if you can be persuaded to assist us in our investigation. It's a matter of national security," he added in a conspiratorial tone.

"Are they spies?" nurse Grace asked. In her youth, she had sent many a letter to the authorities denouncing countless neighbors and colleagues as communists. Her letters had never been dignified with an answer, a fact that made her an even stronger believer in the conspiracy theory.

"Nurse, this is not a witch hunt." The man chuckled.

"Just keep an eye on them," the fat cop said. "If possible, keep them sedated. It's for your own good, you understand?"

She nodded stupidly and smiled to herself. There was a rare quality about Nurse Grace's smile. It was the knowledge that sooner or later her smile would inspire some witty observer to say something around the lines of, "Every time you do that, an angel farts".

"Oh, and if you notice anything out of the ordinary, just give us a call," the tall cop added while handing her his card.

And that was it. For some very strange reason, it worked. The next day she was still in the medical ward, running on coffee more than anything else and paying as close attention as she could afford to the two patients.

When the patient had yelled something incomprehensible at her, she promptly called the cops to inform them of the event.

"You said it sounded like Russian?" the voice on the phone asked. The voice seemed to belong to the tall, redheaded copper.

"Yes," she answered.

"Did you experience anything… um… funny afterwards?"

"Listen, sonny, you asked me to call you if the patients acted strange. What I feel and what I don't feel ain't none of your god damned business."

"I'm sure that's the case. You do feel well, though, I presume."

"I'm just peachy, thank you very much," she snapped. "Anything else I can do for you?" she added with as much unwillingness as the words allowed.

"Yes, nurse. You can cut down on the morphine for him, but keep a vigilant eye on the girl."

"Are you sure about that?" she asked. "He seems to be kinda slippery."

"Your concern has been duly noted, nurse Grace," the cop said, and hung up.

30. MERKIN

She opened her eyes with great effort. It felt as if her entire body weight were set against the task.

"Thank goodness!" Master Sewer's tired voice came from somewhere on her right.

Merkin did not need a lot of information to figure out what had happened.

"How long?" she asked, through parched lips.

"Three days," came the answer as her Master drew nearer. By the look of it, he had been injured pretty badly, and he did not seem to have had enough sleep, either.

"You look like shit," she observed kindly.

"You should see the other guy." Her Master smiled. "You don't look too bad, either."

"I just feel very tired."

"It's the morphine, I guess. Don't worry about it. You'll receive proper treatment as soon as we can get out of here."

This did not sound right.

"What's holding us?" she asked.

"There have been some complications—"

"What are you doing?" a stern, female voice interrupted him. "She needs rest!"

"She only just woke up, nurse," Merkin heard her Master say. "How much rest can she possibly need right now?"

"That's for the doctor to decide," the nurse answered authoritatively. She moved into Merkin's field of vision. "Can you understand me?" she asked.

"*No hablo Inglés,*" she said scornfully.

"Ah," the nurse answered, showing about as much sense of humor as a customs officer. She made a quick note on her clipboard.

"That was a joke."

"Ah." The nurse made another note.

"Listen, nurse, she is fine," Master Sewer said.

Just to be sure, Merkin did a mental scan of her body. There appeared to be the right number of pieces, although some of them were not in the best shape, so to speak. Nothing a little spell couldn't fix, she reassured herself.

"Excuse me, sonny, are you a doctor?" the nurse asked Master Sewer in that pedantic tone that begged for a kick in the ass.

"Are you one?" her Master retorted sharply.

Touché, Merkin thought. The nurse's face colored a shade known to the keen eye as failed-medical-school-crimson.

"I don't have to take cheek from you," she said through gritted teeth. "As for you, Miss, it's time to say nighty-night." She fumbled with something that Merkin could not see, and a few moments later everything went dark and quiet.

***

"…up!"

"…k'up!"

"Wake up!" Master Sewer's voice finally came through.

"Mmm," she said. Her mind still floated dreamily in morphine land.

"You've got to wake up! This is very important," her Master insisted.

"All right, all right," she mumbled. "Whassup buttercup?"

"Listen, we don't have much time. Can you think clearly?"

He sounded uneasy, which was very odd for him. Merkin took a deep breath as she tried to concentrate.

"I'll do my best," she said, although she felt as if she had just smoked a cigar-sized joint.

"It will have to do." He sighed. "You've got to tell me, does your Magic still work?"

"What?" she asked in a whiny voice. "What kind of question was that? She took a closer look at her Master. He seemed to be in even worse shape than the last time she had seen him. Heavy bags of weariness hung under his beautiful, dark eyes and his once-styled hair was now a mess. It was a tribute to Merkin's twisted mind that the first thought she had after seeing her Master like this was that she would still do him.

"Your Magic," he said. "Try a simple spell, anything!" There was no mistaking the sense of urgency in his tone.

"What, like now?" she moaned. It was really hard fighting the drug, almost as hard as telling your ears not to hear.

"Yes, now! She might be back any minute."

A spell. Any spell. Ah, of course, something to clear her mind, that would probably be the best.

"SA.ZALAG();" she intoned in Sumerian.

"Did it work?" Master Sewer asked impatiently.

"Peter Piper picked a peck of pickled peppers," she said quickly, then smiled her sweetest smile.

He let out a huge sigh of relief, then much to her surprise, he leaned over and kissed her forehead. "Excellent idea, but a couple of inches off target," she thought.

It was then that she realized her left hand was clenched into a fist and, by the way, it hurt − it must have been so ever since the accident. It felt as if she was trying to conceal, or perhaps protect, something in her hand, but it was hard to tell. Whatever it was, it was best if she checked on it later.

"You've got to get—" Master Sewer was interrupted by the sound of the door being swung open.

"What the devil is going on here?" the evil nurse asked, only an orchestra stab away from dramatic perfection.

But Merkin was wide-awake now, and her mind quickly put the puzzle pieces together.

"DORMIO();" she ordered.

The nurse's expression did not change, but as sleep instantly settled in, her body folded and fell on the floor with a satisfying thump.

"Now, then, was there anything you wanted to tell me?" Merkin turned to face her Master.

31. MASTER SEWER

He knew she knew, but that didn't absolve him at all from having to admit it out loud. Still, there was no reason why he should make a scene.

"It seems I am unable to cast spells for the moment," he said in as calm a voice as he could muster.

"Oh, really?" she acted surprised. "And how did that happen?"

"I'm not quite sure, but I suspect the accident might have something to do with it."

"Why would you say that? Is there any precedent in recorded history?"

"Not really, but it's just a case of applying Occam's razor. Two unlikely events happened in a short span of time, namely the accident and my predicament. The likelihood of the two events being unrelated is far outweighed by that of their actually being. That said, I still don't yet see how."

"So, you're really, how should I put it, incapacitated at the moment?" she asked, this time hardly concealing her amusement.

He nodded.

"There, there, honey," she said. "I'm sure it happens to everyone." She patted his shoulder in mock affection.

It was too much. His hand sprang like a snake towards hers, and he was about to do something very stupid, when his self-control resumed command over his body. He gently removed her hand from his shoulder and looked into her eyes. To his surprise, she was blushing, and her pupils were dilated. If he hadn't known any better, he would have guessed that she was more aroused than afraid. But luckily for him, he did know better.

"There will be plenty of time later to discuss this," he said in a calm and tired voice. "Right now we have to cover our tracks and get out of here."

"What do you mean, 'cover our tracks?'" she asked, this time in a much more respectful manner.

"Let's just say it's best to play it safe. For a start, please cast an oblivion spell on the nice nurse. Do you know the code?"

"I'm sure I can work something out. How many days should I erase from her memory?" she asked eagerly.

"Three, three-and-a-half days should be enough."

"And what will you do?" she asked. "You don't want me to do all the heavy lifting, do you?"

"You'll find out in a minute. Now, please, either figure out the spell or ask me to teach it to you. At any rate, cast it!"

"Fine, fine." She sighed. Then, after mentally compiling the code for this improvised spell, she turned to face the nurse and said "OBLIVISCARIS.DIEBUS(3.5);"

"Sounds good," Master Sewer said as he got into the hallway. "You might need to use it again pretty soon, so have it ready."

"Yes, Master, I will protect you," she said in a fake robot voice. Her derision hurt him, but he took comfort in the knowledge that he could count on his Scriptling to see him through this rough patch. At least, he hoped that was true. Magicians were notorious mood swingers, but compared to twenty-year-old girls, they were downright stolid.

"The honor will be mine, I assure you," he answered. "Now, we need to delete our medical records, so I suspect we'll have to locate a computer. Where do you normally find computers in a hospital?"

"At the Reception desk?" she ventured.

"Too many people. What about a doctor's office?"

"You mean like this one?" She pointed towards a door labeled Dr. Maison, M.D.

He nodded, reached for the door, and tried the handle. It was locked. Good, that meant that no one was inside.

"Merkin, if you don't mind…" He gestured towards the locked door.

"I most certainly don't… DVER.OTPERET();" she said, moving her hand through her hair and shaking her head shampoo-commercial style. The slowmo was particularly convincing, Master Sewer thought. An extra credit for style.

"Thanks," he said and entered the office.

Sure enough, they found the computer crammed in the corner of the desk. Further archaeological investigations revealed the coffee-stained keyboard under a heavy pile of papers.

"It's not even locked," Merkin remarked, slightly disappointed.

"The paper must have been pressing a key on the keyboard, preventing the screensaver. But don't you worry about it. I'm sure you'll have your chance to shine."

"Speaking of which, if you could just step aside, I will most awesomely hack into the medical records."

"Hold your horses, young lady," he raised his hand. "I can handle this on my own." He opened a browser window.

"Without Magic? Ha! It will take way too long. Here, let me—"

"Almost there," he said, typing furiously. "Aaand... done. I'm in!"

Her jaw dropped. "But... how?"

"It's just a neat little program that I wrote a while ago. It hacks through anything."

"But..."

"And I've posted it online, for convenience. All I have to do is type the IP Address from any computer hooked on the Internet and there you have it."

"Ah, but does it work on a Mac?" she asked.

"Of course, it does. Even on newer operating systems. It's what you would call, forward-compatible."

"You've got to show me how that works one day," she said, defeated.

"I promise I will," he answered kindly. Normally he would have teased her on the matter and provoked her to figure it out herself. But right now he was, more or less, at her mercy, and it didn't pay to act cocky.

"Have you found those records?" she asked.

"Yes, I have. I'm deleting them as we speak."

It wasn't entirely true. He deleted them, indeed, but just before that, with the kind of mastery that can come only from playing endless hours of Mortal Kombat, his fingers went into a blur of motion on the keyboard and he uploaded all her medical records to a safe location on the Internet[13]. Luckily for him, his deed passed unnoticed by Merkin. He was sure he would have known by now if it hadn't.

"All right, then let's get out of here," she said.

"What about the other nurse?"

"What other nurse?"

---

[13] Hey, if you are ready to believe in Magic, then you must believe in such a thing as a safe location on the Internet, too.

"There was this intern. I don't know his name. I don't even know if this is his shift or not."

"So, we're looking for a guy who might or might not be here and whose name you don't know. It seems too easy to be true."

"You're right, maybe we should just go."

"It occurs to me," she drove the painful point further, "that his name might have figured in those forms you just deleted."

"Yes, indeed," he mumbled. "Too bad about that."

"Cheer up, Master!" she said, and this time her voice did not bear any trace of irony. "Let's just find our clothes and get out of here".

32. MERKIN

Given enough determination, they might have eventually located their clothes in one of Toronto's dozens of waste management facilities. It had been Master Sewer who reminded her that doctors dealing with an emergency tend to have a very direct approach towards stuff, such as clothes, that gets in their way. And if that something happens to be labeled Armani or Gucci, the fact has very little importance to them. Very ethical, indeed, but that had been a three thousand dollar dress, god damn it!

"So, what do you suggest?" she asked her Master, leaning forward just to make the already-revealing hospital gown even more so.

His eyes followed the motion, and she could see his pupils dilate at the sight of her petite, but perfectly shaped, cleavage. It all lasted for less than a moment.

"Well, we could wait until two persons having about the same build as we do show up, and then we could ambush them, knock them out, and steal their clothes," Master Sewer said.

She smiled. The fact that he relied on humor meant either confidence or panic. She hoped it wasn't the latter because that would have made two of them. She was not well — her spell had cleared her mind, but her body was still weakened after the accident. More than three days of lying in bed had drained away her muscle tonus, and she was sure some of the bones were in a pretty bad shape, too. Still, she would have to carry on until they got home. Healing Magic was far too complex and risky to attempt while on the run, especially when performed on oneself.

"Sounds like a plan," she replied. "Where shall we wait for our doppelgangers?"

"It occurs to me that the best place to do so would be in the locker room," he said in mock wistfulness.

Ah, the locker room — just like a mall for shoplifters who enjoy a little challenge.

"Oh, you know how I love shopping." She laughed, and this time she knew one of her ribs was definitely in the wrong place.

"Are you all right?" Master Sewer asked when he saw her face twisting in pain.

"It's just a woman thing. No need to worry about it."

He did not seem to be entirely persuaded by her explanation, but hers was the kind of argument men had been hardwired not to pursue even if their lives depended on it.

"Sorry, I didn't mean to be indiscrete," he replied. "Come, let's find a floor plan and see where the locker room is."

They found both the floor plan and the locker room without facing any major obstacle. Luckily, there had been very little traffic in the hospital's corridors at this time of night. Unfortunately, little traffic also meant less staff, and less staff meant less variety of clothes to choose from in the locker room.

In the end, Master Sewer had to settle for a baggy pair of blue jeans, a stained green and orange t-shirt, and a pair of sneakers that had seen better days. Her options had been equally as bad, but at least she was able to find colors that matched better.

They were now facing another sensitive issue, at least as far as her Master was concerned: the room was pretty small, and it offered nothing in terms of privacy.

Merkin decided to end his misery. "Tell you what, why don't we both turn around and slip into the new... um... into these clothes? I'll let you know when I'm done, and you'll do the same. How does that sound?"

"It sounds good enough. All right, on three: one, two, three," he said, and they both turned, except that while he turned the agreed upon hundred-and-eighty degrees she went for the full three-sixty.

Ah, so he did wax all over, she thought. Gluteus maximus indeed! If she had doubted it before, now she knew that she would have to have him. But she would have to do it the proper way, which was to lure him into making the first step, thus allowing her to act totally surprised when he did.

She remembered about the thing hidden in her hand, and judging this to be a safe time to do so, she unclenched her fist with great pain and took a look at the shriveled brown thing wrapped in a napkin and lying in her palm. Ah, excellent, she thought. But still... yuck!

As she undressed, she noticed the collection of bruises on her skin and the ugly stitch under her right breast. No wonder her ribs hurt so much. Nevertheless, the bones would heal, and the scar would vanish. She didn't know all the necessary spells, but she was sure her Master would teach them to her.

Poor Master. If only his condition could be so easily alleviated. He was handling it very well, she had to admit. Compared to her own experiences of being grounded, when the loss of magical abilities would aggravate her to the point where maintaining her reason was nigh impossible, Master Sewer was a veritable study in self-control. Maybe it was his Germanic heritage or simply something that came with age, but at any rate, it was something to look up to.

Seeing that he was almost done dressing, she turned around noiselessly and did her best to catch up.

"I'm done," he said.

"Of course, you are. Men always are," she answered. "Anyway, I believe I'm decent now," she added after a pause.

"Excellent," he said as both of them turned to face one another. "We should head out now."

"You lead the way, Master."

"Right. Now, let's see. The best option would be the back door. A good Magician always finds the backdoor."

"I thought a Magician is never late and that he arrives precisely when he means to," Merkin said in a voice she thought sounded like Sir Ian MacKellen's.

"That, too. But by the same token, we should just jump out of a window and expect a Gwaihir[14] to pick us up before we fall," Master Sewer replied, scoring one for the geek team.

"You can't just *expect* the Lord of the Eagles to show up. You summon him by whispering the words of command in the ancient language to a butterfly," Merkin outgeeked her Master.

"And what happens if there is no butterfly?"

"You take the backdoor?" she said sheepishly.

***

In the event, it was a side door through which they got out of the hospital, but given the circumstances, neither of them had any objections.

"Uh… Master?"

"Yes, Merkin?"

---

[14] Come on, just Google it!

"Which way is home?"

"I'm not quite sure, to be honest. Why don't you use your powers?"

"Sorry, Master. I would try clicking my heels and saying, 'There's no place like home,' but it doesn't work well with flip-flops," she said. Her patience was wearing out. Truth be told, she was as tired as she had ever been, and every passing second marked a new all-time record. Still, she'd be damned if she'd admit it.

"I see," he said kindly. "Then let's take a cab."

"What with? We don't have any money."

"Ah, this is where you are wrong," Master Sewer said, flourishing a stack of banknotes from his pocket, and having the decency not to look very smug.

There was no point in asking where he'd gotten the money from. Silly of her not to have thought about it, too. It was the one disadvantage of relying too much on Magic, you forgot how to use your brain. She knew that, of course, or else she would not have succeeded in killing her old Master. If she didn't want to finish just like him, she would have to pay more attention to the non-magical options from now on.

33. BUGGEROFF

Whoever said that the most effective way to turn fascination into dullness was to turn it into the object of intense study must have been very wise. Between the one-on-one tutoring with Master Loo and the private drilling with Stapley, Buggeroff's overworked brain was on the verge of shutting down.

Were it not for the afternoon walks with Gertrude, he might have easily lost his marbles by now. Not that his marbles were safe, in any case. He was, after all, a Magician's apprentice, and he had a magical goat for a pet. These were not quite the types of environmental factors normally associated with marble safety — or safe marbling — whatever the term was.

Exactly how and why Gertrude switched owners was a bit of a puzzler. She was still, technically, Master Loo's pet, but there was no denying her strong attachment to Buggeroff. Moreover, while she insisted on maintaining her trademark herpetophilia around Master Loo, she hardly ever showed any signs of it around Buggeroff. And since the Master was too absentminded and polite to protest this change of fealty, the relationship between her and Buggeroff had quickly become de facto.

Best thing about it was that, despite their initial bad start, both goat and Scriptling seemed to enjoy each other's presence. It became clear that they were in for the long run one morning when a delivery of one hundred green towels was made to Master Loo's mansion, and Buggeroff explained that he had ordered them so that Gertrude would have something nice to chew on.

***

Later that day, they were climbing down the path to Don River when, out of the blue, Gertrude stopped in the middle of the trail and stuck out her tongue to taste the air. Then, having apparently identified what she was looking for, she turned towards a thick copse of trees and charged at it, disappearing from sight in three, long strides. Cursing himself for taking off her leash (Master Loo had insisted that Gertrude should wear one while on the streets), he called after her to come back.

Alas, it is a well-known fact that nothing surpasses the determination of a goat, with the possible exception of tectonic plates. Seeing that his verbal command had no effect on his single-minded friend, Buggeroff had no choice but to follow Gertrude on the treacherous path. Like many men before him, he went in search of his lost goat. There was something deeply ancestral about this, and he could almost feel the dormant shepherd gene silently kicking into action.

The trees let enough light pass through, but somehow Buggeroff still managed to walk into, quite probably, the only briar in a two-mile radius. Its thorns cut through his jeans and deep into his skin, but Buggeroff did not mind it terribly. He was used to this kind of luck. It had a pleasant familiarity.

He could not see Gertrude, but at least he could hear her tantalizing bleat in the distance. He pressed on, but after a few more minutes his sense of direction started to give him mixed signals.

Stapley, where am I? he asked.

There was a pause.

"I'm sorry, Chief, but I'm afraid I can't locate us," the personal assistant answered in a miserable voice.

What do you mean? I thought you had built-in navigation capabilities.

"I do, but, it's like… by my calculations you've either crossed the Don River without knowing it—"

Kind of hard to cross it without knowing. I'm sure my feet getting wet would be too strong a giveaway, Buggeroff thought.

"Yes, that's what I thought. Anyway, either you crossed the river or you somehow dug your way under a shopping mall… um, without knowing it."

Some help you are.

"Don't be mad, Chief. I'm doing my best," Stapley whined.

I'm not mad at you. I'm just mad. Hey, can you teach me any spell that might be useful here?

"Let me look it up, Chief."

There was another bleat, but this time it came from somewhere closer. Buggeroff ran for it, and before he knew it, he found himself in a lush, green meadow patched with dandelions. Six feet from him, Gertrude was grazing unperturbed.

"Sorry, Chief. I couldn't find any useful spell that you could cast at your current level," said Stapley.

Oh, forget about it, he thought.

113

He kneeled down in the grass, giving Gertrude a hug. He wanted to chide her. He wanted to tell her never to run away like this. But as he looked into her big, golden eyes, he felt his rage melt away. Without a word, he laid back in the soft grass and shut his eyes. Mere moments passed before his loud snore vibrated through the forest.

***

There is this to be said about Toronto: wherever you might find yourself in the city, you can't be more than a fifteen-minute walk from some sort of green patch of nature. What's more, some of these oases can actually extend for miles, following a river's course all the way to Lake Ontario. If such be its wish, a squirrel could easily branch-hop its way from Richmond Hill to downtown Toronto without once encountering a sign of civilization.

Peering through half-closed eyelids, Buggeroff saw a white squirrel take an effortless ten-foot leap between two, neighboring oaks. His mind was still numb with sleep, but he wondered if there were such a thing as a secret forest animal marathon.

"What do you think, Gertrude?" he asked in a lazy voice. "Do they have little hydration stations every couple of miles or so? Do they have charities to run for? Have you any idea how they go about fundraising?"

A noncommittal belch was all that Gertrude saw fit to reply.

"You're right, of course," Buggeroff said, curling her hair with his fingers. "But, you know, I would rather think silly thoughts than hear one more word of Latin. *Natura, naturae, naturae, naturam.* Why on earth do I have to learn all those stupid declensions? You don't need to know grammar to write computer code, so why would it be any different for spells?"

"Chief, but you are making amazing progresses." Stapley tried to make himself heard.

Not now, Stapley, Buggeroff dismissed him.

He stood upright, his face level with Gertrude's muzzle. Her breath was warm and filled with the sweet aroma of fresh-cut grass.

"You know, Gertrude," he said, "this was the best sleep I've had in ages. We should come here more often."

She said nothing.

"All right then." He stood up. "Let's go home. I'm sure by now Master Loo has started to fret."

With Gertrude by his side, the journey back to the beaten path took less than a minute, and they were soon back home.

34. MASTER LOO

"Sorry we're late, Master," Buggeroff apologized as Master Loo opened the front door.

"What do you mean, late?" he replied. "You've only been away for fifteen minutes."

"But..." Buggeroff turned to face Gertrude, who appeared to wink. "Um...I mean. I might have lost track of time."

"It can happen," Master Loo admitted. "You've worked yourself too hard this week. Perhaps you need to take a break."

"But I'm fine now," his Scriptling protested. "I feel more relaxed than I've felt in a long time."

"Ah, surely that's the dopamine speaking. Too much work can do that to you."

"I must admit I'm surprised by his progress," the inner voice said.

You are? That doesn't sound like you, he replied inwardly.

"What? Just because I'm the cynic of the group doesn't mean I have to be blind."

So, you really mean it? he asked the voice.

"Do I have to spell it out for you? The boy is learning fast. It's like he has not one, but many, tutors."

Well, he has Stapley, doesn't he?

"Stapley is a spellchecker at his best. He is not really capable of teaching him anything. You should know. You made him."

You are right, of course.

"Of course, I'm right."

That's what I said, he reminded the inner voice. *At any rate, what puzzles me is that, although he shows all the signs of hating Latin—*

"Sensible boy."

As I was saying, although he hates it, he seems to be learning it at an incredible pace.

"Maybe he's gifted with languages," the inner voice suggested

Perhaps. But still—

"Yeah, I know. He acts like he's in one of those Hollywood movies where after spending a couple of weeks with the natives in a remote Amazonian village the white explorer is already debating the nature of the universe with the Chief in passable lingo."

Yes, almost like that, Master Loo agreed.

"Except that in the movie, he ends up shagging the prize virgin whose body looks as if the jungle is really just a spa. What he doesn't know is that ten years down the road, she will wind up looking like all the other women in the village: saggy tits, rotten teeth, and about as supple as a mother of eight can be."

Well, I never!

"I know. You would never use these words. But I can, so live with it," said the inner voice.

"Master, are you OK?" Buggeroff asked.

Master Loo harrumphed. "Never been better. I was just thinking about your vacation."

"Seriously, a vacation?"

"Yes, why not?"

"Because there's so much to be learned?"

"Good grief, boy. You do realize you can't just learn on an on, don't you? It's like building a house. If you don't allow time for the cement to dry, then the whole structure will shift and crumple under its own weight."

"Ah, you mean I should let the old nugget archive all that junk I've been shoveling in?"

"Rather colorful, but well-put," the Master nodded.

"So, how many days are we talking here?"

"Two, perhaps three. Do you have any favorite place you'd like to go?"

"Yes, I do. Right here," Buggeroff said after a moment's thought.

"I beg your pardon?"

"If it's all the same to you, I'll take a couple of days off, but spend them here."

Master Loo watched his Scriptling with uncertainty.

"Are you serious about this?" he asked.

"I am. To be honest, your mansion looks better than any hotel I've ever afforded to visit. As for the staff, well, they might kill and resurrect you without asking permission for either, and they might spy on you in the shower, but they are really nice chaps when you get to know them."

Despite himself, Master Loo's eyes moistened.

"You are welcome to stay here as long as you like, Buggeroff, dear," he said in a trembling voice. "And because this is your vacation, let me officially declare you exempt from the house chores."

"Thank you, Master," Buggeroff said, still smiling. And then, a shade seemed to pass over his face. "Master?" he asked.

"Yes, boy. What is it?" Master Loo replied kindly.

"Oh, it's nothing." He hesitated.

"Come on, out with it!" the Master said in a firmer, but still kind, tone.

"Back when you were young... What I want to ask is, were there any... How did the young Scriptlings socialize?"

Master Loo's mouth opened and shut wordlessly.

"In case you don't get it, it's about a girl," the inner voice supplied in a nasty tone.

Yes, I do get it, thank you very much!

"Master?" Buggeroff asked.

"Um, yes. Let me see. Well, there were the funerals, of course. There were plenty Magicians in those days, a fact which, of course, translates into a steady turnover for funerals, if you know what I mean. Then there were the solstice and equinox celebrations. Old pagan habits die hard, you see." He shuddered. "And yes, let us not forget the occasional social calls," he finished.

"Social calls? What were those?

"Ah, well, you see, Magicians do visit one another from time to time, apparently for a game of chess and a glass of brandy, but in reality only to see if there is any gossip worth learning about, or any spell worth stealing. Anyway, on these occasions it is customary that the visiting Magician be accompanied by his or her Scriptling, if he has one, of course."

"So, while the Masters play their spy game, the Scriptlings watch and learn?" Buggeroff observed.

"It doesn't necessarily have to be an unpleasant process. Both Magicians and Scriptlings might actually enjoy the time spent together. Indeed, many a strong romance has kindled under such circumstances."

It was clearly what Buggeroff needed to hear. Dilated pupils never lie.

"Master, I don't know if I should ask, but... Is there a Mrs. Loo?" Buggeroff enquired coyly.

"Ha! I'd like to see you introvert your way out of this!" the nasty inner voice smirked.

"You are right," Master Loo said in a chill, but not unkind, tone. "You shouldn't have asked this."

"I'm sorry." His Scriptling lowered his head.

"But since we've been through so many things together..." he started.

"Come on! It's only been like a week and some change," the inner voice protested.

"I suppose we can do with fewer secrets," he finished.

"I... I..." Buggeroff stuttered.

"So, to your question, no, there is no Mrs. Loo. There never has been."

"Oh," Buggeroff said as if disappointed by what he was hearing.

"Look at him, poor bugger," the mocking voice whispered in Master Loo's mind. *"You can't just leave him like that. Tell him the whole story!"*

"That's because she died before she had the opportunity to become Mrs. Loo," the Master said in a dejected tone.

"Good, good. Now tell him how she died, you old fart!"

"I'm sorry to hear that," Buggeroff said in a low voice. "It must have been terrible for you."

"Beyond comprehension," Master Loo said, and then quietly excused himself, turned around, and walked to his private study, his mind set on an old bottle of Scotch that he kept in the liquor cabinet.

35. STAPLEY

"A vacation? The little sod needs a vacation like the Comic-Con needs more nerds. Why do I even bother, Stapley? Why?"

Master Dung was in a foul mood, but this, in itself, was no news for Stapley. What was new, though, was how the wretched intruder was beginning to use ideas that were not his own, such as the Comic-Con reference.

Granted, Buggeroff's head had been designed with the intended capacity of exactly one Buggeroff. The fact that, at the moment, it was also occupied by a magical personal assistant and a malicious spirit only meant that unexpected consequences were definitely to be expected. No wonder, then, that Master Dung was beginning to create similes using Buggeroff's own vocabulary and references. A crowd is the best place to lose your identity, and Stapley could not imagine a more crowded place than his Master's head.

But the real question was this: if Buggeroff was leaking into Master Dung, how long before Master Dung would start leaking into Buggeroff?

"I asked you a question," said Master Dung.

"I am sorry, Sir. I was struggling to find an answer. Quite frankly, I don't know why you bother, Sir," Stapley answered. Master Dung had insisted that Stapley should address him using the Butler mode. It showed respect, or so the foolish impostor thought.

"I'll tell you why I bother."

Good, a megalomaniac too, Stapley thought bitterly.

"I bother because the miserable weakling is my ticket to revenge," Master Dung finished.

"Oh, I see, Sir. Jolly good!"

"Alas, he is so unprepared that even if I had full control over his body I could not take revenge on a fly."

"Agreed, Sir. However, he does appear to possess a natural talent for Syntax. You said it yourself."

"That he does," Master Dung admitted. "Although I blame it on the university's curricula more than on his aptitude."

"And let us not forget that he is learning at an amazing pace. Wouldn't you agree, Sir?" Stapley pressed on.

"Learning my foot! Even a chimpanzee would learn Latin if someone poured it right into his head while he was asleep," Master Dung spat out, metaphorically speaking.

"And what a remarkable teaching method that proved to be, Sir. I must congratulate you on the idea, most sincerely!" Stapley said.

Stapley was honest in praising Master Dung for this. True, Buggeroff had made a decent progress by following the traditional teaching techniques with Master Loo and Stapley. But, for all that mattered, this was negligible when compared to the amazing leaps made thanks to Master Dung's unorthodox approach.

Learning is normally a convoluted and fragile process involving concentration, assimilation, questioning, judgment, and most important, a good memory. Except that it doesn't necessarily have to be like that. Not when the teacher happens to have unlimited access to his pupil's mind.

Following several failed attempts, Master Dung had decided that the best time to go about overhauling Buggeroff's brain was when the subject was asleep, relying on the notion that the numbness of a sleeping mind made it more suitable for such an undertaking. It was, in Master Dung's own words, the difference between modeling with putty and attempting the same with water.

But while the results were, as previously stated, extraordinary, something was not entirely right as far as Stapley was concerned. Learning was supposed to be a cathartic experience, a transforming journey, and an enlightening transition toward wisdom. Knowledge should shape the mind, not the other way around.

This realization came as a surprise to Stapley, primarily because software is not expected to take an interest in philosophy. After all, he was nothing more than a clever piece of code, and that made him, technically, software. Still, having a conscience is thought to be the rich soil from which the dense and thorny shrub of philosophy sprouts. Stapley had, he was forced to realize, not one, but two, consciences contaminating his mathematical inner core.

"What I don't understand is why we were not able to access his memory just now when he was asleep in that meadow," Master Dung said.

"Indeed, Sir, this unlikely occurrence poses some intriguing questions. I would also remark upon the fact that both Master Loo and my internal timer have confirmed

another strange detail. I'm referring, of course, to the fact that no time seemed to have passed while Mast... Err... Buggeroff was in the meadow."

"And what do you make of it?"

"Nothing, Sir. I am merely presenting the facts," Stapley lied. He had a pretty solid theory about what had happened there, but since his loyalty lay with Buggeroff, he thought it best not to share his findings with Master Dung.

It was also interesting to see that, for someone with such a vast knowledge of Magic, Master Dung was remarkably incapable of connecting the dots.

"Hey, Stapley!" Buggeroff's thoughts resonated through him with such strength and authority that, if Stapley had had a tail, he would have wiggled it.

"Yes, Chief!"

"Cum est altera solstitium?" Buggeroff asked.

Ah, here is someone who can put one and one together. Too bad he still had to work on the form, though.

"You mean to ask, 'Quid proxima solstitium dies est,' Chief," Stapley replied, after passing Master Dung's censorship.

"Grrr!" said Buggeroff. "And in case you have any doubts, I really meant to say, 'Grrr!'"

"No harm done, Chief. To answer your question, the next solstice is five days from now."

"Good, good. Then I'd better prepare."

"Prepare, Chief?"

"Well, you know. I have to do some research into pagan rituals, for a start. What if I'm expected to perform some sort of fertility rite? Is wearing a condom considered appropriate in the circumstances? Stuff like that."

For a moment Stapley toyed with the idea of teasing Buggeroff with some plausible but totally made up facts about the solstice celebrations, but then he thought better of it. He could guess that behind his Master's prurient interpretation there hid an overgrown infatuation with that Merkin girl. He also knew, from what Master Dung allowed to transpire, that the girl was dangerous. Admittedly, the exact words had been "a bloody succubus", but Stapley had doubted the accuracy of this description on the grounds that succubi were supposed to have larger breasts. Exactly how he knew that was a bit of a mystery to him.

"I'm sorry to ruin this for you, Chief, but my database inquiry suggests that a formal dinner followed by too many drinks is about as much as you could optimistically expect," he said.

"Oh, my! Master Loo must have fed a lot of information into your database. You never cease to amaze me, Stapley!" Buggeroff said.

Indeed, Stapley was surprised about that, too. He could not recall this particular record being stored in his database, and if he could not remember it, then by all rights it should not have been there. He then wondered if he had once again inadvertently tapped into Master Dung's reserve of knowledge, but seeing as the annoying trespasser had not protested, had, instead, allowed him to convey the information without censoring it, Stapley decided to rule out this possibility.

"Just doing my best, Chief," he said for lack of a better explanation.

"Still, I like the part about too many drinks," Buggeroff commented. "I guess I'd better learn the hangover spell."

36. NURSE GRACE

"Would you look at that!" a man said. The voice permeated her mind slowly, like molasses through thick wool. For a moment it seemed familiar, but then the memory slipped away.

"Whatever happened in here, I'm sure it's nothing we haven't already anticipated," another man said.

"Not quite. You predicted they would kill the paranoid nurse. As it is, she only seems to be asleep."

Were she not still dazed with sleep, nurse Grace might have let out a shriek. She was not sure the two men were talking about her, but she was a nurse, and she was a bit paranoid. She'd better pretend to be asleep, too, just in case.

"An interesting development," the other voice commented. "Why do you think that is?"

"They might be growing cautious…"

"And isn't this what we always wanted?"

"I might have chosen the wrong word here. What I meant to say was afraid, not cautious."

"Ah, that's an entirely different matter. What makes you think so?"

"Well, for a start, they were really shocked to see us at the funeral. I'm not saying we shouldn't have gone, but…"

"But?"

"It's just that, as far as they were concerned, it came out of nowhere."

"Oh, did it now? I daresay it was equally shocking for us when we realized we had to organize a funeral."

"That's what happens when you take your role too seriously."

"What you mean, *take lole seliously*?" said a woman in a thick Chinese accent, and then the two men burst into laughter.

"You always crack me up when you do that voice," the first man said, still laughing. Anyway, there's no point in looking back now. What's done is done."

"I agree."

"Would you also agree with me when I say we've scared them?"

"I agree they are scared, but I will not blame it on us. There was the accident, too."

"But that wasn't our fault. If anything… Oh, I see it now. You're right. It wasn't our fault. So, where does that leave us?"

"We don't really have a choice. Cautious people, I can handle, but frightened people, now that's a different dish. It reminds me of a story—"

"Is it the one about the hunter who chased a wounded tigress into her den?"

"Yes, it is," said the man in an almost embarrassed tone.

"Then I gather we won't be paying them another visit any time soon."

"Correct. But there is nothing to stop us from watching from a safe distance."

"My thoughts exactly."

"Now, that leaves us with just the problem of nurse Grace and her assistant. What do you think we should do with them?"

"Funny you should ask that. I believe I know just the thing!"

SECOND TRIBAL INTERLUDE

By the time the Tribe members had completed their second world tour, they could no longer ignore the signs. It had started as something amusing in its randomness, but as its incidence continued to increase, it evolved into an almost life-threatening issue.

It all began one unusually warm, spring evening when the Tribe members were gathered around the fire listening to Ram, the storyteller, unravel his most recent yarn. Although in the fullness of time Ram would become a refined and celebrated[15] storyteller, for the moment, he was prone to telling the kind of stories that made children run away from the village and adults look for a length of rope and some soap.

However, it wasn't the quality of Ram's tale that made this night so special, but rather the way in which a pound of steamy elephant dung materialized from thin air as Ram was telling his story about the pedantic stork and the rude elephant. What made the event even more interesting was the fact that the shit − as it were − happened exactly after Ram uttered the Mama word for steamy elephant dung, which was ¢ã[16].

Following this rather ludicrous episode, the Tribe members began experiencing similar occurrences in their everyday lives. In some cases these have proven beneficial for the Tribe, like the time when Ping told Pong[17] how much he loved honey and how he could eat four baskets of the stuff. In other cases, though, it was less so, such as the time when Pong told Ping that those four baskets of honey that had just appeared in front of them would surely attract a lot of angry bees.

By and by things had gotten so out of hand that the Mama had become understandably reluctant even to whisper about things such as spiders, volcanoes, or athlete's foot. The only Tribe member who seemed content

---

[15] Surely you must have heard some of his stories. He usually goes by the name of Unknown Collective Author.

[16] Please don't read this out loud if you are a Magician.

[17] No relation.

with the situation was Ram, whose newly found ability to conjure a rather decent thunderclap had gone a long way towards impressing his ever-demanding and otherwise-jaded audience.

In the end, it was Rack, the Tribe's historian, who proposed that they should stop using Mama for mundane conversation and that they should, instead, learn to harness its power for other purposes. There had been some who argued that Mama was more than a language, but a living cultural artifact that should be celebrated rather than put behind bars. However, a resolute growl from Spike had settled the matter once and forever. From that day on, the Tribe adopted what later became known as the *When in Three-Rivers act like the Three-Riverites* policy, which stated that the Tribe's day-to-day language should be that of the place they were visiting. It proved a sensible policy, and the Tribe had instantly experienced a dramatic decrease in accidents caused by inappropriate use of language.

37. MASTER SEWER

He was tired. So tired was he, in fact, that the spellchecker was throwing errors at him as if he were some kind of amateur.

He typed two more lines of code and hit the *Check* button. The program crunched at it for a couple of nanoseconds, then the screen went black and the following text appeared, in white system fonts:

OUT OF EUPHEMISMS ERROR!

CODE: #thisisjuststupid

APPLICATION LOCKED DOWN: #12hours

DEVELOPER_NOTE: #getsomesleep

Funny thing, he had built that spellchecker himself, a few years earlier, as a simple means to test Syntax before actually casting a spell. So, while he was upset at the program for making him look bad, he was also proud for having created something that worked so well.

The thing was right, though, he needed to get some sleep. It's just that he also wanted to have the healing spells ready for Merkin first thing in the morning. Well, it was too late for that now. The program would not work for twelve hours, and there was no way of bypassing this nuisance. A piece of software would normally have a kind of backdoor, a combination of keys or a certain sequence that would enable the programmers to debug it. Not this one. Master Sewer had been smart enough to realize that trusting no one was a process that had to start with himself.

Reluctantly, he closed the lid of his laptop and went to bed. He still found sleeping in Master Dung's bed discomforting, but he knew he would have to get used to it. He also knew that, in a way, this served as a reminder that he should be on guard, lest he and the late Master share a similar fate.

And thus his thoughts swerved back to Merkin. They – his thoughts – had gotten into this habit lately, especially before he fell asleep, and, more than once, during sleep. And while he had been able to maintain his claim of being a gentleman while awake, his dreams were an entirely different matter.

In his dreams he was wild, and by gods, she was wilder. In his dreams he had her, and yes, she had him in ways that only a mind tortured by self-imposed abstinence could conjure up. He could allow himself this luxury in his dreams. That much he could. To take the same kind of liberties in real life would be tantamount to compromising their student-teacher relation, and that was simply inconceivable.

"Inconceivable, that's such a long word," he heard Merkin whisper in his ear.

Ah, the dream had already started. Well, he'd better make the most of it.

"You know what else is?" he whispered back and threw away the blanket.

Yes, he could be wild in his dreams.

***

When he woke up, he was surprised to see Merkin standing by his bed with a breakfast tray in her hands. For just a moment he felt that stroking her breast would be the most natural thing in the world, but then the dream washed away, and he was a gentleman once again.

"I should be the one taking care of you," he said and sat up.

"You're welcome." She smiled as she laid the tray on his lap.

"I'm sorry, my manners..." He cleared his throat. "Thank you very much! That's very kind of you."

"Like I said, you're welcome." After a pause she added "Oh, don't look at me like that! You've been in bed for almost a day. I fixed you breakfast only because I was getting bored. Now, shut up and eat, or I promise I'll mash it all together and deliver it straight to your bloodstream with a syringe."

He surveyed the contents of the tray and came to the frightening realization that if Merkin were to put her threat into action it might actually be an improvement. Having travelled all over the world, Master Sewer thought he had seen all the ways in which a perfectly simple dish could be murdered by a clumsy chef.

He could not believe his eyes. With their whites so burnt that you could mix them with water and make ink, and their yolks so raw you could collect DNA samples, the over-easy eggs appeared to defy even the most fundamental laws of physics. As for the sausage and potatoes, they were a sight too horrifying for anyone with Germanic blood to behold and not cry blasphemy. In short, the contents of his plate were simply atrocious. No, they were what you get when you take atrociousness and distil it until only its purest essence remains.

The orange juice looked safe, though, so he took a cautious sip, which he immediately regretted.

"You like it?" Merkin asked, her face beaming with anticipation.

"It's… good. A bit salty, if I'm not mistaken," he managed to say.

"I'm glad you noticed. Salt is a flavor enhancer, so I thought, you know, it would bring the orange taste forward. Also, I'm sure you need the minerals."

"Oh, I see. A flavor enhancer. So is sugar," he commented, half under his breath.

"I know. That's why I used it to caramelize the eggs," she said brightly.

That, at least, explained their color.

"Quite astonishing," he said, and then, because she was watching him so intently, he took his fork, made a dent in the caramelized egg and brought the yucky thing to his mouth, wondering if he should chew or simply swallow it. Neither option appealed to him.

"I'll leave you to it," Merkin said as she headed for the door. "Oh, I almost forgot." She turned around. "I left you some newspaper cuts on the nightstand. They are about our accident. You might find them amusing to read."

38. MERKIN

She closed the door and forced herself not to burst into laughter, partly because it would give her away, and partly because her ribs still hurt like hell when she inhaled too deeply. The look on her Master's face after he drank the one-part-salt-three-parts-orange-juice had been simply priceless. And then the torture through which he went with the caramelized egg! Ah, that really made her day. She wondered whether she should go back and shame him into trying the sausage and potatoes, but in the end she had to decide against it. After all, what use would she have for another dead Master?

Two years earlier, when she had offered Master Dung the same treatment, the old fart had chugged the juice, gobbled the eggs, and stuffed down half a sausage before his stomach took charge of the situation and ordered a mass retreat. She later learned that the poor bastard had long since lost his taste buds in a failed alchemical experiment and that as long as the food smelled OK, he would just eat it. Still, her plan had worked, and following that fateful breakfast, Master Dung had never again asked her to cook.

True, her new Master had not asked her to do any chores yet, but that was no reason she should not be proactive in showing him what kind of danger hid behind such a request. Besides, she had somehow got it into her twisted mind that men are more prone to be sexually attracted by women who are terrible cooks. There was, of course, a simple rationale for this theory, as simple as the man's mind itself. It was this: a woman is only good for two things, and if she is not good at cooking, then surely she must compensate with an increased talent for the other skill. Q.E. friggin' D.

She hated herself for having to rely on such flimsy theories to justify his lack of physical interest in her. It made her look desperate, not to the world, but in her own eyes, which was far worse. It wouldn't be long before she would start thinking that he was gay, and that would really make her a sore loser.

No! She would not allow this to happen. She would have him even if it meant tying him to the bed and shagging the soul out of him. And once she'd had him, it would be he who would ask for more. She was sure of that. And who knows, if he behaved, maybe she would even indulge him.

The silver medallion around her neck gave a tiny vibration, enough to pull her out of her daydream. She pulled it out from under her blouse and read the dials — half a mile north and stationary. Interesting. So they were actually stalking them. Well, two can play that game.

She had come up with the idea of crafting the device concealed within the medallion the previous afternoon while Master Sewer was still recovering. Knowing she could not do anything about the broken rib other than magic some of the pain away, she addressed the less threatening but aesthetically unpleasing bruises, and then set to work.

It had been a rather ingenious, if a little guesswork-based, enchantment. She started by placing a small, brown, foul-smelling object in a cast iron mortar. It was the cigar butt that the fat cop had discarded in the cemetery four days before, and which she had been holding in her hand while unconscious in the hospital. Whispering a Slavonic nursery rhyme, more to keep track of time than for any magical effect, she added honey, hairball essence, and spittle. Then, using a heavy-looking, rusty pestle she mixed the ingredients until they formed a gooey paste.

She let the concoction rest for a couple of hours under a UV lamp while she assembled the clockwork. This wasn't her forte by any stretch, and sure enough, she destroyed a couple of cogwheels before anything resembling a working mechanism came out of her hands.

With all the preparation out of the way, the final step had been little more than a formality. A simple infusion spell took care of imprinting the device with the cigar's morphic signature, and that was pretty much it. She was now the proud owner of a Magical device that went *buzz* whenever it came within a mile of the fat cop.

And it had just buzzed.

Without a moment's hesitation, she stepped into a pair of sandals and got out on the street. No subtlety this time. She would confront the cops and give them a piece of her mind. If that wouldn't make her Master proud, then nothing else would.

Keeping an eye on the silver medallion, she navigated the streets with the confidence of a native setting up an ambush against the cocky foreigners. Her plan was to catch them from behind, cast a paralyzing spell, and then drive them back to the house for interrogation. She was getting closer. According to her tracking device, her target was less than thirty yards away, just around the corner. They had sure picked a good spot for stalking her. This street was part of her regular route. There was a good chance this was not the first time they had stalked her.

She paused, bracing herself for the next step. Most likely the cops would be hidden in an unmarked car, eating doughnuts. She peeked around the corner for confirmation, and sure enough, a white Ford sedan was parked at about the right distance, facing the other way. The car seemed to be empty, but Merkin knew better than to trust appearances. Making the car appear empty was as easy as reclining the front seats, and it was the oldest trick in the book.

Rushing toward them would have been the best maneuver, but it was also impractical in her current condition. She opted instead for a slower but safer pace, knowing that if she stayed in the blind spot she still had a pretty good chance of taking them by surprise.

She kept her attention fully focused on the car as she drew nearer, her right hand ready and itchy to cast the spell. Twenty yards, fifteen yards, ten, seven, five... She knew her plan had worked. If they hadn't noticed her so far, it was too late for them now. She crossed the remainder of the distance and raised her hand.

"TORPOR();" she said, before seeing the empty seats.

"Is everything all right, ma'am?" an elderly voice asked from behind her.

She spun on her heel, ready to throw another spell, only to see a white-haired man smoking a cigar on his porch. He looked like everything you would expect a grandpa to be.

"It's the heat, Elroy," said a nice old lady from the door. "Come inside, sweetie. I'll get you some water."

Merkin stood on the curb with her mouth open. Of course! The cigar! Her device was not only tuned to the morphic resonance of the cop who smoked the cigar, but also to all cigars coming from the same plantation. Maybe even the same factory. It all made sense now. A few minutes ago, when the medallion had started to vibrate, it had already indicated a distance of half a mile when it should have normally picked up the signal within a full mile. It must have been the moment that Elroy, the white-haired grandpa, lit his cigar. Blast it!

"Ma'am?" asked Elroy.

She cleared her throat and said, looking extremely embarrassed "I... I'm all right, thank you very much! I should be going now."

"Are you sure you don't want a glass of water, darling?" asked Elroy's wife. "Perhaps some iced tea?"

"No, no, I'm fine," Merkin said. "That's very kind of you," she added, not wanting to be rude to these nice people. Why? What was wrong with being rude?

"The girl said she was fine, Mildred," Elroy said, coughing a blue cloud of smoke.

"You're right, Elroy. When you're right, you're right," Mildred said, winking at Merkin. "Send our regards to your granddad, will you, darling?" she added.

"My granddad?" Merkin stopped in her tracks.

"I mean Mister Dang. Isn't he your granddad?" Mildred asked in a pleasant voice.

Mister Dang? Well, of course. These people must have lived here for ages, plenty of time to know a little bit about their neighbors, even the grumpy ones.

"No, he was just a distant relative," Merkin said.

"Was?" both members of the couple asked, with that keen interest only death can arise in people past a certain age.

"He... he passed away last week," she babbled. "He died peacefully in his sleep," she added for good measure, knowing this detail would be important for her audience.

"Poor Mister Dang." Mildred sighed. "And he was so young. A very nice gentleman, I always said. Hey Elroy, didn't I always said what a nice gentleman Mister Dang was?"

"Yes, yes, that's what you always said. Although I'll be damned if I know why you'd say such a thing."

"Elroy!" Mildred chided her husband. "You must excuse him, sweetie. He gets agitated," she said to Merkin as if that explained everything. "Please receive our deepest condolences for your loss, darling!"

"Thank you," Merkin said, feeling miserable. "I'm really sorry, but I have to go now. Have a good day!"

"Come visit us anytime," Mildred shouted after her.

39. MASTER SEWER

As soon as Merkin left the room, Master Sewer rushed to the ensuite and flushed the dubious contents of the breakfast tray down the toilet, animated by a deep, unshakeable feeling of righteousness. He let out a sigh, feeling somewhat better for having performed this exorcism in the name of the holy cuisine. The problem remained that he was still hungry, and he couldn't just go down to the kitchen to fix himself a nice sandwich, for fear of hurting Merkin's feelings.

It was then that he heard the front door open and close. From the bedroom window he spied Merkin as she headed into the alley in a manner he could only think of as a furtive. Well, this was not an opportunity to miss. He descended the stairs with understandable alacrity and before long he was surveying the shelves of the huge fridge. He had been half-expecting the thing to be empty, or at least to be filled with week-old groceries. Instead, he was pleasantly surprised to see that Merkin had done a pretty good job of restocking their food supplies while he had been asleep. Good girl! Too bad her cooking could only be lucratively used in biological warfare. But hey, she had other qualities, he caught himself thinking in an ungentlemanlike way.

Not knowing how much time he had before her return, he went straight for the low-volume, high-caloric food group. Ten seconds later he regarded the ham and Swiss wrapped candy bar, took a cautious bite and decided, against all odds, that it was actually quite good. He grabbed an apple as a minor concession to dietary norms and headed back to his bedroom. The whole search and rescue mission had been conducted in under two minutes.

Master Sewer considered rewarding himself by resuming his work on the healing spell, but on a second thought[18] he had to concede that a shower might actually be a better idea.

---

[18] Read "smell".

By the time the much-needed ablution had been completed, Merkin had already returned. By the way, her passage through the house was marked by slamming doors — he could tell she was obviously upset about something, and if Master Sewer knew one thing about women (and about meteorological phenomena in general), it was that the best way to deal with such wrath was to lock yourself in a safe place and wait for it to subside. Besides, he really needed to work on that spell.

But before that, there were some medical records to be perused. With child-like curiosity, he downloaded the files from their safe location and started skimming them.

The first interesting piece of information to surface was that Merkin was not really twenty, but rather nineteen-and-a-half. Not that it really mattered. It wasn't as if he had to argue this point to a jury or anything. Oh, and what was this, an on-going prescription for contraceptive pills? Kids these days…

And then he saw it. It had been right there, before his very eyes, yet he could not bring himself to believe it. The paragraph read:

Mother: Beatrice Long (1972 – 2009)

Father: Bartholomew More (1971 – 2009)

Of course, Silvia Longmore! The name itself did not ring any bell, but Long and More rang enough bells to make the Kölner Dom seem like a toy rattle. If genealogical trees could be classified in terms of Magic, these two would definitely be Ents. No wonder Merkin was such a potent and precocious Magician.

Master Sewer had known Merkin's parents, if only from a distance, although they had been the same generation, his own, murky pedigree had prevented him from meeting them in person.

"You'd have found out sooner or later," Merkin said from behind him in a sad, quiet voice.

He almost jumped, but years of self-composure kept him nailed to his chair.

"I…" he began, turning to face her.

"You thought I'd live under the same roof with someone as paranoid as Master Dung and not learn a thing or two about sneaking? Oh, and by the way, I saw when you copied the medical files from Dr. Maison's computer. The only reason I didn't say anything about it was that, well, I kind of wanted you to know. Besides, you're smarter than the rest and, like I said, you'd have found out anyway."

"I didn't know."

"It's not really a conversation piece. Hi, my name is Merkin, and I'm the sole heir to the Long and the More estates," she said in a mock posh voice.

"You are?" Master Sewer was surprised. "Then why—"

"Why am I not a spoiled brat living off the family's huge pile of money?"

"I never said you were not a spoiled brat," he said before remembering that in his current condition this was like teasing a bear with an unloaded shotgun.

"For someone who's lost his magical abilities, you really have some balls," she said angrily, then burst into laughter. "I'm just fucking with you, that's all."

Somehow her words triggered a flashback from his recent dream, and Master Sewer turned instantly red.

"Oh, come on, you know I don't really care. You're still my Master with or without your Magic," she said, misjudging his embarrassment for anger.

"I appreciate that." He tried not to sound relieved. "Still, I'm intrigued. Why did you choose a low profile?"

"I guess deep down inside I knew I wasn't ready for a high profile."

"That's wise of you."

"You wouldn't say that if you knew the entire story." She smiled, then appeared to hesitate. "When my parents died—"

"Excuse me, but I need to interrupt you. It might sound inappropriate, but I believe it is a legitimate question. Your parents—"

"No, I didn't kill them. Not that I didn't think about it a couple of times. You know how teenagers are."

"I'm sorry"

"Oh, don't be. You're right. It was a legitimate question. But that being said, I don't believe it was an accident, either. Both of them were experienced sailors, and they were also powerful Magicians."

"A thunderstorm is not something to be taken lightly," Master Sewer, who had heard scattered details about the sad accident, said. "Nature is—"

"Neither is a car crash!" she cried. "And yet we're not dead!"

"We had medical help, of sorts, more or less," he tried, but even as he spoke, he realized he was not entirely convinced by this explanation. Their survival had been a lucky one, no matter how he looked at it. "And I've lost my Magic in that accident."

"You think that happened to them, too?" Merkin asked, trying hard to control her fury.

"It's just a conjecture. I cannot really posit—"

He stopped when he saw Merkin was crying. He stood up and clumsily offered her a box of tissues from his desk. She ignored his offer and instead pressed herself to his chest and wrapped her hands behind his shoulders.

"There, there," he said, putting an arm around her waist and gently stroking her hair with his other hand. They stood like that for a while, Merkin sobbing quietly and he, because nature has endowed men with unsophisticated albeit very sensitive triggers, trying his best to think of dead puppies.

He spoke first.

"You were about to tell me what happened after your parents'… is it all right if I call it an accident?"

She broke the embrace and sat on the bed with her legs on her side in what Master Sewer instantly recognized as the little mermaid pose. Her eyes were red and she still looked vulnerable. He fought back the urge to hug her again.

"Well, for six months I pub-crawled my way through Europe, and the funny part is that no one ever asked to see my ID. You got to love the old continent! Anyway, there's much I don't recall from that period, and I'm sure that's just as well."

"Did you—"

"No, I didn't do any spells. In fact, I was so upset at the world that I actually took a vow to forswear my magical heritage. It didn't last, as you can see, but at least it saved me from some serious trouble."

Master Sewer nodded approvingly. A rogue Magician with an alcohol problem has a very limited shelf life. Magicians were very good at covering their tracks, and by extension, at covering other people's tracks.

"So, what happened?"

"What happened is that someone who went to great lengths to remain anonymous had picked me off the streets and put me in a rehab center in Austria."

"When you say great lengths…"

"Trust me. I could not track this person down, no matter what I tried."

"A Magician?"

"What else could it be?"

"Just because it is the most likely explanation doesn't make it true," he commented, becoming the Master once again.

"You'd think that, wouldn't you? But what do you think was the first thing I tried when I found myself trapped?"

"You tried to escape, of course."

"By means of?"

"Umm, Magic?" He paused and then realization dawned. "Oh, no!"

"Oh, yes! It didn't work. It was the first time I ever experienced grounding, and it hasn't been a nice first experience, let me tell you that."

"So, what did you do?"

"Nothing. For almost a month I didn't want to do anything. I didn't eat, I didn't drink, I didn't want to talk. I didn't do a thing. They kept me on perfusions for fear that I might starve to death. To tell you the truth, I was kind of aiming for that anyway. And then it occurred to me that if I had to go, at least I should go with a big bang rather than with a pathetic fizz. I started responding to the treatment, and, before long, I cleaned up my act. My powers came back the day I left the wretched place as if whoever had put me in there decided I was no longer a threat to myself."

"That didn't stop you from becoming a threat to others." Master Sewer smiled.

"That didn't happen until much later." She smiled back. "I decided to return to Canada, partly because it seemed like the sort of quiet place I needed at the time, but mostly because I knew Master Dung by reputation, and I was ready to resume my training. You know the rest."

He nodded, trying to assimilate all this new and fascinating information.

"Aren't you going to tell me your story now?" She made a pouty face. "It would be the polite thing to do."

"Perhaps some other time." He sighed. "I really have to work out that healing spell for you now, wouldn't you agree?"

"Yeah, I guess you'd better do that." She sighed, too. "Do you think I'll be back in top shape in time for the solstice festivities?"

Master Sewer closed his eyes and did the math.

"I don't see why not. Although, to be honest, I didn't picture you as the type."

"And why not, if I may ask?"

There was a hint of menace in her voice and Master Sewer became aware he was treading on dangerous ground.

"Well, I mean, you seem very modern and all that," he replied, his usually composed demeanor slowly wilting under her steady gaze.

"All that? And what exactly do you mean by 'all that?'" If she were a volcano, this would have been that time when the peasants in the valley decided to either flee or learn very quickly how to breathe lava.

"Excuse me." He decided to play a risky card. "Are you fucking with me?"

She leaned forward, her anger instantly turning into seduction but maintaining all its momentum. She said nothing, but her eyes seemed to ask, "Do you want me to?"

For a brief moment his senses were overwhelmed by her presence, and his heart responded by picking up the pace, pumping blood to his cheeks, ears, nose, fingers, and other, less mentionable, extremities.

He wanted to shout YES to the unspoken question, but just as he was about to, she stepped back from him and said, "You'll have to fix me first. I can be pretty amazing, even in my current state, but I'm sure you would expect nothing short of the best from your Scriptling. Isn't that so, Master?"

She turned and cat-walked out of her room, leaving him fully and thoroughly dazzled.

40. BUGGEROFF

It hadn't been the vacation he had expected. To Buggeroff, the ideal vacation meant playing endless hours of *Diablo* or *Gothic* and the occasional classic, like *Day of the Tentacle*.

It wasn't that he didn't have the right conditions. On the contrary, Master Loo's magically tuned game station was nothing short of a nerd's dream, and the sound system was simply mind-blowing. No, the reason his vacation did not go as planned had been precisely the fact that he did have the right conditions. Buggeroff could not quite put his finger on it, but it seemed to him that half the thrill in playing video games derived from its being a clandestine, forbidden affair. It was one thing spending your night squinting at a fifteen-inch CRT monitor, the CPU fan vrooming louder than a tumble dryer, when you had an exam the next morning, and you didn't even know the professor's name. It was a completely different thing sitting in a state-of-the-art ergonomic chair, playing 3D games at an insanely high frame per second, with no homework waiting to be done. It was too perfect, too sterile.

So, when this activity failed to deliver the anticipated kick, Buggeroff decided to switch his attention to something else. The question was, to what? And then, as his eyes gazed emptily at the frozen battle scene on the screen, an idea sprouted in his mind. Why wallow in the virtual territory of Role-Playing Games when he could play the game in real life? He was, after all, a Scriptling aiming to become a Magician. Wasn't this what all games were about? Building a character, learning skills, choosing between right and wrong, killing goblins? OK, maybe not the latter, but the point remained valid.

Stapley, can you teach me how to create a fireball? he asked his assistant.

"Umm... *that sounds a bit dangerous, Chief,*" Stapley faltered.

What about chain lightning?

"*Definitely dangerous, especially without rubber boots.*"

Perhaps a healing spell, then? That can't possibly hurt anyone.

"You would be surprised, Chief," Stapley shook his head.

Life drain, courage, slow, curse, summon, stone skin, paralyze, frenzy, minor ward, telekinesis, raise zombie? Nothing?

"I'm sorry, Chief, but none of that is part of your curricula." Stapley sighed.

Then I'd better add them myself, don't you think?

"What do you mean, Chief?"

You'll find out pretty soon, Buggeroff thought, and then he added out loud, "Gertrude, I know you're hiding somewhere around here. I can smell you."

And there she was, dangling from a foot lamp that only a moment ago seemed perfectly ordinary. She blew a raspberry and slithered down to the floor.

"Come on," said Buggeroff. "I know you're upset with me for playing video games during your walk time, but I'm on vacation, and I thought I'd break the routine a little bit."

She looked at him with eyes that seemed to say she might be persuaded to let this one go if only the right incentive were presented to her.

"Now, go find your leash. We're going out," he said and watched her as she scampered down the stairs, so excited that for a moment she was not able to figure out how four feet were supposed to work together.

"So, where exactly are we going, Chief?" Stapley asked.

Out, where else? You don't expect me to risk setting this place on fire, do you?

***

A few minutes later, as they drew closer to the ravine, Buggeroff squatted so he faced Gertrude.

"Now, I'm going to take you off the leash," he said. "But you have to promise not to run away again. Is that clear?" he asked in a firm, but friendly tone.

She nodded curtly, and then, because she was within perfect distance, gave his face a slobbery, rasping lick.

"Yeeew, cud!" he exclaimed, still not quite used to her ways of showing affection.

He released her from the leash and started walking down the path to the river. As they reached the place where Gertrude had run off the other day, he turned right and started walking towards the meadow. A couple of steps later he was forced to stop, taken completely aback by a rare case of overnight geography. He blinked, rubbed his eyes, and whistled a perfect up and down glissando, not wanting to believe what he saw.

141

"Gertrude, you have some explaining to do," he said in a singing voice as he pointed at the sheer rock cliff where only a day before there used to be a copse of trees.

She had the decency to look embarrassed for a moment before letting out a frail, apologetic bleat that softened Buggeroff's heart as if by magic.

"I had a feeling that wasn't your run-of-the-mill meadow," he said. "That's why I wanted to perform my experiments over there. Could you please show me the way to it again?"

In response, she tilted her head, pointing knowingly to a place behind him. Slowly, as if not wanting to scare whatever it was that stood behind him, he turned his head. There was still no sign of trees, and the barren cliff was still there. Well, most of it, anyway.

"Funny, I don't recall using the words 'Open Sesame,'" Buggeroff said, and then he stepped into the cavern mouth.

"Chief, my Navigation Module is sending mixed signals again." Stapley's face appeared in the bottom, right corner of his vision, looking genuinely perplexed.

That's a good sign, Stapley. It means we're heading in the right direction. By the way, could you increase my ISO sensitivity to around sixteen thousand? It's pitch black in here.

"No problem, Chief. I'm installing an infrared layer as we speak. Here, how does it feel?"

Buggeroff blinked a couple of times and then, as shades started to resolve themselves into shapes, he said *"Hey look, a stala-ct-t-gm-m-thingy!"*

"Ctite, Chief. It's a stalactite. It helps if you think the 'c' in stalactite stands for ceiling while the 'g' in stalagmite stands for ground."

No, it doesn't.

"Beg your pardon, Chief?"

It doesn't really help. Anytime someone comes up with a clever way of remembering stuff, it turns out the memory doesn't do clever. It's like trying to impress a chick in a pub by memorizing her phone number: yes, three-eight-two, it's easy because eight is two to the power of three, and then thirty-one, which is a prime number, not hard at all, followed by zero-one which is impossible to forget.

"Fascinating thing, the human mind is, Chief. Anyway, I've been meaning to ask, why are you doing this?"

Doing what?

"This spell experiment you mentioned. I thought you were taking a vacation. Look, it even says so in my calendar: sixteenth to seventeenth, June vacation." Stapley displayed the relevant calendar page.

I still don't see the problem.

"It's your vacation, Chief. You're not supposed to do anything work-related. Perhaps you should do the exact opposite."

By the same token bartenders should not drink on their holidays and policemen should always exceed the speed limit when off-duty.

"I agree, there might be a flaw in my reasoning," Stapley said after a pause.

Looks like we're getting closer, Buggeroff remarked upon seeing a flickering light in the distance.

41. MASTER LOO

"Would you look at yourself? You are fidgeting. You are actually fidgeting, and you're as drunk as a skunk," the inner voice sniggered.

For the first time in years, Master Loo had nothing to keep his mind occupied, and as a result, his mind had started wandering places, leaving the old motor functions on their own. Indeed, following the years of exhausting and heart-breaking attempts to perfect the Ritual, the unexpected success with Buggeroff came more as a shock than a relief. At the time, Master Loo took comfort in the knowledge that this was merely the first phase of the big plan, and that tutoring the freshly minted Scriptling in the ways of Magic would be just as rewarding.

Huh? he asked absentmindedly.

"Good grief! Get a grip on yourself, will you? Next thing I know you'll be wetting yourself."

But pretty soon after that, things took a wrong turn. OK, not wrong per se, but still quite different from what Master Loo had expected. He was not afraid of progress. He was, if such a nametag could be put to it, a progress-junkie. But if there was something he prized more than progress, then that thing was the road that led to it. And this was exactly where he felt cheated by Buggeroff and his fast-track approach to learning.

There's nothing for me to do. He sighed.

"Says the one who practically begged the boy to take a vacation. And you call me a masochist."

But it was the right thing to do, said Master Loo

"For you or for him? No, don't answer that. I know what you're going to say. Let me ask you this, though — don't you think you deserve a vacation, too?"

Me?

"And people think you're bright! Seriously, how did you manage to fool them for so long? Yes, of course you!" The inner voice snapped.

But you know I don't like vacations, Master Loo protested.

"That's because you've always approached them from the wrong end. Seriously, your idea of a vacation is to do exactly the same things you are doing now: sink deep into self-pity, get drunk, and force me to take charge. You know how I don't like being in charge."

Yes, you've always regarded yourself as a sort of éminence grise, operating behind the scenes, knowing the ropes and pulling the strings. I can't say I liked it.

"But it suits me well, doesn't it?" the inner voice beamed.

I can't argue with that. So, what exactly are you suggesting? Master Loo asked.

"Surf the net, bathe in the shallow waters of social media, download porn."

You know I'd never, Master Loo protested.

"The last part was for me. You never do anything for me, you know that? Actually, scratch that. You do a lot of things for me, like the fact that you never cease to give me irrefutable reasons for staying a cynical and bitter bastard. Thank you very much for that!"

The reason you are a cynical and bitter bastard is, quite simply, because I'm not either of those things. That's how split personalities work, by being opposite. He did not enjoy this conversation, but at least it was beginning to sober him up.

"I can't say that I agree with that. You and I are not so different, you know?" said the inner voice.

Don't flatter yourself.

"Anyway, go for a hike, learn to canoe, or camp out for a night. Yes, you're an old fart, but you have Magic on your side. How hard can it be?"

You know me better than that, Master Loo said.

"Yeah, you never were the outdoorsy type, and neither was I, to be honest. See, we're not as opposite as you would like to think. No, don't interrupt me because we both know you don't have the right arguments. Good! Now then, let us try something basic and more appropriate for our age."

***

An hour later, Master Loo was feeling considerably better.

You were right about this. It is actually quite enjoyable. I'm surprised I haven't tried it before, thought Master Loo.

"Careful there! I know it seems harmless, but it can become extremely addictive. Many specialists agree this can lead to personality disorders. On second thought, I suppose it's too late for you to worry about those."

Yes, fascinating, Master Loo said, his attention not entirely extended to the conversation with his inner voice.

"Don't you dare do that to me! I will not be ignored! I knew I shouldn't have told you about the TV."

Yes, yes, quite. Oh, my! Would you look at that?

On the TV screen a fat, perplexed woman wearing excessive makeup was looking into the camera. Next to her, a young man, as thin as she was fat, had a similar look on his face.

"These are the winners of the forty-two million dollars lottery jackpot," the news lady's voice proclaimed. "Although they work together at a downtown hospital, they have played the winning numbers on their own, following a premonitory dream that came to them during their night shift. At least, that's what they claim."

A previously recorded footage showed the fat lady recalling how an angel with hair of fire came to her in her dream and told her the lucky numbers. This was shortly followed by a similar recollection by the dazed young man, whose only point of divergence to his colleague's story was that the angel's hair was not on fire but merely red.

"More about this story on newstoday.ca/luckybastardsgetfilthyrich," the news lady concluded. "Now, back to traffic news."

"What do you reckon are the odds of that?"

You mean the fact that two co-workers independently won the jackpot? Master Loo asked.

"No, that's statistically probable."

What then? The fact that they were both sleeping during working hours? What can the hospital do now, fire them?

"I'm talking about their actually receiving the winning numbers in their dream," said the voice.

Well, I suppose some intimate knowledge of Arcana Actuariorum might enable a nimble and ill-intended spell-caster to look into the future and have a glimpse at the winning numbers. But that would be simply preposterous when there are plenty of better and more discrete ways to become rich.

"You're missing the point here."

Oh, am I? he thought, but then his attention was drawn back by the television. *Hey, look, there was another accident on the 407. When will people learn how to drive safely? When?*

"Fine, have it your way, you fool! See how long it takes before this TV thing fries your brains. Speaking of which, can you smell something burning?"

I… Yes, I think so.

"Hey, Master, look what I can do," said Buggeroff as he entered the room excitedly.

Master Loo watched incredulously. Floating inches above Buggeroff's open palm, a crimson-red fireball crackled joyfully.

THE SCRIPTLINGS

42. BUGGEROFF

For the first time since Buggeroff had met him, Master Loo was genuinely taken aback. He looked as if he wanted to say something, but somehow the words were incapable of freeing themselves from his mind.

Stapley, do you think he's OK? he asked.

"I think so, Chief. I would guess he's being torn by mixed feelings and also a bit drunk."

What kind of mixed feelings?

"Well, on the one hand, we have pride at your being so successful, but on the other hand he might feel frustration at not being directly responsible for your remarkable success."

What do you mean, not responsible? I owe everything to him.

"Yes, but he isn't the one who taught you how to cast a fireball."

Oh.

In the meanwhile, it seemed that Master Loo had regained his voice.

"H... How did you do that?" he asked.

Buggeroff chose his words carefully. "I guess I've worked it out from general principles. It was just a question of applying what I learned from you towards the end goal."

This had the intended effect on Master Loo, who looked slightly mollified by the reference to his own contribution.

"Tell me more," he said. "And by the way, unless you mean to set the carpet on fire, I suggest you put that thing out. It dribbles."

"Actually, I'm not sure exactly how to do that, Master," Buggeroff said sheepishly. He said nothing about what a challenge it had been to get back from the park while trying to conceal the fireball in his hand. For one thing, reaching for the keys in your right pocket with your left hand is much harder than it ought to be. "I tried shaking it off, but it's stuck."

Master Loo's face illuminated at the prospect of being needed again. "I don't suppose you bothered to include a User Abort procedure?"

"No, Master," said Buggeroff, obviously mad at himself for his mistake. "I... You know what it's like when you write code. I mean on a computer. You don't have to worry about this kind of stuff until later. There's always a STOP button in the debugging menu, and if that fails, you can never go wrong with CTRL + Break. Except that..."

"Except that since you are the *machine* on which the spell code is being executed, going for the CTRL + Break option might have... fatal consequences. Is this what you were trying to say?"

"Yes, Master," Buggeroff replied, his previous excitement now completely vanished.

"Before we go any further, I'd like you to understand something about priorities and about doing things in the right order. For instance, while a propeller is a very useful device to have on boat, the important thing to remember is that you should affix it before going into the water. Especially when the particular model requires a hole cut through the keel."

"I understand," Buggeroff's shoulder sagged.

"On a brighter note, I must congratulate you on having the sense and skill to render your skin impervious to fire beforehand. You would be surprised to learn how many fail to take this minimum precaution."

"How many?" Buggeroff could not keep his mouth shut.

"Oh, I don't know. That was just a figure of speech. Now, the good news is, you have two options," Master Loo said, scratching his chin.

"Why do I have the feeling the bad news is concealed within one or both of these options?"

"Oh, don't be like that. Let's just say the bad news has already happened."

"Ah."

"I don't really mean bad news," Master Loo replied, seeing the sad expression on his Scriptling's face. "What you've done is quite astonishing, if only a little bit reckless. That's the mark of a good Magician, if you really want to know."

"Thank you, Master." Buggeroff sighed, not entirely convinced. "So, you mentioned there are two options?"

"Ah, yes. The first and easiest option is to wait until your power runs out and you faint. This should take care of the on-going spell and should have no harmful effects on you."

"How long would that take?" Buggeroff asked. He was not too crazy about fainting after the episode at the funeral. He found it somewhat demeaning.

"At your current level, let's say about twelve hours," Master Loo replied.

"*Actually, Chief,*" Stapley began, "*if you remember, your Master doesn't know your true level. My calculations indicate roughly two days before you run out of juice.*"

Ouch! thought Buggeroff. "What is the other option?" he asked his Master.

"The other option is… Well, it's not that simple. It requires a lot of concentration and extreme delicacy. On the other hand, you had to learn this sooner or later anyway."

"What is it?"

"To use an analogy with which you might be more familiar, your task is to build something like a test environment inside your mind. This is the hard part, but at least I can teach you how to do it. Sadly, that's not all there is to it."

"Let me guess," said Buggeroff, who had a knack for sensing impending narrative doom. "The part you cannot teach me, the part that requires extreme delicacy, is transferring the spell session to this test environment without losing myself in the process."

There was a pause.

"As a matter of fact, I think you captured the essential. Well done!" Master Loo said.

43. STAPLEY

"I beg your pardon, Sir, but do you have any thoughts on how to handle this?" Stapley asked with false concern.

"Quiet, worm! I'm thinking," replied Master Dung with all the tact of a bulldozer.

Stapley muttered something unintelligible.

"What was that?" Master Dung inquired in the authoritative tone of a teacher.

This was lost, however, on Stapley. Well, not entirely lost, but seriously diminished by the fact that, while perfectly capable of decoding the message, Stapley did not possess the proper mechanisms for experiencing anxiety. He could, on the other hand, experience pain, like that time when he had the displeasure of making Master Dung's acquaintance. Still, whereas in normal people, the memory of pain causes fear, Stapley was not normal, nor was he people.

"It was nothing. Just a random system message caused by Buggeroff overloading the mainframe," he replied, radiating honesty.

"You think you're smart, do you?" Master Dung launched one of those retorts that didn't really mean anything but had a menacing ring, nonetheless.

"I couldn't say, Sir. Sir, if I may be allowed to shed some light on the current predicament..."

"I don't need you to shed any kind of bloody light over any damned predicament!"

That much was true. The situation was quite clear in all its dreadful details. There was no doubt the intruder deserved his fate, and, in his heart of hearts, Stapley rejoiced in anticipation. It was a joy made twice as intense by the irony that Master Dung had brought the whole thing upon himself.

In short, Master Dung had been so blinded by Buggeroff's determination to craft an offensive spell that he failed to recall just how inexperienced the kid was in the ways of spell casting. Of course, Stapley had a pretty good notion that the idea of including a User Abort procedure or that of using a test environment would not cross Buggeroff's mind. Normally, he would have done everything in his power to prevent the disaster. But this had not been a normal situation. Not by a long shot. In fact, it had been the perfect opportunity to get rid, once and for all, of Master Dung.

Consider two environments, A and B, both occupying a clearly delimited brain space. Environment A is the live environment, the one where any change, say, casting a fireball, is reflected in real life. B, on the other hand is the test environment, where actions are mere virtual representations of their real life counterparts. The typical way to go about creating a new spell is to build it in environment B where all bugs can be safely tested and all errors can be fixed and only then run a copy of the final code in environment A.

Code is easy to copy because it's just words. On the other hand, transferring a running program, or in this case, a spell, between two environments is a completely different business. It requires a temporary buffer, a large chunk of free brain space. The only catch was that, as far as Buggeroff's brain was concerned, the much-needed chunk of free space was already occupied by Stapley, specifically by that part of Stapley that stored Master Dung.

"How much time have we got?" asked Master Dung.

"Us, Sir?" Stapley smirked. *"I don't recall my being in any kind of danger."*

"Why you!"

"Relax, Sir! You still have about two minutes to come up with a brilliant plan before Master Loo teaches him how to transfer the spell. I believe the first step would be clearing the buffer, Sir."

"You knew about this?" Master Dung said furiously.

"I can't say the notion didn't occur to me, Sir. Still, I recall how you went to great lengths to teach me not to question your judgment. I daresay you succeeded. Time is ticking, Sir."

"Can't you just make more room for me?"

"Ah, yes. How do you fit an elephant into a refrigerator? An interesting riddle, I must agree. But you see, the correct question right now would be, how do you fit an elephant into twenty-three refrigerators? Hmm. Where shall we make the first cut, Sir?"

Master Dung groaned.

"Of course, it would have helped if you would have allowed me to do a little bit of defragging like I asked you to. That way, instead of having twenty-three small-sized, disparaged memory spaces available, I'd have had a large one, just good enough to fit your Lordship. Alas, it's too late now. There's simply not enough time."

"There must be a way," Master Dung moaned.

"*Well, Sir, you've heard Master Loo. There's either this, or fainting,*" Stapley said before realizing what it was that he had just said.

"Say, this fainting option… What's the worst that can happen?" Master Dung tried to suppress the tremble of hope in his voice.

"*Before we move any further, it is important to acknowledge that fainting will not occur for another two days,*" Stapley smiled nervously.

"Of course, of course. Even so, please, humor me."

Stapley was beginning to choke under the strong grip exerted by his captor. "*I believe the spell will be broken, Sir.*"

"And while poor Buggeroff is recovering, you will…" Master Dung smiled.

"*I will…?*"

"De…"

"*De…?*"

"De…fr…" the grip got stronger.

"*Defrag, Sir?*" Stapley choked out.

"What a charming notion! I must commend you for your initiative, old chap!" Master Dung released the grip, but not all the way. "Now, listen to me, worm! You will make him faint, or I'll make you wish you were never born!"

"*Cast, Sir. I was never born. I was cast-eeeeey,*" Stapley's voice drifted in response to Master Dung's grip being suddenly increased. "*I… I'll see what I can do, Sir. But remember, we've already told him it will take two days for the manna to run out. How will he continue to trust us if-eeeeey…*"

"Why don't you blame it on a calculation error? The lad is simple and gullible. He will not even think to suspect you. Now, make him faint!"

Stapley looked desperately around for a way out. In the world outside, Master Loo was teaching Buggeroff about the transfer procedure. In about fifteen seconds, Buggeroff would make the first attempt at applying it. Fifteen seconds: that was how long he had to withstand the pain. But with every second that passed, the pain increased. At this pace, Stapley reckoned, within ten seconds the pain would surely kill him. At least dying would mean that Master Dung would die, too. The question was, would he, Stapley, be brave enough to perform this sacrifice?

Less than four agonizing seconds later, he knew the answer. It was not an answer to be proud of, but it was the only one he was capable of.

Reluctantly, Stapley placed a layer of white light in front of Buggeroff's vision and switched it on, then off, then on, then off, then on again. He kept doing it, tuning the frequency while at the same time monitoring his Master's brainwaves until, three seconds later, he found the sweet spot he was looking for.

The pain ceased.

"See, that wasn't so hard." Master Dung sniggered. "A seizure. I must say I'm surprised that a worm like you could come up with this idea. Now, let us not waste any time. Proceed with the plan!"

44. MERKIN

"Teasin' you, it's easy 'cause you're kind of dumb. Makin' love with you feels just like sliding on a—" Merkin hummed her own, dirty rendition of Minnie Riperton's song, accompanied by her music box.

For the first time since she had met her new Master, she was sure that his self-righteous composure was beginning to shake. If the day before was any indication, then it wouldn't be long before the inevitable would knock on the door. And the best thing about the inevitable knocking on your door was that it always used a battering ram.

But until then, there remained the problem of her recovery. The spell should have been ready by now, but for some reason, Master Sewer's concentration seemed to falter. It was, Merkin could not help thinking, partly her fault, and although that helped her ego to no end, it did nothing to soothe her pain.

As if on cue, there was knock on the door and Master Sewer's weary voice said, "It's me, Master Sewer. Are you decent? Can I come in?"

"Not entirely, but yes," Merkin answered, quickly adjusting her clothes to the point of not-quite-arguably indecent.

There was a pause, and then Master Sewer coughed politely and said "I'd rather wait until both answers are positive."

Well, she had to try, didn't she?

"Oh, all right," she sighed, pulling her pants back on. "I'm decent now."

There was another pause.

"Are you sure?" her Master inquired.

"Oh, for the love of gravy!" she exclaimed as she moved to the door and opened it. "Of course I'm sure, you—" She stopped. His face looked as tired as she had ever seen it, and his entire posture spoke of tremendous fatigue. "What the hell have you done to yourself?" she asked, sliding one arm under his shoulder and helping him in.

"Does it show?" He smiled wearily.

"Yea-ha-ah!" she let him slide on a chair. And then a thought struck her. "It's the Magic, isn't it?" she asked.

"In a way, you're right. But it's really the bad habits," he replied.

"What do you mean?"

He sighed. "Many years ago, I reached the conclusion that sleep, while useful, is a very ineffectual process. So, I came up with a spell that helps concentrate a night's sleep into just a few minutes. Dangerous stuff. You should never try it, by the way."

"And so your body got used to it, and now it can't sleep properly without the spell," Merkin filled in the blanks.

"So far, since I lost my Magic, sleep has been mostly a hit and miss affair, if I can call it that. For instance, the other day when I slept for over twenty-four hours or last night when I couldn't sleep at all."

"Poor soul," she said while stroking his hair with what she was shocked to discover was genuine concern rather than lust.

"I'll adjust," said her Master, straightening his back. "On a brighter note, the healing spell is ready." He pulled a folded paper from his pocket. "Here you go. You'll have to learn it by rote before you cast it, but I have all faith in your fascinating ability to memorize all sorts of things."

Merkin took the paper and unfolded it. She gave it a quick inspection to make sure everything was in order.

"It seems legit," she said. "Thank you!"

"Don't mention it. After all, it's my fault you're in this situation. Anyway," he said as he stood up, "I'll leave you to it. I suppose you need a bit of privacy for this."

"Yes, indeed," Merkin smiled. "Now, go and try to have some sleep. Thanks again!"

"Good luck," Master Sewer said, leaving the room.

As soon as he was out, she locked the door and sat down at her desk. With a pen in her hand, she skimmed the code until she found what she was looking for, and then she carefully marked the passage with a big X. It had been a cunning plan, and she couldn't blame her Master for trying. It might have actually worked were it not for the fact that she had expected it. Frigidity, indeed!

With that little thing being taken care of, she allowed herself to relax and let her mind compile the code. When she was done, she stood up and walked to her bed where she laid back and waited. While fast, the healing process was potentially painful, and so the spell had been designed to anesthetize the subject, Merkin, prior to the actual procedure. According to the code, she should start feeling drowsy in about a minute after casting the spell. Well, there goes noth...

***

The shadows in her room shifted slightly, indicating the passage of two, maybe three hours. Had it worked? Yes, she could tell by the way her ribs did not hurt when she breathed. She felt a wave of relief wash over her, and for a moment the sun seemed to shine brighter. She jumped out of the bed, and before her feet touched the ground the music box started playing "Walking on Sunshine." Merkin danced, not like a Scriptling and certainly not like a witch, but like a carefree, young woman whose life had just gotten better.

A few minutes later when the high of the Eighties subsided to a somewhat less euphoric level, her mood gave way to an unexpected sensation of gratitude. Merkin chose to direct this strange, new feeling entirely at her Master. She wondered how she could ever repay him. Well, there was, of course, a very straightforward answer to that, but for once she decided to put prurient matters on the back burner, at least for a while.

And then there was the other option, the difficult one, made no less difficult by the fact that she had no idea how to go about it. Sure enough, if there was one thing her Master needed now, that thing was getting his Magic powers back. But how? Magic was something you were born with, not something to grant upon a wish.

Or was it? Come to think about it, her old Master used to switch her Magic on and off quite often, and that had been, as far as all but very few people were concerned, impossible. Of course, Master Sewer's condition had nothing to do with being grounded, but still, it made her wonder. It was, she mused, a safe assumption to make that grounding might not be the only closely guarded secret in the trade. What else was there?

She paused, her mind conjuring a memory of something Master Sewer had told her a few days before, when talking about their old Master. "He did not have to know everything, he had to know only where everything was."

If that was true, then all she had to do was find someone who knew all the secrets. Where do you find someone who knows all the secrets? Correction, where do you find someone who is not a drug dealer or a charismatic leader of some ecclesiastic order, and who actually knows all the secrets?

And then she realized she was not asking the right question. There was no single person in the world who knew all secrets, but the world was full of people and each one of these people knew at least one secret. If someone knew how to restore Master Sewer's powers then all she had to do was find that person.

She thought that this should increase her chances, or at least in theory. It was true, in an insignificant sort of way. It actually did to her chances what buying a thousand lottery tickets did to the chances of winning the jackpot[19].

Still, there might be a way.

---

[19] Everybody knows the chances of winning the big prize in a major lottery are roughly one in fourteen million. What people fail to see very often is that buying a thousand tickets only means you have a thousand tickets, each with a one in fourteen million chance of being the lucky one. But people need hope, and one in fourteen thousands sounds much better, however poor the math.

45. MASTER SEWER

He opened his eyes only to find her staring at him in deep concentration. His first reaction was to panic at the thought that another sample of her extreme cuisine might be forthcoming, but this fear was soon replaced when he saw that what she held in her hands was not a silver tray, but a book. Not just any book, but a spell book. And just to be more accurate, not just any spell book, but an old one, one that he did not recognize.

"Hold still," she ordered in a level voice, as if in a trance.

He knew better than to argue. She was, now that he had had more time to assess the situation, clearly casting a lengthy and convoluted spell, probably the kind that required constant user input. Interrupting her now was bound to have unpleasant consequences to the subject of the spell, and he had every reason to believe he knew whom the subject was.

He relaxed, or at least he relaxed as much as someone being stared at by an attractive young woman with thoroughly proven murderous tendencies could relax. As he continued to look at her, he noticed a tiny jerk of movement at the edge of his vision. Master Sewer was about to dismiss this as mere speck of dust on his retina, but then the thing took a course of action fundamentally inconsistent with established eye floater behavior: it continued to lurch towards the center of his vision, and then, with an audible click, it locked into position midway between his face and Merkin's.

This triggered a brief smile from Merkin, as if confirming that her spell was actually working. She resumed her casting with renewed confidence, and, before long, a thin wisp of grey smoke materialized out of nowhere and floated towards a point a few inches above the first apparition. This was soon followed by a variety of oddly-shaped lines and isolated particles that, by and by, contrived to coalesce into what looked more and more like a black and white, or rather greyscale, portrait of a young man.

The man in the portrait was not particularly becoming, nor was he, in any distinctive way, homely. If anything, he emanated that air of

159

averageness found in police sketches and anatomy manuals. With a sudden shock, Master Sewer realized he had seen this person before.

"I've seen him before," he said, forgetting that he was supposed to stand still.

"Oh, good!" said Merkin, dismissing the spell with noticeable relief. "I don't know if I could have held it much longer."

"What is this spell?"

"First, you tell me who that was," she said. It was not a request, but an order, and Master Sewer had no choice but to comply.

"I don't know his name. He's just a guy I met at the funeral. He almost fainted when he got to the coffin. I suppose no one warned him about how unsightly our dear Master really was. Why is this important?"

"He is the key to solving your problem," she said with hesitance in her voice.

"What, him? But he is not even a Magician!" he said.

"At the moment, neither are you," she replied in a bitter tone. "And for that matter, nor am I, but that did not stop me from looking after you, now, did it?"

"I'm sorry, I didn't mean it that way." He cursed himself for not seeing how his previous remark would hurt her. Master or not, there were some limits to how far you could push someone before they snapped.

"I know," she said in a tired voice. "I was expecting someone else, too. Not someone who looks as if he can't even count to ten in Sumerian, to be sure."

"There now, I'm sure any Scriptling can do that. But I see your point. If the portrait was at all accurate, then this guy is not the sharpest knife in the set. To be fair, he is not the honing steel, either." He paused, then continued in a cautious tone. "So, you say he is the key to my—"

"Problem. Yes, I think so. I have little reason to doubt my casting."

"I should think not, but what about the spell? How confident are you in the actual spell?"

"As confident as I could be in a pool of infested water when I have to choose between immediate dehydration and delayed poisoning."

"Ah, that kind of spell." Master Sewer tried to smile.

"But don't worry, the spell is not invasive. It's a read-only thing. Worst case scenario, it will send us on a wild-goose chase."

"Then I must say, your choice of metaphors for describing it was rather misinformative," he remarked, not unkindly.

"Got you scared, though, didn't it?" She smiled sweetly.

He thought quickly of a way to deflect her words. "Hey, you're healed!" he remarked joyfully.

Her expression changed in the blink of the eye. She was still smiling, but it was no longer the ironic smile that came with delivering a spicy comment, but rather the beam of abandonment radiating from a happy memory.

"I most certainly am," she said and leaned to kiss him on his cheek. "Thank you, Master!"

"Don't mention it," he replied, hoping his blood would not do something embarrassing in response to her kiss, like cause a blush or... or worse.

Still, despite his own, crude interpretation, he could distinguish nothing untoward behind her intention. He congratulated himself for concealing those lines of code in her healing spell. This should make matters easier to handle.

"Do you mind if I have a look at the spell book?" he asked after a moment's pause.

"Not at all," she said. "Here, careful with it. It's quite old."

She handed him the book.

"It certainly smells old. Ah. Divination. I should have guessed."

"You don't have to be so condescending," she said defensively. "An entire field of analytical sciences is based on Divination techniques."

"You don't mean Data Mining, do you? That's just statistics hocus-pocus for commoners."

"OK, so maybe I did not choose the best line of argument here, but Divination has its merits. Come to think of it, Arcana Actuariorum is nothing but a sophisticated form of—

"Arcana Actuariorum? Are you really comparing Divination to Arcana Actuariorum? That's like comparing Astrology and Astronomy."

"Look, it's the best lead we have. At least the spell revealed someone who is connected to Magic, and not some random person. Furthermore, we can actually get hold of this guy. Fluke? I don't think so."

"And how do you intend to find him?"

"That's easy. We'll use the guest list from the funeral."

"May I remind you that the guest list does not come with pictures?"

"And may I remind you that this pretty face comes with a rather awesome brain?" she said, gesturing towards herself.

Master Sewer said nothing as he waited for her to make her point.

"All you need to do," she continued, "is look for names you don't recognize."

46. MERKIN

They were sitting in the study and they had been scanning the list for the last half-hour. Merkin kept herself busy by asking plenty of questions about the Magicians as her Master crossed their names off the list. It had been a seemingly educational exercise, in that while Master Sewer did not endeavor to answer all her questions, she felt wiser for having asked them.

"Old Master Dung didn't really show you around. You hardly know anyone," Master Sewer had remarked after her first five or so questions.

"Perhaps he was afraid I would say something smart," she replied coyly.

"Or maybe he—" He was ashamed, perhaps having realized that what he was about to say was not entirely appropriate.

She thought it would be best to ignore his unspoken remark. Any other approach might have been inconsistent with those lines of code hidden in the healing spell, and for the moment Merkin had no reason to reveal that she had bypassed them.

After that, her Master became slightly more generous with details about the Magicians and their ties. Guilt can be, as many religious figures would tell you, a very effective means to facilitate cooperation. Merkin was not a religious figure, but she was a woman and thus naturally qualified to exploit the rich deposits of dark feelings that make up guilt.

Alas, Master Sewer knew a surprising number of things about a surprising number of people, and roughly two hours later, when she thought her head would explode from too much information, she decided to point out the obvious shortcut.

"If you don't mind my asking, do you happen to have this list as a soft copy?" she said.

"No, I don't mind you asking, and, yes, I do have it somewhere on my computer. Why?"

"It's just that I thought we could speed things up a little bit."

"How do you mean?"

"Well, we could start by filtering out the unlikely candidates. It's not easy to do it on paper, but a spreadsheet should handle this in a jiffy. It sounds like something you would do, if I'm any judge."

Her Master thought for a second with his mouth open.

"Why did I not think of that earlier?" he exclaimed. "Of course, I can just ask the computer to remove all Magicians from my search criteria instead of going about it the old way. Why, oh, why did I not see it?"

"You've been through a lot lately, and you haven't had a decent sleep since the accident," Merkin said soothingly and patted his arm. "Here, just sit back in your chair and let me take over," she added, smiling inwardly at the hidden connotation.

"Sounds good," he said, stifling a yawn. "Let me locate the file for you."

"All right," she said a minute later, "so I filtered out the Magicians. That leaves about seventy guests who are most likely Scriptlings." She paused and then continued in an excited voice. "Hey, according to these numbers I was right when I said that only a third of the Magicians had Scriptlings."

"Yes. You have a good eye for such details," her Master said proudly.

"Thanks! Now, let's take away the weaker sex," she said. "Don't look at me like that. It's OK if I say it. Did the guy have any noticeable accent?"

Master Sewer looked upward, searching for the memory.

"Not that I can remember," he said at length. "Mind you, I don't think he said more than a few words."

"Did he say enough for you to be comfortable removing the East Europeans from the list?"

"I'm not sure I approve of your methodology. Just because someone doesn't have an accent doesn't mean he can't be from another country."

"Oh, really? Tell me, Master, how long since you moved out of Germany?"

"Are you saying I still have an accent?"

"I would not call it an accent. It's more of an intonation if you ask me, but, yes, there's just enough of it to betray your origins."

Her Master paused for a moment, apparently having difficulties digesting this piece of revelation.

"In that case, we can also cross the Brits and Aussies from the list. The guy sounded North American as far as my uneducated ear can tell. Just joking." He raised an arm in defense when he saw the protest forming on Merkin's lips.

"You'd better be." She giggled. "OK, so if I remove all those, then I'm left with eight, nine, ten Scriptlings. That's not too bad."

"Well, if we are using this criterion, then I guess you can just as well remove the guy from Texas."

"Good thinking, but that still leaves us with nine," she said.

"Not bad for a two-minute job," Master Sewer commented.

"It's easy when you use a computer. Which reminds me…" her voice trailed off.

"Yes?"

"I haven't forgotten about the challenge. You know, the one about writing the ultimate virus that would destroy all the computers in the world."

"I certainly hope you haven't forgotten about it," he said in a suddenly cold and serious tone.

"Master, why is this so important?" she asked, rather confused by his abrupt change of mood.

"Do you want to do it or not?" he snapped.

"I do, of course, but I need to know more details. You said this would set things straight, and from that I can surmise that you want to take all this power away from regular people and thus enable Magicians to once again be in control of all things awesome. This is all very noble and jingoistic[20] of you, but there must be more to it than just re-establishing the balance of power, or tipping it our way, as it were."

"I… You're not ready for this…" he faltered.

"Come on, trussst in me," she said, lengthening every sound and rolling her eyes in a pretty good impersonation of Kaa, the python.

Several thoughts appeared to form at the same time on Master Sewer's face, but Merkin could read none of them.

"Who am I to judge?" he said eventually. "All right, I'm going to tell you something that very few people know. And because very few people possess this knowledge, you must understand this makes it extremely dangerous." He paused. "Do you understand this?"

"Yes, Master. I understand," she said petulantly.

"I had no doubt." He smiled while his voice remained grave. "Magic is…" he started. "Computers are…" he struggled to continue. "Well you

---

[20] Same thing, as far as Magicians are concerned.

see, computers use Magic. A very diluted form of Magic, but Magic nonetheless. It's not an intuitive conclusion, especially since it took decades to witness it, but it is true all the same. It is not true just because I say so, but because I, along with a handful of others like me, have thoroughly tested this theory and proved it right beyond any doubt. Are you with me so far?"

"I am," Merkin said slowly. "But I can't say I understand you yet. My intuition tells me you are right, but how can the computers use Magic? Programming languages are mostly based on modern day English, which is not a dead language."

"But the Syntax is there. That's why I said the Magic that computers use is very diluted. Extremely diluted, if you wish. But even a smidgeon of Magic makes a world of difference."

"Because there are so many computers, and they all use a little bit of Magic every nanosecond. It all adds up," Merkin understood. "Oh, shit!" She understood some more. "So, that's why—"

"Yes! That's exactly why Magicians are in decline. There's not enough Magic left in the world for us to use it. The computers are devouring all of it. The decline started slowly, too slowly for any of us to see, but now it's happening at such an accelerated rate that by the time more Magicians understand what is going on, there will be no Magicians left." Master Sewer concluded.

"If that's really the case, why keep the knowledge secret? Why is it that you refer to it as extremely dangerous knowledge?" she asked.

"Aha, a very good question, indeed! Suppose no one believes us? What if we are regarded as some sort of apocalyptical cult nurturing a secret agenda? And that is the optimistic scenario. It would be even worse if they believed us. Why, think about what a horde of panicked Magicians could do to this world."

"Just playing the devil's advocate here," she interjected. "You do realize that what we plan to do will have a dramatic effect on... this world, as you put it. I went through this mental exercise, and either way you look at it, many people will die. Not that I have any misgivings about that," she added quickly, so as not to disappoint her Master.

"I have no reason to believe you would have any misgivings. However, what we are endeavoring to do is akin to a delicate, but precise, surgical intervention. I do not need to draw the metaphor with regards to what the others would do, do I?"

"Nope. I guess I see your point very clearly."

"Excellent." He smiled. And then, before Merkin could press him for more details, he added, "So, you said you haven't forgotten about the challenge. Were you going to say more about it?"

"I… No, that was all," she said, still pondering over what she had just learned. "I haven't forgotten. I did not do anything about it, either. I guess you could say I was busy with other things."

"Can't blame you for that." He smiled gently. "You were making good progress, though, if I recall correctly."

Merkin's memory played back the conversation in the car, just before the accident. She shuddered at the thought, and immediately felt like a stupid little girl for having shown weakness in front of her Master.

"If it's any help, I feel the same about it," he said, having guessed her thoughts. "Even more so, as it was entirely my fault."

There was a deep pause, in which all the things that hadn't been said since the accident continued to remain unsaid, only in a strangely, more enunciated way.

"So, anyway," both of them said at the same time, and then they laughed.

It is believed that laughter is psychosomatic, which is just a fancy way of saying that the brain links happiness with laughter, but it doesn't really care which one comes first. Causality can sometimes be a two-way street.

The tension in the air dissipated in an instant, and even the sun seemed to shine brighter through the window (which is just another wonderful example of psychosomatic Magic).

"About the list," she said.

"Yes, the list," he replied. "I think we've narrowed it down as much as possible."

"I agree. We need a new angle."

"I think I might know just the thing," Master Sewer said, and there was a glint in his eyes, indicating the birth of a new idea.

"What is it?" she asked, curiosity blending an electrifying harmonic to her voice.

"I guess the real question is, what shall we wear?"

47. STAPLEY

When Buggeroff came to his senses and saw his Master's face looming concernedly into his field of vision, his first words were, "Is anything wrong with you, Master?"

"With me? Why would you say that?"

"Well, it's just that the last two times I woke up in your presence you felt obliged to point out that I was alive. The fact that you are not saying it now, coupled with my first-hand observation that I am, indeed, very much alive, make me wonder what the reason is for interrupting the established pattern."

"Excuse me," Master Loo said slowly, as if every word had to be built from scratch, "but do you realize you've just said all this in fluent Sumerian?"

"Did I?" Buggeroff asked, equally surprised.

"Oh, my! Not only that, but I asked you the last question in Sumerian and you understood it. What on Earth is going on here?" he said, shaking with excitement and anxiety.

Stapley? Buggeroff addressed a mental question.

"Worm?" Master Dung asked at the same time.

"*I—*" Stapley hesitated. He knew very well what the cause of this sudden attack of polyglotism was, but he was also understandably reluctant to share it with the wretched usurper. On the other hand, the memory of the recent pain Master Dung had inflicted upon him still echoed loudly in his inner core. "*I think you might be leaking, Sir,*" he said cautiously.

"That's preposterous! I believe I would be the first to know if I were leaking," Master Dung shouted. "I've got no holes, so how could I leak?"

"*Then you are infusing, merging, permeating, percolating, or even soaking, Sir,*" Stapley tried to explain. "*Some part of you is trickling into Buggeroff and—*" no, he would not point out that the opposite was also true. "*And that's all there is to it.*"

"You... You..." Master Dung seemed on the verge of exploding. "You might be onto something," he conceded, still fuming with unresolved anger. "But why so sudden?"

It was the one question Stapley was trying to avoid. Actually, it was the answer that he dreaded rather than the question.

"There might have been a teeny-weeny glitch during the defragmenting process, Sir. Yes, just a glitch. Not even a systematic error and certainly not something that could have been foreseen. A random occurrence which had, if I may say so myself, positive consequences," he squealed.

"A WHAT?" Master Dung shouted.

"A glitch, Sir. An algorithm hiccup. A trifling anomaly. A slight irregularity," Stapley swiftly adopted the desperate faith of redemption through synonyms. *"A minor malfunction that, as I'm confident I pointed out earlier, had a rather constructive outcome."*

"You mean to say you accidentally picked all the pieces that make up my entire knowledge of a dead language and – I will repeat it for emphasis – accidentally placed those pieces into Buggeroff's mind?" Master Dung asked with blood-chilling composure.

Stapley would have preferred if the usurper had been shouting. It is not good to store anger behind a barrage of tranquility if the design of the barrage does not include an escape shaft of sorts.

On the other hand, Stapley was quite proud of his achievement. It had taken several days (well, nights, actually) for Master Dung to clandestinely teach Buggeroff the fundaments of Latin, and that had been no little task. But it had taken him, Stapley, just a few minutes to copy the sum of Master Dung's fluency in Sumerian to Buggeroff's mind while he was unconscious. It had been a spur-of-the-moment experiment, just to test if the idea worked. And oh, how it worked!

"Well?" Master Dung insisted.

"I believe you are right, Sir. This strange event bears all the markings of an accident," Stapley assumed his best poker face.

"Absolutely! No doubt about it. And apparently this *accident* was thoughtful enough to copy my knowledge rather than to transfer it. Am I right?"

"Indeed, Sir. Information does seem to be one of those things that can be distributed without being wasted."

But thanks for the idea, Stapley thought. It is actually easier and far more destructive to move than to copy. As any computer geek would point out, copying a file implies taking a chunk of empty storage space and changing many of its zeroes into ones, following the exact same pattern of the original file. This can take quite awhile. However, moving a file, no matter how large, is an entirely different business. It requires a single step, and that is to change a relatively small tag that contains the file's address. Of course, this only holds true when the source and target files are located on the same device, but that was all right, because as far as Stapley was concerned, there was only one device, namely Buggeroff.

"I see," Master Dung said levelly. "Just to be on the safe side then, let it be known that from now on I will personally supervise all defragmenting tasks. We don't want the next *accident* to be less... what was the word I used? Ah, yes, thoughtful."

Bummer! Stapley thought. There goes that window of opportunity. Even though Master Dung wasn't very creative, he had enough imagination to understand danger when it lurked around.

"A splendid idea, Sir!" Stapley managed to sound enthusiastic. He was sure he would come up with a new plan, sooner or later. Maybe next time he would be luckier.

"Good. Now—" Master Dung started.

Stapley, can you hear me? Buggeroff interrupted the covert dialogue.

"Ah... Yes, Chief. Of course I can hear you," Stapley answered.

Then why didn't you answer when I first called you?

"I was thinking, Chief," Stapley said gingerly and then, addressing Master Dung he asked, *"What should I tell him?"*

"Surprise me," Master Dung replied with a wry smile. "Something tells me you have a genuine knack for bullshit."

Busted! Stapley thought. Well, no point in letting down the man. If bullshit was required, then he might as well summon the herd. *"You see, Chief, it is my uneducated but far-reaching opinion that what we have here is a case of spontaneous erudition caused by a triumvirate of occult resonances, opportunistic causality, and pyromania–induced fatigue... In other words, thermodynamics happens."*

"Very well put." Master Dung smirked.

Does this sort of spontaneous eructation happen often? Buggeroff asked, as usual completely oblivious to the third resident of his own brain, as well as to his own vocabulary blunders

"It's spontaneous erudition, Chief. As for its occurrence, we can say that technically it has a one hundred percent success rate," Stapley said.

Huh?

"It could only have happened once, and it actually did happen. Like I said, one hundred percent success rate."

Oh, that kind of thing, Buggeroff mused. *Too bad it won't happen again then. I could really use some kind of boost.*

"Well, now, Chief, don't say that. You know what it's like when you play a game and you level up too fast? You lose interest, right?"

I suppose so.

"So, then, consider that you've just jumped up ten levels, the equivalent of having mastered a whole branch of Arcane Knowledge. You don't really want to do this too often, right?"

Fair enough. And there is the other thing, too.

"What thing?" Stapley asked.

You know, when you level up, the monsters level up, too, to keep the game in balance. Except that I didn't really increase any of those skills that would help me fight monsters.

"Lucky for you, then, that there are no monsters in this game. There is no game to speak of, anyway."

There's always a game, Buggeroff thought.

"So, what does Stapley have to say about it?" Master Loo asked from the world outside of Buggeroff's head.

"How—" Buggeroff was taken aback.

"Well, I know you two communicate at the speed of thought, but sometimes there is a perceptible gap in the conversation if you know what to look for."

"I guess that makes sense. By the way, am I speaking English now?"

"Yes, you are."

"Good, just checking." Buggeroff smiled. "So, anyway, Stapley says this is just a spontaneous *Euro-diction* thingy, although, I can't see what currency has to do with it."

"Indeed." Master Loo smiled kindly. "Alas, we shall have to solve this riddle some other time."

"Something's the matter?"

"Not as such, no. It's just that I think we should get ready for tomorrow."

"Tomorrow? What is happening tomorrow?"

"Err, Chief?" Stapley whined. *"There's something I forgot to tell you."*

What's that? Buggeroff asked cautiously.

"You've been out for quite a while." Stapley did his best to delay the answer.

"Why, the solstice, of course," said Master Loo.

"THREE DAYS?" exclaimed Buggeroff after a brief moment of astonishment.

"Hungry?" asked the Master, producing a bucket of fried chicken from thin air.

48. BUGGEROFF

When Merkin made her appearance, looking like a hunting goddess in her green and gold dress, Buggeroff's stomach sank so heavily that it actually dragged his jaw to a record low in its wake. Buggeroff had known she would be there, and he had been expecting some kind of unusual activity in his stomach, perhaps even butterflies. What he did not expect was a brick. In its defense, the brick[21] had not expected this either.

In the space of a few seconds, the brick went quickly through Kübler-Ross's five stages of grief. However, since it was no expert in handling an existential crisis, it did it in reverse order: acceptance, depression, bargaining, anger and denial. In the end, the unbearable strain of self-denying proved too much for the poor thing and it promptly disappeared into oblivion, leaving a brick-shaped empty space in Buggeroff's stomach. In its turn, the stomach, now freed of unwanted masonry, reverted to its original volume. Unfortunately, the force and suddenness of this maneuver had the effect of sending all its contents upwards, much to the chagrin of Buggeroff and the other guests.

It should not be technically possible to throw up without hunching, but this detail had little importance for Buggeroff as the grotesque display, to which he was both helpless spectator and prodigious main character, scrolled before his eyes.

"It's the shrimp," he explained to no one in particular.

---

[21] Many things have been compared to a brick, mainly as a tribute to their intellect or to their aerodynamic characteristics. Bricks themselves are not particularly happy with this arrangement that they regard as demeaning and stereotypical. If asked, the average brick will describe itself as having humble origins (because you don't get any humbler than mud) and as being naturally capable of performing its function under a lot of pressure. Bricks will take pride in their team-working skills and will often seek to fill a support role rather than engaging on a competitive career path. You know where you stand with bricks, and they pretty much know where they stand with you.

"I knew there was something off about it," commented a lady Magician who wore enough makeup to make a peacock envious. "It's a good thing I had only a bite."

"What kind of restaurant is this?" asked someone else. "Serving spoiled food to its guests. I demand to see the manager!"

"Are you all right?" asked Master Loo as the chorus of discontented Magicians grew louder and attention shifted to the unfortunate restaurant manager.

"Just a little bit smitten," Buggeroff admitted as he wiped his mouth with a cloth napkin.

And then, as he looked up, he saw Merkin detaching herself from her Master and walking in his direction. She did not so much walk as meander. If photographed at a slow shutter speed from above, Merkin's passage through the room would have resembled that of an undulating snake. Hips can do that. Well, that too.

"Quick, pretend like you're talking to me," Buggeroff urged Master Loo.

"But I am talking to you," the Master was confused.

"Ha ha, how very amusing," Buggeroff threw his head backward and laughed genially. "I can't believe you've never told me this story before!" he continued, slapping his Master on the shoulder.

"Well, then you would probably want to hear the one about the three imbricate sequences and the golden ratio," Master Loo caught on to the act.

"Oh, pray tell! It sounds most fascinating!" Buggeroff exclaimed.

"Hi, my name is Merkin," said a silky-smooth voice.

For a brief moment Buggeroff felt as if the brick had made its way back to his stomach, but this time he was able to fight the unwanted sensation.

Stapley, help! he moaned in his mind.

"No worries, Chief! My Romance Module will sort this out in no time. Just follow my lead."

Buggeroff was not entirely convinced that a Romance Module created by Master Loo would deliver any positive outcome, but then he had no better choice. He turned to face Merkin and leaned forward to kiss her extended hand.

"Buggeroff, enchanté!" he repeated after Stapley, realizing just how incongruent that sounded. "And this is my Master." He pointed towards Master Loo, who was no longer there. "Ah…"

"It's lovely to make your acquaintance. Although I can't shake the feeling I've seen you before," she added, most charmingly.

He recalled the fainting episode at the funeral and prayed that Stapley would have a decent reply to this.

"Is that so? How very interesting. I don't recall seeing you before, and I am most sure I would have remembered such a remarkable occasion." He thanked his assistant for the save.

Was that a blush on her face?

"Oh, you don't really mean—" she started.

"Aren't you going to introduce me to this nice gentleman?" Merkin's Master materialized into the conversation, much to Buggeroff's annoyance.

"Why, of course," she replied, not showing any sign of being taken aback. "Master Sewer, this is Enchanté, Enchanté, this is Master Sewer."

"Quite an unusual name," Master Sewer commented.

"Buggeroff, actually," Buggeroff said.

"Excuse me?" Master Sewer raised an eyebrow.

"That's my name, Buggeroff. Enchanté is just the way I feel about meeting Miss Merkin."

"Oh, it's entirely my fault. I feel so embarrassed," Merkin covered her mouth with her bejeweled fingers.

"At being called Miss?" Master Sewer smirked.

"And why would I find that embarrassing, huh?" she snapped sharply, and then immediately regained control of herself.

"Excuse me," Buggeroff tried to interrupt them.

"I don't know, it just sounds—" Master Sewer began.

"Excuse me," Buggeroff insisted.

"Yes, how does it sound exactly?" asked Merkin in a patient tone.

"EXCUSE ME!" Buggeroff shouted. A number of heads turned in his direction, and he immediately froze on the spot. They regarded him expectantly for a while, but then seeing that no interesting follow-up was forthcoming, they resumed their private conversation, not bothering to conceal their disappointment with the lack of entertainment value.

"That was a close one, Chief," said Stapley.

"That was a close one, Ch " Buggeroff repeated out loud, before realizing his assistant was not actually feeding him a line.

"Indeed," Master Sewer nodded. "So, what is it you wanted to say?"

"I forget," Buggeroff replied lamely.

"I see. Well, why don't you tell us something about yourself then?"

"Yes!" Merkin's face lit up, and she applauded like a little girl upon receiving a pet unicorn.

This gave Buggeroff pause. Why were they — why was she, especially — so interested in him? He hadn't done anything special in their presence other than fainting and hurling and that was hardly anything worth this kind of attention.

What do you make of this, Stapley? he asked.

"Well, Chief, you are a good-looking young man, well-dressed, well-spoken and the whole whatnot. Perhaps they are simply happy to find someone in the under-fifty age group to talk to."

Yeah, you might be onto something, he replied as he surveyed the other guests. True enough, most of them could have been easily placed anywhere between fifty and undead.

"Well?" Master Sewer asked.

Buggeroff cleared his throat. "So, like I said, my name is Buggeroff... Umm... what else? Oh, right! I'm Master Loo's Scriptling."

"Ah, Master Loo," Master Sewer's face lit up excitedly as if he had gotten Australia in an early Risk game. "I've heard many things about him, of course, but I've never had the pleasure of making his acquaintance."

"He's around here somewhere." Buggeroff craned his head in search for his Master.

"Perhaps we could invite Buggeroff and his Master to dinner over the weekend. Please, Master! I'll even cook," Merkin suggested.

For a moment, Master Sewer's face turned a sickly pallor, and Buggeroff wondered if it had been Merkin's invitation that upset him or something else. But what?

"That's a wonderful idea." Master Sewer recovered quickly. "However, as a host, I consider it my duty and honor to cook for my guests."

Buggeroff could barely conceal his excitement at this turn of events. Less than five minutes earlier he had been throwing up in front of Ontario's most prominent Magicians, and now he was the lucky winner of an invitation to spend an evening with the most beautiful girl in the world. Things were looking up.

"I—" he said.

"How's Saturday working for you?" Merkin asked, touching his arm.

"You mean like this Saturday? Geesh, I don't know. I guess I'd have to ask Master Loo if he has any plans," Buggeroff said, knowing very well that coaxing his Master into attending yet another social event so soon after the solstice would be a herculean task.

"Fair enough," said Master Sewer. "Here is my address." He handed Buggeroff a black card that felt velvety to the touch.

Buggeroff took it and inspected it carefully because he'd read somewhere this was the polite thing to do. The front side had a simple jester hat motif etched in gold, and even through the restaurant's din, Buggeroff could hear faint harmonious bell sounds coming from the drawing as he moved the card. Flipping it over revealed something that he instantly recognized as a QR Code, also etched in gold:

"The contrast ratio is pretty messed up, Chief, but I was able to decode it anyway," Stapley said. *"The place is not far from where we live. A fifteen minute walk at most."*

Buggeroff thanked his assistant, and then repeated the words out loud to Master Sewer. "I will do my best to honor your invitation. It's not far from our place."

"Capital!" Master Sewer was impressed. "Now, if I'm not mistaken, I think the festivities are about to get started"

"Would you like to join us at our table?" Merkin asked.

"Sure, I would love to!" Buggeroff felt his heart rate accelerate. "Let me see if I can find my Master. I hope you don't mind if I extend your invitation to him."

"By all means. See you soon, I expect." She smiled, and then suddenly her expression flickered, and she placed her hand on her chest. "Excuse me," she babbled. "I need to go somewhere. Do join us at our table, please!" She ran for the exit.

"What was that?" Buggeroff asked.

"Women." Master Sewer smiled knowingly, although even Buggeroff could tell he had no clue whatsoever.

Stapley?

"Reporting for duty, Chief! A split second before the peculiar event, you heard a muffled buzz coming from her chest."

Did I?

"Yes, Chief, you did. Like I mentioned before, there is a huge gap between what your senses perceive and what your mind accepts as useful sensory information. Anyway, the sound grew slightly louder, and it continued to do so over time."

And you said it came from her chest?

"To the best of your aural perception coupled with my own triangulation algorithms, yes."

Chests don't buzz, Stapley, Buggeroff pursued his point further.

"Indeed, Chief, they don't. She did wear four necklaces, though, and one of them descended all the way under her dress. Perhaps it might conceal a small cell phone."

Yes, maybe, Buggeroff thought, his mind entangled in the four Magic syllables of un-der-her-dress.

49. MERKIN

This was it. The vibration had started low, and then it had grown steadily, a sure sign that whatever had triggered the alarm had been moving towards her rather than popping into existence. This felt completely different from the sudden buzz caused when her neighbor Elroy lit up his cigar.

This might be just some random person wandering in the vicinity while smoking a cigar that came from the same plantation as the cigar left behind by the cop. But this felt different. The vibration had a slight edge to it, a mellow harmonic that told Merkin what she wanted to know.

She rushed through the dining hall doors, and then, as she was about to get out on the street, she stopped to consider. If she got out now, the cops might spot her and play the vanishing act. This would not do. No, what she had to do was add a little bit of cunning to her game. You don't catch the slippery fish by wrapping your bare hands around it.

The vibration stabilized at a steady, high pitch, which caused Merkin to take out the silver medallion and read the dials. The cop was fifteen yards away, probably parked on the street with a good view of the door. She peered behind a window curtain, and she recognized the black sedan that she had last seen speeding away from the funeral. Good thing she hadn't gone out on the street!

Her mind raced, trying to decide what to do next – figure out how the cops knew where she was or formulate a plan to get close enough for a strike. While the first choice held an undeniably important role in the high scheme of things, the latter had the intrinsic advantage of providing, amongst other things, a framework for solving the first.

Now that her mind was clear about what she had to do, there remained only the trifling details of how she would do it. Merkin tried to remember how much she knew about this neighborhood. Not much. Very little, in fact.

"Does this place have a back alley?" she asked a passing waiter who happened to walk by.

The waiter looked her up and down before his eyes settled somewhere up, but not quite above the chest.

"Of course," he said in a sleazy voice. "Every restaurant has a back alley. It's one of those architectural prerequisites."

"Can you take me there?" she asked, and then, reading the implications of what she had just said into the waiter's suddenly dilated pupils, she added "I meant, just show me the way."

"I can show you the way, and then take you... there." The wannabe Romeo raised his eyebrows with what passed for subtlety in his monomaniac mind.

How about you just show me the way, and in return, I won't turn you into a common batrachian? she wanted to say as her low level of patience was rapidly running out. "How about you just show me the way. In return, I won't mention this conversation to your manager?" she said instead. "I'm sure that's just what he'd like to hear after the shrimp incident. It will make his day, and no mistake about it." She smiled sweetly.

The mathematics of hierarchical wrath flickered on the waiter's face for a split second before he reached a decision.

"If the lady would be so kind as to follow me," he said, all milk and honey.

She nodded and followed him through the kitchen, the staff area, and then finally through a metal door that lead to the back alley.

"Not so fast," she said as he was about to close the door behind her.

"Ye-es?" he lengthened the vowel just a little too long for Merkin's taste.

"What's the shortest route from here to the front street?" she asked.

He thought for a moment before answering, "Through the restaurant, of course."

Fair enough, she thought, but that's no reason for not giving him hell. Her face shifted into the well-rehearsed, annoyed-predatory look and her right foot started thumping that menacing thump that seemed to say, "If I reach the count of ten there will be trouble, Mister."

The waiter started to sweat. "Go left and then left again. The path is shorter if you go to your right, but the alley is blocked by an old dumpster. A real safety hazard if you ask me." He paused for a moment. "You're not with the Fire Department, are you?" he asked the disappearing shape of Merkin.

She followed his instructions, and she was soon surveying the street from behind the corner of a brick wall adorned with tasteless, washed-out graffiti. The black sedan was still there, but unfortunately it was facing towards her. There were people on the street, but hardly enough of them to conceal her, especially in her current attire.

Merkin had chosen her outfit with the unmitigated intention of broadcasting her delightful presence. And while it is said that green is one of the best camouflage colors in nature, it is worth, given the context, exploring the subtle difference between the jungle as seen by Sir David Attenborough and the jungle as envisioned by, say, Axl Rose. She could, if absolutely necessary, alter the color of her dress by Magic, but Magic colors are such a pain to wash, and besides, she really did not want to ruin yet another expensive dress.

"Yous pretty, missus," said a slurry voice from somewhere close to her feet. "I can seez yous got them nice pair of legs under that skirt."

"It's a dress," Merkin snapped, out of sheer fashion sense.

She looked down. Peering at her through milky eyes and covered by a blanket that gave a whole new meaning to the word dirty, there lay a man. The long, unkempt beard made it difficult to estimate his age[22], but Merkin guessed around forty.

"Piss off," Merkin said in a shushed voice.

"Way ahead of you, Missus. I'm as pissed as Pierrot, the clown."

"How much is that?" she asked, despite herself.

"Baaaah… Tragically drunk, Missus!" The hobo made a sound that bore all the organic richness of something oozy struggling to crawl out of his lungs. To her irreversible loss of appetite, Merkin realized that he was laughing. She also realized that all his upper teeth were missing, a detail that did not make her feel any better.

"What does a hobo know of Commedia dell'Arte?" she asked absentmindedly as her eyes were locked on the black car.

"What does a floozy know about it?" The hobo shook away the hillbilly affectation, but not the slurry timbre, which was apparently built in.

Merkin opened her mouth to say something, probably a castration spell, but then reconsidered. At length, she said with condescension, "I've heard of people like you, people with a university degree in particle physics, or art history, or, I don't know, field theory or something. Educated people who live perfect lives up to the point where they find themselves in a tight

---

[22] The beard is one of nature's most democratic implements when it comes to perceived biological age. It makes everyone look older. Had it worked the other way around, we would have seen more women wearing one.

corner and have to file for bankruptcy. Stop me when I get too close," she added dismissively

"You think you know me?" the hobo shook an accusatory finger at her. "You think you KNOW me?" he spattered. "Well, I know you too, Miss!" He lowered his voice and continued in a pedantic tone. "You come here all dressed up and smelling of roses, and there's something out there on the street you need to get to, but you can't get there because you're afraid you'll be seen. Your precious flashy clothes now sit in your way, and for all that you think of yourself as smart, you can't bring yourself to see the obvious solution. Do stop me when I get too close," he finished in mock affectation.

"How dare you!" Merkin's face flushed red with anger. "I should—"

"When you're as low as I am, Miss, everything you do is an act of daring, even breathing. I take it, by the way you look all red and flustered now, that I hit the mark. No one speaks to a hobo, Miss, so the hobo has to learn to read body language. A hobo needs to know who will take pity and who will take offence. A hobo needs to recognize the hint of disgust and see it evolve into righteous charity as people with sensitive noses and unresolved guilt complexes pass by. And right now this hobo knows how to help, but he won't share his knowledge with you unless you pay the price."

Merkin considered her options: (a) Give the hobo a serious thrashing. (b) Place an excruciating and embarrassing curse on the hobo. (c) Think.

"I don't have any cash on me, and these jewels are worth more than you can drink in a lifetime," she said.

"Ah, the lady is mistaking my intentions." The hobo grinned. "I have all the money I need, but what is money good for? All the money in the world will not buy me a glimpse at those silky legs. All the jewels bolted in the Tower of London will not guess me the color of those precious panties. But perhaps something else will."

"You…want to look up my dress?" Merkin asked, too shocked by the whole strangeness of this situation to actually be outraged.

"You make it sound so prosaic. Is there no place left for poetry in this world?" the hobo complained.

"You bastard!" She regained just enough composure to remember to act offended.

"I wouldn't know about that, Miss, although, in all fairness, my mom did enjoy a little flirt, as my father learned just before he shot her brains out."

Merkin looked once again around the corner. The car was still there, but for how long?

"All right," she said. "What's your game?"

"First thing first, Miss. You hold your end of the bargain and I'll hold mine."

"Don't you trust me?" Merkin asked in a sweet voice.

If the hobo's proficiency in reading verbal language had been at least half as good as the proficiency that he possessed in interpreting body language, he should have, right about then, soiled his pants[23].

"I will not offend the young lady by saying I don't trust her. But there's a chance she might not like my brilliant plan, and then I'll be left, as it were, in the dark."

"You have my word. I will hold my end of the deal whether I like your plan or not. That's my best offer," she said in the same, sweet voice, with an added layer of urgency.

Her word! Yeah! What a joke!

"Fine, fine then," the hobo said. "I will teach you how to move unseen on the streets."

He told her. She suppressed a gag reflex.

"And now, I guess it's time for you to lift the veil of mystery surrounding those panties," he said in a hopeful voice.

"There are many things I would enjoy lifting," Merkin mused as she lifted her dress to the knee level, "but the mystery surrounding my panties is not one of them," she continued, punctuating her remark with a powerful low kick that caught the hobo right behind the ear, sending him straight to La-la Land.

She savored the elation of the moment, and allowed the wave of joy to wash through her tense body. Next, for no better reason than that she felt like it, she changed her mind and did the hobo a good turn. Damn it! She could be such a softie sometimes.

A few moments later, hating the fact that she had to sink so low, but seeing no other way out, she applied herself to the task of becoming street-invisible.

***

To say that the blanket smelled bad was to do an immense injustice to the multi-layered cacophony of sordid emanations reeking out of its fouled fabric. But it was, Merkin had to admit, the closest thing to an invisibility cloak she could find for the time being. Besides, not to put too fine a point on it, it kept her nether regions shielded from the cool, evening breeze.

---

[23] Some more.

The hobo had been right. No one gave her a second glance, and she was not entirely sure if anyone had bothered giving her a first glance anyway. Misery and poverty are real life tragedies, and the thing about tragedies is that, in order to acknowledge them, people have to be just the right distance away, not too far and definitely not too close.

Merkin opened and closed her fist under the protective blanket in anticipation as she drew closer to the car. First, she would cast a paralyzing spell through, yes, through the open window,[24] and then she would slip unseen into the backseat where she would proceed unhindered to the medieval component of her plan.

She could feel the vibration of her silver medallion increasing with every step she took, but strangely enough, this had a calming effect on her. Things were finally aligning themselves, and she knew it.

Merkin heard the muffled sound of the starting engine, and before she could make sense of it, the car was already doing a dangerous U-turn. With a blood-chilling screech, the car stopped again across the street, right in front of the restaurant.

From her vantage point, Merkin could see how the fat cop stuck his head out the window and waved at an old gentleman who was leaning against a wall, smoking a cigarette. As the man detached himself from the wall and started talking with the cop, Merkin realized she had seen him before. The chat continued for perhaps another minute or so and then, without any warning, the car left the curb and disappeared into traffic, leaving the gentleman in an obvious state of perplexity.

Merkin cursed as the medallion ceased to vibrate at her chest. What the Hell had just happened? On the opposite sidewalk the gentleman dropped his cigarette, crushed it under his shoe, and then entered the restaurant. Panic took over her senses as Merkin finally remembered where she had seen him before.

---

[24] As Greek mythology would teach you, paralyzing spells have a tendency to bounce off reflecting surfaces.

50. MASTER LOO

"*Well, you wanted a sense of purpose, now you have it,*" said the inner voice.

That's the last thing I needed, Master Loo replied.

"*But you are going to do it anyway, right?*"

I don't have any choice, do I? I can't say no to these people.

"*You can... But then you will have to be ready to face the consequences,*" said the inner voice.

Right. So where do I start?

"*How should I know? Being a cynic doesn't mean I have better ideas. It only means I'm better at spotting the stupid ones.*"

You know, there are times when you are nothing but an intolerable pain in the arse, and then again there are times when you... you... times when you...

"*Times when I'm a slightly more bearable pain in the ass?*"

That's not it. I wanted to say that there are times when you can actually produce a rare pearl of wisdom, said Master Loo.

"*A pearl, you say. Perhaps that's what's causing the pain in the ass, you know?*"

Master Loo ignored this last remark, as his attention was forced to shift to a more urgent matter. Someone was waving franticly at him. It was Buggeroff, and he was sitting at a small table in the company of a man.

Master Loo had never quite got the meaning of the word "playboy" when used to describe a person, but he now knew without a shadow of a doubt that the man sitting next to Buggeroff was the precise embodiment of said descriptor. It wasn't that the man was handsome or that he was well groomed. It wasn't even the fact that he exuded confidence or that he sweated charisma. No, it was all of those things together.

"You must be Master Loo," the man said in a slight German accent. He extended his hand as Master Loo got to the table. "My name is Master Sewer. I had the privilege to..."

"Now, that was easy," said the inner voice. *"You were wondering where to start, and I believe you have your answer now. If only the rest of your assignment would be so easy…"*

"… such a fine gentleman," Master Sewer concluded.

"My humblest apologies," said Master Loo. "My mind was elsewhere. What was that last bit you just said?"

"No worries whatsoever," Master Sewer said magnanimously. "I was merely saying how I had the privilege to sit down and chat with your Scriptling, Mr. Buggeroff, here, and how you, as his Master, should feel immensely proud of having modelled and inspired such a fine gentleman."

"Oh, I… That is to say… I guess…" Master Loo tried.

"Ah, modesty. What finer virtue could have complemented your noble qualities?" Master Sewer said, bringing his hands together as if half-applauding, half-praying.

Master Loo was mildly aware that the words he had just heard were, when you got right down to it, utter bullshit. But somehow the manner in which the words had been said, the gestures, the posture, and not least, the enunciation, all contrived to make them sound genuine and undeniably heartfelt.

"You must have been imparting your knowledge to him for years, surely," Master Sewer said in a warm voice.

"Well, actually," Buggeroff started to say, but then his mouth dropped open and continued to stay that way, while his eyes stared somewhere behind his Master's shoulders.

Master Loo was a fast learner, so he did not have to turn back to know that the girl was there.

"Seriously, if he's going to go catatonic whenever he sees her, I don't think there's a future for their relationship," the inner voice commented. *"And what on Earth is that smell?"*

"Ah, Merkin, so good of you to join us again," said Master Sewer. Master Loo thought he heard him utter an almost invisible question mark, but since there was no apparent reason for one in the conversation he ignored the thought.

What he could not ignore was the smell, and he could see how the others at the table wrinkled their noses, too. It was the kind of smell that took you all the way to the point of gagging and then kept you locked there, right on the edge between the world of in and the world of out.

"How could I have missed such a distinguished audience?" she said, looking questioningly towards Master Loo.

"My apologies," Master Sewer said. "Merkin, this is Master Loo, Buggeroff's Master. Master Loo, this is Merkin, my Scriptling."

"How do you do?" said Master Loo.

"Very nice to meet you," replied Merkin. "Your Scriptling was looking for you earlier," she added as an afterthought.

"I was outside, having a cigarette," Master Loo answered. He did not feel at all comfortable being the center of attention, even if said attention came from only two people. Two too many.

"Oh, I see," Merkin nodded. There was a little bit too much amplitude to that nod, Master Loo couldn't help remarking, but then again, who was he to criticize other people's public behavior?

"Can anyone do something about the smell?" Buggeroff asked.

Master Loo smiled inwardly. If there was someone who could embarrass the elephant in the room by pointing at it and then ask what the fat thing with a trunk was doing inside, then that person was Buggeroff. Social faux pas, as far as Master Loo understood them, were something that came natural to his Scriptling.

"We should ask the manager to investigate a possible sewage failure," Master Sewer said.

"Or we could try a spell," Master Loo suggested.

"Indeed," replied the other Master. "Merkin, if you will—"

"I... I don't think I know the right spell," she replied, and this time there was definitely something else in her voice. It sounded like alarm.

"FEBRIZIUM();" said Buggeroff, and the foul smell immediately disappeared as if by, well — Magic.

OH! MY! CODE! the inner voice reacted, while Master Loo's outer voice remained silent.

"I don't believe I've heard this spell before," Master Sewer's smooth voice tore away the silence. "Is it from one of your Master's books?" He addressed the question to Buggeroff.

"Not really," Buggeroff replied. "I sort of, like, you know, came up with it," he continued, as if unsure whether he had done a good or a bad deed.

"As part of your extended curricula, no doubt," Master Sewer pressed on in what, were it not for his charisma, would have been considered a rather impolite manner.

"Not really," Buggeroff said, obviously puzzled by the question. He then sought his Master's eyes in search for help.

"Ahem," Master Loo harrumphed. "I must claim fault for this. You see, young Buggeroff here is what you would call an experimentalist. That is to say, he has proven a natural inclination towards trying new spells, and by new, I mean really new. He makes up spells, is what I'm trying to say. Indeed, only a few days ago he — but I digress. What I wanted to say is that, although I have recognized this tendency in my Scriptling, I have sadly neglected to inform him that it is considered a health hazard to cast uncertified spells in public."

Master Loo watched his table companions carefully while he delivered this speech, not for reasons of suspicion, although after the conversation he had just had outside the restaurant, he had many reasons to be suspicious, but out of sheer habit. What he saw on their faces was gratitude in Buggeroff's case, a deep pool of inscrutable blackness in Merkin's eyes, and finally, a pixel-perfect conciliatory look on Master Sewer's face. The latter beamed.

"Where would we be now if we followed rules all the time? In fact, I truly believe it is people like your Scriptling to whom we owe the elevated state of our craft. Granted, bureaucrats have their merits in solidifying the establishment, but like I said, it is the experimentalists who drive us towards a better future," he said.

I couldn't have said it better myself, Master Loo thought.

"Yes, that's exactly what bugs me," answered his inner voice.

"I'm glad you think that," Master Loo said out loud.

51. MASTER SEWER

"All in all, I believe we were lucky to find him so fast," he said, keeping his eyes on the road and driving the new Mercedes SLK-Class as cautiously as he could.

"I guess so," Merkin replied.

The preoccupied look had not left her face yet, and that worried him. He spoke again. "What is it that you did back there? You know, the mysterious absence, the smell. Everything."

"I would rather not tell you just yet. There are things I need to figure out first."

"Fine," he replied. He knew he was being too soft with her, but somehow this did not bother him that much. Even so, the dinner had given him the opportunity to act his old, confident and charismatic self in public, and by contrast, he was currently acting like a wuss. Perhaps Merkin had earned her right to this. "So, what did you think of the boy?"

"He is not what I had expected, to be sure. And by the way, I don't think you should refer to him as 'the boy.' He is older than I am, so, unless you would consider calling me 'the girl,' then I suppose you shall have to find a different appellative."

"Why so protective?" he found himself replying faster than he had intended to.

"Because I have to learn this role. Why do you think?" she replied.

"I'm not sure I follow you," he said, still doing his best to keep his eyes on the road. He really did not want to cause another accident.

"Well, I thought this would be clear," she said. "I will have to seduce him." She spoke as if she were discussing groceries, yet her words stirred something deep inside him, something he did not want to be stirred.

"Seduce him? Couldn't you see that the boy... the... err... Buggeroff was... is already head over heels with you?" he replied in a voice that he did his best to keep level.

"Infatuation is one thing, and trust is something entirely different. There are too many things at stake right now to rely solely on the first."

"It appears you have been giving this some serious thought. I will let you do what you think is best," he said, more for the benefit of convincing himself than for anything else.

"Can I ask you something?" Her voice sounded so innocent that Master Sewer could not help foreseeing that a bomb was about to drop in the conversation. "You know, as a man?" she continued hesitantly.

Yes, he could definitely hear the unmistakable Doppler sound effect made by a heavy projectile plunging from the sky.

"Sure, by all means."

"Do you think I should go straight to third base with him or let him steam for a while? I mean, they say the longer the chase the stronger the commitment and all that, but I don't know if that is really true."

And there it was. The bomb might as well have been launched from an airplane called Enola Gay for all the grief it portended.

"Master?" she asked, when a few seconds had passed without an answer.

As if dragged from a distant reverie, Master Sewer pulled the steering wheel and parked negligently on the curb less than a hundred yards from their home.

"This shit has to stop!" he said, pulling the hand brake. He turned swiftly and leaned towards Merkin only to be abruptly stopped midway by the seatbelt's automatic locking mechanism.

By all rights, it should have been a ridiculous scene, were it not for Merkin, who apparently guessing her Master's intentions and evidently agreeing with his point of view regarding the cessation of the metaphorical bowel movement, met him halfway and, cupping his face into her hands, French-kissed him like he had never been French-kissed before[25].

It was a sensation so rich and warm, so sweet and wholesome, so wet and powerful, that it seemed to him that it was not a woman who kissed him, but rather the quintessence of all that was a woman, folded countless times within itself like Damascus steel. He thought all that while they kissed, and then, realizing that thinking was not of utmost importance in the current circumstances, his instincts took control of his body. A mere two, euphoric seconds later, thinking forced its way back to the surface.

He remarked, "You're not wearing panties, you kinky thing, you."

---

[25] Not even if he counted that winemaker's daughter in the Loire's valley, twenty summers in the past.

"Would you believe I took mercy on a smelly and erudite hobo and offered them as a gift to him in return for his immeasurable help?" she said between kisses.

"Right now I would believe anything," he said, achieving the amazing feat of delivering more kisses than syllables in one sentence.

"Good," she giggled. "Then believe me when I say there's an old man called Elroy watching us from his porch in a confused, but rather elated, manner. Hey, I didn't say you have to stop!"

Extricating his hand from under her dress at great expense of willpower, he grabbed the wheel and pushed the gas pedal. The car did nothing for a moment, then slowly jerked forward.

"Your hand brake is still on."

"Right," he said, and released the leaver, causing the car to jolt forward and to miss a parked Corolla by a hair's breadth.

***

The brief garage episode had been a delightful study in the ergonomics of a sports car coupled with a thorough, multi-point test of the suspension system. Following suit, the bedroom had been a triumphal duet of acrobatics and animal instincts, resulting in a broken chair and a totally unusable pillow. By contrast, the shower had been a mellow mix of intimacy and hot steam, setting up the perfect ground for a long and well-deserved night's sleep.

It was thus a merciless pity that sleep refused to come. Too soon had the oh-yes-I-did-it been replaced by the what-have-I-done. Awash in a syrupy cocktail of endorphins, dopamines, plus who knows what other -ines, and at the same time tortured by deeply rooted guilt, Master Sewer could not have been more torn apart by the two, strong feelings pulling his conscience in opposite directions.

Spooned against his body, Merkin moved in her sleep and the motion had a decisively uplifting effect on his − amongst other things, spirit.

"I'm sincerely impressed, really, but you should seriously get some sleep," she moaned half-asleep. "But just because I don't want you to think I'm a bad girl, I'll just point out that you know where everything is." She snuggled closer.

And with that impressive spell of articulated wording she went back to sleep, giving way to a soft, rhythmic purr.

"She even snores sexy," Master Sewer thought, very much entranced by her suggestion. Alas, by then the guilt had a sufficiently powerful grip on his mind to bypass even a desire as strong as this one. Something had to be done.

"Merk… Uh… Silvia?" he whispered.

She continued to snore her sensual, dainty snore.

"Silvia?" he tried again, this time nudging her thigh.

"One night of awesome sex and we're already on the first name basis?" she murmured. "Very well, then. What is it, Cornelius?" she asked, turning to face him.

"I can't be your Master any longer," he said a minute later, when the inevitable kiss was, if not concluded, then at least put to the side for the time being.

"Yeah, I know," she replied simply.

"I don't think you've heard me right," he insisted. "I said I can't—"

"Yeah, yeah, yeah, I already said I know." She yawned. "It would wreak havoc with your moral backbone if you were still my Master. Do not think I haven't considered this plenty of times before, as I'm sure you have, too. But tell me, Cornelius — by the way, I like the taste of your name on my tongue," she mused, licking, then gently biting, her lower lip. "So, as I was saying, tell me, Cornelius, would you rather have me as your Scriptling or would you rather have me — well, just have me?"

"You know very well," he replied, and squeezed her soft buttock for unneeded but absolutely delightful emphasis.

"Then here is the deal: why don't we agree I will no longer be your Scriptling, but that I shall keep on calling you Master? We'll sort out the rest of the details in the morning. How about that?"

"All right." He sighed, quite pleased by her relaxed attitude. "But why do you want to continue calling me Master?"

"It gives me a lusty kind of pleasure. It turns me on, as it were. I'm sure you will have no problem with this, will you, Master?"

"No, not at all," he managed to say.

"Aren't you happy that I chose to bypass the frigidity subroutine you had so callously hidden in my healing spell?" she said, gently caressing his cheek with her fingers.

"I was beginning to wonder about that," he admitted. "Although I'm honestly surprised you found it."

"I wouldn't have found it if I hadn't been looking for it. But you didn't answer my question."

"Of course, I'm happy you changed the spell. These last hours would have been very different, not to mention awkward, if you hadn't."

"You're right about that." She giggled. "Speaking of which, I'm awake now, Master."

52. BUGGEROFF

He had not exchanged a single word with his Master on their way back home.

Buggeroff really wanted to talk with someone about, about everything. About the intoxicating effect Merkin had on him, about the startling amount of attention Master Sewer had unloaded on him, or even about how embarrassed he felt when he had cast that improvised spell in front of everyone. Alas, his Master had an unshakeable inclination towards silence, and that meant that if Buggeroff wanted to have a conversation, he would have to be the one to spark it up. But that was not what he wanted, and nor was it what he needed. What he needed was for someone to empathize with him, to perceive the state in which he was, and subsequently offer a helping hand, or at least a helping ear, if nothing else was available.

"What is bothering you, Chief?"

Not now, Stapley. Buggeroff sighed inwardly.

"What have I done this time?" his personal assistant complained.

You're cheating. That's what you've done. I don't need pity, only sympathy.

"I don't understand, Chief. What are you talking about?"

I'm saying I know you've been reading my mind, so there is no point in your acting so caring all of a sudden, Buggeroff said sharply.

"But I can't read your mind, Chief. I thought we'd already had this out of the way."

Then—

"Please don't interrupt me," Stapley raised his voice in anger for the first time Buggeroff could remember. *"It doesn't take mind reading to see that something is troubling you, Chief, and I surely don't have to act so caring all of a sudden when all I've been doing for the last few weeks was busting my ass to cover for you, teach you, assist you and, yes, care for you, Chief."* Stapley threw the last word as he would a hand grenade.

Stapley, Buggeroff said, barely containing an avalanche of laughter behind a composure stretched thin, *"you don't technically have an ass."*

He hoped this would work. Humor, even the low quality variety, has an amazing ability to diffuse tense situations. It also has an even more amazing ability to offend those who are not in the proper mood at the time it is being delivered. Especially so when irony is mistaken for humor.

"Oh, yes, I do have an ass," Stapley said bitterly. *"I'm talking to him right now!"* Any subsequent attempts to resume communication with Stapley proved fruitless. Buggeroff was conscious of his assistant's presence in his mind in the same way that he was conscious of electricity flowing through cables buried underground. He knew some kind of force was there, but as long as said force did not materialize in any kind of tangible form, it might as well not have existed.

To no avail had Buggeroff swung back and forth between friendliness, spitefulness, dejectedness, and remorse, sometimes in the same sentence. *Come on, Stapley, you know there is no ass in assistant. Oh, wait a minute, there is, and you're it. You're an ass! Why don't you talk to me, asshole? Please talk to me, Stapley. Please! I feel lonely without you. Oh, Stapley, I'm so sorry!* All his efforts were met by resolute silence.

***

When they had finally arrived home about ten minutes later, Master Loo invited Buggeroff to his study and offered him a generous measure of what he referred to as "a wee dram". Buggeroff, who had just enough cultural awareness to infer that McDonalds did not constitute traditional Scottish food, was left completely unmoved by the reference. But the drink was fine, in a stiff sort of way, and it did have that universal effect of alcoholic beverages, which was to loosen one's tongue.

"What exactly is a wee-wee drum?" he asked. He would normally have asked Stapley, but he was sure it would have been to no avail.

"It's not a *drum*," Master Loo emphasized the w sound of the English r. "It's a *dram*," he continued, swiftly rolling the 'r' through a quick series of steep peaks and valleys and modulating the 'a' to the point where it was not yet a question nor was it a statement anymore. "Dram is the Scottish word for drink, and a wee (not a wee-wee) dram means a little drink."

"A wee dram," Buggeroff tried to imitate his Master's pronunciation, but for all that he had a splendid mane of red hair, which the kind nuns at the St. Patricide Orphanage insisted was a sure sign of Gaelic ancestry, his brogue gene must have completely washed out from the DNA pool.

"Close enough," his Master said, taking a sip from his own, large, crystal glass. "So, what did you think of tonight's events?" he asked, seemingly without any real interest.

Buggeroff knew his Master sufficiently well to know that this was not just some random question. Clearly his Master had already made a series of observations, and now he wanted to see if his Scriptling was able to match them and perhaps even contribute some new ones.

What have we got, Stapley? he asked, but his question was greeted by silence and, unless he was mistaken, the faint echo of a derisive snort.

Well, a snort was marginally better than absolute silence, but it was still a far cry from what Buggeroff wanted to hear. What he wanted to hear was a marvelously aggregated collection of facts, layered with deep insights and sprinkled with witty observations.

"Umm…," he said out loud, forcing his mind to think. After all, didn't Master Loo say that everything that Stapley did, he did it by using his, Buggeroff's, own brain? "I guess Merkin and her Master seem to be a curious bunch," he continued, congratulating himself for the vagueness of his conclusion.

"What do you mean by that?" his Master pressed on.

Damn it!

"What I mean is… what I am trying to get through when I say that… when I say that I find Merkin and her Master, that is, Master Sewer to be more precise… uh… like I said, by suggesting that they appear to be a curious bunch, I don't really mean… Well, of course, I mean precisely that, but…" Buggeroff blabbered like a schoolboy who hasn't learned the lesson but who nevertheless thinks that salvation can be achieved through sheer volume.

"Oh, for crying out loud," Stapley said. *"Repeat after me—"*

Stapley, I'm so sorry, Buggeroff interrupted his assistant. *I don't know what came over me. It's not really my style to act like that.*

"I know it's not. That's why I'm helping you. But apologies, should you have more where that came from, can wait, Chief. For now you would do well to repeat after me, unless you want to disappoint your Master."

Thank you, Stapley! Buggeroff replied, and then resumed his explanation out loud, for the benefit of his Master. "Yes, they seem contradictory, inconsistent if you will. Let us take Master Sewer for instance. While he does seem to broadcast nothing but affability and genuine interest, this is hardly consistent with his career choice, no offence meant. You, yourself, mentioned how Magicians are not the kindest of persons, and I, therefore, infer that if one acts kindly then it is because he has a secret agenda. How am I doing so far?"

"Go on, go on." His Master nodded encouragingly.

"As for Merkin—" He stopped and sighed the unmistakable sigh of the desperately hopeful, "As for Merkin, despite her astonishing looks and sharpness of mind, it is hard to ignore the one or two, odd facts."

He stopped again, only to consult with Stapley. *What do you mean by odd facts? I don't remember seeing anything out of ordinary.*

"*Oh, yes, you've seen plenty of unusual things, but you were too mesmerized by her astonishing looks and, ahem… sharpness of mind, to catalogue them properly,*" Stapley replied. "*Lucky for you, my attention is not likely to succumb to such charms. Now, if you please, do continue to repeat after me, and kindly refrain from improvising.*"

All right, all right, Buggeroff agreed, not wanting to risk upsetting his assistant again.

"Two, odd facts?" asked Master Loo.

"Indeed," he nodded. "Where do I begin? Well, I am sure you remember the terrible smell, right?"

"Wish I knew how to forget it." His Master wrinkled his nose at the memory. "I, too, found it suspicious that the smell seemed to appear at the same time as Merkin returned to the room. But while this is an odd fact, it is not significant."

"The smell in itself is not significant, I agree. However, in this case, the smell plays the role of a mnemonic device. In very much the same way as Proust's *mad lane*, it allows us to segue to the truly interesting matter, which is the fact of her unexpected departure," Buggeroff explained.

Then, as he paused for breath, he addressed his assistant, *Stapley, I gather you must have a Private Detective speech mode somewhere in that intricate system of yours, and I will be the first to congratulate you on its eloquent usage, but I just want to point out that I don't talk like that.*

"*What do you mean, Chief?*"

Well, if you want me to repeat everything you say then at least try to use words I would normally use, too. I have no idea who this Proust guy is and what is so famous about his mad lane. Also, may I remind you that affability, mnemonic, segue and contradictory do not, oddly enough, belong in my day-to-day vocabulary?

"*Understood, Chief. But since we are on the topic, neither do gather, intricate, and eloquent, if you know what I mean.*"

That's exactly what I meant! See, your poshness is rubbing on.

"*On the other hand, it does suit you rather well, Chief, if I may say so myself. But this being said, point taken. I will downgrade the quality of my discourse to better accommodate your patently non-posh persona.*"

"What departure are you talking about?" Master Loo asked.

"Oh, I almost forgot," Buggeroff said, slightly taken aback, as usual, by the fact that he had to handle two conversations at the same time, only one of them outside his own mind. "You were not there when she left," he added.

"I sneaked outside for a cigarette when I saw her begin talking to you," Master Loo explained. "I did not want to be in your way, you know," he added in the embarrassed tone used by old people when talking about what they believed to be intimate issues. "What happened there?"

"Well, shortly after the introductions were made, and just after Master Sewer invited us for dinner, she excused herself and ran outside," Buggeroff said.

There was a pause.

"What invitation to dinner are you talking about?"

"Funny how that slipped away," Buggeroff said sheepishly. "Master Sewer, that is to say, Merkin on behalf of her Master, invited us to dinner on Saturday. Master, are you all right?" he asked when he heard the agonizing groan and then saw his Master's blank face.

There was no answer.

"He is panicking," Stapley said. *"You know how he feels about social events."*

53. MASTER LOO

"Gimme an L! Gimme an O! Gimme another O! Loo, Loo, Loo, this is something you can do." The inner voice tried to cheer him up, or, failing that, at least to antagonize him.

Shut up! Master Loo hissed inwardly.

"Hey, Loo-Loo you're so fine, you're so fine you'll have to dine, hey Loo-Loo! Hey Loo-Loo!" his inner voice continued to cheer with renewed energy.

"Master?" Buggeroff asked again.

"Don't settle for number two, have dinner with Master Loo!" the nagging voice kept pouring its second-rate slogans. *"I can do this all day, you know? You would be surprised how many words rhyme with Loo. You don't even need to step outside the subject area, if you get my meaning. Hey, check this out: if you dine with Master Loo you will surely have to—"*

"I see," Master Loo replied to Buggeroff, shaking himself free from his moment of social anxiety and mercifully diverting his attention away from the last word in his inner voice's chant just in time. "I guess we shall have to honor the invitation," he added, forcing himself to sound optimistic.

"We will?" his Scriptling asked.

"Indeed, we will. It's part of the etiquette. Incidentally, I would appreciate if next time you would do me the favor of informing me of such invitations as soon as they become apparent to you."

"What good would that do?"

"Well, you see, etiquette also dictates that an invitation between Magicians can be refused within the first twenty-three minutes of its being issued if the total age of the invitees surpasses that of the inviters by a ratio larger than one and a quarter. I am quite certain we could have qualified for an exemption under these peculiar, yet nevertheless extremely legal, terms. I know it's ludicrous, but I don't make the rules," he felt compelled to add upon seeing Buggeroff's distrustful expression. "If anything, it tells you a lot about the history of our noble profession."

"Probably more than I wanted to know." Buggeroff shook his head as if trying to expel this newly gained knowledge.

"A sensible attitude, if you want my opinion. However, you might find that it pays to know some of these rules, especially the odd ones[26]. I'm sure there are about two shelves concerning the topic in my library. A largely incomplete collection, I have to admit, but nevertheless, a good starting point if you are ever interested. Now, I do believe I have interrupted your interesting exposé regarding this evening's events. You were just saying how the girl, Merkin, rushed outside."

"Ah, yes." Buggeroff drew in a deep breath, gathering his thoughts. "We were just talking when her expression changed completely, and she left the room, excusing herself. Just before that, though, I thought I heard a buzzing sound coming from − well, I believe it was from under her décolletage. A miniature cell phone, probably, but I couldn't tell for sure. As soon as the buzzing started, she cupped her hands over her chest and kept them there as she ran away."

"I'm sure it must have been a device of some sort, perhaps even a cell phone, as you suggested. At any rate, I don't find anything unusual about her behavior other than its inherent impoliteness, of course," Mater Loo commented.

"You are most certainly right, Master. I can only recount what I saw. As for the interpretation, I leave it all to you. It is worth remarking, however, that the atrocious smell was not the only interesting fact associated with her return."

"Really? Do tell more," Master Loo asked in anticipation.

"I don't want to offend anyone, but I am talking about her obviously hostile attitude towards you, Master," Buggeroff replied in such a manner that it seemed to Master Loo that he was not entirely convinced. He even sounded a little bit surprised at what he had just said.

"Is there anything wrong?" Master Loo asked.

"It's just that I can't believe anyone would have reason to be hostile to you, Master," his Scriptling said quickly. "Other than me, that is. But that's only to be expected seeing as you tried, and actually succeeded, in killing me," he added with a lopsided smile.

---

[26] Master Loo had first discovered his fascination with rules, especially odd rules, when he was in his twenties. It had been an embarrassing moment, like the one you get when you realize for the first time that you have what it takes to become an accountant, but since embarrassment was something Master Loo had lots of experience with, he managed to fight it, and in the end, overcome it.

"Who knows, dear Buggeroff," he replied, deeply moved by his Scriptling's display of loyalty despite the ironic twist at the end. "I, too, have witnessed Merkin's lack of courtesy concerning myself, but truth be told, this was not an isolated occurrence, and over time, I have developed quite an immunity to it."

"What do you mean, Master?"

"Come on, boy, I'm sure you see it very well. There are people like Master Sewer, charismatic, easy-going, and instantly likeable, and then there are people like me. All right, I might not be at the completely opposite pole, such as the late Master Dung whose funeral you have so recently attended was, but I know I'm not that far from it, either."

"Yeah! It makes total sense that the Loo should stand between the Dung and the Sewer," the inner voice made a witty, but otherwise pertinent remark.

"Master Sewer is indeed charismatic," Buggeroff said. "Nevertheless, charisma has but a temporary effect on relationships. You, on the other hand, are kind and generous. I would rather have these qualities in the long run."

"Brown nose! You wouldn't talk like that if you'd really known your Master. Hey Loo-Loo, why don't you tell him about your fiancée? Come on, make my day!"

"Thank you, Buggeroff," Master Loo said. He then paused for a few moments before speaking again in a slightly hesitant voice. "There is one more matter I wish to discuss with you with regards to these recent events."

Buggeroff sighed and his shoulders sagged.

"Is it about the spell?" his Scriptling asked.

"It is, indeed, about the spell," he agreed.

"I shouldn't have done it. I know. Truth is, I wanted to impress Merkin."

"And you very well succeeded in that, be sure of it. In fact, I would not exaggerate if I were to say you managed to impress everyone at that table."

Buggeroff clearly did not expect this.

"What do you mean?" he asked. "It was just a simple spell..." He didn't know what to say next.

"Perhaps you are right about that. But just as a side note, it is simplicity rather than complexity that is the mark of genius. At any rate, this was not the point I wished to remark upon."

"Then what was it?"

"Well, correct me if I'm wrong, but last time I checked, 'febrizium' was not a Latin word, despite its neutered singular, morphological suffix."

"Ah, you're perfectly right about that," Buggeroff replied quickly, obviously happy to have found a familiar grip on the conversation. "It's just a word I made up. It's a *port-man-toe* of a popular air-freshener and the *anthropomorphic singularity* suffix thingy," he finished enthusiastically, completely oblivious to the way in which he had just butchered the good old English vocabulary in doing so.

Master Loo harrumphed. "Yes, quite. Just out of curiosity, though, doesn't that strike you as unusual?"

"I... I suppose the advertising industry might have played a role in it. That explains the word association between fresh air and this particular brand of freshener. Funny thing, that."

"That's not what I was pointing at," Master Loo pressed on. "The unusual thing about your spell is that it actually worked."

"I don't understand you, Master. Of course it worked. I might be inexperienced, but at the very least, I can be counted upon to cast a decent spell, can't I?"

"I never challenged that, but—"

"Don't do it! Trust me when I tell you it's best not to say anything to him about it," the inner voice interrupted him.

What are you talking about? Master Loo replied.

"You know very well what I'm talking about. You want to tell him how spell words, or invocation words, as you so pompously like to call them, have to be in the same language as their actual code."

All right, so what if I want to tell him this? He should be aware of it, or else who knows what sort of accident might happen?

"And you call yourself a novocrat! Boo! I thought you were all for experiments and stuff. And what if an accident happens? That never stopped you, did it?" said the inner voice.

But the spell shouldn't have worked! He didn't even use the gesture of power.

"He doesn't know that. Why would you want to change this? Didn't you always say that our progress is only impeded by our refusal to part with what we already know?"

No, I didn't! But blast it! You are right.

"Of course, I am," the inner voice snorted.

Master Loo turned his attention outwards and saw that Buggeroff was still waiting for an explanation, or at least for something better than an ellipsis.

"I... Forgive me," he babbled. "My mind wanders off these days more often than it should. What I meant to say with regards to your spell was, good job, Buggeroff, dear! I am very pleased with you."

"Oo-key," his Scriptling replied, clearly confused by the spiraling way in which this conversation occurred. "Thank you, Master," he added as a polite afterthought.

Not wanting to prolong this awkward moment, Master Loo stretched his back and stifled a yawn, but not so much as to make it unnoticeable. Answering to an empathic reflex stronger than his willpower, Buggeroff yawned in reply.

"You crafty, old fart," the inner voice congratulated Master Loo and, in as much as a split personality could, he too yawned.

"Perhaps we should call it a day," Master Loo spoke. "What say you?"

"I guess you are right, Master. Besides, I have to wake up early in the morning to take Gertrude out for walkies. Speaking of which, have you got any idea where she might be? I haven't seen her tonight, and you know how she always likes to greet us at the door."

"I'm afraid we won't be seeing her for a week or so. No, don't be scared. It's nothing serious, well, nothing to be frightened of anyway. I believe she locked herself in her room, and it would be best if we would offer her some privacy. It's that time of the month, you know?"

54. MERKIN

"Good meowning, Master," she purred, adding just the right amount of velvety touch to her voice.

"Mmm." her Master and her lover, who were, of course, the same person, moaned. "I could get used to this."

They were still in bed, and despite the long-imposed Hollywood tradition, Merkin's beautiful torso was not covered by a PG[27] grade, white sheet.

"What else could you get used to?" she asked, shamelessly insinuating something that needed no amount of insinuation. Her words did not, however, have the desired effect.

"What I could use right now would be a hearty breakfast. After that, I'm sure I'll have a better answer for you, whether you'll ask for it or not." Master Sewer smiled, proving once and for all that men are beings of simple desires, with food and sex at the top of the list constantly fighting for the pole position.

"Fine." She pouted her perfect lips. "Then why don't you doze off for a few minutes while I fix you the hearty breakfast of your dreams. I need you strong and well rested."

Ah, the joy of being in control! No sooner had she mentioned fixing him breakfast than his entire demeanor underwent a radical change. If the

---

[27] PG (Parental Guidance) is a TV rating system whose single role is to warm the audience to the idea that a woman who had just engaged in a serious amount of sexual debauchery will, come morning, suddenly feel extremely self-aware about the shape, colour, and general existence of her breasts. In its most extreme form, PG will also force the female character who has just finished making sweet love to roll on her back beaming with fulfilment, covered in a white sheet that has either magically appeared or that has been there the whole time, in which case said love making must have been severely obstructed, and, consequently, the beaming of fulfilment must have been, alas, definitely fake.

house were on fire, her dear Master would not have moved any faster. Food and sex: simple pleasures, indeed. But simple pleasures only meant bigger and easier targets. It might seem like exquisite guile from where the man is standing, but really, all a woman needs to do in order to have control over her man is to adjust the flow and temperature of these two taps. In her case, Merkin had made sure her man would never lack fine, home-cooked meals, provided, of course, that her man would take the hint and cook them himself. This was nothing but another aspect of the flow and temperature concept.

She would have loved to spend the rest of the morning in bed, but this was not the time for laxness. With an instinct found only in smiths, women, and smiths who were women, she was aware that she should strike the iron while it was hot.

A minute later, she entered the kitchen and perched on a high stool, hugging her legs to her chest in a carefully practiced, vulnerable posture. She wore one of her Master's shirts with nothing else underneath and only two of its seven buttons strategically fastened. She could have worn a large t-shirt, or a transparent nightgown or she could have just as well shown up naked. Any of these accoutrements, or lack thereof, would have had a bludgeoning effect on her Master's concentration. However, Merkin was not the bludgeoning type, but rather the stiletto-wielding kind, and that was precisely why she had chosen to wear his shirt. Looking up at him through puppy eyes, she grabbed his coffee mug in her hands, blew gently on the deep, molten darkness, inhaled the rich aroma, and then, slowly closing her eyelids, took a cautious sip. And that, she thought, is how you twist the blade.

"The sausage is burning." She indicated the frying pan from which thick smoke rose when she considered she had allowed him to stare at her long enough.

"Indeed, it is," he replied automatically, and then, as he realized what she really meant, coughed and turned his attention to the stovetop.

She smiled and made no comment, although inside she was very proud of the way in which she could so easily manipulate him.

"Did you sleep well, Master? No more misgivings and moral issues giving you trouble?" she asked.

"Excellent, thank you!" he answered, not turning his attention away from the sizzling pan. "As for the misgivings, I believe we reached a conclusion last night, the details of which I would be more than curious to learn from you."

"How do you mean?" She leaned forward on her high chair.

"Well, just before you so emphatically explained why you should still call me Master, you promised to discuss more about our... about... to discuss more in the morning."

"Yes, I did, didn't I?" She eased back and smiled. "I will, indeed, no longer be your Scriptling, but that is not to say I will neglect my education. In fact, I have already found a new Master, and I shall go to live with him very soon."

To see a man as self-possessed as Master Sewer noisily dropping a fork on the plate was a sight for the most sadistic of hearts.

"You have?" was all he could ask.

"Of course, I have." Her eyes were bright with unilateral merriment. "You have met him, too, and made many a positive comment regarding his results."

At last, the penny dropped, and her Master's expression turned from fretfulness to disbelief.

"You don't mean that old fart, Master Loo?"

"Why the sudden change of opinion? Judging by your display last evening, I thought you admired and respected him to no end."

"Which is more than I can say about your display. Seriously, when you don't like someone, especially when that someone is a Magician, you should try to hide your feelings. Half a century ago, you would have been slaughtered on the spot for giving a Magician the evil eye."

"Was I that obvious?" She fluttered her eyelashes, faking skepticism.

"You know it very well. Actually I've been meaning to ask, but I've been caught in other activities. Why did you do it?"

She sighed. "Well, you might as well know. It's because I saw him talking to the cops, and you don't need to ask me which cops I am talking about. Not only that, but he acted as if he knew them well."

Master Sewer stopped chewing his food, a sure sign that he was thinking very hard.

"When did you see this?" he asked after a few moments of concentration.

"You always have to ask the best question, do you?" she complained half-heartedly. "All right, I saw this last night when I went outside."

"What is it that you are not telling me?" he pressed on.

So, she told him about the device concealed in her medallion, about her first attempt to catch the cops unaware, and about what she had seen the previous night.

"I guess that explains the smell," he said when she was done.

"Is that what you take from my story?" she asked angrily.

"No, that was what psychologists call a tension diffuser. An attempt, which, I must say, didn't seem to work at all. Anyway, if that's the case, then why do you want to go to live with him? It seems both annoying and dangerous."

"Ah, let me see...." She rolled her eyes upwards, pretending to think. "Several reasons, actually. I should start with the fact that someone couldn't keep their Magic wand in their pants last night and thus made it impossible for me to continue as their Scriptling. However, I will not insist upon this because I have reason to believe I, too, am at fault here. Besides, it's not like I can complain or anything."

"Magic wand?" he asked in an insecure tone that caused her to giggle.

"Excuse me. I should have said *wizard staff* instead. My bad. Wouldn't have worked well in the sentence, although I must say it worked well everywhere else," she finished with a grin.

He coughed. "Quite... yes... point taken. So, what other reasons can you bring to mind?"

"Well, on the one hand there is the old, keep-your-enemies-closer argument," she said, holding one hand in the air. "On the other hand, there is the obvious fact that this will bring me closer to Buggeroff and his secret." She raised the other hand.

"I see," he said, rubbing his chin. "Are you still planning to seduce this Buggeroff guy?"

"I plan to go as far as need be." She put on a brave face as if she were heading to war rather than to Buggeroff's bed. Of course, things would not go so far, but that was no reason for not roasting her Master a little bit. "And if it's any comfort, bear in mind that I am doing it for you," she said to add guilt to jealousy.

"I would rather—"

"You would rather what?" she prompted him. "Stay powerless for the rest of your life? Have me all for yourself? You don't own me, you know that?"

She could tell by the angry fire in his eyes that she had gone too far this time.

"Believe me," she added quickly, trying to mend what could still be mended, "if there were another way, I would be very happy to try it. If you really want me to stop and be safely yours, than I can do that. But I know how much you love your Magic. I know it because I've known all too often what it feels like not to have it. Can't you see? I want you to be happy, and I know the only way you can be happy is if you have your Magic back." She could see that her words had the desired calming effect. And then, because she would not have been Merkin if she had have left it at that, she added "Besides, I'll make sure he wears a condom."

THIRD TRIBAL INTERLUDE

Imagine, if you will, thirty-seven immortals for whom curiosity is a built-in imperative being given the most remarkable and most powerful toy in the universe. Alas, even this audacious comparison is off the mark by a few orders of magnitude when it comes to describing the following fifty or so generations in the Tribe's history. What we're talking about here is big scale Magic, climate changes, and even the advent of early religions (although trying to get any Tribe member to admit to the latter would be quite a tremendous challenge).

Let's just say that once the party was over, the Tribe had the decency to put most of the things back into place with the possible, and otherwise notable, exception of the platypus and a moronic drinking game that later evolved into the imperial measurement system.

However, this is not where the unforeseeable consequences of the Tribe's accidental discovery of Magic came to a full stop. The foremost of these consequences had been, without any doubt, the sudden realization that the aptitude for Magic was, by no means, confined within the esoteric boundaries defined by the Tribe and its members. If anything, this remarkable aptitude was, in a rather twisted way, hereditary.

It must be said that the Mama are as partial to romance and its treacherous traps as any other human beings. They had, to put it bluntly, over the course of their numerous incarnations, mothered and fathered quite an abundance of children. And while they seldom chose to incarnate into their own progenies, they did somehow pass on a gene responsible for turning their mortal offspring into natural Magicians.

These Descendants, as the Tribe called them, had children of their own, and these, too, were Magicians by all rights. Of course, as the generations multiplied, the talent diluted – up to the point where it would disappear completely.

However, and this is the important bit, while the Tribe itself continues to fornicate its way around the world, a new batch of first-rate Descendants is bound to pop up in every generation.

55. STAPLEY

When Buggeroff woke up, he went through his usual routine: stretch in bed, swear vengeance at the sun rays coming through the blinds, perform unmentionable – but nevertheless enjoyable – shower activities, dry up; stretch some more, get dressed, walk the goat.

He paused.

Stapley, what did the Master mean when I asked him about Gertrude and he said that it is that time of month?

"*Got no clue whatsoever, Chief,*" Stapley replied.

Can't you, like, search your reference dictionary or whatever neuronal thingamajig you have at your disposal? There is one, obvious meaning to his words, but I refuse to believe that's what he really meant. It would be low-hanging fruit, and besides, it's not really the Master's style. It's a mystery wrapped in riddle wrapped in an enema.

"*Yeah, I don't think that's the right interpretation either,*" Stapley agreed. "*Also, I think it's an enigma, Chief.*"

That, too, Buggeroff replied, oblivious of his own slip.

Right, Chief. I'm going to initiate a heuristic search of my neuronal thingamajig for a valid reference. Be right back.

Sure thing, take your time.

"*Do you know anything about it, oh, brilliant Master?*" Stapley asked Master Dung in the privacy of his own mind.

"I might," the usurper replied, obviously enjoying this.

"*Then would you be so kind as to share your superior knowledge with your miserable servant?*" Stapley asked in a tone that was more impatient than obsequious.

"And why would I want to do that?" Master Dung replied with enough anger to make it clear that Stapley's attitude had been noted.

"*Because helping Buggeroff would help consolidate my, but ultimately, our, position,*" Stapley thought quickly.

"Helping him do what? Figure out what his lame Master told him about that crazy goat? You know what I think of their relationship? I think it's sick, that's what I think!"

"What relationship would that be, Master?"

"The one between the boy and the goat, obviously! Where did you ever hear of such a thing? It's not normal, I'm telling you," Master Dung spoke like a monomaniac prophet announcing the imminent wrath of god.

"He is treating her like a pet." Stapley was conciliatory. *"Were she a dog, I am sure you would have been more tolerant."*

"You're just as sick as he is." The usurper nudged forward a last word.

"Be it so, Master, what harm would it do you to tell me what you know about the goat?"

"Ha! All right, I'm going to tell you, but it won't make any difference," Master Dung sneered.

He was right about that. When Stapley learned the details of what his evil master had been so reluctant to tell him, he actually wondered why all the fuss.

"I might have something, Chief." He coughed politely. *"But it's not high quality stuff. At any rate, please allow me to engage the cynical storyteller mode for a richer narrative experience."*

Let's hear it, Buggeroff thought.

"This is a little embarrassing. Apparently there is an obscure and farfetched reference to this matter in old, Balkan fairy tales. Please, don't ask me how I know this. In the story, the main hero, a young man of humble origins who is regarded by everyone as a dimwit and a coward, goes around accomplishing miscellaneous tasks. You know — feed the chicken, find the treasure, and slay the wyvern for no better reason than that the poor, mythical animal is unwilling to part with said treasure. Those kinds of tasks. In the end, our by-now-wise-and-kind hero gets to marry the most beautiful girl in the land who is usually of royal blood. This notion, alone, proves just how unlikely the story is."

Yeah, I know. Social class differences and stuff. It would never work, Buggeroff pitched in.

"That and the grinding effects of inbreeding, a practice which is the questionable privilege of aristocracy. What I'm saying is that it is highly unlikely that someone of royal blood would be the most beautiful girl in the land unless we are only counting the land within the castle walls."

Perhaps she can afford better dresses, Buggeroff remarked. *Personal trainers, beauticians, a yoga parlor, and stuff. These things can really make a difference.*

"Perhaps," Stapley had to agree, not to the historical details, which were completely out of place, but to the general idea that a princess might have been more presentable than a peasant daughter. Perhaps this could be

explained by the fact that the princess bathed in goat's milk while the peasant daughter had the hard job of sustaining the whole, messy process – at the end of which goat milk became available. *"Anyway,"* he continued, *"so the unlikely couple sets out to live together in the castle as the new king and queen of the land."*

Wait, what happened to the previous king and queen? Buggeroff asked. *You know, the princess's parents? Don't they normally have to die before the royal succession takes place?*

Stapley quickly invented an explanation, annoyed by all the interruptions but not letting it show. *"In an extremely atypical monarchical gesture, they stepped aside and gave the young couple all the prerogatives of the crown. To keep themselves busy, they invested all their savings in an organic turnip garden that proved so successful that it actually doubled their money within the first, two weeks. As I was saying, the newlywed couple embarks on the ultimate leadership career and everything works just fine for a while. The queen spends her day embroidering and playing the harp while the king strengthens the borders, reinforces the law, and lowers the taxes. Completely unrealistic, I know. Things also work really well in the royal bedroom where the couple has endless hours of good time, night after night."*

So, when do they get to sleep then? Buggeroff asked

"Beats me, Chief," Stapley tried very hard to keep the exasperation out of his voice. *"But the story gets more complicated, probably on account of the collective author trying to introduce some kind of imbalance to this nauseating utopia. One evening, while they are having supper, the queen informs the king that they will not be sharing the bed for the following week and that she will be sleeping in the tower, a tower that had never been part of the story until that moment, but which, miraculously, makes its appearance in the castle's architecture. Furthermore, the queen asks her beloved husband and king not to attempt to visit her in the tower because that would spell the end of their marriage. Of course, for all his wisdom and kindness, the king cannot contain his desire for more than three nights, and on the fourth night he sneaks to the tower and peeks through the keyhole into his wife's room."*

The bastard! Buggeroff exclaimed. *Why couldn't he give her some privacy?*

"On the other hand, he could have done what every other king would have done in this situation, which is to find a temporary replacement or two for his wife from the ranks of noble women clustered around the palace. He did not, however, do that, so, credit where it's due. What the king sees through the keyhole varies from story to story, but the most common elements are: his naked wife who now has goat legs instead of her perfectly shaped own, an emerald snake curled on top of a small egg mound, and a small hippopotamus farting copiously. As a side note, I think this whole scenario is a rather misdirected allegory for a woman's menstrual cycle, undoubtedly conceived by a very sick bunch of misogynists."

Yes, very gory indeed, Buggeroff replied, as usual, navigating his way around the unfamiliar words and finding some kind of relevant meaning. *So, what happens next?*

"*Well, the king gasps in shock at the sight so loudly that the queen hears him, prompting her to jump out of the window, guided by irreconcilable shame. The king then quickly descends the spiral stairs of the tower and heads outside to where the squashed shape of his wife should be. Except she is not there. Haunted by remorse, he sets out looking for her. The search goes on and on for years and years, during which time the kingdom falls apart and the wandering king manages to wear out ten pairs of iron shoes.*"

Come again? Buggeroff asked for clarification.

"*Ah, the iron shoe is a common element in fairy tales. Apparently one has to wear out their stiff, iron soles ten times before finding what they are looking for. A good business opportunity for blacksmiths. I would imagine a hero would pay extra for thin and poor quality iron soles if he had sufficient guile. Eventually, the king finds his wife, whom he fails to recognize despite the fact that she had not aged a day. She lives in a small hut in a very dark forest and offers him a place to sleep for the night. As the night gets deeper, it turns out she is willing to offer him more than just a place to sleep, but our righteous hero adamantly refuses her offer, claiming that he is a married man. It is then that she reveals her true identity, and they both cry and renew their vows of eternal love and loyalty.*"

What, just like that?

"*Yeah, apparently those were simpler times.*" Stapley sighed. "*In the end, they both return to their castle and, through the Magical force of applied leadership, they succeed in restoring the kingdom back to its original glory. The end,*" Stapley finished.

You are right, Buggeroff said after a long pause. *It was not high quality stuff, but at least it offers a lead.*

"*What do you mean?*" Stapley asked, hurt by the not-high-quality-stuff remark, especially after he had done his best to spice up the story with witty comments and startling interpretations.

Well, we learned that it would be, indeed, very wise not to disturb Gertrude. For all we know, she might have even turned into a human, perhaps even a beautiful woman. It would be only fair to respect her privacy.

"*Then why are we... I mean, why are you climbing down the stairs towards her basement room as we speak?*" Stapley asked in alarm.

Oh, you're right, you're right. Although I don't suppose a little curiosity ever hurt anyone. After all, it's not like she is big on other people's privacy, Buggeroff mumbled.

"*No, Chief!*" Stapley shouted. "*Please, don't do it!*"

But Buggeroff was now too close to his destination to even consider going back. Stapley desperately sought for a solution, and having no other option, he reluctantly engaged the stroboscope-induced seizure procedure.

Not knowing what happened to him, Buggeroff fell down a mere two feet from the door.

"Ha ha! I love it when you do that!" Master Dung laughed his sadistic laughter, which made Stapley feel even more miserable.

"You don't have to rub it in," the latter said morosely. *"I only hope I've done the right thing."*

56. BUGGEROFF

"What happened?" he moaned as he came to.

"I'm not quite sure, Chief, but it seems like there's a spell protecting Gertrude's room from invasions of privacy. Do you feel all right?"

Yeah, I guess so. Thanks for asking. Well, I'd better leave it at that then. I don't know what came over me, he thought, trying to blink away the strange sensation in his brain. *I should go upstairs and fix myself some breakfast.* He started moving up the stairs.

"Ah, there you are," Master Loo's voice came from the top of the stairs, carrying unconcealed signs of relief. "I've been looking all over for you."

"I'm sorry, Master. I came down to see if Gertrude was all right," Buggeroff lied.

"Oh, my." His Master sighed. "You couldn't stay away, could you? Not even after I specifically told you we should offer her some privacy."

"I've learned my lesson, though." Buggeroff rubbed his temples.

"And what lesson is that?" Master Loo asked while gesturing to his Scriptling to follow him upstairs.

"That I should mumble mumble more respectful of mumble mumble privacy," Buggeroff muttered as he climbed up the stairs.

"I didn't quite catch that, but it's not really all that relevant anyway. Breakfast is ready." He pointed towards the eggs-and-ham plate resting on the countertop as they entered the kitchen. "I've eaten already."

"Thank you, Master." Buggeroff started forking down the delicious food.

"Tell me, Buggeroff," his Master began in his pedagogical voice. "Do you know what the trademark of a successful Magician is?"

He tried his best to answer the question. "Ambition? Stealth? A steady hand with deadly miniature crossbows?"

"Close enough, but the answer I was looking for was curiosity. Not many of us agree, but I believe curiosity should be a Magician's greatest asset. I am happy to see that you have plenty of it. Enough, I should say, to get you in trouble, but that's the way we learn."

"We learn from our mistakes," Buggeroff said for lack of a better answer.

"Not really, Buggeroff, dear, not really. Mistakes prompt us to learn, that much I can agree with, but it is from our successes that we really learn our lessons."

"I'm not sure I follow you, Master," he said while cutting a slice of ham.

"Let's start with something simple. When you first tried to hammer a nail, how did that go?"

"I managed to drive the nail into the board, with my finger serving as a buffer between the nail head and the hammer. I guess deep in my mind that is when I decided to become a programmer."

"Fair enough, but I suppose now you are perfectly capable of hammering a nail without injuring yourself, right?"

"Sure. I guess I'm a decent nail driver now," Buggeroff replied, not knowing where this was heading.

"And how did that happen? How do you take a person who can't drive a nail, without having a career-related epiphany, and turn him into a decent nail driver? Was it the mistake that taught you?"

"I... I don't think so." He rummaged his memory for an explanation. "I guess the next time I tried to hammer a nail I paid more attention, took my time, and after a number of trials I was able to do it right, and I kept doing it right." He paused, and his face lit up. "Oh, my god! You are right! I did learn from my own success!"

"I'm sure there is a health risk in dropping too many exclamation marks in one breath. But I believe you got it. Just to clarify, making mistakes is important because this is what provides the incentive for our learning process. However, it is only by doing something right that we learn how to do it right. Actually, I should not even call this process learning, but rather forming a habit. Learning implies that we are memorizing facts, when what we are really doing, in the case of hammering a nail or speed typing – or even driving a car – is storing habit sequences. Habits are there in order to keep us from making mistakes. So, to summarize, it is not correct to say, 'We learn from our mistakes.' It would be more accurate to say something around the lines of, 'We form habits by succeeding,' although I must agree it doesn't have quite the same ring to it."

Not for the first time, Buggeroff watched his Master in awe. It was not what he had said, even if that had been very informing and educational, but it was the way he said it.

Hey, Stapley, just out of curiosity, how many words was that?

"One hundred and fifty-seven, Chief," Stapley replied promptly.

Doesn't that strike you as weird?

"It is a significant statistical deviation from his usual speech pattern," Stapley agreed.

Right, I'm sure you have that calculated to the third decimal.

"Sixteenth decimal, Chief. The actual value is—"

I really don't want to know all the details. I just find it so unusual that someone as introverted and... and soft-voiced as he is can sometimes suffer from such a severe case of explosive logorrhea. Buggeroff sighed.

"Chief, you've actually used the right word," Stapley beamed.

What do you mean? I always use the right word, Buggeroff replied.

"Yes, of course, Chief. That's not what I meant. In more colloquial terms. I would rephrase my last statement as, 'You've nailed it, Chief,'" Stapley explained. He was not entirely convincing.

"Buggeroff?" Master Loo asked gently.

"Sorry, Master. I was having a little chat with Stapley concerning what you were saying." This was not exactly a lie. "As a matter of fact, I have a question. I don't wish to challenge your reasoning, but what about all the stuff we learn... sorry, all the habits we form without making a mistake first? I'm talking about crossing a street in high traffic, or *jailwalking* as it is also known."

"It's 'jaywalking,' Chief," Stapley stage-whispered.

That's what I said, Buggeroff whispered back.

"A very good question," Master Loo sighed. "Indeed, you don't necessarily have to be hit by a car in order to learn how to time your illegal crossing just right. If anything, this proves my point even more by taking the necessity of committing a mistake completely out of the equation. Thank you for this wonderful example! I shall use it next time I deliver my theory on Habit Forming Through Successful Attempts. Does this name sound any better than the old one?"

"It's more academic and less personal. It sounds more like a dissertation title than a thing grandparents would tell their grandchildren."

"Right, right, of course." The Master nodded approval. "Now, before I forget, why don't you tell me more about the dinner invitation we have been tricked into accepting. Where is this place exactly?"

57. MASTER LOO

Just as Buggeroff had told him, the place was easy enough to find. In fact, it was so close that they could have walked there. Of course, this was not a sensible option for two reasons. The first reason was that Magicians were required by their status to travel in style, a rule with which Master Loo did not necessarily agree, but which he followed, nonetheless. The second reason — and quite a hard reason to dismiss — was the fact that, although Toronto was enjoying its hottest summer since Pleistocene, outdoor air conditioning had yet to be invented.

At the intersection of these two reasons there stood only one mode of locomotion: his modified Tesla Model S car, which was, indeed, very stylish and which also sported an A/C system capable of kick-starting an ice age all by itself.

"This is so easy to drive," Buggeroff said contently as he pulled out of the garage.

"I'm sure it is," Master Loo replied. He had been reluctant to allow his Scriptling to drive this jewel of a vehicle, but had just finished installing a collision prevention system of his own making, and this seemed like the best way to test it. Even though he was confident in his design, Master Loo could not help grabbing and holding his seatbelt as Buggeroff accelerated through the stop-all-way sign.

At least, that's what Buggeroff was on course to do when the car overruled his enthusiasm and braked with a terrible shriek. Master Loo made a mental note to calibrate the collision prevention system for gentler braking. After all, it is good to avoid an accident, but having your brain eager to escape through your nostrils was not a desirable course of action.

"I'll take that back," Buggeroff said. "The car is not responding well."

Master Loo coughed politely. "Tell me, Buggeroff, dear, do you see that octagonal, red sign to your right with the text STOP written in capitals on top of that diminutive, but perfectly readable, red label that says ALL WAY?"

"Of course, I see it, Master. You don't have to be condescending. But I also saw no car coming either way, so then what was the point in stopping?"

What exactly do you answer to that? Master Loo has always asked himself who those people who never stopped at the Stop sign were, and now he had his answer. It was people you knew, people whose opinion and judgment you otherwise respected. It was people who, once behind the steering wheel, abandoned all reason and turned into highway monsters, the same way a werewolf would react to the sight of the moon.

"Karronthropy," the inner voice remarked.

Say what? Master Loo replied curiously.

"Kàrron + ànthrōpos, which is old Greek for car-human, the inner voice explained. You were thinking about werewolves and I remembered how they are technically called lycanthropes, a word that comes from old—"

Old Greek. Lycos + ànthrōpos. Wolf-human. Indeed, an interesting point.

"Master?" Buggeroff said. "Was Tesla one of us?"

"You mean, Canadian?" Master Loo replied. "No, not really. He was born in what was then a Serbian territory occupied by the Austrian Empire."

"Ah, an Aussie," Buggeroff commented knowingly. "Do you know, the legendary rock band AC/DC comes from Australia, too. There must be something on that continent inspiring people to have an interest in electricity. AC/DC, you see? Alternating current / direct current."

"I said the Austrian Empire," Master Loo tried to clarify matters.

"And I heard you," Buggeroff replied. "Mind you, I didn't know they were ever an empire. Aren't they part of the Commonwealth, just like us? Anyway, that's not what I meant when I asked if Tesla was one of us. I was asking if he was a Magician."

Master Loo nodded as the car swerved automatically to avoid hitting a suicidal groundhog. "I can't tell for sure, but I suspect he was not a Magician."

"Why is that?"

"Well, you see, innovation usually comes out of struggle. You start with an idea, and then you rack your brain in search of a way to make that idea come to life. If Tesla were a Magician, he would not have had to struggle because Magic would have been the simple and readily available answer for all of his ideas."

"But he might as well have been a Magician struggling to make people's lives easier without having to rely on Magic."

"Perhaps, but that would have been an immensely selfless gesture for a Magician. By the same token, Babbage could have been a Magician, but it is hard to tell."

"Was Babbage the one who invented the *deference* engine?" Buggeroff asked as they reached their destination.

"It was the difference engine, not the deference engine. And no, what he actually designed was the analytical engine. Anyway, in case you are wondering why the car won't switch off, it's because you are attempting to park too close to that fire hydrant. Why don't you drive forward six feet or so?"

58. BUGGEROFF

Buggeroff had managed, during the last weeks, to get over the awe that Master Loo's mansion inspired in him, but he was in for another surprise. Master Sewers' house, which had until very recently belonged to Master Dung, was not necessarily bigger, but it was definitely more imposing. It was hard to tell exactly how the effect was achieved, but it seemed to Buggeroff that this worked in, more or less, the same way as the comparison between a giant panda and a gorilla, where both animals weighed roughly the same, yet anyone would know instinctively which one they shouldn't mess with.

"What are you doing?" his Master called after him.

"Trying to gain access to the house?" he replied in that floating-question sort of way, normally reserved for the slowest of interlocutors. "Traditionally, the door is considered a safe approach," he continued sarcastically.

"Of course, but not the front door," his Master ignored his cheek, as usual. "Magicians don't use the front door when visiting unless it is Halloween night on a leap year. Oh, it is also acceptable to use the front door when bringing terrible news or when planning an assassination."

"Yikes! All right, then by all means let's use the backdoor," Buggeroff said. "Maybe I should start reading those rules you keep mentioning."

"I don't see why not. It's fascinating reading," his Master commented.

They followed the alley of slab stone to the back, and soon enough they were facing a simple door whose only decoration was a sorry-looking welcome mat laid negligently in front of it.

Stapley, what is that stain? Buggeroff focused his attention on a dark, brown stain that occupied the center of the mat.

"Looks like a burn mark, Chief," Stapley replied. *"If you would just lean down a little bit and perhaps collect a sample, I could tell you more."*

Say what? Buggeroff replied, not exactly sure what Stapley meant by collecting a sample, but he could follow this train of thought no longer as the door opened, revealing a breath-taking and very animated Merkin.

"Come in, come in. I saw you when you parked. That's a gorgeous car, by the way. Isn't the backdoor rule just stupid?"

"Thank you, I see, thank you, and it's not for me to tell," Master Loo replied punctually to her invitation, two statements, and one question.

There was a moment's hesitation in Merkin's eyes as she forced herself to switch mental gears to an arrangement better suited for communicating with Master Loo.

"She appears to be making an effort, Chief," Stapley remarked. *"It could be that her Master chided her for the way she behaved last time."*

Buggeroff heard his assistant's words, but he treated them the same way one would treat background street noises or an academic lecture on the topic of advanced nose-picking. His entire attention was sucked in by the space-time singularity called Merkin, a space-time singularity that was now doing something that would have puzzled scientists all over the world — it winked. Yes, it definitely winked, and to his great surprise and relief, Buggeroff found enough strength to wink back.

"I shall mark this as remarkable progress, Chief. Not only did you not throw up upon making contact, but you have actually managed to establish the rudiments of a viable communication mechanism by reciprocating her friendly gesture. I am proud of you, Chief!"

***

After the initial shock of seeing her, a shock that always swept him off his feet, things got gradually better to the point where he could actually make decent conversation and even drop the odd joke or two.

To her credit, Merkin was a wonderful listener, and she knew exactly how to make him feel at ease. She had invited him, nay, dragged him by his hand to her room, giving him no better explanation than that the two Masters needed to deal with their Mastery things. She was now sitting on the top of her bed with her legs folded sideways, little mermaid style, and was laughing at his clever comment about the ablative case and circular references.

"So, what's your Master like?" she asked when her laughter had subsided.

"What do you mean?"

"Well, is he laid-back, or is he very demanding? Does he let you get away with things or does he punish you? Stuff like that."

"Oh, no, he is very nice and relaxed. Perhaps just a little bit weird sometimes, but I guess we all are. Why do you ask? Does your Master punish you?"

"Ah, no, absolutely nothing of the sort," she replied with a dreamy look to her face. At the same moment, as small music box on her nightstand started playing a soft tune that Buggeroff did not recognize. He was about to ask her about it when she added, "But the old Master did punish me a lot. He was an evil son of a bitch, that old bastard."

Buggeroff was about to say something comforting to Merkin when a sudden pang of terrible pain flashed in his head. It had gone as soon as it had come, but it was enough for Buggeroff to miss the entry point into the conversation.

"So, how long have you been studying with Master Loo?" Merkin asked.

"Just a few weeks," he answered, rubbing his temples as if still fighting the echoes of that pain.

"How very interesting," she remarked, her face, a study in fascination. "And before that? Who was your mentor before Master Loo?"

"Amy Sharkowicz?" he answered, unsure whether that was the right thing to say.

"I don't think I've heard this name before. Is she Russian? What is her specialty?"

"I think she's of Polish heritage, and as for her specialty, she does make a mean Chai Latte."

"I'm not sure I follow you," Merkin curled her beautiful lips into a universal sign of doubt.

"Amy was my coach at the Second Cup store where I held a job for almost a year," he offered, aware that this was not going well.

To his surprise, the next thing Merkin said was not, "What the hell are you talking about?" Instead, she leaned close to him and asked in a soft, whispering voice, "Was she pretty?"

Her new posture revealed just enough cleavage to get the blood flowing out of Buggeroff's cognitive brain and straight into the other. His eyes lingered on the petite details of her stunning anatomy, but unlike those prudish girls he usually stared at in the subway, she did not seem to mind.

He managed to find his voice. "She was prettier than Master Loo, that's for sure."

"Ha-ha!" Merkin rolled her head back and laughed wholeheartedly. "You are such a goof! I like you!"

"I like you, too." His words came so fast that it took a while for the mind to analyze what he had just said, and then to come up with a suitable reaction, which, in this case, was a sizeable, crimson blush.

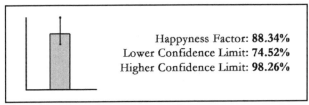

Happyness Factor: **88.34%**
Lower Confidence Limit: **74.52%**
Higher Confidence Limit: **98.26%**

"Well done, Chief," Stapley commented.

You don't need to be sarcastic about it, Buggeroff replied bitterly.

"Oh, but I'm not. Just look at her. She seems pleased with what you've just said." Stapley supported his statement by superimposing a transparent green layer over her eyes and mouth and displaying a legend in the bottom, right corner.

"At least according to my Facial Expression Reading Module," he added proudly.

Is that for real? Buggeroff could not believe his luck. *By the way, Stapley, just how many Modules do you have?*

"Following the last upgrade, I have been furbished with a total of fourteen individual Modules. However, at the present I sustain no less than twenty-three Modules. Before you ask where the difference comes from, you must know that one of the fourteen Modules installed by Master Loo was the Module-Designer Module which, as the name implies, is responsible for creating new Modules. I hope you find this explanation useful, Chief. Would you like to rate it in terms of usefulness with a mark from one to five, one being utter bollocks and five being the pinnacle of enlightenment?"

But before Buggeroff could think more about this newly found, extraordinary feature of his trusted assistant, he was interrupted by an outside stimulus he could not ignore.

It was a soft knock on the door, and Buggeroff had enough dramatic sense to know that whoever was doing the knocking would not wait for an invitation before opening the door. He was right, of course, and this fact became apparent when the door swung open and revealed the smiling, but, nevertheless, prying, face of Master Sewer.

"Dinner is almost ready," he announced ceremoniously, and then, in a more relaxed attitude he added, "Perhaps you two would like to join us downstairs for a nice appetizer."

***

It was a really nice appetizer, better than anything Buggeroff could remember. The drink was sweet, spicy, and very potent. Its most interesting characteristic, however, was that it presented the imbiber with the peculiar effect of double vision, an effect that lasted for several seconds following each sip.

"This is very good! What is it?" Buggeroff asked hesitantly. If this was something Magicians drank all the time, then the fact that he did not know what it was might reflect badly on him, but that was no reason to remain ignorant.

"I'm glad you like it." Master Sewer smiled genially. "It's a little cocktail of my own invention called the Parallel Port Wine. You will find it listed on the menu amongst the rest of the culinary delights I have assembled for the dinner."

"Oh, thank you," Buggeroff replied. He cast his eyes around in search for the menu.

"It is on the dinner table, Chief," Stapley whispered, understanding his boss's predicament.

There it is. Buggeroff pointed towards the dinner table and picked up one of the four, identical menus.

It was, as he had come to expect, printed in golden letters on a pitch-black, velvety paper. Of course, the jester hat motif had to be present, and Buggeroff now had sufficient information to deduce that this was Master Sewer's coat of arms just as the mouse with the Egyptian eye was Master Loo's.

The menu read as follows:

Parallel Port Wine

***

Unicode Soup

***

Arctic VarChar

***

Hexadent Chocolate Cake

"These are all computer puns," he remarked to the double image of Master Sewer as he took another sip of the delicious Parallel Port Wine.

Both Master Sewers seemed pleasantly surprised by Buggeroff's perspicacity. "Indeed, they are. Your Master did not tell me you were also skilled in the art of Computer Sciences."

59. MASTER LOO

"Well, yes, he is very talented," Master Loo said proudly but a little cautiously.

He had plenty of reasons to keep his guard high following the conversation he had just had with Master Sewer and especially in light of what he had learned outside the restaurant a few nights before, during the solstice festivities.

Do you think this will work? he asked his inner voice, who, despite being an annoying git, was also a good confidant.

"You will have to make it work," the inner voice replied.

At least the boy will be happy.

"Happy? He will be as excited as can be. Then again, I guess he is the one who will suffer the most. You can tell a mile away that the girl is one hell of a cock-teaser."

I am sure I would not put it quite like that, but I understand what you mean. She is, I am given to understand, a real prodigy, though, Master Loo replied.

"Capital!" Master Sewer exclaimed. "Then let us start with the first course and see who can identify the most characters."

For those unfamiliar with the peculiar game of Unicode Soup, here is how it is played. Each player receives a bowl of soup (traditionally tomato soup is used, but chicken soup works just as well) that contains exactly thirty-two pasta figurines representing different Unicode characters. The purpose of the game is to identify as many characters as you can and to call out their alphanumeric codes. While this is a fun game to play, in a geeky sort of way, Master Loo had always thought it made for a lousy culinary experience.

"My money is on Buggeroff," the inner voice called.

And the inner voice was very right, indeed. Although this had been Buggeroff's first ever Unicode Soup contest, he had scored an outstanding 96.88%, dwarfing everyone else's attempts. He had undoubtedly been taking unfair advantage of Stapley and his vast database, but it was not up to Master Loo to point that out, especially since Stapley's existence was supposed to be a secret known only to him and his Scriptling. Buggeroff could have very well scored a perfect 100% were it not for the altering effects the moisture in the soup had on the Telugu character CHA (చ).

When Master Sewer and Merkin exploded into a loud string of cheers and congratulatory remarks at Buggeroff's performance, Master Loo decided it was time to phase out of the conversation. It was high time for that, too, seeing as the next item on the menu was the Arctic VarChar.

Different versions of this dish had been a culinary attraction amongst Magicians for millennia. Whether it is called Poison Surprise, Omnes Pisces In Unum, or Fischüberraschung, this recipe has always delivered a fascinating experience to the brave gourmand. The dish has the deceiving appearance of a generic fish fillet and is normally served with freestyle garnishing. However, this is where similarities to any preconceived knowledge about fish cuisine stop. What makes the Arctic VarChar so unusual and popular is that each bite has a different taste. As you carve your way into the ersatz fillet, you might find yourself chewing on smoked salmon, tender tuna, marinated mackerel, seared snapper, raw roe, baked barracuda, grilled goldfish, or even pickled perch, to alliterate just a few.

Having the kind of brain to which sensory information comes screaming all at once like an endless barbarian horde, Master Loo regarded this recipe with mixed feelings. The taste explosion had a mind-numbing effect, effectively cutting out any form of communication with the outside and inside world of Master Loo. It was like blissfully blacking out in between bites. Of course, this, while a pleasant experience, presented plenty of risks, especially while in public. Master Loo decided to take the risk, counting on his natural talent for fading out of the conversation to the point of near social invisibility.

For the next minutes, fragments of conversation such as "…this is unbelievab…" or "…could eat this for the rest…" or "…be happy to show you…" or "…more wine?" came and went like annoying punctuation marks into the gastronomic dialogue between the Arctic VarChar and Master Loo. When the last bite of ubiquitous fish sang its flavored farewell song to his overexcited taste buds, Master Loo sighed appreciatively and eased back into his chair.

"This was a-ma-zing, Master!" Buggeroff exclaimed. "Can't wait to see what the Hexadent Chocolate Cake is all about."

Master Loo blinked rapidly in an effort to touch base with the outside world.

"Where is everyone?" he asked as he saw that only he and Buggeroff were present in the room.

"Huh?" his Scriptling's eyes bulged in surprise. "Weren't you here when they left?"

Master Loo felt embarrassment as he tried to find a decent explanation.

Buggeroff continued, "Stapley tells me you must have had one of your special moments. Don't worry, Master, I bet no one noticed."

Master Loo harrumphed for lack of a better answer.

"Anyway, Master Sewer is plating the dessert and Merkin went to help him."

"Thank you, Buggeroff! Thank you very much. I take it you are enjoying this dinner."

"Enjoying it doesn't even begin to tell the story. I love it! I can't thank you enough for introducing me, albeit quite violently, into this secret world of Magic."

"I'm glad you like it so much, although I must warn you that not every aspect of a Magician's life is so glamorous, or safe for that matter."

Buggeroff nodded and emptied the glass of Parallel Port Wine.

"By the way, I wanted to ask you something, you know, man to man," he said a couple of minutes later as he leaned closer and lowered his voice. "I don't want to jump to conclusions, but I think Merkin is beginning to take a shine to me. Could you keep an eye open and tell me what you think? Stapley tells me the numbers indicate an encouraging outcome, but you and I both know numbers are not enough when it comes to matters of the heart."

"I don't mean to be mean. Well, to be honest, I kind of do. Wouldn't you say they are taking an awfully long time plating the dessert? Just saying, you know? Completely out of context. You'd have to have a really dirty mind to draw any sort of facetious conclusion. I'm sure it's nothing," the inner voice said and then finished with nasty laughter, the kind of laughter you would expect from an old man who had just jumped into the alley from behind a thick bush, wearing a trench coat with nothing underneath.

"I am hardly an expert. I wish you the best of luck, though." After a short moment of hesitation, Master Loo said, "Just be careful, whatever you do. You have a young heart, Buggeroff, and to a young heart, love can be just like hot peppers, exciting on the way in and agonizing on the way out."

"That was uncharacteristically deep and metaphorically sound. Did you come up with it all by yourself?" the inner voice whistled appreciatively.

"Thank you, Master," Buggeroff nodded. "But I am not that young," he added with a slick smile.

"The fact that he is choosing to ignore a perfectly valid piece of advice shows just how young he is."

He will learn, sooner or later, Master Loo commented to himself. *After all—*

But his soliloquy was interrupted by the arrival of the Hexadent Chocolate Cake, which did not come by itself (although it would have taken a rather simple spell to achieve this feat), but rather accompanied by the two, smiling hosts.

60. MERKIN

Merkin knew exactly why Master Sewer was smiling. She would have taken it as a personal offence if he had not smiled.

As for her, her happiness derived from the way things were evolving. Indeed, as she applied herself to the task of offering her dear Master a piece of dessert sweeter than even the Hexadent Chocolate Cake, part of her mind had been paying attention to the eavesdropping spell she had planted under the dining table. Everything had been going according to plan, with Buggeroff falling head over heels for her, and with his Master incapable of instilling even the most basic common sense into his lustful mind. There were still a couple of things she did not understand, like who the hell Stapley was and what a Master Loo "special moment" meant. Still, this was nothing a little investigation during the next few days couldn't reveal.

But enough of that. For the time being, there were more immediate tasks at hand for her, tasks such as serving the dessert, for instance. Following the routine they had agreed upon, Merkin and her Master placed the four plates on the table and lifted the dome-shaped silver covers with well-practiced flourishes.

"Hexadent Chocolate Cake!" Master Sewer announced with great ceremony.

In contrast to the Arctic VarChar, there is nothing intrinsically Magical about the taste of Hexadent Chocolate Cake, although, in all fairness, most people will agree that sixteen layers of chocolate can hardly be called anything but magical. However, what with chocolate being such a finicky and time-sensitive material to work with, some degree of Magic is recommended, if not absolutely necessary, during the preparation process.

The fact that her Master had insisted on baking this special dish the traditional way, in other words, without accepting Merkin's offer to cast the occasional supporting spell, made it even more spectacular. But Master Sewer had not stopped there. As if the sheer amount of chemistry involved in this complex recipe were not enough, he had decided to up the ante by fashioning those sixteen, delicate layers of chocolate into seemingly solid golden ingots marked, of course, with his jester hat insignia. It was a veritable work of art, and it made Merkin very proud of her Master, who somehow managed to stay ahead of the game despite his handicap. If anything, it made her even more determined to do whatever she could to help him gain back his powers.

For a while, the diners were quiet as they made enthusiastic dents into the twenty-four carat, chocolate ingots. Merkin was surprised to see that no one, including herself, was making any comments about the awesome taste and presentation of this wonderful dessert, but then, as she was formulating the thought, she realized that the deep silence and the way in which it was punctuated by occasional lip-smacking, made a much more compelling argument in favor of everyone's satisfaction than a mere congratulatory remark would have made.

The spell lasted for a few more minutes. By that time, everyone was in such a mellow state that not even a family of earthquakes doing a conga line could have shaken them. It was then that, proving once again to be a great strategist, Master Sewer stood up and said, in a perfectly balanced and earnest voice, "Honored guests, loyal Scriptling, I have an important announcement to make."

He paused, as if trying to make sure he had everyone's attention. He need not have worried. If he had told them to take their clothes off and do a belly dance, they would probably have done so with only the slightest hesitation. Of course, Merkin knew for a fact that she would have very well done it, chocolate or no chocolate, but that was an entirely different matter.

"When the dreadful news that my dear, old Master Dung had passed away, it was like taking an irreversible plunge into the deep, black waters of despair and regret. With one merciless blow, Death had taken away from me a father, a friend, and a mentor. In moments such as this, it is only understandable if one allows dark thoughts to push their poisonous claws into the very essence of the soul. It seemed like nothing in this world could undo the damage, and I remember the little ember inside of me that was still sane facing the cruel decision of whether to switch off the lights. And then, as I was a hair's breadth away from flicking the switch, an unyielding force reached into the gloomy depths I found myself in and pulled me out, cleaned me up, and then set me on a right track."

He paused, allowing the drama to permeate his audience.

He continued in a trembling voice, "That force was the call of duty. In my selfishness, I did not realize that I was not the only one stricken by this tragic loss. Indeed, my late Master's Scriptling, who now sits beside me, was in an even drearier state than I was."

Sensing that it was required of her, Merkin nodded forlornly.

"Whereas I had status, a career, and – why be modest about it – the financial means to live my life the way I wanted, poor Merkin had none of these things. To her, everything was lost before it could even begin. But like I said, her curse had been my blessing; her misery, my salvation. In committing to take care of her, I found the reason for taking care of myself. In hindsight, I daresay we both benefitted from this arrangement." He turned and smiled at Merkin. She smiled back, sharing the private joke.

"Alas, I am afraid things are not meant to continue this way," he resumed. "When I took Merkin under my protection I pledged an oath to always do what is best for her. And now, I stand here and ask you this: how can I live up to my promise, when by keeping Merkin with me, I am actively preventing her from having access to the best possible form of education?"

He paused again, this time in order to allow a heavy sigh to escape from his chest.

"I will beat around the bush no longer. It was with great regret but with even greater hope that, less than an hour ago, I approached my most distinguished guest and friend, honorable Master Loo, with the request to take my promising star pupil, Merkin, under his knowledgeable and protective wing."

Merkin watched Buggeroff as her Master delivered this news, and she was pleased to see his pupils dilate to the point where he started bearing an uncanny resemblance to those manga cartoon characters.

"It is a credit to Master Loo's wisdom and kindness that he not only accepted this burden that I have forced upon his shoulders, but he did so with infinite grace. Merkin, I know it is not easy to switch through three different Masters in less than a month, but I have all confidence this is for the best. It is time for you to leave this house and all the lingering memories behind. Go and make your old Master Dung proud!" He finished his speech with the glint of a tear in the corner of his left eye.

Merkin did not see the tear. Her eyes were still on Buggeroff, and she was astonished to see him instantly reach for his forehead in an agonizing gesture that came and went in less than a second.

61. STAPLEY

"Aaaaaaaaarrrrrrrrggggghhhhhhh!" Master Dung cried. "The hypocrite! The demagogue! The maternal, fornicating bastard!"

"Calm down, Master," Stapley whimpered. *"You're hurting Buggeroff, and it shows."*

"Screw Buggeroff! Who cares about the little twit? Didn't you hear what this phony creature just said?"

Stapley had to admit that the usurper had tried, he really had, to keep calm while his former Scriptling delivered the speech. He even went so far as to force himself to regard the whole thing as a ludicrous affair, nothing but a light amusement, and the restraint had been effective until Master Sewer's last remark.

"Make me proud! Would you listen to that! Make... Me... Proud! Proud of what? Proud of having killed me?"

"Master, please," Stapley cowered.

"In my own house! Oh, wait 'til I get my hands on the two of them!"

"Precisely," Stapley intervened in a calm and persuasive voice. *"The time will come, and I am sure it will come pretty soon. But not now. We don't know if Buggeroff is ready. Can he face Merkin? Can he face her Master? I mean to say, her former Master."*

Master Dung took a deep breath and clenched his fists. For a moment, it seemed as if he were going to explode, but then, as he let out a long sigh, it became apparent that the danger had been averted.

"Well done, Master! Now, let us look on the bright side," Stapley said quickly, before the usurper changed his mind.

"There is no bright side," Master Dung groaned.

"Oh, but there always is. As the song goes—"

"Sing one note, and I will make sure you spend the rest of your life wishing you hadn't!"

There was one nanosecond in which Stapley struggled to bypass the *play* command. It was, in more mundane terms, like trying to beat the network speed in a game of Cancel the Print Job.

"I can see how singing might not be the best idea at the moment," he burbled. *"But there still is a bright side to all this, and it is the fact that you will now have Merkin under much closer observation."*

"I suppose so," Master Dung admitted reluctantly.

FOURTH TRIBAL INTERLUDE

It is the year 1975 and the Tribe have decided to spend their summer following Pink Floyd through their North American tour. Fop, the Tribe's foremost musician had come up with the idea, and they had all welcomed it wholeheartedly. They have all had millennia to refine their tastes in music, and these four English lads were playing just about the most sophisticated songs the Tribe had heard in centuries. It would have been a pity not to keep close to them and their boundary-pushing creativity.

Even so, the Tribe members knew one another too well not to suspect something else was going on. It is for this very reason that one warm, June afternoon in Montréal, Ina casually approached Fop and asked, "What are you up to, Fop?[28]"

"What do you mean?"

"Come on, man. You can lie to me if you want, but you can't lie to Spike," Ina said, holding the white Bichon Frisé, which was the Tribe leader's current incarnation, in her out-stretched arms as if he were some kind of holy relic, which he was, in a way.

Fop fell silent, a strategy that offered the double advantage of not having to lie to his leader, while at the same time not unveiling his secret.

"I saw you, you know? And it wasn't just me. Whenever you're close enough to Waters you start whistling this catchy, two-bar tune. Na-na-naah-na na-na-naah-na. ♪ D-E-F-E D-E-F-E ♪. So, I'm going to ask again. What are you up to?"

Fop remained silent. His face showed that she had hit the mark.

"Here is one more fact," she continued. "Less than eight years ago you and Rack ran into Paul McCartney in a public washroom. Of course, McCartney was wearing a disguise, but that never fooled you, did it? Now, Rack seems to remember how you stood two urinals away from the Beatle

---

[28] They were, for the sake of blending in, speaking Québécois French peppered with the occasional English neologism.

and how you started humming a simple, repetitive tune. Do I need to tell you what happened next?"

At this, Fop shrugged noncommittally.

"I'll tell you what happened. A few weeks later, their new tune hit the charts and went straight to the top. Interestingly enough, the song has this peculiar structure, with a coda that comes out of nowhere and then stretches for a few minutes. It integrates quite well with the song, though, and it is extremely catchy. Now, you know Rack. He has a very good memory. This is a rather important detail because, you see, Rack believes this coda, the na-na-na na at the end of the song, bears an uncanny resemblance to what you had hummed in that washroom. Note for note," Ina added, placing the shiny bate into the hidden trap.

"Note for note my foot!" Fop snorted before realizing what he was doing.

"Indeed," Ina beamed. "Although, The Beatles' version sounds amazing, Rack tells me yours had a slightly different cadence and two extra notes, which made it even better."

"So, what does that have to do with anything?" Fop asked.

"Well, it wasn't the first time, now was it?" Ina answered with another question. "I can think of a number of classical musicians who had a sudden stroke of genius around the time we passed through their towns, and, in some cases, villages."

"I'm not breaking any rules," Fob said defensively. He was right, of course, but that was only because the Tribe had no rules.

"I never said you were." Ina smiled benevolently. "My only question is, why don't you start your own band? The Tribe wouldn't mind[29] if you roamed free for one or two incarnations and followed your muse."

"I… I don't know, Ina. I'm not sure I could handle the fame. I would rather just whisper my tunes into the ears of accomplished musicians and then see what happens." He paused, and then added in a conspiratorial voice, "I only do it with the best, you know?"

"Yeah, I guess you do." Ina grinned while Spike, obviously satisfied with the results of this friendly interrogation, jumped from her lap and wandered off. "I will share my findings with the rest of the Tribe, as it is the custom," Ina said. "As for your tune, I would hurry up if I were you. The tour is coming close to an end."

"You're right about that," Fop said and turned to leave.

---

[29] Actually, the Tribe encouraged this. When you travel with the same thirty-six people for thousands of generations, things can get a little itchy.

"One more thing." Ina put her hand on his shoulder and held him in place as he turned to face her again. "The tune you're trying to plant into Waters' mind is not really what I would call Pink Floyd-ish. Aren't you afraid you might be missing the mark with this one?"

At this, Fop smiled wryly and tapped his nose knowingly.

"We shall have to see about this. It might yet become their most popular song ever, Floyd-ish or not." He chuckled, and then took his leave.

Ina did not try to stop him this time. She had satisfied her curiosity. No need to spend more time on the topic, especially now that the concert was about to start.

Time to mingle with the natives.

***

Ina was a woman. Not once, not twice, but many, many times a woman. Over time, she had given manhood a few, half-hearted tries, but she had long since decided she would stay a woman. It simply suited her better, just as it suited Aur, the Tribe's accountant, to be a man, or the way it suited Ping and Pong to reincarnate as twins all the time. Ina strongly believed that being a woman was an art form, and she considered herself the most accomplished artist in the world. She certainly had more experience than anyone else. Seduction, compassion, sacrifice, empathy, lack of sense of direction — she had mastered all these traits and many more. She was equally as proud of her contributions to the Kama Sutra as she was of her role in founding the Plakalshchitsy.

And right now, Ina was in a mood for random, carefree, inebriating, rock concert love. She cast around for a lucky guy but saw no suitable candidate. All the men were either too handsome or not handsome enough, too obviously in a relationship or too desperately not in one, too high or too serious.

So much for the random factor, she thought, just as the bleat sounds accompanied by the jazzy Rhodes piano tune announced that the concert was starting with "Sheep." A few seconds later the iterative bass riff made its subtle apparition, and by the time the drums signaled their fulsome presence, Ina was already banging her head to the hypnotic rhythm.

"Oops, I'm terribly sorry," said a voice as its owner bumped into her.

Ina turned her head, ready to throw a sharp remark, but stopped when she saw the impossibly thin, goofy-looking guy that sat meekly in front of her. She could also see the two fancy dudes sniggering beyond him, obviously very amused by this situation. She was ready to bet they had pushed the poor, defenseless guy into her as some sort of a practical joke and were now racking their brains for a way to turn this into a pick-up line.

She looked again at the guy who stood apologetically in front of her and decided that he would do.

"Don't be," she said, wrapping her arms around his neck. Then she planted a wet kiss on his open mouth. It had been a kiss of her own devising, a kiss that had been around for millennia before it became known as the French variety. "I'm Ina, by the way," she added when they broke free. She was not sure why she had given him her real name, but somehow it made sense at the time.

Behind him the two, slick guys gawked wide-eyed for one more moment and then shuffled somewhere else with their metaphorical tails between their legs.

"I'm Dave, Dave Watters," the dazed guy babbled.

"Are you kidding me? Dave Watters? At a Pink Floyd concert? Why not Roger Gilmour?" she laughed.

He did not appear to be upset by her joke. Instead, he nodded his head and said, "Indeed, this is a very apt association, what with two of the band members being called Roger Watters and Dave Gilmour, respectively."

Ina did not normally enjoy having someone explain to her why exactly her joke had been amusing, but something in the geeky way Dave delivered his remark made her smile.

"Besides, my other name is Singular," Dave continued. "I guess that kind of ruins the pun," he finished dejectedly.

She made her next move, knowing very well that men liked a direct approach. "Wanna go behind the trailers, Dave Singular Watters?"

"You know," he swallowed rapidly, "I really, um… really want to, but I'm here for the concert. I really want to, though. You know? For real! Can it just wait until after the concert?"

Now, that's unusual, she thought, *but intriguing nonetheless.*

"It's just that I came a long way by train to see the band," he continued, evidently feeling that he needed a very good explanation for refusing her unveiled proposal. "Hopefully I'll be catching up with them again in two days, but every experience counts, you know?" He watched her with begging eyes.

She smiled again and took his hand into hers.

"Let's enjoy the concert," she said. "Those trailers aren't going anywhere, at least for a while."

62. MERKIN

Saying goodbye to her Master had been a heart-breaking thing to do, and the fact that she had to conceal her emotions did not make matters any easier. She had known it would come to this ever since the plan's early stage. If there was one comforting thing about this, albeit in a rather twisted way, then it was the knowledge that Master Sewer was bound to suffer even more than she. At least she had the slight advantage that came from having to keep herself busy with the mission. He did not have that, and consequently, he would have much more time to pine over her.

The worst thing was that she could not tell how long this mission was going to last. Before making any sort of assumption, she would have to find out what it was about Buggeroff that could benefit her Master. Only after that would she be able to formulate a more precise plan. This whole uncertainty did not have a positive effect on her mood, not by a long shot; but no matter how she felt, she knew she would have to face the world smiling her best bimbo smile.

That, at least, was not hard at all. In fact, it had always worried Merkin just how naturally this whole thing came to her. Even now, as Master Loo's car took a left turn, she instinctively leaned her body towards Buggeroff and accidentally gave him a portion of what men cryptically called an "elbow boob." It had been an inconspicuous act, made even more natural by the fact that they were both sitting on the back seat of the car and that she was not wearing her seatbelt. The only unlikely factor (and one would have to possess a very keen mind to notice it) was that, what with her sitting on the right seat, the centrifugal force shouldn't have thrown her into Buggeroff, but away from him.

Master Sewer would have definitely noticed this, and he would have undoubtedly been very jealous. Merkin herself was not sure whether she had a good explanation for her desire to push the envelope further than necessary as far as Buggeroff was concerned. She was pretty sure she could get what she wanted from him without having to step out of the read-only zone of seduction. A smile here, a suggestive remark there, and she would have him eating from her hand. There was really no need for her to do more than that, yet she found herself unable to resist the temptation to use the heavy artillery. To make matters even worse, she was perfectly aware that there was no single way in which Buggeroff could outscore Master Sewer, whether in terms of physical or mental prowess. However she looked at it, her Master was more of a man than Buggeroff could ever hope to be.

But this was not a good time to start challenging her own morality or lack thereof. By now, Master Loo's electrical car was pulling into the garage. Buggeroff, out of the car first and then quickly around to hold the door open for her, held his chest high and was ready to utter something pompous, perhaps around the lines of "Welcome to your new home!"

"Welcome to your new home!" he said, as she got out of the car.

"Yes, welcome," Master Loo said with substantially less enthusiasm than his Scriptling, although, in all fairness, Buggeroff's enthusiasm could have outshone that of an incontinent puppy whose owners had just got home from a very long trip.

Merkin delivered a reply that was as charming as it was untrue. "It is an honor and a great pleasure to be here."

She followed her new Master through the mudroom into the kitchen while Buggeroff stayed behind to get her luggage, and – she did not have to verify to know it – to take one lingering look at her ass.

Master Loo stifled a yawn. "If you don't mind, I think I might be calling it a night. It has been a very exciting dinner, and I am not as young as I used to be."

To his credit, he did not pause to allow his Scriptlings to fake protests about his age, the way Master Dung would have surely done.

"Buggeroff, dear, please be so kind as to show Merkin around. Good night, everyone!"

"Good night, Master," the two Scriptlings chorused.

Buggeroff started the tour of the mansion for lack of anything better to say. "So, this is the kitchen and dining area. Down the hallway you have Master Loo's study and library plus the living room. There is a two-piece washroom next to the pantry that we don't use for hygienic reasons, the washroom, not the pantry, that is. There is also a three-piece washroom between the study and the library in case you ever feel like taking a shower in the middle of any captivating reading. Ah, yes, the library – it can be accessed only through the study or through a secret latch door from Gertrude's room in the basement. Gertrude is indisposed at the moment, so you will have to use the study door, but that's OK because the Master doesn't mind being interrupted. In fact, he would probably not even notice it if you passed through quietly enough."

Merkin felt her mind spinning under the whirling effect of too much information. It was pretty obvious that Buggeroff was in desperate need of someone to talk to, and while this bore clear benefits for her mission, it was also wearing.

"Gertrude?" she asked, trying to make sense of at least one, hazy item in his odd depiction of the main floor.

"Oh, that's Master Loo's goat. She thinks she is a snake, though. I used to call her a Chupa-Cobra for that reason, but she is actually very friendly in a woolly sort of way. She likes to chew sleeves... er... any sort of fabric, to be honest, so be careful where you leave your clothes."

Merkin had heard of such animals before, but it had been a long time since she had been so close to seeing one. There was a time when Magicians had been very keen on keeping a familiar around, but the popularity of the practice had been slowly decreasing over the last century for reasons of increasingly harsh city sanitation rules. There was a definite mystic aura about having a familiar, and Merkin felt strangely attracted to the idea despite the fact that, as a little girl, she had resolutely refused the unicorn her parents had bought for her five-year anniversary. She had specifically asked for a fire elemental, and even though her parents had patiently explained to her that fire elementals had been banned ever since the Library of Alexandria incident, she had remained adamant. The little unicorn had been returned to the magical pet store the same day, and the subject had never been mentioned again.

"You said she was indisposed?" Merkin asked.

"Um, yes," he said, showing some mild signs of discomfort. "It's that time of the month, if you know what I mean." His voice implied that it was expected of her to know what he was talking about.

No, she did not know what he meant, and, judging by his mannerism, she was quite sure he didn't, either.

He fell back into his realtor persona. "Anyway, that's the main floor. The basement is fully sound proofed and it consists of Gertrude's quarters, a state-of-the-art gaming room, the lab, laundry facilities, a two-piece washroom, and a wine cellar, which, although modest in size, is anything but modest in its contents."

"I should very much like to see that." Merkin smacked her lips in anticipation.

"I'm afraid we would need Master Loo's permission for that. However, there is cold beer in the fridge, and then, of course, there is always the liquor cabinet in the study, of which I don't recall any rule against using."

"That's OK, it's really wine that I had in mind, but it can wait." She yawned, "Actually, I think I might want to catch some z's myself. I'll take whatever bedroom is closest to yours," she added, knowing very well how prone guys were to interpreting this kind of statement as something it was definitely not.

"A… Are you sure?" he babbled, unable to control the excitement in his voice. "I mean, there are four bedrooms on the second floor and a large apartment in the attic," he offered, trying to play the gallant.

"Let me guess, each bedroom has an ensuite bathroom, right?" she asked.

"How did you guess?" he replied, and to her surprise, he did not seem to be facetious.

"Oh… I suppose… I mean, that's the way most houses are built," she said.

"Magician houses, perhaps, or houses belonging to very rich people," Buggeroff commented.

"I—" For as long as she could remember, except for her junkie time in Europe of which she did not remember a lot, she had been surrounded by Magicians and rich people. To her dismay, she realized that she had never been in a *regular* house. Sure, she had seen them on TV, but somehow she had never made the connection. Buggeroff on the other hand…

"Before moving here, I shared a basement apartment with a friend of mine," he explained. "There was a bathroom, but trust me, you don't want to know the details. It was still better than what I had before, though…"

"Excuse me. Just how exactly did you come to be Master Loo's Scriptling?"

63. BUGGEROFF

"What do you mean?" he replied defensively.

"Careful here, Chief. These are things she mustn't know. You have already allowed her to learn too much," Stapley warned him.

"Excuse me," Merkin said demurely. "I didn't mean to offend you with my question. It's just that you appear to be different. Not in a bad way. Just different, you know?"

"Is this a class difference issue? Is it because I don't come from a wealthy family the way most Scriptlings do?" Buggeroff's words came straight from his proletarian soul.

"That is exactly why I tried to stay away from this question. It is all too easy to strike that sensitive chord in people of your background."

The last words had a harsh, chauvinistic ring to them, but the way she had spoken them was gentle. Buggeroff did not know what to make of this mixed signal, and he was even more confused by the turn this conversation was taking. It wasn't as if he had been expecting hanky-panky, not that soon at any rate, but he had also not been expecting quarrelling either.

"All right, let me try to fill in the blanks here," she said in an almost maternal tone. She took him by the hand and seated him in one of the chairs at the big table in the dining room. She sat next to him, still keeping his hand in hers.

"Obviously you haven't been in this for too long, although even as I use the word 'obviously,' I realize that I am doing it rather liberally. Allow me to explain. I can only infer from the scarce details you have seen fit to share so far that you have been studying under Master Loo for a few weeks. On the other hand, you exhibit the kind of magical prowess that would normally take more than a year to develop. Faced with this conundrum, I naturally had to assume Master Loo was not your first Master, only to have my assumption contradicted by your story about working at Second Cup. I was then left with the unlikely scenario in which you had been born into a well-known Magician's family, which would account for your talent. In this case, your job at Second Cup must have been just a self-appointed lesson in humility, meant to increase your willpower. But then I saw the way you marveled at things that I, who had been lucky enough to be raised by a well-off family, had always taken for granted. It then follows that you do not come from a wealthy family, which automatically excludes the possibility that you would come from a Magician's family."

She paused, as if inviting him to take the lead and turn this monologue into a conversation, but Buggeroff was too fascinated by the cold, precise way in which she had just dissected his persona to say anything.

"So, I suppose you must be one of those very rare people to which Magic occurs naturally, without its running in the family, as it were. Is that so?" she asked.

What do I answer to that? Buggeroff mentally inquired his assistant.

"Say something non-committal, or something that's true without being the whole truth," Stapley suggested.

"I've never met my parents," Buggeroff said levelly. "For all I know, they might have been Magicians, but there is no way I would ever know for sure."

"Not fair, but a great move, nonetheless."

64. MERKIN

Damn it! Damn, damnity, damn it! With one sentence he had blown away all her carefully built scaffolding. She took a deep breath and considered her position. It did not look good at all. Not only had she lost all momentum, but she had been left completely exposed. She had slowly worked her way up to the point where she could ask him the really important questions (such as how did Master Loo find him or how come he had learned so many things in such a short time), and in the process she had assumed this gentle, friendly, and caring persona that she was now forced to maintain lest he become suspicious.

She did not fancy looking him in the eye right now, so she cast her glance down, only to realize that she was still holding his hand. Where do you go from here? What would a truly gentle, friendly, and caring person do now?

And then it came to her. It came from the same place her other identities came, and although she had far less practice in this role than she had in her slutty, tomboy, or sophisticated skank roles, it still fit her like a glove.

She gave him a hug, which was a rather cumbersome move to attempt from her seated position, but she managed to include the core elements[30]: one hand around his neck, her warm cheek next to his, and their knees touching.

"I am sorry, Buggeroff," she whispered in his ear. "I didn't mean to upset you."

"It's not your fault," he said kindly. "And by the way, it's Simon."

---

[30] We don't normally think about it, but our bodies know on an intuitive level that there must be at least three points of contact for a hug to claim any sort of legitimacy. Professional climbers know the three-points-of-contact rule very well, but in their case, the choice is simple: if they don't embrace the rock wall, gravity will embrace them instead.

It took a moment to understand what he had meant, but when the meaning became apparent, her first thought was, "BINGO!"

The balance of power had unexpectedly shifted back in her favor, thus proving there was some merit, after all, in playing the nice guy, or girl, as it were. Contrary to popular belief, knowing a Magician's true name will not grant you limitless power over him, nor will it render you immune to his spells. There is, however, a subtler form of Magic in a name, and it lays hidden in all those little things we unknowingly associate with our names. It is the kind of Magic that glues society together, the Magic of trust, willingness to help, peer pressure, and mild obedience.

"Thank you, Simon," she said and patted him on the knee. And then, before he had a chance to ask her true name, she knew she would have to deploy the *pièce de résistance*. She sighed, deeply and passionately. It was a sigh that women have passed on from mother to daughter since the dawn of time, crafting it to perfection. It was the sigh men had been genetically programmed to respond to with, "Are you all right?"

"Are you all right?" Buggeroff asked, right on cue, suddenly worried.

"Oh, I'm fine," she said whilst displaying all the signs to the contrary. "It's just that…" She sniffled.

"Yes, what's wrong?" he pressed on like a clueless, but determined, insect marching into a Venus Flytrap.

"My parents…" Merkin drew in a spasmodic breath. "They, too, are gone," she said and instantly hated herself for doing it. It had been a strong card to play, and she wasn't even sure it had been the right moment to deal it. But strategy aside, she felt dirty for having used the memory of her parents in this manner.

Buggeroff stood silent for ten, very long seconds, apparently caught in the struggle caused by too many words begging to be spoken at the same time from only one mouth.

When he eventually opened his mouth to answer, she knew even before his words came out that she had lost this round. She saw it in the way in which his entire posture made the split second shift between a boy and a man.

"It has been a long day," he said. "I'd better show you to your room."

His voice was warm and kind, but Merkin felt the unfamiliar cold shivers of defeat putting her strong ego in check. This was supposed to be her own game, her main specialty. She should have mopped the floor with Buggeroff in this battle of guile, but somehow he had managed to stay on top and deflect all her blows. If anything, she had defeated herself. She had lit the fuse, but, in the end, he could not be tricked to take the stick of dynamite from her hand.

"I guess you're right." She nodded, fighting for control over her reaction. She wanted to do something that would turn this whole thing in her favor, but nothing came to mind. Her usual responses — be sexy, be mean, and be clever — simply did not fit the bill. She had tried being clever, but she had been outclevered by Buggeroff, who didn't even seem to have a clue as to what he had just done. Being mean was out of the question, at least for now, because that was the path of no return. Sexy? Well, there was no doubt Buggeroff would have done anything to have her, yet somehow Merkin knew it would be unwise to deploy her most powerful weapon so early in the game.

For now, she would have to lick her wounds and think things over. As she climbed up the stairs to her bedroom, Buggeroff leading the way, her thoughts flew to Master Sewer. She could really use some of his resourcefulness right now, not to mention some of his other qualities.

65. MASTER SEWER

Because Narrative is such a finicky lady, at the exact same moment, Master Sewer was not thinking about Merkin. Master Sewer had been thinking about Merkin for the previous half-hour, and he would resume thinking about her in a minute or so, but just at the moment, his mind was overwhelmed with pain, a pain that had been indirectly caused by thinking of her.

Whoever said that love hurts must have been a wise person, but as Master Sewer rolled on the floor with his hand cupped around his toes, he was willing to bet that said wise person did not have domestic accidents in mind – accidents such as stubbing one's toe on the table leg because one's thoughts were somewhere else. It was astonishing, he thought, how evolution had neglected the obvious task of strengthening such a sensitive piece of anatomy as the pinky toe, especially when the little bugger was so prone to accidents in the first place.

If only he could Magic the pain away. That thought brought Merkin back into his mind. Merkin!

Like anyone who has ever been in that early stage of being in love, he was incapable of coalescing the object of his passion into a single idea, and thus his mind was caught in the never-ending whirlwind of images and sensations that made up his interpretation of Merkin. He could not tell which he loved more, her sexy mind or her sexy body, the way she walked or the way she curled up lazily in a sofa, the way she smiled or the way she pouted – so he kept dedicating fervent odes to each of Merkin's traits as they came to his mind.

By the time Master Sewer was done praising the perfection of Merkin's bellybutton for the twenty-third time, his common sense had finally gathered sufficient strength to get a solid grip on the steering wheel of focus. It had taken over an hour, and it hadn't been an easy task. Even so, the fight for control was not yet over. What Master Sewer desperately needed now was something to keep his mind occupied, something that would provide both purpose and relief. In one word, what Master Sewer desperately needed, was work.

Ah, good old hard work! Nothing quite like it to hijack one's mind from matters of the heart, bladder, and stomach. A good, solid day's work can leave someone hungry, dehydrated, and abandoned by all friends, but at the same time, strangely elated. It is a secret well known by big corporations and other slave herders alike, and it has been distilled into a science often referred to as Project Management, or Resource[31] Allocation.

The first job Master Sewer applied himself to was to clean up after the party, but the task was soon over, and it naturally failed to provide a satisfactory kick. Time to think big.

Then it came to him. After so many weeks of neglect, he finally had time to dedicate himself to his big project, that of building the ultimate computer virus, with the distribution method issue out of the way, thanks to Merkin's elegant solution.

Oh, Merkin. Sweet of lip, smooth of skin and silky of hair. Merkin.

All right, FOCUS!

He could start working on the first code draft, and the beauty of it was that he didn't even need his magical powers for that. His trusty spellchecker would be just the thing for the job.

He rubbed his hands together and headed upstairs to his room where his laptop, should it have known what laid in store for it, would have purred its CPU fan in anticipation.

---

[31] What a cynical term!

66. MERKIN

"SECRETUM.REVELARE();" she whispered, to no apparent effect.

"YAVIT.PAROL(); BUZUR.DAH();" She deployed the heavy Slavonic and Sumerian guns in frustration, but again, to no avail.

She hadn't really expected the spells would work, but it is one thing to make a pessimistic assessment, and it is an altogether different matter to find out that you have been right in doing so.

***

At this moment, it would perhaps be worthwhile to rewind Merkin's story to about five minutes prior to this scene.

She woke up with that feeling of gratitude reserved chiefly for when you realize that all those monsters chasing you were just part of a dark dream that was now over. She took a deep breath, forcing herself not to fall asleep again. She knew that if she succumbed to sleep, the nightmare would resume with renewed strength.

A car drove slowly down the street, its lights casting unfamiliar shadows on the ceiling of Merkin's new room. She checked her phone for any missed calls or messages, but apparently Master Sewer had been serious when he had declared radio silence. Stupid rule! Would it be so wrong if she were to send him a sext right now? Surely he would appreciate it. Perhaps just a little one, something around the lines of "I'm not wearing—" No! If she allowed herself to start thinking about that kind of stuff she would soon find herself calling for a cab, and… and the rest of it would look really desperate on her behalf. Nope, she was better than that. Desperate acts are patently part of a man's emotional toolkit, and they should never be attempted by a self respecting woman. Come to think of it, they shouldn't even be attempted by men, but would they listen?

She was wide awake by now, so she got down from her bed and walked to the window. Glancing absently at the empty street she tried to make sense of the last day's events. No matter how she looked at it, one thing was sure: she needed more data, and there surely was none to be found in this room.

She cast her favorite noise-cancelling spell. "SONITUS(FALSUS);." Then she snapped her fingers to test that it had worked.

Satisfied that all was fine, she proceeded soundlessly downstairs towards Master Loo's study. Once there, she paused and weighed her options. She could not investigate the room in the dark, but at the same time none of the obvious choices, such as turning the lights on or casting a night vision spell, were appealing. Switching on the light would attract unwanted attention, while casting another buff spell on top of her existing noise-cancelling spell was not an easy trick to pull off[32], even for someone of her skill.

Reluctantly, she cancelled the muffling spell and cast the night vision one instead.

Moving as quietly as she could on the tips of her toes, she started rummaging through the pile of papers on the desk and through the cabinets. Her heart stopped for a moment when an old floorboard creaked under her weight, but after ten, long seconds during which she dared not breathe, she had to concede that she was probably safe.

The papers revealed nothing of importance. They were mostly bills, random pieces of code, and doodles of various shapes and sizes. She closed her eyes, trying to concentrate on what to do next.

The laptop! She lifted the lid and was instantly blinded by the bright colors on the screen. Cursing under her breath, she revoked the night vision spell and reactivated the muffling spell for good measure.

She blinked rapidly to adjust her eyes to the new conditions. Then she read the message on the screen. Not surprisingly, it said, "Please enter the password," followed by an input field and two buttons that read, "OK," and, "I forgot my password".

This is where Merkin found herself at the beginning of this chapter. When the three hacking spells failed to deliver, she shook her head in a bitter gesture and grudgingly clicked the "I forgot my password" button.

A message window popped up, with text written in jolly capital letters.

"YOUR MEMORY'S A STUBBORN ASS,

PERHAPS YOUR BRAIN'S BEEN HURT.

THE WORD YOU SEEK SO YOU MAY PASS

---

[32] It is relatively easy to cast a powerful spell that lasts for less than a second, but maintaining a buff spell for a long time is actually quite tiresome. Some practitioners are capable of sustaining two such spells at a time, but Magicians are generally encouraged to of think alternative options rather than risk spell fatigue.

IS BUT A NINE-LETTER TROLL DESSERT."

"Yeah, that was really helpful," she thought, putting a mock inflection on "really." All she had to do now was find an encyclopedia of culinary traditions amongst mythical folk. A piece of cake…

Cake: now that was a dessert, to be sure. Alas, it was not a trollish dessert. Besides, didn't everyone know that trolls eat humans? She concentrated, looking for obscure word associations or anything that might provide a clue, but her mind was weary, and in response to her queries, it chose to present a long bill of recent activities, at the bottom of which stood a total sleep balance of ten hours (gratuity not included).

Merkin knew better than to argue. She also knew that solving a puzzle was not the kind of activity where brute force held the answer. No siree! Puzzles are sneaky little bastards, and, therefore, it stands to reason that you need to be a sneaky big bastard if you want a fair chance at unraveling them. You need to look away and act as if you don't care, while at the same time allowing your subconscious mind to observe through the rearview mirror of intuition.

Right when Merkin was about to break into megalomaniac laughter caused by this self-proclaimed, profound stream of consciousness, her attention was drawn to something so incongruent, yet intimately familiar, that her voice choked with bewilderment.

Hardly believing her eyes, she got down on her knees, then slowly extended her arm and gingerly picked the dark piece of fabric from under the corner of the carpet. She pulled gently, taking her time, as if not wanting to recognize the object. Alas, when the words "Small Opening" written in a circus poster font crawled into view, she could no longer deny the reality.

"What are you doing here?"

It was not, sadly enough, the voice of Merkin speaking to her discarded pair of panties about their current whereabouts in relation to where she had last seen them, namely in a dark alley behind a restaurant.

67. MASTER LOO

"What are you doing here?" Master Loo asked in his usual, level voice as he switched on the light.

"What does it look like she's doing?" the inner voice commented. *"I can offer three possible answers: (a) She is chasing butterflies. (b. She is baking a cherry and poppy seed strudel. (c) She is spying on you. There, SEE if you can spot the right one."*

Merkin raised her eyes from the floor, looking so frightened that Master Loo began to feel a pang of guilt at having caused this reaction.

"There, she put something in her pajama pocket," the inner voice jumped up and down. *"Ask her what it is! Ask her to hand it back!"*

It looked like a pair of panties, Master Loo replied calmly. *I'm sure they weren't mine, so why should I bother her about it?*

Merkin opened her mouth to speak, but no words came out. For a moment, confusion joined panic in the eerie dance that played across her face, but then a new emotion entered the stage, outshining all others. It showed only for the breadth of a second, but so bright was it that it remained visible on Master Loo's face-reading retina for a long time. It was the emotion so often depicted by cartoon artist as a light bulb popping into existence above the character's head.

"Where am I?" Merkin regained her voice.

"Oh, p-lease!" the inner voice scoffed.

"You are in my study," Master Loo said patiently. "A little bird told me I might find you here," he added, looking to his side where Gertrude made a sudden appearance, made even more dramatic by the fact that she was slithering on the carpet in Merkin's direction.

"You... You must be Gertrude," Merkin said with surprising calm, although she could not help taking a step back at the sight of the approaching goat. "Very nice to meet you. As for me, I must have been sleepwalking again," She continued to press backwards.

"Ah, sleepwalking." Master Loo nodded. "Well, I guess that clears the mystery. By the way, are you sure you haven't meet Gertrude before? She acts as if she knows you." He indicated the goat who was now coiling around Merkin's legs, climbing upwards.

"I.... I'm sure I would have remembered."

Just as Merkin finished speaking, Gertrude's muzzle reached into her pajama pocket and, with no small amount of tugging, extracted the pair of panties Merkin had been trying to conceal. Still holding them in her mouth, Gertrude looked up into Merkin's eyes while Merkin looked back into hers with terror.

68. MERKIN

She recognized those milky eyes and that unkempt beard even though last time she had seen them they had been affixed to a hobo's face. Even the smell seemed familiar now, although to be fair, it carried only a hint of the blanket she'd had to wear a few days ago.

As she continued to look into Gertrude's eyes, she somehow became aware that they were broadcasting the unmistakable message, "These are mine!"

This, Merkin had to conclude, must have clearly been in relation to the panties.

"Of course, they're yours," Merkin's eyes beamed back, still confounded by this whole new development. "You've won them, fair and square."

"Square behind the ear," Gertrude's eyes sparkled bitterly in an amazing feat of ophtalmopathy.

"I'm sorry about that," Merkin whispered.

"Excuse me?" Master Loo asked.

Gertrude gave Merkin one last, meaningful look, then she winked and uncoiled from her waist and elegantly slithered down her legs to the carpet.

Those pajama pants will need a thorough washing and no mistake about it, Merkin thought.

"I said I was sorry about that," Merkin repeated, louder this time. "I did not wish to wake you up, Master."

"That's all right," Master Loo waved his had dismissively. "It wasn't you who woke me up, but rather Gertrude, who was only doing her job. Good girl, Gertrude!"

"I shouldn't be here." Merkin looked around.

"Nonsense! You were sleepwalking. Besides, please feel free to come here as often as you like. There are lots of interesting books for you to read, some of them pretty rare, too."

"Thank you, Master," said Merkin, who couldn't believe how gullible the old man was.

"Oh, and by the way, if you want to use the Internet, the guest password is severalspeciesofsmallfurryanimalsgatheredtogetherinacaveandgroovingwitha pict. One word, no capitals." Master Loo pointed towards the laptop whose lid was still up.

Was that a subtle attack or just another manifestation of Master Loo's naivety?

She decided to continue acting the innocent. "Thank you, Master. I didn't even notice there was a laptop in here."

"That's curious." He rubbed his chin. "I always leave the lid closed. Well, never mind. It may very well be that you suffer from a rare form of somnambulism."

"What do you mean?" she asked, trying to keep him talking while she thought of the next move.

"Well, now that you ask, I believe a more suitable term would be *parasomnia*, as it encompasses more than merely somnambulism. I suspect you might be afflicted by a newer type of sleep disorder, characterized by an urge to use the computer. Humanity evolves in mysterious ways. I wonder what the name should be for this new condition, should you indeed suffer from it."

"Youvegotmailitis?" Merkin tried to sound serious.

"Not bad, not bad at all," Master Loo nodded approvingly. "No one said it has to be a Latin or even a Greek word. It's as good a name as any other. Quite catchy too — youvegotmailitis. Yes, a good one!"

Is he for real? Merkin asked herself.

"Thank you, Master," she said for the third time since this unlikely conversation had started, for no other reason than that she couldn't find anything better to say.

"You don't have to thank me, it was your idea. I suppose I should go back to sleep, now that everything seems in order." When he saw her move as if to follow him, he added, "You don't have to do the same, I'll leave the light on if you want me to."

"I—" Merkin began. Then she felt something tugging at her leg. She looked down and saw Gertrude, whose eyes beckoned her to wait. "I think I'll stay for a while."

"See you in the morning, then," Master Loo replied. "Don't keep Gertrude up for too long, though. Now that she is back amongst us, I'm sure Buggeroff will want to make up for lost time, and that would require a lot of energy on her behalf. Good night to both of you!"

"Good night, Master!" Merkin said to the disappearing shape of Master Loo. She felt, not for the first time since arriving to this house, as if some facts were actively and purposefully eluding her. What on Earth did he mean by Buggeroff making up for the lost time with the goat?

"Before you get the wrong idea, he means taking me out for a walk," the spiffily dressed man said from next to the drinks cabinet where Gertrude had stood just a moment ago. "Brandy?" he added, giving the leather-bound canteen in his right hand a meaningful shake.

The last time Merkin had seen this man, he had been knocked out on the cobblestones of a side alley with a pair of panties, her panties, tucked under his chin. It had been her roundhouse kick that had put him on the ground, and it had been her tormented conscience that had pushed her to leave him the unlikely souvenir.

"Sure, what the hell." Merkin accepted the bottle and took a long swig from it. "Gertrude, I presume?"

"Actually, it's Gerhardt when I'm wearing this form. And you, although we've never been properly introduced, must be Merkin. I knew your mother."

"So, you're not just a goat who thinks she is a snake, but you are also a goat that turns into a man. *Aiganthropus Aigafidi*," Merkin tried her hand at taxonomy.

"You forgot to mention that I can become invisible," Gerhardt observed. "As for turning into a man, I can only do it for an interval of a few days each month, six days if I'm lucky. Still, it's better than nothing, I presume. Did I mention I knew your mother, by any chance?"

At this, Merkin's heart stopped and her mouth gaped. She had heard him the first time, but his words had been so out of place that her brain had decided to choose the sensible option, which was to ignore them completely.

She finally managed to speak. "H... How?"

FIFTH TRIBAL INTERLUDE

It was winter, and it was Canada, but Ina had seen far worse than that. She and Dave had been living happily together for the last six months, and that was all that mattered. Despite his goofiness and sporadic weirdness, he made her happy and she, in turn, made him happy as only she knew how.

They had recently moved into a large, Torontonian house that Dave bought for cash. Yes, it turned out he was pretty wealthy, an inheritance of sorts, of which Ina had never learned all details, despite scarcely concealing her curiosity. But that was not the whole story of how he came to afford this gorgeous house. The real story was that Ina had played a rather significant role in making this possible. In short, what Dave had taken for amazing negotiating skills on his behalf had actually been a few words spoken by Ina in Mama, the Tribe's language. Not only did her words get him the house, but they also produced a success that had worked wonders on his self-esteem.

And now, Ina was sure that Dave was working up the courage to ask her to be his wife. Thousands of marriages, and an even larger number of proposals, had taught Ina how to recognize the signs way before even the confused wannabe husband had any clue about his own intentions. Far from being bored with this ageless ritual, she absolutely loved it. It was one of the most beautiful ways in which a man could surrender his power to his woman. It wasn't the kneeling down that came with the proposal, but rather the emotional ordeal that led to this conclusion. It was the stuff life bonds are made of.

Of course, Ina was an incurable romantic and thus the reader should be warned to take some of her interpretations with a grain of salt, and perhaps a teaspoon of powdered chili peppers for good measure.

That day, Dave came home later than usual. His breath carried the fine, woody aroma of old scotch, but he was not drunk, perhaps just a little bolder than his normal self — about one-and-a-half ounces bolder, to be more precise.

261

Ina knew what this meant, and her heart skipped a beat as he took her by the waist and gave her a big, sloppy kiss.

"And how was your day, honey?" she asked him in response to his kiss.

He was taken aback. He had obviously rehearsed a nice, little heartfelt speech, and maybe he had even anticipated some kind of dialogue that would lead to said speech. But it was now clear that her opening line did not feature in his script. Poor thing.

She decided to lend him a helping hand. "You look as if you want to tell me something." She could have toyed with him some more, but he really didn't deserve it.

"Yes," he said, sounding relieved. "Would you mind if we move to the library? I don't like standing in the door like this."

For all that his intentions were as transparent as thin air, she had to give him credit for going out of his way to try being cunning. The library, now that he mentioned it, was a great choice. Very romantic place, the library, and not just because there was scarcely a square foot in that room that they hadn't already consecrated to one erotic activity or another. It was also the room in which they had spent endless hours engaged in fascinating conversations on a beautiful multitude of abstract and mundane subjects.

"Sure thing, honey," she replied, taking care to add just the right amount of confusion in her voice so as not to raise suspicion.

They walked hand in hand. Dave almost dragged Ina behind him, so excited was he. Once in the library, he could bear it no longer, so he dropped his act and also dropped on his knee.

"Ina," he began, and his face relaxed into a dreamy smile, same as it always did when he spoke her name. He hit the play button on his rehearsed speech. "These past six months have been the most..." The speech didn't sound as great as he had imagined it would. "Gosh, Ina," he broke into the freestyle alley, "sometimes, when you're gone for even a minute, I sit there and wait fearfully for you to come back just to make sure you still exist and that all this is not just a dream."

"Oh, you sweet thing, you." She caressed his cheek with loving fingers.

"I want us to be together," he resumed in a trembling voice. "I want us to be the same. I want us to share everything." He reached into his coat's chest pocket.

She could hardly contain her excitement now. In hindsight, perhaps she should have.

"Ina, my dear, I want to make you a gift that no other man can offer you," he finished as he pressed the miniature crossbow under her left breast and released the trigger.

There was joy and excitement in his eyes as he caught her before she could hit the floor. Animated by pure bliss, he carried her down the stairs to the basement.

"Soon, my love," he whispered. "Soon we will be united in the power I was sworn to hide from you. But no more! I shall raise that power in you and there will be no more secrets."

"What the hell is he talking about?" Ina's ghost howled angrily as she followed him.

Gently, he placed her body on the basement floor and took a reverential step backward.

"INCIPE.RITUM();" he said, making a pompous hand gesture.

And then she understood. How could she not have seen it before? How could she not look for it? Her vulnerable, little Dave was one of them, one of the Descendants.

She stood there, watching his spells unravel, and she was completely taken aback when she finally realized what it was that he was trying to do. He was trying to imbue her with his own power. He wanted to make her a... what was it that they called themselves in these parts? A Magician. Oh, dear, sweet, kind, devoted Dave! How could she be upset with him when it had been his pure, loving heart that had pushed him to do this? True, in not telling her what he was, he had lied to her, but she couldn't really blame him. After all, she hadn't told him what she was, either, and even though her secret was far greater than his, the principle remained unchanged. He had tried to breach the gap between the two of them. That was true love.

Too bad it would not work. Whatever Dave had concocted in that brilliant mind of his, there was simply no way this would work. Even so, it was still touching to see him try so hard.

She wanted to stay longer, to see more, but the unyielding force of life compelled her to start looking for a new host. She cast her mind around, enveloping the city in search for a good fit. Ah, yes! She could feel her out there. A three-year-old girl named Beatrice. And what was that she could feel as well? Could it be? Another Descendant? Things were looking up.

She placed a ghostly kiss on her Dave's cheek, feeling sad for him and for the sorrow that was sure to follow in his life. Then, taking one last look at her former, beautiful body, she floated up the stairs.

Waiting atop the stairs, stood Gertrude, Dave's pet goat, whom Ina had liked so much that she had actually given her a gift other Tribe members would have surely frowned upon. In her clear state of mind that came with being dead, Ina could now see that Gertrude was not an ordinary pet goat, but a familiar, of all the things. Damn it! She must have really been very much in love with Dave if she had allowed herself to be so blind to obvious things like that. If only she had known sooner that he was a Magician, she could have easily acted like one herself, and then this whole mess would never have happened.

Gertrude stared at her with sad eyes and followed her movement. Of course she could see her. She was a Magical creature, and a cute, fluffy one to boot.

"Take good care of him," Ina said as she leaned to pet Gertrude's shaggy hair. "He's going to need it, poor thing."

69. GERHARDT

"How, indeed?" Gerhardt flashed his eight-incisor grin. "Well, that's probably one story you will not learn from me. But then again, who can tell for sure? Let's just say your mom is the one to whom I owe this rather useful ability to change into a man. To be completely honest, I never knew why she did it, but it hardly matters now. Besides, this whole thing happened before she became your mother."

"So, you owe her big time," Merkin said.

"That's what I said." Gerhardt combed his goatee with his stubby fingers.

"Then I guess you owe me now," she replied in a resolute voice. "My mother is dead."

"Baaaah!" he said dismissively. "This is not how it works." He smiled goatishly[33]. "Besides, death is overrated."

He paused, looking Merkin up and down, and then sighed.

"Nevertheless," he continued, "while I don't exactly owe you anything, allow me to give you a little piece of advice. I don't know what your game is, but trust me when I tell you there is only grief to be found in there." He gestured towards the laptop.

"What exactly is in there?" she asked, looking thoughtfully at it.

"Nothing but grief. I just told you."

"Whose grief is that? And how do you know it is not grief that I am looking for?"

"Look, Merkin. I wasn't born yesterday," Gerhardt threw in the neonatal refutability argument. "I have seen better advice than this being flouted, and chances are you will pursue your curiosity despite my warning. I could very well stop you. No, don't give me that look!" he raised his voice in response to Merkin's protest. "You might be very skilled, but I graze girls

---

[33] Same as sheepishly, but with a pair of horns and some hints of authority issues.

like you for breakfast. As I was saying, I could stop you, but I will not do it. Fate is a murky business, and the surest way to bring about the unwanted outcome is to try to prevent it."

"Then why did you give me that advice?" Merkin asked.

"Because that was something I was expected to do. Refraining from warning you would have been the same, if not worse, than actively stopping you from meddling with what's in there," he said, pointing again towards the laptop.

"Oh, I get it now. You're one of those people who believe that playing by the rules is a kind of virtue, right?" she said condescendingly. "You cower behind your self-professed righteousness and invoke seemingly wise arguments such as, 'You don't stop a war by making more weapons,' or, 'The forces of good are so much cooler and stronger than the forces of evil, but it would be absolutely wrong if the first would simply destroy the latter'. For all that you might be stronger than I, you have no power over me!"

"Be that as it may," Gerhardt replied calmly, "just remember, when you do find what you're looking for, whatever that is, I urge you not to hurt the kid, or you will see the wrong end of this goat."

"Oh, yeah, and which one is that?" she asked, waving a finger at him.

"The one who will refuse to give you the antidote." Gerhardt flashed his lower teeth in a mysterious smile[34].

"What antidote?" Merkin asked, not quite alarmed yet, but definitely on the tipping point.

"I don't think this is the right question to ask."

"Very well, what poison then?" she asked, seething with anger.

"Oh, I don't know." Gerhardt closed his eyes in mock concentration. "Would you care for another swig of brandy?" He picked the leather-bound canteen from his pocket.

Understanding dawned.

"You... you tricked me!" she said, more surprised than anything else.

"And what if I did?" Gerhardt studied his fingernails.

"So much for not intervening," she said bitterly.

---

[34] A goat's smile is naturally mysterious, the mystery being, where did the upper teeth go? The answer to this riddle is actually quite simple: the goat's upper teeth went up a different evolutionary branch along with a prototype fifth stomach, a webbed hoof, and a completely impractical four-blade propeller that would, nevertheless, have been the envy of NASA's engineers today, despite the fact that it came only in pink.

"Oh, that. I was just biding my time. I wanted the potion to settle in before you decided to throw up or anything," he explained.

Her voice was level. "So, what's in it?"

"Oh, you know, this and that, the usual stuff," Gerhardt waved his hand vaguely.

"What does it do then?" By this time she had probably worked out that if she wasn't dead yet, then the potion had a less obvious effect.

"Do you know what a time bomb is?"

"Yes?" she replied, using the question mark as a replacement for "go on."

"Well, this is not one of those." Gerhardt's smile would have made a dentist want to pull his own brain out through his nose with a hawksbill forceps.

"How do I know you're not lying?" she pressed on.

"You know what, this is getting too stereotypical for my taste," he said tiredly. "Merkin, you should go to bed now. But remember, I am serious about the kid. Don't hurt him!"

He did not wait for her reply. Instead, Gerhardt quietly changed his shape into that of an invisible goat named Gertrude.

"Fine, but this is not over!" Merkin warned the empty air as she left the study.

70. CHAPTER

He woke up with the distinct feeling that he had been dreaming the complete *Epic of Gilgamesh* in Sumerian, and that somehow he had understood all of it. He had particularly enjoyed the ninth tablet, although he felt that the unknown collective author could have spiced up the debate between the two scorpion-beings concerning Gilgamesh's affiliation to the race of gods.

Thus speculating on the relative merits of the literature of the eighteenth century BC, Buggeroff took a quick shower and headed down to the kitchen. He wanted to cook a big, hearty breakfast to make a good impression on Merkin.

It was, however, his Master whom the enticing smells of his cooking had attracted first.

"Good morning, Master." He held the spatula up in salute.

"It sure smells like it," Master Loo replied brightly. "Like a good morning, that is," he explained hesitantly as if trying to apologize for being too cheerful.

"It's just ham, bacon, potatoes, eggs, herbs, toast, coffee, and muffins." Buggeroff smiled modestly. "Oh, and the sun seems particularly jaunty this morning, but I can't really take credit for that."

"Actually, that would be quite an easy spell to cast," Master Loo mused. "I can show it to you later if you want me to."

"I might like that," he nodded. "Coffee? You seem kind of tired. Did you not get a good sleep last night?"

"Oh, you know how it is at my age. Sure, I'll have a cup of coffee if you'd be so good to fill one for me."

Buggeroff took a small cup from the cabinet, then on second thought, put it back and chose a large one instead, which he filled to the brim.

"Here you go, Master. This should do the trick."

"Thank you, Buggeroff." Master Loo took a sip of coffee before putting the cup down. "Did you have a good time yesterday?"

"A good time?" he scoffed. "I had an amazing time! And to learn that Merkin is going to live with us! That was just... I mean, wow! How awesome is that?"

"I know, isn't that something?" Merkin said, leaning casually on the doorframe. She must have moved really quietly if not even Stapley had been able to detect her and warn him about her presence.

Master Loo broke the silence before it had a chance to become awkward. "I am privileged to have both of you as my Scriptlings. I only hope I can live up to the expectations."

"I have no doubts you will," Merkin said. "By the way, this," she gestured as if to encompass the whole kitchen, "smells delicious. Who is the talented chef?"

Buggeroff's face grew instantly hot, and his eyes were suddenly incapable of looking anywhere but down.

Master Loo picked the wrong moment to be helpful. "She means you, Buggeroff."

"It's nothing really," he mumbled, his eyes still glued to the floor. "Just some ham—"

"And bacon," she interrupted him, holding one finger up and sniffing the air, "eggs, sage, thyme, cayenne pepper, mmm... potatoes and... ah, yes, toast. Also, something rich and sweet coming from the oven," she finished her olfactory assessment.

"That's chocolate chip muffins," Buggeroff said proudly, finally summoning the courage to look at her again.

"And I'm impressed." Master Loo nodded as well. "That's a good nose you have there. I bet you'd make a great Alchemist."

"Oh, an amateur at best," she said, trying to sound cheerful, but Buggeroff could see her eyes were looking elsewhere, and, if he was any judge, elsewhen.

"Is everything OK?" he asked her.

"Um, yes." She blinked rapidly as if to shake away whatever it was that had been troubling her. "Just something I remembered." She waved her hand in a universal gesture of unimportance. "Could I have some of that yummy omelet of yours?"

"Sure, let me get you a plate," Buggeroff said. He then took the muffins out of the oven and let them rest on the cooling rack.

He was no Anna Olson, but his experience at Second Cup had taught him a great deal about baking and cooling times. He knew, for instance, that by the time he and his breakfast guests finished their omelet, the muffins would be just perfect to serve.

Ten minutes later, Merkin had her first bite. "These muffins are just perfect! Crispy on the outside, fluffy on the inside, and molten chocolaty in all the right places. Master Loo, I think you've found your Alchemist!"

"Well, I—" said Master Loo.

"I mean, these are absolutely amazing!" Merkin continued enthusiastically. "I feel like I could kiss you right now!"

"I—" Buggeroff said.

"What am I saying?" Merkin resumed her spiel. "I'm actually gonna do it. There!" she said as she brought her face close to Buggeroff's.

71. MERKIN

He was not a bad kisser, and the fact that he still had some chocolate left on his lips certainly made the experience even better. She allowed herself to enjoy this kiss rather than to feel guilty about it. Yes, it was definitely a good kiss, and she made a mental note that she might want to sample more of Buggeroff's talents later.

However, all she could hope for the moment was that her plan would work and, most importantly, that she hadn't made the wrong assumption about the nature of the troll dessert.

By the time she broke the kiss, several things had happened in their immediate vicinity.

Master Loo had, after a polite cough, left the room in embarrassment. By the sound of the garage door, he was now leaving the mansion as well, presumably to "give them some privacy." Excellent!

One Master Loo out of the house: check.

The other thing that had happened was that Gertrude was now staring angrily at her from behind Buggeroff. Perfect! She thought she had distinguished her smell among the overpowering aromas of breakfast. The crafty, woolly thing enjoyed sneaking around under the cover of invisibility, but she had met her match in Merkin's sensitive nose.

I'm not hurting him, Merkin, who wasn't still sure how eye-to-eye communication worked, tried to broadcast in Gertrude's direction. *Here, he is all yours now.*

For a moment, Gertrude's eyes flickered with something resembling confusion and reluctant acceptance soaked in residual anger.

"Um... Thank you," Buggeroff said dumbly in response to the kiss. "That was very unexpected."

He was mercifully saved from having to continue making a fool of himself when he realized that Merkin was looking somewhere behind him. He turned his head quickly and gasped excitedly when he saw Gertrude.

"Gertrude, you're back!" he exclaimed and gave the goat a suffocating hug that somehow contrived to make Merkin a little bit jealous. "Merkin, this is Gertrude. Gertrude, this is Merkin." He made the introductions quickly and rather awkwardly, like a man who suddenly finds himself in the uncomfortable situation of having to introduce two of his lovers to one another. "I'm sure you two will get along just fine."

"Very nice to meet you, Gertrude." Merkin extended her hand, arranging her face in a big, sincere smile. She wanted to add, "I was expecting someone taller," but checked herself in time.

The expression of confusion on the goat's face grew even deeper, much to Merkin's satisfaction. Nevertheless, she took Merkin's sleeve between her lips and nodded a greeting.

"We should all go for a walk," Buggeroff suggested. "Gertrude loves her morning walks, and this would be a great chance for you to see the surroundings."

"I would love nothing more," Merkin said. "But I still feel like I could use some rest after yesterday. I don't know where you find all this energy."

"Oh, I… I am a morning person, you know? Trying to keep in shape and all that," he boasted. "Don't worry about us, then. I'll take Gertrude for a walk, and you can just sleep in."

"Are you sure that's all right?" Merkin asked.

"Absolutely!" Buggeroff smiled genially.

"You're such a sweetheart," Merkin said dreamily and kissed him gently on his cheek. A kiss on the mouth would have looked downright manipulative at this moment, whereas the kiss on the cheek seemed perfectly innocent. That didn't make it any less manipulative. Merkin smiled inwardly at the thought.

Still, as Buggeroff and Gertrude left the mansion, she was a little bit surprised that the goat had not seen through her scheme. Gerhardt would have definitely not been tricked by such simple maneuvers. Perhaps Gertrude was not as smart as Gerhardt, although, with the unknown poison flowing in her veins, she did not take a great deal of comfort in this revelation.

All in all, at least her plan was on the right track.

One snooping goat out of the house: check.

One infatuated Buggeroff busy with the snooping goat: check.

The house all to herself: check.

A couple of minutes later, Merkin stood in front of Master Loo's laptop. She cracked her knuckles in anticipation, and then, with the kind of reverence normally reserved for scratching a lottery ticket, she typed in the password:

C-H-A-L-K-L-A-T-E

Nothing happened. Could it be that she was wrong?

It was true, trolls did eat humans, but it was a lesser-known fact (a fact which Merkin had all but forgotten the previous night) that the only reason trolls were interested in humans was their bones. Trolls have no need of the flesh, skin, and miscellaneous gore that humans are made of. Instead, their diet is rich in minerals such as calcium and phosphorus, both of which are incidentally found in large volumes in, yes, bones. But humans are an unreliable food source, mainly because they tend to be vengeful and also adept at using a variety of sharp, agricultural implements, and, worst of all, fire torches. Sedimentary rock[35], on the other hand, presents none of these disadvantages, and, therefore, it has always been a staple food for trolls.

This last paragraph represents the analysis that Merkin's subconscious mind had worked on during the night. It was a relevant piece of work, but it had been largely incomplete until Buggeroff mentioned the word chocolate. Buggeroff's reference was exactly what her imagination had been awaiting – a spark to ignite the explosion. Within less than a moment, Merkin had her answer.

"Chalklate" had seemed like the perfect choice, in that it was both elegant and that it made perfect sense. Then why was it that it didn't work?

Of course! With a sudden realization, Merkin slapped her forehead and then hit the Enter key.

She was in.

---

[35] For an interesting collection of trollish culinary art please see *The Pinnacles* (Australia), *The Stone Tree* (Bolivia) or *The Delicate Arch* (USA).

72. MASTER LOO

"How could you forget?" the inner voice spat out the question.

What gives you the right to blame me? Master Loo protested. *You have forgotten as well. If it wasn't for the kiss none of us would have remembered until—*

"Until what? Until someone accosted you politely on the street and said, 'Excuse me, sir, did you know that it was exactly thirty-six years ago that you met the love of your life at a Pink Floyd concert in Montreal? No? Well then, happy to oblige, sir.' Is that what you had in mind?"

Until I checked the calendar, that's what I meant to say.

"And what would the calendar have said to you?" asked the inner voice.

Twenty-sixth of June, that's what, Master Loo replied simply.

It had been the right answer. It had to be, or it would not have shut off the inner voice. For the last thirty-five years he had observed the twenty-sixth of June religiously. It was the one day in three hundred sixty-five during which he allowed himself to remember the good times. For the remainder of the year, the only image of Ina he was able to summon was that of her face turning accusingly from joy to bewilderment as the crossbow bolt pierced her heart.

He might never be able to explain what kind of madness had driven him to shoot the bolt. Wasn't it enough for the young Dave that he was in love with a beautiful woman who loved him back? Why had he tried to improve upon perfection? Would it have been so bad for him, a Magician, to marry someone like her? But no! He somehow got it into that little mind of his that he could help her become a Magician, too. All he had to do was...

Alas, his Ritual spell had been so poorly conceived that it had actually taken him thirteen trials to make it work. Thirteen! A lifetime marked by a body trail. If only he could go back in time and use what he had learned about the Ritual. No, that was not the right thing to do. If he were ever be able to go back in time, the first thing he would change was to not attempt the Ritual in the first place.

He shook his head, chasing the dark thoughts away. Today was not the day for sorrow. Today was the day he would remember her kisses, her embraces, her morning smile, her smell, and her walk. Today was the day he would cherish her. There was plenty of room for regretting her during the rest of the year.

To think that he had almost forgotten about today. Was it the fact that he was getting old, or was it the fact that there had been more excitement in his life during this last month than during the last thirty or so years? Perhaps it was both, but that was still no excuse.

As he walked through the cemetery, he eyed a bench, apparently at random, and sat down on it. It was the same bench he had sat on for thirty-five years on the twenty-sixth of June. He wished there had been a grave where he could visit her, but he did not have this luxury.

He remembered that cold, December day when they had come for her body. Who they were and how they knew about her death, he had never learned. They simply showed up at his door — three, well-built men in dark clothes — and asked for her. At first, he had pretended that he had no idea what they were talking about. Seeing this, two of the men, whom young Dave could swear were twins, had silently moved past him and climbed down the stairs to the basement where Ina's cold body lay on the floor, surrounded by hundreds of her favorite flowers: white roses. The other man stood and watched him grimly for a minute until his partners came back. One of them was carrying Ina in his strong arms, while the other pulled a large, black sack filled with the white roses. The twins left the house without a word, and young Dave was about to say something when the other man, who had stood behind, raised one finger in the air and said, "One day one of us will ask for your assistance. You will know that day when it comes."

And didn't he just know it.

He shook his head again, this time succeeding in clearing his mind. He leaned back and relaxed. From deep within his mind, six months of happy memories slowly started their journey to the surface. Master Loo took a deep breath and smiled.

"Ina," he whispered.

"Ina," young Dave whispered back, for once, in agreement.

73. MERKIN

On a scale ranging from very little to too much, Merkin could just about categorize the amount of personal data stored in Master Loo's computer as a shitload[36]. To her new Master's credit, though, it was all very well organized, with no small number of tags, keywords, and Gantt charts.

Why anyone would invest so much time and passion in recording all the minutia of their lives, especially when it was filled with incriminating evidence, Merkin could not venture to guess. People were, after all, entitled to their little kinks, whether they were collecting toenail clippings or simply indulging a penchant for taking long, relaxing baths in aardvark milk.

Organized as it was, the data was still too much for Merkin to parse in the little time she had before Buggeroff and Gertrude would return. Nevertheless, she had come prepared with a 64 GB flash drive the size of her fingernail and worth about forty bucks. Only fifteen years ago, this storage capacity would have required a number of floppy disks that could have easily filled a small room. It would have also set you back about nine thousand bucks. Merkin mused about this and other astonishing technological leaps for a couple of minutes, while the shitload of data was being copied to her USB key.

When the data transfer was complete, she logged off and closed the lid with the satisfaction of a job well done. Stopping in the kitchen for a still-warm chocolate muffin, she strolled back to her room humming a happy tune.

Once there, she locked the door and cast a protection spell just in case Gertrude decided to try something funny. The thought of Gertrude reminded her of the poison she had so foolishly self-administered last night. In response, her music box started playing The Prodigy's "Poison,"

---

[36] The shitload is one of those exotic units of measurement expressed as a function of perception rather than (the more traditional) size, volume or mass. Other examples include the handful, the smidgeon, the just-enough, and the morality.

although for some reason it chose to use a symphonic orchestral sound bank rather than the synth kit. She paused grimly and ran a quick system check on her body, the same as she had done the night before and that morning. The poison was still there, a blur of darkness flowing through her veins, completely ignored by her antibodies, and utterly impervious to her own, magical investigations. The bloody bastard hadn't bluffed, that much was sure. She would have to tread cautiously.

"I got the poison," went the tenor choir.

"I got the remedy," replied the baritones.

"I got the pulsating, rhythmical remedy," insisted the mezzo-sopranos.

"I ain't got shit!" said Merkin bitterly and shut down the music box.

Still, the sense of imminent doom instilled by the poison's presence had somehow contrived to boost her determination. She switched on her laptop and plugged in the flash drive.

Two hours later, she picked up her cell phone and, without fearing for one moment that she would sound desperate, she sent the following text message to Master Sewer, "Pick me up in ten. Found it!"

She would help her man to be a Magician again even if she had to kill him first. The only question was, where could she find a miniature crossbow? It seemed, after all, an important piece of the Ritual. Also, she noted with satisfaction, that she now knew who Stapley was. That still didn't explain Buggeroff's impressive growth in skill in such a short time, but she was sure she would crack that problem eventually.

"Address, pls?" came Master Sewer's reply before a minute had passed. He had obviously been waiting by the phone, poor thing.

She sent him the address, and, after some fumbling under her blouse with the phone, a picture of her breasts, just in case he needed the reminder.

Then, having just had a new idea, she snatched her knapsack, threw in the laptop, then flew out of her room and down the stairs.

***

Once in the study, she closed the double doors behind her and proceeded with her investigation.

"Looking for something?" Gerhardt's voice came from right behind her.

"Just the miniature crossbow," Merkin replied automatically before her brain caught up and ordered a full system double take. "What the hell are you doing in here?" she asked, placing an open palm defensively between her and the goat man.

277

"Seriously, are you really going to ask that?" Gerhardt said in a tired and slightly disappointed voice. "I told you already, I can stretch this turn-into-a-man thing for up to six days, and this is the sixth day. I thought you would be happy to see me." He almost sounded convincing.

Merkin frowned. "Why would I be? Do you think I have some kind of fetish for being poisoned by scheming goats?"

"Well, if anything, I am the one who holds the antidote. That, at least, should make our encounters an exciting and much-anticipated event for you, don't you think?"

"Believe me, nothing you hold could excite me in any way."

"Too bad, too bad." Gerhardt shook his head. "Then I don't suppose you would be interested in this?" He pulled the miniature crossbow from his green, tweed jacket.

"You—" She looked for the most hurtful appellative she could throw at him.

"Yes?"

"You... bitch!" she settled for the time-honored insult.

"Come on, there's no need for name calling. Here, you can have it if you want it that badly." He held out the weapon.

"Why?" she asked. But she took the crossbow.

"Because it won't help you in any way," Gerhardt said simply.

She gave him a calculated look, but said nothing.

"I can only surmise you found out about the Ritual," said Gerhardt. "It won't work, that's all I'm going to tell you."

Merkin, whose initial shock had subsided by then, decided to use her brain for a change.

"You mean to say," she said slowly, still working out the fine details, "that there is something more to the Ritual than what Master Loo has documented."

"I'm not saying anything," Gerhardt replied distantly.

"But," she pressed on, "Master Loo is not one to omit important details, so it follows naturally that if there is something missing, then it must be something he is not aware of."

"Ha!" he scoffed.

"Something you know," she concluded, poking his chest with her index finger. "So, what is it then?" she poked him again and took a lot of pleasure in doing so.

"Merkin, who is this?" came Buggeroff's voice from the door.

She watched him in surprise and saw that he was pointing at Gerhardt.

"This?" she asked, turning her eyes slowly on the goat man, trying not to smirk. Was that panic she read on Gerhardt's face? Could it be that Buggeroff did not know about his pet's transformation act? How very interesting. And now Gerhardt's eyes were begging her.

It should probably be clear by now that Merkin was, when you got past the wanton cruelty and gratuitous frivolity, a manipulative bitch. Her answer, therefore, should not surprise anyone.

74. BUGGEROFF

"This, Simon, is a spirit of the Third Circle I have summoned as part of my preparation for advanced Enchantment," Merkin said. "I'm afraid I'm still not very good at it. In fact, it might disappear at any moment, what with my concentration faltering and whatnot."

Even as she was finishing her sentence, the strange man dissolved into thin air. He must have been a demon, no doubt about that, with such goat-like teeth.

Stapley coughed politely. *"Chief?"*

Yes, Stapley, what is it?

"You know how we have established that your eyes can see invisible things but your brain can't?"

Yes, go on.

"Well, I just thought I'd mention that your eyes have witnessed the spirit of the Third Circle tiptoeing past you and outside the study. Also, I would like to point out that, at this moment, it would be of great social importance if you could just keep calm and refrain from turning around brusquely," Stapley said matter-of-factly.

Sure, of course, I can do that, Buggeroff replied. But might I just ask what you make of this?

"Well, Chief, it could very well be that the spirit was looking for a way back home. There is a high chance that the closest passageway to the Third Circle is not located in this room, but rather in some thorn bush out on the street, or even a rusty manhole. I am hardly an expert, though, so don't take my word for it."

So, if I were to just turn around right now, what do you think I would see?

"Beats me, Chief. I'd guess you would see the hallway."

Buggeroff turned around slowly and saw instantly that Stapley's assumption had been both right and incomplete. Before his eyes stood, very much indeed, the hallway. It stood there resolutely, unmistakably conveying the message that it would stay there for another century or so, if that was all right with everyone. Something else stood there, though, and it watched Buggeroff with big, questioning eyes.

"There you are, girl!" Buggeroff dropped on his knee and gave Gertrude a hug. "I was wondering where you'd been."

In response, Gertrude planted her warm muzzle on his neck and sniffed a couple of times with delight.

"O-o-key," Merkin said, somehow managing to squeeze three syllables out of the word. "If you'll excuse me now, and I don't want to be rude or anything, but I really have to go. There's an errand I must run. She walked past them and into the hallway.

"What? You can't leave like that," he protested.

"You're right," she smiled and hurried back a couple of steps to where he stood. "How could I forget?" She pressed her lips onto his.

He gasped for the second time that day, hardly believing his luck, and now that his mouth was open, he could feel Merkin's tongue probing shamelessly for his.

Too soon, oh, way too soon, they were interrupted by a sound that has been the relentless bane of so many couples caught in the heat of their love. It was the sound of the front door being unlocked. Guided by an instinct as old as guilt, they both jumped backwards, trying to put as much distance between themselves as possible and managing not to break any oversized, priceless, porcelain vase[37].

"Relax, Chief," Stapley's voice came calmly. *"Master Loo has seen you two kissing before."*

Yeah, and you've seen the way he reacted. He went straight out of the room and drove away, Buggeroff replied.

The door stood open, revealing Master Loo and, much to both Scriptlings' surprise, Master Sewer.

"Hello, hello, hello," said Master Loo with uncharacteristic joy. "Look what I found outside." He pointed towards Master Sewer who seemed a bit puzzled, but who was still as confident and full of machismo as ever.

"Hello, there," he said, shaking Buggeroff's hand and giving Merkin a curt nod.

"Imagine, he was sitting in his beautiful sports car with the roof let down right in front of this house," Master Loo said.

---

[37] That is because the ever-practical Master Loo was not the type to be bothered about such decorative items. Should he ever need a vase, he would get one made of titanium, a material known both for its high endurance and its light weight.

"I got lost on my way to the new shopping mall." Master Sewer raised his shoulders and eyebrows together in a self-ironic gesture. "Can you believe it?"

"So, I asked myself, what are the odds?" Master Loo resumed, still as blissfully and energetically as if he had been taking a coke and ecstasy mix. "But then, I thought, who cares about the odds? What better thing to do now than to invite my new friend for a glass of brandy and perhaps lunch?"

Friend? Lunch?

Stapley, does he look all right to you? Buggeroff inquired.

"He looks... Well, blimey, Chief, if the old man doesn't look great!"

"A splendid idea," Master Sewer commented. "How could I ever say no to that?"

"Excellent!" Master Loo rubbed his hands together. "Now, why don't you two," he pointed to his Scriptlings, "try to see if you can think of a main course and appetizer that would impress our guest, while the two of us retire to my study. Don't worry about the dessert, though. I've already got some wonderful Belgian ice-cream in the trunk of my car. Buggeroff, here are the keys." He tossed them.

Buggeroff caught them, baffled at his Master's unusual behavior.

"If you'll excuse me," Merkin said. She stepped in front of the two Masters as they headed for the study. "There is something the three of us need to talk about."

"Sure, come on in," Master Loo said magnanimously. "Just don't be long, though. You don't want Buggeroff to handle the lunch preparations all   by   himself   now,   do   you?"

75. MASTER LOO

"So, my dear Merkin, what is it that I can do for you?" he asked.

She gave him a cold look and said, "I want you to perform the Ritual on Master Sewer."

"Wah wah wah waaaah," Dave, the inner voice, imitated the sad trombone sound effect.

"The what?" asked Master Sewer.

"Well, apparently our mad genius, here, has perfected a way to turn a normal person into a Magician," Merkin explained in a cold voice.

"Hmm, that's intriguing." Master Sewer rubbed his chin, not showing any discernible emotion. "How do you know it works?"

"Would it help if I told you that less than two months ago Buggeroff was about as magical as a bag of doorknobs?" She smiled conspiratorially.

"Oh, I see," Master Sewer replied.

"Now, wait a minute." Master Loo managed to wedge a crowbar into the conversation. "Why would Master Sewer need me to perform the Ritual on him? And, come to think of it, however did you find out about it?"

"That's none of your business," Merkin hissed.

"Oh, my, if she isn't a feisty one!" Dave giggled excitedly.

By now the cheerfulness had abandoned Master Loo, leaving him with an emotional void that quickly started to fill with anger.

"Don't give me that, young lady!" He waved his finger at her, but his voice was as demure as ever. "You said it yourself, the Ritual turns normal people into Magicians. Do you have any idea what the Ritual turns Magicians into? I'll tell you what it turns them into. It turns them into dead Magicians. So, now I'll ask you once again, and this time you'd better think before you answer: why does Master Sewer need the Ritual?"

"Wow, I never knew you could be so tough," Dave remarked, almost admiringly.

Master Sewer intervened calmly. "Perhaps, I should answer this. There is scarcely any point in withholding information now. I lost my magical abilities a few weeks ago, in a car accident. I'm afraid I can't tell you more than that simply because this is all I know about it, myself. Now, about this Ritual of yours, what does it involve, exactly?"

"Let me see if I got it right," said Master Loo. He was still possessed by anger, but it was a calculated anger now. "You can't cast any spell, right?"

"Indeed, I can't," admitted the other Master with rather more dignity than he, Master Loo, would have done in his situation.

"And now this Scriptling of yours has discovered my secret, a secret which incidentally might be the cure for your ailment. Under normal circumstances, I would have been curious as to what tipped her. However, my curiosity is otherwise engaged with a different issue, and that is, how do you intend to elicit my help? If you have, indeed, lost your powers, then there is only Merkin, who counts as half an opponent, against me. Need I say more?"

"Come on, you know you have to help them," Dave said. *"You promised."*

That is no reason not to be curious, Master Loo replied to his inner voice.

"First of all, let it be known that I resent your comment about my being only half an opponent," Merkin said. "I might not have your criminal record when it comes to sheer numbers, but I've taken on more serious challengers than you and lived to tell the tale. Well, one challenger, but the principle remains. As for your willingness to collaborate, the matter is quite simple. You will do it because if you don't help us, then your cop friends will learn about all your crimes." Merkin smirked.

"Crimes? Criminal record? Sheer numbers?" Master Sewer raised three questions and one eyebrow.

"Cop friends?" Master Loo was also taken aback.

"Oh, well," Merkin turned to face Master Sewer, "to be completely blunt, the Ritual starts by killing the subject in a... um... ritualistic manner with a miniature crossbow. It should pose no danger now, but let's just say that Master Loo underwent a rather long trial-and-error phase before he managed to make the Ritual the safe procedure it is now."

"I see," Master Sewer replied. "Killing the subjects, you say."

"Yes, but it should be perfectly harmless," Merkin said reassuringly.

"Right," Master Sewer nodded, apparently not entirely convinced by her sales pitch, a state of mind that perfectly mirrored Master Loo's.

"As for your friends, the coppers," Merkin turned back towards him, "I saw you that night in front of the restaurant talking to them, so I would drop the denial act if I were you."

"The... the restaurant?" Master Loo staggered, not knowing what she was talking about.

"Come on, the Solstice festivities. Does that ring any bell? You went outside for a smoke, and then the cops drove their car to your side of the street where you chatted like old pals for a minute or so," Merkin said impatiently. "What is it that you talked about anyway?"

***

Five days earlier...

The car drew right in front of him and a jolly-looking fat man of Asian persuasion waved his hand at him from the passenger seat. Master Loo chose to ignore him, but the man insisted and called him by his name, his Magician name.

He quickly stepped forward and leaned forward to the window. Before he could say anything, the other man spoke again, "Or should I say Dave Singular Watters? Relax, we're friends of Ina. We came to collect our debt. Name's Liu, by the way, and this is my brother Chuck." He pointed towards the driver who was as redheaded and fair-skinned as you would expect a trademark leprechaun to be.

"Different mothers," Chuck explained, seeing the question in Master Loo's eyes. "Pleased to meet you," he added jovially.

"And fathers, too," the inner voice observed.

Master Loo was still unable to speak. If Liu's intention had really been to put him at his ease, then he had failed miserably. How could these two men be friends of Ina when neither of them looked older than thirty?

"How—" he tried to voice his perplexity.

"Listen, we don't have time for explanations, nor, quite frankly, are you entitled to ask for any," Chuck said. "Here's the deal, there is one sassy girl who calls herself Merkin and who is most likely attending the Solstice dinner in this restaurant. Do you know her?"

"I... that is..." Master Loo tried.

"A simple yes or no would suffice," Chuck said. "We haven't got much time."

"Yes," said Master Loo.

Liu said, "Good. We have reason to suspect she and her Master are up to something big. Really, really big stuff, understood?"

"Um... no," Master Loo replied honestly.

Chuck took over. "That's perfect! Now, what we want you to do is to keep an eye on them, especially on her. Actually, if you could somehow infiltrate their household and learn what their plan is, that would earn you extra credits. Can you do that?"

"I can try…"

"Fair enough," said Chuck. "There's one more thing we will ask of you – you must be there for her. I'm not asking you to be nice to her, because that would be too much to ask, even from a saint. I'm just saying that you must offer her your support if she asks for it, and even if she doesn't. This is how you will clear your debt. Will you do it?"

"Yes," he replied resolutely. He had no idea how he would do it, but he knew he needed to do it if he could ever dream of redemption.

"There's a good Magician." Liu laughed, but to Master Loo's surprise it wasn't an ironic laughter.

"Why would I be ironic about it, eh?" Liu took him once more by surprise by apparently reading his mind. "I always thought you were one of the good guys. If it weren't for the whole mess with Ina, we might have even been friends."

"Who are you?" Master Loo's voice whined under the stress of so many things that he could not understand.

Liu smiled kindly. "I already told you. We're friends of Ina. Now, off you go and do what you promised you'd do. Oh, and try not to kill anyone this time, unless specifically asked to, all right?"

"I…" he hesitated. "How will I get in touch with you? If I find out what Merkin is up to, that is."

"You'll find a card with our phone numbers on it inside your pocket," Chuck said. "Don't ask me how I did it. Professional secret." He tapped his nose.

Master Loo took out his wallet and looked into it. Sure enough, the card was there. He searched his mind for something to say, but the black car was already moving away, taking with it the answers to so many of his heartburning questions.

***

Master Loo looked Merkin in the eye. "What I talked to them about is none of your concern."

"Why would she think they were cops?" the inner voice asked, but Master Loo ignored him.

"All right, I'll help you," he continued, "But at your own risk."

"OK," she said with disconcerting ease. "I'll go get Gertrude. She owes me one." She turned and started for the door.

Gertrude burped, her equivalent for "ahem," as she cast away her invisibility spell. She held her head high and lifted one of her front hoofs in the air, as if posing for the *Goat to the Rescue* magazine cover.

Master Loo frowned. "Why would we need her? No offence meant," he added quickly as Gertrude turned to give him one of her scolding looks.

"Don't bother yourself with that," Merkin said dismissively. "Just make sure you don't screw it up this time, understood?"

"A good smack behind the ear, that's what this girl needs."

"Merkin, are you sure about this?" Master Sewer asked. There was no fear in his voice, but rather some kind of fatherly concern.

"Trust me," she said and kissed him, long and hard, forcing Master Loo to avert his eyes.

76. MASTER DUNG

"Typical! My enemies drink brandy behind closed doors while my puny host is playing Cinderella," Master Dung exclaimed. "Is this why I bothered to teach him all this stuff, so he can slave in the kitchen?"

"Come on, Master, he is not really 'slaving,'" Stapley said in his annoying, pacifist tone. *"You know how he enjoys cooking. Besides, your teachings are safe. I'm sure none of the things you taught him will be lost just because he is preparing an excellent course of Duck Poutine a l'Orange. Seriously, just smell it."*

It smelled delicious.

"What of it? So, the boy can cook. How is that helping me?"

"He did show some rather creative spell work with the recipe, didn't he?"

"So?"

"Well, I'm not what you would call a military strategist," Stapley began, *"but I do think originality and an ability to improvise are attributes to look for in a combatant."*

Master Dung paused to reflect on what his obsequious slave had just said. "You know what, you're right," he said.

"I... I am?"

"Why, yes, you are." He smirked. "This is as good a time as any. They have been in there for over an hour, and with a little bit of luck, they should be pretty intoxicated by now. Not exactly sitting ducks, but not alert fighters, either."

"What are you talking about, Master?" Stapley's voice quivered.

"I'm talking about my revenge!" he said in a booming voice. "We're going in!"

"But, Master, wait!" Stapley cowered.

"No! I've waited enough. You're right. The kid is not perfect, but he is good enough. And you know what, no one said he has to make it out alive. Come, I want to take these new wheels for a drive." He burst into manic laughter.

What Master Dung referred to as *new wheels*, others less given to classic displays of psychopathy might have referred to as Buggeroff.

Indeed, over the course of the last, few weeks, the disembodied spirit of Master Dung had managed to plant an inordinate number of triggers straight into Buggeroff's brain, triggers that he had then wired together into an immensely complicated control panel. His main focus had been around the primary motor cortex and Broca's area. In layman's terms, what Master Dung had done could roughly be translated as having gained control over his host's movement and speech.

Sitting at the stirring knobs[38] of his intricate contraption, Master Dung let out yet another roar of dramatically suited laughter. If there was something more intriguing than the grotesque appearance of his creation, then it must have been the fact that it actually worked. It was, by no means, a smooth ride, but a ride from A to B it was, nevertheless; even though the trajectory accounted for brief and painful intersections with the points C (corner), D (door), E (erotic carving of an elephant), and F (fucking stairs).

"Wh-az diz?" Master Dung's words came from Buggeroff's mouth, curious, in spite of himself, about the strange tableau unfolding before his eyes in the basement.

His question was met with indifference by Master Sewer and Master Loo on account of the first lying on the floor and busying himself with being quite obviously dead, while the latter showed all the signs of being engaged in a spell that required all of his attention.

"You shouldn't be here," Merkin gasped.

Beside her, Gertrude hissed and spat furiously, apparently understanding that something wrong was happening to her pet human.

"Sss'lence!" Master Dung ordered.

Merkin's eyes glowed with anger, and she raised a hand to slap him.

With a jerky, but nevertheless, lightning-fast movement, Buggeroff punched her in the jaw, sending her sprawling on the floor. He turned his eyes on the lifeless body of Master Sewer. How dare they deny him the pleasure of killing him, himself? Time for a little purifying, fire action.

But then, even as he formulated this angry thought, something happened. Where the darkness of death had stood only a moment before now sparkled a tiny ember of life. Master Dung watched, transfixed, as the ember erupted into a blinding inferno that engulfed Master Sewer in a

---

[38] Seeing as this device resembled what could only be described as the mutant offspring of a church organ and a milking machine, no one could possibly have expected a stirring wheel. It also makes perfect sense that some of the levers would start squirting at the most inappropriate times.

protective cocoon. And then, he felt something else. He felt the irresistible attraction this new life force exercised on his frail essence. He had not felt like that since the day of his funeral when he had met Buggeroff and invited himself in. But even that blissful episode had none of the intensity he was experiencing now. He let go and allowed himself to drift out of his host. Behind him, he could hear Stapley's cry of freedom, followed by the sound of Buggeroff promptly folding at the knees and dropping down.

A moment later, Master Dung's spirit melted into that of his new host. Immediately, he felt a familiar presence that caused him to smile his evilest of smiles.

"Fancy meeting you here, Stapley," he said, getting ready to give his old acquaintance the spiritual equivalent of a wedgie.

"*I ain't no Stapley,*" the presence said in a steel voice. "*I'm his big brother, beyotch!*"

There was a soft, pathetic squeal, and then there was nothing.

77. MASTER SEWER

It had worked!

Only a moment before, his mind had been roaming a psychedelic vision of Toronto and trying to determine if this was heaven or hell and being infuriatingly unable to formulate a satisfactory conclusion. But now, he knew for certain that he was alive.

"You're alive!" Master Loo's voice confirmed his conviction beyond any doubt.

What about the Magic, though? Had that been restored to him?

"It appears you are interested in the status of your magical abilities," said a robotic voice that seemed to originate somewhere deep in his mind. *"The name is Bolty, by the way. I'm your new personal assistant. Before we proceed any further, do you find this voice to your taste or would you prefer something different?"*

Meanwhile, the voice had also been taking a shape of sorts. It looked very much like a stick figure of a man wearing a pointy hat, except that his arms and legs were awfully short and close together, while his neck was disproportionately long. On second thought, it looked exactly the way a crossbow bolt would look if someone had been trying to make it look alive.

Oh, what the hell, I could use a personal assistant, thought Master Sewer. *Speaking of voices, can you do my own? I'm rather fond of it.*

"Absolutely, Boss," Bolty replied in Master Sewer's own timbre. *"As for your magical abilities, they are currently operating at seventy-two percent and steadily rising. I expect you should reach your top peak in about fifty-eight seconds."*

Good! Now, I should very much like to know what's going on in here. Why are Merkin and Buggeroff sprawled on the floor, and why is Master Loo hopping excitedly from foot to foot? Also, where did that goat go?

"It is a great joy to have a Boss so keen on putting me to good use." Bolty saluted and tried, without any discernible success, to inflate his chest.

I haven't asked you to do anything, Master Sewer replied. *I was merely listing out the items that seemed out of place.* After a brief mental calculation, he added, *Hey, this*

291

whole conversation between the two of us is actually quite fast. Is this what is called the speed of thought?

"*Precisely, Boss,*" Bolty said. "*As for the items you have just listed, nothing would please me more than being of assistance. Merkin, for instance—*"

Just a moment. If you must be obsequious, then you are free to do it, but don't use my voice for that.

"*I shall make a rule out of this,*" Bolty replied, using a butler-type voice.

Right, now tell me about Merkin and the others.

"*As I was saying, Merkin appears to have suffered a blow to her lower maxillary. The position in which she collapsed on the floor, along with the barely perceptible bruise on her left chin all point to this conclusion. She should regain consciousness in less than a minute.*"

That's a pretty in-depth analysis, Master Sewer said appreciatively. *But who would punch my Merkin, and why?*

"*Thank you, Boss. Judging by the color of his knuckles, I would presume the culprit is Buggeroff. I can't really tell why, but he seems to be unconscious now. He, too, should be fine in a minute or so.*"

I will be there when he wakes, and we'll have a little chat, Master Sewer said menacingly.

"*Very well, Boss. If I may continue answering your list of questions, Master Loo's little happy dance might have something to do with his recent remark about your being alive. By the way, you might consider replying any time now.*"

I will, of course. I owe him that much.

"*Very nice of you to think so, Boss. As for the goat, she disappeared the moment you opened your eyes. I caught a glimpse of her for merely a hundredth of a second before she completely vanished. Pretty odd stuff, too.*"

I see, Master Sewer thought, although he didn't exactly see, per se. *Thank you for your assistance, Bolty. I will now talk to my unwilling benefactor, Master Loo.*

78. MASTER LOO

"You're alive!" he said excitedly.

Master Sewer moaned, rubbing his temples. "I must admit, I'm surprised to see you so cheerful about it." He rose to his feet, still looking slightly wobbly.

"Call it professional pride," Master Loo replied.

"You could have just left me for dead. I know I would have if I had been in your position."

"Call it integrity," Master Loo replied sharply.

"Ah, integrity, that wretched feeling that lurks on the seabed of our souls with all the maddening might of a circular reference. I know it all too well."

"Do you really?" Master Loo snorted.

His question gave his interlocutor some pause. "Yes, very much so, although I can understand how you may not see it that way," Master Sewer said amicably. "At any rate, you have my humblest thanks for what you've done today!" He took Master Loo's unresisting hand and shook it vigorously. His charisma shone through, once again.

"It's nothing, really," Master Loo babbled, his Canadian genes compelling him to play the modest-politeness card.

"Quite the opposite, I should say. This Ritual of yours has a lot of potential, although I can't think of one practical application off the top of my head."

"Alas, I can imagine a couple of applications that would spell doom to the world as we know it. If it is not too much to ask, I would prefer that the Ritual remain a secret."

"Agreed! You have my word on it, for what it's worth," said Master Sewer.

In the meanwhile, judging by the low moan she made, Merkin seemed to have come back to her senses. She opened her eyes, took in the scene, and without any hesitation, jumped into Master Sewer's arms crying "You're alive!" and smothered him with kisses.

"She's a flirty little thing, isn't she?" Dave commented.

"Of course, I am alive," Master Sewer said when Merkin's lips had finally given him room to do so. "Didn't you say it was a safe procedure?"

"I was so worried," she replied and kissed him again. "Tell me, did it work? Are your powers back?"

In response, he snapped his fingers and whispered a silent spell that caused a beautiful display of fireworks to sparkle through the air. She giggled and gave him yet another kiss.

It was during this scene that Buggeroff, too, came to his senses.

"Merkin?" he asked in a trembling voice as he tried to stand up. "Why?"

She detached herself from Master Sewer and watched Buggeroff with guilt in her eyes. Master Sewer, on the other hand, stepped forward, and without a moment's hesitation, punched him so hard that poor Buggeroff was knocked out before he hit the ground.

"That's for punching my girl!" Master Sewer explained in a cold voice. "Sorry about that," he added genially, addressing Master Loo. "Integrity, you know?" Then, taking Merkin's hand in his he said, "Come, we're leaving," and started walking towards the stairs.

As he reached the bottom of the stairs, he turned his head and said, again in his unresistingly warm voice, "Thanks again for everything! Perhaps we'll meet again one day and laugh about all this."

79. BUGGEROFF

"Chief, are you OK?" Stapley's voice came bearing strange harmonics, as if preceded by its own echo.

I... I'm not sure, Buggeroff groaned. *What's going on?*

"A lot, actually. Chief, I need to tell you something very important," Stapley said, barely containing his excitement.

What is it?

"We are free, Chief! Free at last!"

Huh? Haven't we been free all along?

"You don't understand, Chief, but that's OK. I'll try to explain. You see, for the last few weeks, ever since that funeral at Mount Pleasant, we have been... how should I put it... possessed by Master Dung's spirit. Are you with me so far?"

Master Dung? Isn't he the guy whose funeral we attended? Merkin's late Master?

"Yes, the same. He has been parasitizing your body until only a few minutes ago."

That's ridiculous, Buggeroff thought. *I'm sure I would have known if such a thing had happened.*

"It's not that easy, Chief. He has been hiding himself from you, and only I knew of his presence."

Why didn't you warn me then?

"Wish that I could have," Stapley said miserably. *"The usurper had me in his clutches and I was powerless. I did try to shake him off a couple of times but to no avail, although I did come very close once."*

But what did he want of me? Buggeroff asked.

"To live! Oh, and to have his revenge on Merkin and Master Sewer. She killed Master Dung. Did you know that? Also, Master Sewer had helped her cover her tracks and then he took over Master Dung's estate. Pretty solid foundation for revenge, I'd venture to say."

But if he was dead, then...

"Not entirely dead, Chief. Somehow his spirit survived, and it remained attached to his lifeless body. If you hadn't shown up when you did, then he would have had to spend eternity buried six feet under. Now, I'm not at all clear about the details, but something in the fact that you are technically undead made you a perfect host as far as he was concerned."

The bastard!

"Well, it's not all that bad, to be honest. He did help you a lot by shoving volumes of knowledge into your brain while you were asleep. Didn't you ever wonder why it was that you always woke up smarter than when you went to bed?"

Oh, Buggeroff thought, suddenly humbled by this revelation, *but why would he do such a thing?*

"To train you as his weapon, of course," Stapley explained. *"This brings us to what happened today."*

This should be interesting to hear, thought Buggeroff.

"Quite. Seeing as both his former Scriptlings were within reach, the usurper decided this would be a perfect chance to get his revenge. Sitting ducks, or so he thought. This is where things might get a little bit hazy for you."

No kidding. I was in the kitchen, and then, all of a sudden, I was on the basement floor watching Merkin making up with Master Sewer and… did he actually punch me?

"I'll get to that in a minute. The reason you don't remember anything is because Master Dung took full control over you and drove you, yes, I believe this is the right term, drove you down here. Down here, interestingly enough, Master Loo was busy performing the Ritual on Master Sewer. Of course, the usurper Dung had no idea what was happening. To him, it appeared as if someone had denied him the pleasure of killing Master Sewer himself, and that had a rather aggravating effect on his already dark mood. It was then that Merkin picked the wrong moment to speak. Not surprisingly at all, the brute reacted by punching her senseless. Only, it was you who actually punched her, understand?"

With great difficulty, Buggeroff admitted. *Go on, please.*

"And then the miracle happened. When Master Sewer came back to life as a result of the Ritual being complete, the stupid idiot — I'm talking about Master Dung, here —thought it would be a good idea to jump bodies again. I'll be damned if I can understand why, but the good news is that he is gone now! We're free at last!"

That's all very well, Buggeroff thought, feeling as if he should probably be more excited about the news, but, above all, feeling extremely confused. *So, what happened next? You still haven't explained the punch and the making out.*

"I'm getting there. You passed out as soon as Master Dung got out of your body, and understandably so. I am hardly an expert, but it seemed to me that splitting one's soul in two can be very painful, even if the part being removed is actually a tumor."

That's a beautiful, if rather disturbing, metaphor, Stapley, Buggeroff remarked.

"Thank you, Chief! Just trying my best. Sadly, I, too, have been affected by your pain, so I was unable to record the events that followed. All I know is that as Master Sewer punched you he said, 'That's for punching my girl.' Chances are, and I understand how you may find this more than a little upsetting, that there is more between Merkin and Master Sewer than meets the eye. The kiss only adds further support to this suggestion."

I guess I should have known, Buggeroff thought sullenly.

"I must say, you're taking it quite well, Chief," Stapley said reassuringly.

I always thought she was out of my league. Buggeroff sighed. *I just want to know why she pretended to like me.*

"I don't think she pretended, Chief. I'm not just saying this to make you feel good. I could really tell that she liked you."

It's just that she also appears to like Master Sewer.

"I am given to understand by my Social Module that this is not such an unusual state of affairs. Both men and women are victims of, more or less, acute forms of polygamy. It's in your genes or something. Haven't you ever been in love with more than one woman?"

I suppose…

"See, there you have it. Anyway, I hope that clarifies things a little bit. I suppose now would be a good time for you to come back to your senses and open your eyes."

80. MASTER LOO

"Good! I was beginning to worry. That was quite a punch you took," Master Loo said as he saw his Scriptling open his eyes. "I suppose you want an explanation."

"Stapley explained quite a lot," Buggeroff said in a low voice.

"I'm sorry you had to go through all that." Master Loo shook his head sadly. "I believe some of it is my fault."

"I find that hard to believe," Buggeroff said. "The only thing I don't understand is why you performed the Ritual on Master Sewer?"

"It's quite a long story, and I shall share it with you in a minute. But before that, I need to ask Stapley a favor."

"He's all ears, or so he says," Buggeroff said.

"Actually, there is a patch I need to install first. I'm giving Stapley an upgrade I'm sure he will enjoy having."

"Sure, go ahead."

Master Loo closed his eyes to better concentrate on the spell, then cast it.

"Now, Stapley," he said, "can you feel something different?"

"He says he can feel another presence of sorts."

"Excellent," Master Loo rubbed his hands. "Stapley, I'd like you to meet your brother. He is Master Sewer's magical assistant, and he secretly works for us. You should be able to communicate with him now."

There was a brief moment during which Buggeroff's eyes seemed to phase out.

"This is awesome!" the Scriptling said when the moment was gone. "Stapley tells me his brother's name is Bolty and that Master Dung is gone for good now."

"Of course, he is gone for good." Master Loo raised an eyebrow. "He's been dead for a few weeks now."

"I'll come back to that after you tell me your part of the story," Buggeroff said with a sly smile.

"Fair enough. What else is Stapley saying?"

"That Master Sewer is currently driving back home, and Merkin is with him."

"Ha! It's always fascinating to see new technology at work!" Master Loo clapped his hands in a rare display of childish excitement. "Just one more question, before we share stories. Has Bolty managed to secure Master Sewer's trust?"

"He says he is not one hundred percent there, but that there is no sign of distrust, either," Buggeroff replied. "Now, please tell me about the Ritual."

Master Loo told him. He told him everything, starting with Ina, continuing with the two, mysterious men in the car outside the restaurant, and finishing with the day's events.

"I'm sorry I did not tell you any of this earlier," he said when he was done.

"That's OK, I would have done the same in your place. It's just that…"

"Yes?"

"I would never have figured you for a rock fan." Buggeroff made the sign of the horns with his fingers and started banging his head to an imaginary tune.

"Oh, no?" Master Loo pretended to be upset. "Then I suppose I must show you some pictures from my youth." He smiled and imitated Buggeroff's gesture.

They both laughed. It felt good.

"Rock on!" growled Dave.

"Look," said Buggeroff, "before I go ahead and tell you about Master Dung, shouldn't you be calling the two guys Chu and Lang to tell them the news?"

"It's Liu and Chuck. But you are right. Come, let's go upstairs to the study, and I'll give them a call. I want you to stay close in case I forget anything."

81. MASTER SEWER

"So, that's how I found out about the Ritual. It went pretty well, all things considered. I'd like to see others doing better in such a short time," Merkin said as the car pulled into the garage.

"You really are a force of nature. Devastatingly so."

"Are you, by any chance, suggesting that I should have kept a low profile?" she asked in a hurt voice.

"Perish the thought," he said quickly, afraid that if he upset her now, he might not be *getting any* a little later. "All I'm saying is that you are simply marvelous." He killed the engine.

"Oh, dear, I didn't think I would turn you into a scared, little lamb so quickly." She smiled and ruffled his hair. "I know I should have proceeded with more caution, but you know me – I put a little bit of passion in everything I do." She pulled his hair so hard that his head fell backward. "Like that," she whispered into his ear, and punctuated her remark with a highly agreeable little bite on his neck.

He moaned with pleasure. "Do you think we should have disposed of them?"

"It would have been too messy. Three bodies in the same dissemination area in such a short interval might attract unnecessary attention. Besides, I'm sure they are not the type to squeal."

"You like him – I mean the boy – don't you?"

"No more than I like you." She licked his chin, lips, and tip of the nose in one swift motion.

"And how much, exactly, is that?" he asked in an insinuating voice.

"Why don't I just show you how much?" She reached into his pants.

***

Car, bedroom, broken furniture, shower… If anyone wants to call this a routine just because it had happened once before in the exact, same order, then they are free to do it. Master Sewer would gladly go through this routine for the rest of his life, provided he could keep up with the furniture expenses.

"What's troubling you?" asked Merkin. She lay naked next to him, her head resting on his chest.

"Nothing," he said. "At least, I think it's nothing."

"You might not know that you're troubled, but I can tell. A woman can always tell when her man is not happy," she said, taking his hand in hers.

"But I am happy," he protested. "How can I not be happy when I'm with you?"

"Good answer," she kissed his hand. "But I know something is bothering you. Come, tell me what it is, and together we might make it go away."

"I… I don't know… It feels as if something is missing, but it is not related to you. That much I can tell."

"Unfinished business?"

He frowned.

"Is it the ultimate virus project?" she asked.

"You know what, I believe it is? I didn't even know this was bothering me, but now that you brought it up to surface, it makes total sense."

"Then we shall have to deal with it," Merkin said confidently and stood up, her perfect body filling his vision. "No," she said as she saw his manhood responding to her charms. "No more boom-boom for you until we get this over with."

Then, as if to accentuate her resolve, she took his long shirt and put it on, covering at least some of her nudity.

"You're right, of course." He sighed and drew on his pants.

"So, let's start thinking about the code. I had more ideas while I was away," she said.

"Actually, I think I may have finished writing the code while you were gone. I have been working on it for a long time, over two years I would say, but my code was incomplete. It was your brilliant idea for using electricity as a distribution method that provided the missing piece."

"But I thought this was supposed to be my project. Why didn't you tell me you had it, more or less, figured out?"

"Pedagogical technique," he replied. "You needed something to focus on. Besides, what is wrong with this being our project rather than just yours or mine?"

"I guess…"

"Tell you what," he moved behind her and put his hand around her flat abdomen, dragging her closer. "Why don't we revise the code together, and then we can go ahead and cast the spell. I'll put some champagne on ice to celebrate the occasion, and then…"

"Boom-boom," Merkin giggled, shaking her ass meaningfully.

82. BUGGEROFF

Buggeroff lay on the bed with his eyes closed, trying to make sense of the day's events and feeling sorry for himself.

"Is everything all right, Chief?" Stapley asked.

I wonder what she's doing now, he replied.

"Bolty says Master Sewer and Merkin are talking now, and they just had sex. I probably shouldn't have said the last part."

They had sex? Buggeroff asked in despair.

"Yes. Bolty is asking if you would like to watch the highlights."

What?

"Bolty has this new Psychiatric Module, and he is of the opinion that watching them have sex would be good for you. There are two scenarios, he says: either you will derive pleasure from this POV experience, or you will be disgusted and thus find closure. Either way is better than sitting here sulking."

Well, then, I guess I could give it a go, Buggeroff thought, awkwardly aroused.

The images started flowing into his mind in a level of detail superior to even IMAX 3D. And it wasn't just images, but also smells, tastes, sounds and tactile sensations. Before a minute was over, Buggeroff had one of the best orgasms he had ever experienced.

"Sorry about that," he apologized to no one in particular.

"Don't worry, Chief. I'm incapable of passing judgment in these matters. Just sit back and enjoy the rest of the reel."

Yes, I think I can do that, Buggeroff thought.

A couple of minutes later, just as things were starting to become pleasantly uncomfortable again, he was interrupted by Stapley's alarmed voice.

"Chief, we must go! Get up and get the Master!"

What, what do you mean?

"Get dressed and I'll explain things to you in the meanwhile."

Buggeroff did as he was told, and less than a minute later, he was on the stairs shouting for Master Loo.

"What is it, Buggeroff, dear?" Master Loo's voice came from the study.

"Get the car! Get the phone! No time!" Buggeroff said as fast as he could.

"Fine, I'll get the car," Master Loo said and headed for the garage.

"Take the phone, too, and faster!"

"I have the phone in my pocket," the Master said and picked up the pace. "What is this all about?"

Buggeroff reached into his Master's pocket and took out the phone.

"No time to explain twice. You'll get the news while I inform Luck and Chew over the phone."

"It's Chuck and Liu. That's how you'll find them in my agenda. Now, where to?" he asked as he started the engine.

"Master Sewer's house. And hurry! This might be the end of the world!"

"Chief, I have good news, at least partially," Stapley said. *"Master Sewer is out of the game for now."*

What do you mean? Buggeroff asked.

"I… I taught Bolty how to induce a seizure." Stapley replied meekly.

Good! Excellent! Wait a minute… He paused as he remembered one or two occasions in the past when he, himself, had fainted for no apparent reason.

"No time for this, Chief. Just call Chuck and Liu and we'll talk about this later," Stapley said hurriedly.

Buggeroff dialed the number.

"Master Loo," said the voice at the other end of the line. "What a surprise! I didn't expect to hear from you so soon."

"Hello, this is Buggeroff, his assistant," Buggeroff said hesitantly.

"You mean to say his Scriptling," the voice corrected him. "This is Chuck speaking. Where's the fire?"

"Master Sewer and Merkin have created a virus that will destroy all computers in the world. It's distributed via the power grid through electricity, so it's virtually undetectable by any antivirus programs. They will cast the spell any minute now," Buggeroff said it all in one breath. He gasped for air, then continued, "We managed to disable Master Sewer remotely, at least for a while. We're on our way there to try to stop them."

"Holy crap! I mean, thank you for calling us! We'll be there shortly," said Chuck.

83. MERKIN

"Master, what's happening? Cornelius?" She shook the limp shape of Master Sewer, trying to wake him up.

They had just finished parsing the code and made the final touches. The next moment, making barely a wheezing noise, her Master rolled his eyes back and folded unconsciously over her. She moved him onto the bed with some difficulty and listened to his heart. There was a pulse.

"SALUTEM.INVESTIGARE(MAGISTER.CLOACA);" she cast a diagnosis spell on her Master. The result came back in an instant – a minor seizure. The excitement had simply been too much for him, poor soul, and so he fainted. No problem whatsoever. She could wait for him to feel better.

"I told you not to hurt the boy," came an all-too-familiar voice from behind her.

She spun around, trying to land a blow on that crooked face, but Gerhardt was faster and was already out of her reach.

"Once was enough," he said, referring to the time she had kicked him behind the ear in that side alley a few nights ago.

"What do you want?" she said between her teeth.

"I want to stop you from destroying the world. Oh, and I want to punish you for what you've done to Buggeroff." He grinned menacingly.

"I haven't done anything to him," she protested, suddenly remembering about the poison to which Gerhardt still held the antidote. "He's the one who punched me."

"He saw you kissing Master Sewer. What do you have to say to that?"

"I…" she backed away.

"Enough! It's time for me to activate the poison. This should be punishment enough for you, and it will also prevent you from doing more harm."

"What... What does the poison do?" Merkin asked in a trembling voice.

"Ha! Haven't you guessed yet? It steals your Magic away. Forever." He laughed an annoying laughter, redolent of bleating more than anything else.

"Nooo! Please don't do that! I'll do anything. Anything," she insisted as she stepped forward and took her shirt off.

For a moment there was a wild glint of lust in his eyes, and he seemed to hesitate. But then the moment flew away and gave room to a sight that almost turned Merkin's stomach upside down. Gerhardt's face contorted, then started to shrivel. His mouth and nose crept forward, exposing his ugly teeth. He convulsed, once, twice, then once more. When he was done, what stood in front of Merkin was no longer the man called Gerhardt, but rather the goat named Gertrude.

It took Merkin a moment to realize what had just happened.

"Oww... Isn't that sweet?" she said in a mocking voice. "Who's a pretty goat, then? Who's a silly goat-man who ran out of juice just before activating the poison? Huh?"

Gertrude took a few steps back and turned invisible.

"Oh, no you don't!" Merkin shouted, and got ready to throw a fire bolt where the goat had stood before. Just then, she heard the screech of tires out on the driveway, and following her intuition, got to the window just in time to see Master Loo and Buggeroff jumping out of the Tesla and rushing for the door.

She smiled. Whatever it was that they wanted, it could wait. She had a spell to cast, and she would cast it whether her dear Master were awake enough to assist her or not.

***

A minute later, Buggeroff's head popped into the room, and he shouted, "Found her! Gertrude showed me the way."

"Gertrude?" came Master Loo's panting voice from somewhere on the ground floor. "What is she doing here?"

"Damned if I know!" Buggeroff shouted back, and then his eyes turned again on Merkin, staring widely.

She realized she was still naked, and she decided to use this to her advantage.

"What brings you here, Simon?" she asked in a sweet voice.

"We came to stop you," he forced himself to look her in the eye.

She feigned confusion. "Stop me?"

"That's right," said Master Loo who had joined his Scriptling in staring at her. "That spell you want to cast is extremely dangerous, and it will bring our civilization to the brink of extinction. Many will die!"

"Since when did you become so sensitive to a few deaths?" she asked with a mean smile on her face.

"This is not—" began Master Loo.

"Besides," she interrupted him. "You are too late." She pointed towards Master Sewer's laptop where only a few moments ago the spellchecker program had displayed the ultimate virus code. The screen was now blank, and the computer showed no sign of being switched on. "The virus spreads as we speak, and there's nothing you can do to stop it." She allowed herself a maniacal laugh.

On the nightstand, a small, silver object began to vibrate.

84. MASTER LOO

"How can you laugh about this?" Master Loo asked, despair ringing like a funeral bell in his voice. "Don't you realize what you have done?"

"I've set things straight, is what I've done," Merkin replied haughtily.

"Set thing straight?" he cried. "People are dying as we speak, probably by the thousands!"

"Oh, come on, be serious, will you? It's probably going to take a while before such a high rate is achieved," Merkin replied in a casual tone, as if she were talking about stock markets. "The only casualties we could expect for, now, might be due to traffic lights not working or life support systems failing."

"But why?" Buggeroff asked. "Why would you do such a thing?"

"Oh, you poor soul," Merkin tsk-tsked. "Aren't you quite the innocent? But the reality is, you don't know enough about Magic to understand the reasons."

"I, on the other hand, know a lot about Magic," said Master Loo. "Go ahead, try me!"

"If I may," said Master Sewer who was just recovering from his seizure. "I couldn't help overhearing the conversation, and I believe I might be able to shed some light on the matter. I take it, by the way, that it worked, right?" He addressed the last question to Merkin.

"Most definitely so." She smirked, pointing again at the dead laptop.

"Marvelous! Now, here's the deal…" he stopped, glancing curiously at the door. "Oh! I didn't know we were expecting visitors "

Chuck and Liu stood on the doorway, panting and looking accusingly at Merkin and her Master.

"What the hell is wrong with you?" Merkin shouted at the newcomers. "Why do you always have to show up at the wrong time? I bet you don't even have a warrant."

Master Sewer coughed politely. "Merkin, if you don't mind, please ask these gentlemen if they would like a cup of tea. Oh, and please put something on before the nice policemen get the wrong idea."

"Seriously?" she asked in an offended tone.

"I'm afraid so," he replied politely, but resolutely nonetheless. "Also," he addressed the rest of his mesmerized audience, "I would prefer it if we were to move to the living room, downstairs. This is, after all, my bedroom. One doesn't just invite his guests into the bedroom, right?" He chuckled genially.

"I'm sure there must be some kind of spell," the inner voice commented as everyone responded positively to Master Sewer's suggestions. *"Every time he smiles and acts gentlemanly, people's wills bend to his."*

I don't know. Could be just a lifetime of practice in being liked by people, Master Loo responded.

"Or manipulative. Doesn't he strike you as a little bit of a psychopath?"

Well, now that you mentioned it... Master Loo replied to his inner voice.

"Would anyone like a cup of tea?" Merkin asked meekly once they had all gathered in the living room. She was wearing a long-sleeved shirt that, although quite revealing, was a definite improvement over the stark nakedness she had previously exhibited.

"Not me," Buggeroff said. "Call me old-fashioned, but I find tea and apocalypse don't mix well."

"Apocalypse?" Master Sewer raised an eyebrow. "God bless your soul, Buggeroff! The world is not coming to an end. The only thing that is coming to an end is this era, an era of shame for us Magicians. That's right, we are Magicians," he said proudly in response to Chuck and Liu's sudden reaction. "And you, as men of law, should learn to show us the proper respect if you want to keep your jobs... and lives," he added with a chuckle. "Can't you see? Have we all been so blind as to not understand the danger posed to us by the advent of computers? All the seemingly inoffensive computer does is cast very simple, all-but-diluted spells over and over again. No harm done, I hear you say, but you couldn't be more wrong. The bitter truth is that Magic is not an inexhaustible resource. We didn't know that until recent years. How could we have? Until now there hasn't been anything in the world as voracious as computers constantly feeding on Magic. How else can we explain the decreasing number of Magicians over the last decades?"

"It kind of makes sense, you know?" the inner voice remarked, but Master Loo did not reply.

"It is our duty, as children of Magic, to save our mother from this slow and agonizing death," Master Sewer continued with great pathos. "And this, brothers, is what we have accomplished today. Today, we have unleashed our champion, a powerful virus created by yours truly and by this wonderful woman who sits beside me." He pointed generously towards Merkin. "This virus will soon put an end to the unprecedented threat brought forward by the cursed computers. This virus is the harbinger of a new age, an age of prosperity and reconstruction. And we, the Magicians, will be more powerful than ever. We will rule this world, and this time we won't have to hide behind the throne. Instead, we will occupy it in all our splendor." He finished energetically with his fist high in the air.

Silence descended in the room but the words still echoed in Master Loo's mind. Wasn't that what he, in his small way, had been trying to do? Admittedly, the Ritual could not hold a candle to the virus in terms of sheer magnitude and scope, but the intention was, more or less, the same – to restore Magic to its former, glorious status. Then why did he feel deeply uncomfortable about what Master Sewer was proposing?

"You're wrong!" Buggeroff's determined voice came unexpectedly, making all heads turn to him.

"I beg your pardon?" Master Sewer smiled benevolently.

"You're wrong," Buggeroff repeated, his face a mask of outrage. "Your rhetoric is flawless, but your assumptions are feeble, if not complete *phalluses.*"

"Fallacies," Master Loo whispered exasperatedly.

"Exactly," Buggeroff said. "You blame computers for exhausting the Magic, but you neglect all sorts of other factors. It's what scientists call the availability heuristic – just because an idea sounds good to you doesn't make it right. Have you ever stopped to consider other changes that occurred in the last decades? I'm talking about the population boom, globalization, or even rock music. All of these factors define the last half-century just as much as the computers do. I'm not saying all of them are relevant, but you get the point. You can't just single out one event and turn it into the *escape goat* for everything that's wrong with Magic. For crap's sake, if Magic is a hereditary thing, as I believe it is, then why haven't you considered inbreeding as one of the causes? Also, why would you assume that Magic is simply a resource? You use it all the time, but how much do you really know about it? Can't it be that Magic is a sentient entity? And if so, wouldn't it make sense that Magic is subject to evolution? Perhaps Magic has had it up to its nose with you guys. Perhaps you drove it away with all your stupid, useless spells. Would it be so wrong to assume Magic has seen the computers as a window of opportunity for getting rid of you?"

"But if that's the case," Master Sewer's smile did not falter, "assuming that Magic is not a resource, but an entity as you suggest, then should we just sit and watch as it runs away? Magic is ours. Ours! If your horse runs away, what do you do? Do you let it go and force yourself to feel happy for its newfound sense of community with nature, or do you track it down and punish it for making you waste a good day's work? In destroying all computers we are forcing Magic to return to its rightful, and, I should add, forgiving, owners."

"Enough!" Chuck shouted. "The boy is right. Well, mostly right, anyway. But you, Mister Cornelius Wehr, you are most definitely wrong, and you will face the consequences of your deeds."

RAM'S INTERLUDE

By rights, this should have been the Sixth Tribal Interlude. But seriously now, who in their right mind would deny an old storyteller a little cameo act written in first person? Now, don't rush to answer. After all, I'm only a guy who, less than one hundred fifty thousand years ago, could conjure a decent thunderclap. Really, what are the odds that I might have picked up a thing or two in the meanwhile?

Now that we've cleared that up, here's what I wanted to tell you:

You've probably guessed by now that Liu and Chuck are Tribe members. If you haven't, then please re-read the "75. Master Loo" chapter. You would literally be surprised by how you were able to miss it the first time. What you probably haven't guessed, though, is Liu's and Chuck's roles in the Tribe. Indeed, I would be shocked if you had.

Liu is the Tribe's soothsayer. It's really a vocational thing with him, you know? Even before the Mama had discovered our hidden Magical talents, Liu had always been the guy who, when something really bad happened, was the first to raise his fist in the air and proclaim at the top of his voice, "I told you this would happen, didn't I?" In all fairness, he became quite an exceptional oracle once we learned how to harness the power of our words. He really is the best.

Chuck, on the other hand, is our watchman. He hasn't always been one, though. I remember when his only interest in *watching* boiled down to a rather embarrassing case of voyeurism, much to everyone's chagrin. But all that is water under the bridge. We all have our moments. Chuck evolved so much over the last, hundred millennia that it is now possible for his moral compass to show true north even if you were to drop him in a desert and surround him with lawyers.

Now that we have established their identities, let us rewind back to the year 2009, right after Merkin had lost her parents in that terrible sailing accident.

We found out about the accident a day later when Ina sent a mass email to the Tribe informing us of her new identity and whereabouts. Apparently

Bartholomew and Beatrice's boat had been hit by a storm that could have very well been avoided if only the naughty couple hadn't been thoroughly engaged in a role-play activity involving a lost mermaid and a handsome pirate.

If you recall, Beatrice Long, who, at the time of her death, was thirty-seven years old, was the identity that Ina had assumed after young Master Loo killed her. In her email, she explained how her first intention after dying had been to reincarnate as her daughter, Silvia, who was fourteen at the time. Her plan did not succeed, though, because apparently, Silvia (aka Merkin) was too far away, and another, more suitable and younger host had irresistibly presented itself on the way. She was now a ten-year-old girl living in Auckland, New Zealand, and her official name was Cookie McAdams. She was not ready yet to re-join the Tribe, she continued to explain in her email, and then she proceeded to ask if anyone would be so kind as to keep an eye on her daughter. That is where her letter ended, and that is also the last piece of news we've had from her. I know she will show up, eventually. She always does.

We had, indeed, kept an eye on Merkin, and, despite her continuous transgressions, we thought it best not to intervene for a while. It was only when she had been rushed to a hospital in Salzburg with an alcohol-induced coma that we decided it was time to step up. We sent Liu to act on our behalf, and he did the best he could while, at the same time, keeping a very low profile. He put her in a rehab center and disabled her magical powers in order to prevent her from doing any harm to herself or to the medical personnel. When she eventually decided to clean up her act, Liu let her go and restored her powers.

The story could have stopped then and there, if only Liu had not had one of his notorious glimpses into the future when Merkin walked past him as she exited the rehab center's iron gate. It had been an incredibly complex vision, and even Liu who is the world's expert in such matters, was unable to unravel all of its meanings. It sent the poor soothsayer into shock for a week, and when he woke up, he realized that his eyesight had been completely lost. Sadly for him, no number of spells had been able to cure him of his blindness. In the end, this turned out to be to his advantage because it rendered him immune to most mesmerizing spells, such as the one Master Sewer would attempt later on when they first met.

The vision, or at least the part of it that Liu could make sense of, was this: sometime in the next few years, the world will face a most extraordinary challenge that could spell doom for all but a few of its inhabitants. But that was not all. For some reason, Merkin was part of the vision, and she was destined to play a critical role in this major event. Whether her role would be to prevent or to cause this cataclysm, Liu was unable to foresee. All he knew was that she would be there, right at the tipping point of the delicate balance that would send the world one way or the other.

Liu shared all this with the Tribe, and we all pondered it for a long time. In the end, Spike, having listened to everyone's suggestions and having carefully weighed all the options, made known his decision. Liu would continue to keep an eye, metaphorically speaking, on Merkin, and even support her if necessary, so long as he made sure that, when the time came, he would be there to tip the balance in the right direction. But Liu would not be sent alone on this task. A Tribe member would volunteer to go along with Liu to assist him. It is thus that Chuck became Liu's partner in the quest of saving the world. It's not that others did not volunteer. Indeed, I, myself, had half a mind to raise my hand and join Liu, but Chuck had been faster than everyone else.

They spent the following two years making sure they stood in Merkin's shadow, never revealing themselves. But then Liu had another vision right about the time when Merkin had killed her old Master.

It became clear to him that the critical time was drawing near, and that they could no longer hide. Disguising themselves as policemen, they approached Merkin under the pretext of investigating a missing person case. They had learned about the pizza boy from the police radio, and they had subsequently buried the case under a thick layer of Magic and bureaucracy just to keep Merkin safe.

Well, you know the rest, more or less. It is perhaps worth mentioning that when Master Sewer and Merkin had that terrible car accident, it was Chuck and Liu who saved them from sure death. They were driving cautiously behind them when the crash happened. Immediately, they cast a series of protective spells, but their power soon started to drain, as not even Magic can do much in the face of death. Then, with a stroke of genius, Chuck decided to tap into Master Sewer's reserves of power, and in the end, that was what made the difference. The fact that Master Sewer had lost his powers as a result was all but irrelevant.

And now, having tied together some of the loose threads in this story, it is my pleasure to reveal the last scene.

85. MERKIN

"Seriously, who the fuck are you?" She threw the full blast of her anger at the two cops.

Buggeroff's speech left her more than a little uneasy, and she didn't like that feeling a single bit. Until then, she had been giving full credit to Master Sewer's theory about computers being responsible for the current, precarious state of Magic and Magicians. But Buggeroff's arguments, although peppered with his usual collection of ludicrous *faux amis*, made enough sense to shift her perception to the point of doubt.

"We're... we're friends of your mother," the fat, Chinese cop said.

"Yeah, right," she said with a snort.

"Really old friends of your mom," said the other cop, the ginger-headed one.

"My mother had a lot of friends, but I am sure she would not have befriended cops," Merkin said contemptuously.

The two cops lay quiet for a moment, but then, against all expectations, the first one started to sing. It was a simple song, with made-up words, but it was a familiar song, nonetheless. She had to stifle an impulse to yawn, and she could see that everyone else in the room felt quite the same.

"How the fuck do you know that song?" she asked.

The song stopped, and everyone snapped back to attention.

"It's a lullaby," the cop said simply. "It's the lullaby your mom sang to you when you were little, and it's the same lullaby that women in her family have been singing for as long as they can remember."

She took a step back, seeking the relative support of a wall.

"You two are not cops, are you?" she asked.

"No, we're not," the ginger-headed one said.

"Then you must be Magicians. Are you part of the Oriental school or some other, lesser-known system?"

"In a way," the fat one replied. "Let's just say we are older and wiser than you. Oh, and much more powerful." He smiled kindly as he raised one hand in the air.

Merkin did not immediately see the meaning of this last gesture, but then she turned her head, following everyone else's glances towards Master Sewer. In his right hand he held a small fireball, and his face was contorted in a painful grimace.

"It burns, god damn it!" he hissed.

"So it does," the fat one said. "Isn't it written that he who shall play with fire will get burned? You wanted to make me a gift of fire, but I refused your gift, so now it is yours to do whatever you may please with it," he added with Zen-like clarity.

"I... can't... shake... it... off," Master Sewer whined. Merkin felt disgusted at his tone. She was used to seeing him as a figure of power, and she didn't like his current stance in the least.

"Well, I guess you should have thought about that before trying to throw it at me," Liu − yes, that was his name − said.

"Pleaaaase! It huuuurts!" Master Sewer moaned, tears streaming down his face, a face that Merkin now knew with painful clarity she would never again find beautiful.

"Weakling!" Liu spat the word out and lowered his hand, releasing Master Sewer from his invisible grip. "Mother Magic," he continued as Master Sewer huddled into a corner and started casting a healing spell on his burned flesh, "Mother Magic is not something you lock away and force to work for you. Who would ever do something like that to their mother? The boy was right: Mother Magic is simply evolving, nothing more, nothing less. We all know, or at least should know, that islands are veritable crucibles for evolution. And what were the first computers, if not islands of technology in a huge sea of humans?" He paused for a moment and then asked with a dreamy look on his face "Can't you see?"

Master Loo scratched his head. "So, you mean to say that Magic has found a new home, a new environment, if you will, in the computers?"

"You are correct," the ginger-headed one, Chuck, replied. "But the essential bit is that not all of it has. We can safely say that we have two species of Magic on our hands now, still related to one another, but both going their own, individual ways."

"Not anymore, you don't!" Master Sewer said in a wretched voice. "We killed the ugly sister, and now the remaining one would do well to obey us and never stray." He laughed at his own wit.

"What have I done?" Merkin whispered to herself, feeling like a soldier suddenly stripped of his patriotism and left only with guilt.

"This is where you are wrong," said Chuck.

"How do you mean?" Merkin asked the question that was on everyone's lips. "We've all seen the virus at work."

"Ah, the virus." Chuck chuckled. "Is this the same virus that travels through electricity?"

"Yes," she replied.

"Good. Then I don't think it should have travelled too far. You see, thanks to our young friend, here," he gestured towards Buggeroff, "we learned about the virus just in time to cause a complete lockdown in the whole province. Without electricity, the virus cannot escape. It's—" He was interrupted by an explosion of cheers from everyone in the room, except for Master Sewer. Even Gertrude raised her muzzle in the air and bleated happily. "It's chaos out there," he continued. "People will suffer, and some of them might actually die, but the price, I'm sure you will all agree, is not as high as we would have imagined."

There was a murmur of agreement, interrupted only by Master Sewer's cackle.

"And what happens when you turn the power back on?" he asked with a satisfied smile on his face.

"Nothing," Merkin heard herself answering in an uplifting tone. "OK, so the virus might still lurk in some battery-operated devices, but this doesn't mean a thing because by the time electrical power is restored, we will have an antivirus ready."

"Good luck with that, you traitor!" Master Sewer sneered. "You no longer have the code. It disappeared when my laptop was consumed by the virus."

"You seem to forget who you are talking with." Merkin threw a look of revulsion. "Fascinating memory for details," she said, tapping her temple with her index finger. "Isn't that what you've always said?"

"You—" He formed an all-too-familiar gesture with his burned fingers, causing a sparkling ember to glow in his palm. But before the ember could grow into a fireball, Master Sewer's eyes rolled back, and he collapsed, most ungracefully, on the floor.

"Thank you, Bolty," Buggeroff said, but Merkin was too pumped up to ask what he meant.

"You little piece of shit!" she hissed at her Master. "FINES—" she started, but the words choked in her throat.

Chuck said gently, "I believe once is more than enough. You should learn to control these impulses if you really want to make it in this world." He released the pressure that had been holding her words in. "As for you, former Master," he looked disapprovingly at Master Sewer, "we will deal with him properly." There was a glint in Chuck's eye that spoke volumes about the meaning of the word "properly."

"About that antivirus, now," Liu cast his eyes straight at her, and for the first time since she had met him, Merkin realized that he was completely blind.

EPILOGUE

Merkin and Buggeroff were walking through the park, hand in hand, with Gertrude frolicking carefree around them.

"I am happy," Merkin said out of the blue, squeezing his hand affectionately.

"Me, too," he replied dreamily, and took a deep and satisfying breath of fresh air.

Gertrude burped in agreement.

"It just feels right, you know?" Merkin spoke again. "It feels as if I can look into the future and tell that everything is going to be all right."

"I know exactly what you mean," he answered. "The world is a better place, now, and it is certainly facing a bright future."

"What about us? Do you think we have a future? Perhaps a bright one?"

In the week that had passed between the precipitated events (described in the last chapter) and the present time, Merkin had grown very fond of Buggeroff – more so than she had ever imagined her heart capable of. He was kind, sensitive, and loyal. In a phrase, anything but a bad boy, and to her shame, Merkin had had enough encounters with bad boys to last her a lifetime.

He stopped and took her face in his hands. "Silvia, there is nothing I would love more." He smiled, but then a dark cloud passed over his face, and he continued in a gloomy voice, "We will have to work hard for it, though."

"I know, and I'm sorry." She lowered her eyes. "You have no idea how sorry I am, Simon. Will you ever believe me when I tell you that that part of me is gone?"

This was still an open wound in their otherwise fast-developing relationship, and it hurt badly enough to raise the question of whether time alone would heal it. Merkin was a poacher turned gamekeeper and no matter how good a gamekeeper she became, her past would always stick with her — as annoying as an empty can tied to her leg.

"I want to believe you. I really do. I guess what I feel more than anything is fear, fear that I might lose you, fear that one day you will outgrow me and despise me. I fear that if you ever decide to go back to your old ways, I will follow you against my better judgment just for the sake of being close to you," he said, and his voice quivered as if he was about to break into tears.

"Oh, Simon," she whispered and patted his cheek gently with the back of her fingers. "What girl could ever ask for more? But you will never have to face this option. That much I can vow to you right now. Still…"

"Yes?" he asked worriedly.

"It's just… Speaking of fear, what I fear is that one day he will break out and seek revenge."

There was no need to explain who *he* was.

"You need not worry about that," Buggeroff said resolutely. "I'm sure Liu and Chuck know what they are doing. And even if he escapes, which is impossible, what would he do without his Magic? Besides, Bolty has him in check. Whatever happens, we can nip it in the *butt.*"

"You don't know him, Simon. Even without his Magic, he is a formidable opponent. He is extremely resourceful and he is a better strategist than most Magicians."

"Should I be jealous?"

"You should know better than that. I despise the man beyond words. If there is one thing I disapprove of in Liu and Chuck's approach, it is the fact that they haven't killed him."

"I must say, I kind of agree with you on this one. And you know how set against killing people I am. But everything is going to be all right. Our strength and knowledge will only grow with time, and we will have nothing to fear."

"You are forgetting about the poison," she said.

At that, Gertrude turned her head to face her and blew a raspberry.

"I am sure Gerhardt will provide the antidote when the time is right for him." Buggeroff looked intently at his pet goat. He had learned her secret from Merkin, and he wasn't sure he would like this Gerhardt guy as much as he liked Gertrude. "I will not impose on him, at any rate."

"It is his right to keep me in check, but he can rest assured I will never hurt you, unless you want me to, of course." She grinned and bit his lower lip with exquisite dexterity.

He feigned protest. "Ouch! Gertrude, save me from this beast!" he cried happily as Merkin continued to plaster his face with kisses, and he started tickling her.

Gertrude ignored them, and, instead, chose to take interest in the acrobatic maneuvers of a white butterfly.

"You call that tickling?" Merkin sounded menacing. "I'll show you the meaning of tickling, mister!"

When the couple's antics gradually came to a stop, Buggeroff, still panting with excitement, took a step back and said, "We should learn to control ourselves."

"Is this about the new girl?" Merkin asked, panting heavily. "She won't be here until tomorrow."

"Yeah, the Master will pick her up from the airport early next morning. Who would have thought our dear, solitary Master would have three Scriptlings on his hands?"

"Who would have thought his fame would reach as far as New Zealand, eh?" Merkin replied. "How old did you say the girl was? Twelve? I've heard she's a natural."

The Tribe moves.

GLOSSARY

BUZUR.DAH();
Sumerian
Help me, God of Secrets!

CEPHALEA.IRE();
Latin
Headache, go away!

DORMIO();
Latin
Sleep!

DVER.OTPERTET();
Russian[39]
Unlock the door!

FEBRIZIUM();
Latin
Product placement.

FINES.VITAE(NUNC);
Latin
Finish life now!

---

[39] I couldn't find, for the love of me, a decent English-Slavonic dictionary on the Internet, at least not one suitable for the convoluted purposes of this story.

INCIPE.RITUM();
Latin
Initiate the Ritual!

INTIMUS.CAPILLAMENTUM
Latin
Merkin.

LAVABIT();
Latin
Wash!

MAGISTER.CLOACA
Latin
Master Sewer.

OBLIVISCARIS.DIEBUS(3.5);
Latin
Forget the last, three-and-one-half days.

SA.ZALAG();
Sumerian
Cleanse the mind!

SALUTEM.INVESTIGARE();
Latin
Investigate health!

SECRETUM.REVELARE();
Latin
Reveal the secret!

SHURPU();
Sumerian
Purify by fire!

SONITUS(FALSUS);
Latin
Mute the sound!

SPOTKNUTSYA();
Russian
Stumble!

TORPOR();
Latin
Nighty-night!

YAVIT.PAROL();
Russian
Reveal the password!

ZAPLATKA.NALOZHIT();
Russian
Apply patch!

●

NOTE

Dear Reader,

If you have made it this far, then it is safe to presume that you are possessed of the same strike of masochism that drove me to write this story. In that, we are kindred spirits.

The Scriptlings has crawled through many stages before it got where it is today. Some of its sources are bizarre, to say the least. I will list some of them here, partly to pay tribute to those influences, and partly because I know everyone loves a little bit of trivia.

Simon was initially meant to be a ghoul named Wart, slave to an evil Master who occasionally shape-shifted into a blonde succubus called Ghouldilocks. That I have named him Simon might have something to do with one of the best adventure game series ever, incidentally called **Simon the Sorcerer**.

Speaking of games, I'm sure the geeks out there have recognized references to other classics of the genre. Good for you!

Merkin's entire existence is owed to Tom Sharpe, in whose **Ancestral Vices**, 1980 I have discovered this astonishing word.

I got the idea of Syntax being used by magic and computers, rather tangentially, from Richard Dawkins and his "The machine code of the genes is uncannily computer-like." (**River Out of Eden**, 1995). The very fact that we have discovered this similarity after actually inventing the computer code is remarkable.

The Tribe started as a jaunty band of gypsies. I was more than halfway through the story, and I desperately needed a deus ex machina device that didn't look like one, to serve as some kind of backbone to the plot. The Tribe turned out to be just that, as well as its ribcage and limbs.

What else… Oh, yes – Stapley. Those of you who have had the pleasure of using earlier versions of Microsoft Windows know what I'm talking about. Enough said.

I hope you have enjoyed *The Scriptlings*, and I am pleased to say that its sequel – **The Masters** is already taking shape.

Thank you,
Sorin Suciu

ABOUT THE AUTHOR

A gamer by vocation and an office dweller by dint of circumstance, Sorin lives in the beautiful city of Vancouver with his wonderful wife and their vicious parrot.

Born in Romania, Sorin has stubbornly resisted the temptation to learn English for well over twenty years. When he finally gave up, it was not work and nor was it video games that weakened his resolve, but rather the mindboggling discovery of Terry Pratchett, Douglas Adams and Monty Python. With such teachers, it is no wonder that, much in the same way some lucky people learn to ride before they walk, Sorin has learned to be funny before being fluent.

Now a fluently funny author, he is equally thrilled and terrified to share his debut novel The Scriptlings with the rest of the geeks out there.

If you enjoyed this book,
please take a few moments to place a review online.

This is the absolute best way to support a writer – either by sharing your praise with other readers, or by providing your fair perspective on ways the author can grow and improve their writing ability.

Thank you!

41290764R00192

Made in the USA
Charleston, SC
24 April 2015